PRAISE FOR ARIA CUNNINGHAM'S

THE PRINCESS OF SPARTA

"Masterfully written and pulling from one of the most memorable myths to come out of ancient Greece, *Princess of Sparta* reminds readers that even in the throes of a violent world people can be weakened by love, and will go to great lengths, even risking death, for the ones they love."

- San Francisco Book Review

"Aria Cunningham presents the coming-of-age of a character often portrayed as a mere pawn in the wars of men and expertly re-interprets the "Herstory" behind Helen's legendary tale. Sprinkled with tunic-tearing passion, Cunningham paints this popular story with an exquisite brush and reinvents one of the greatest love stories ever told."

-BTS Book Review

"*The Princess of Sparta* is the perfect blend of history, romance, and action giving this book a broader reach with readers. The characters come alive in this forlorn world of long ago as they share their joy, pain, and struggles. Once you pick this book up, there's no turning back or putting it down!"

-Portland Book Review

“As a reader, I was left wanting to read the next book in Aria Cunningham’s series, so that I can see how she will flesh out this next part of their lives. Legend has taught us how this will end, but the Heroes of the Trojan War series promises to bring it to life for me.”

-Historical Novel Society

“The characters had depth and compassion. I will be honest in saying I started the read without much knowledge in regards to who Helen was, other than the woman who started a war. Now I feel like I have a greater appreciation for her and her struggle.”

-Wolf Majick Reviews

"I quickly found my ideas of Helen the bratty beauty fall away, and be replaced with a more female empowered version. What Cunningham quickly reminded me of, is that there are many sides to one story, and I might just prefer this romantic one the best!"

-Books Hug Back

THE PRINCESS *of* SPARTA

HEROES OF THE TROJAN WAR

by

Aria Cunningham

MYTHMAKERS PUBLISHING

LOS ANGELES

ALSO BY ARIA CUNNINGHAM

The Princess of Prophecy: Heroes of the Trojan War, Vol II (2015)

Cover Art by JR Burningham

ISBN: 0991420101
ISBN-13: 978-0-9914201-0-0

Mythmakers Publishing is a division of Mythmakers Entertainment.
www.mythmakersent.com

To JR, my Prince of Destiny.

Acknowledgments:

This novel could not have been possible without the encouragement and moral support of my friends and family. Writing seems a solitary endeavor until it is time to publish, and then it takes a village of diligent people to bring the tale to its audience. A special thank you to my Betas- to Autumn, my rock of sensible input, to Claire- who's enthusiasm brightens the weary soul, to Dori, Renee, Amanda and Carol, and to everyone who donated to the publishing fund. And lastly, to my Alpha, JR. Your keen sense of story never ceases to amaze me.

May we always live extraordinary lives.

TABLE OF CONTENTS

WESTERN FRONTIER
TROJAN
TROY
SEHA
GREECE
TROJAN ALLIES
MYCENAE
SPARTA
MILLAWANDA
CRETE

The Wolrd of 1250 B.C.

OLD WORLD EMPIRES
HATTUSAS
PHRYGIA
HATTI
TROJAN ALLIES
ASSRYRIAN
CYPRUS
UGARIT
CANAAN
SIDON
TYRE
DAN
EGYPTIAN
JAFFA
BABYLON
MEMPHIS

THE END OF EMPIRE

Prologue

OUT OF DARKNESS, there came light.

Mankind and all its glory was once nothing more than barbaric clans roaming the earth, hunter-gatherers whose power came from shaping stone.

From that primitive landscape came order. Both land and beast were tamed, weapons of bronze forged, populations grew, and eventually an Age of Empire emerged. Mighty kings built temples, pyramids and fortresses to honor the heavens, feats of human achievement that would go unmatched for eons to come.

But such greatness came at a terrible cost. For a thousand years, the drums of war thundered, and the land ran red with the blood of Egypt, Babylon, Assyria, Hatti and the Levant alike.

Each kingdom, emboldened by delusions of their greatness, was eager to claim the world for their own. Entrenched in oppressive regimes, these empires rotted from within. Corruption and political squabbles hindered their societies from advancement. And in their hubris, they failed to see the fearsome truth before them—

They would soon be destroyed.

In the West, a new power was rising. The Greeks of Mycenae lived along the northern Mediterranean at the very edge of the known world. A mere two hundred years young, their fledgling society was a child amongst the giants of the Old World. Fiercely independent and half wild themselves, they sought the two things that eluded them: power and influence.

While their legacy would give birth to classical art, philosophy and mathematics, these Greeks were brutal men, mercenaries who believed heroic deeds were always those of the sword. They had no inkling of the important role they would play in the advancement of mankind, for that was not a future they sought. And, if not for a singular event that changed the tide of human history, the Greeks, and therefore the Western world, might never have existed.

The time was 1250 BC. The world was moving from the Age of Bronze to that of Iron, and warfare was on the brink of a new revolution. As the Empires of Old struggled for domination, the fate of their people remained uncertain. The world needed but a spark to ignite a flame that would consume them all.

That spark would come from the West. Her name was Helen, Princess of Sparta.

But history would remember her as Helen of Troy.

Part 1

The Courtship

CHAPTER 1

THE SUITORS

THE LONELY cry of a golden eagle reverberated throughout the valley plateau of Lacedaemonia. The raptor circled on solar-warmed gusts of wind, its dusky brown wings spread wide while eyeing the open fields below for the telltale signs of breakfast. Though the sun had barely stirred from its nightly rest, the activity below was not the burrowing of voles or muskrats, but that of the hardworking citizens of Sparta setting out to complete the multitude of tasks required for the festivities ahead.

The eagle dove, wings folded alongside its tapered body as it chased thick sunbeams crawling down the slopes of Mt. Parnon. With breathtaking speed, it soared across the vast banks of the Eurotas River, cresting over the numerous masts of longships at dock, ships so great in number the river seemed a forest of billowing sails.

Over the hard-packed earthen streets of the city, the eagle flew, swooping low over free workers carrying woven baskets teeming with fish and large clay amphora filled with wine. It wove between colorful banners lining the streets, past open shutters filled with fresh smoke from the morning cook fires, and up the steady rise of avenues towards the acropolis.

The home of King Tyndareus was more fortress than palace. Built of thick timbers of ash and oak and resting atop a natural rise of granite, the High Seat was rumored to be impenetrable. With Mt. Parnon to the east and the towering slopes of Mt. Taygetus to the west, Sparta was nestled between two natural barriers. The only land access to the province was along the northern mountain passes, a route so narrow no army of size could advance with speed. If an invader was truly desperate, they could approach by river, sailing the Eurotas from the south, an arduous journey fighting trade winds and current. But either passage was folly, as both routes were highly visible from Sparta's defensive walls, a vantage spot where Tyndareus now stood.

The king seemed a man carved of stone, his protruding jawline firm, the dark scowl of his eyes unwavering. Such matters of defense were necessary in times of political upheaval where the claiming of a throne was determined by who best wielded a sword. A careless king was one who did not reign long, and Tyndareus had sat on his throne for more years than he cared to count. He had long disproved any man who thought Sparta easy prey.

Like most men of Sparta, Tyndareus was born a warrior. The king was well into his third score of years and, surprisingly there was no stoop to his frame, no lessening of his prowess. Life on the edges of civilization demanded a hardier stock of men in order to survive. If there had ever been a modicum of softness to his bloodline, it had long since been bred out.

He raised his arm high and the eagle slowed down to land on its master's perch. The leather guard wrapped around Tyndareus' forearm bore deep gouges from his pet's sharp talons.

"Ho, Orion. Easy." Tyndareus spoke in soothing tones. He clasped the small tether attached to Orion's leg in his forefingers and stroked the bird's plumage. The regal creature and the king seemed a reflection of one another. Along the raptor's neck dark brown feathers were speckled with white, much like Tyndareus' own coiled mane. Orion, too, stood proud, gazing over the landscape below, a king of his sky realm.

Tyndareus followed Orion's gaze down to the crowded harbor. From Ithaka and Athens, Argos and Salamis, from all the far reaches of the Hellas, those ships had come. Not to lay siege to Sparta, for only a fool would try that, but at Tyndareus' own calling. A throne would be claimed, but not by conquest. Helen, the child of his heart, the great joy of his silver years, had finally come of age, and every true-blooded Greek had come to court her.

Tyndareus sighed, pushing away a small twinge of remorse. He could no longer delay the inevitable. He could not keep Helen here forever, no matter how much he would rue losing his daughter. But if she must wed, she would wed well. That much Tyndareus could provide.

He could almost hear the rough planks of the dock groan under the weight of his guests' boots. Mighty men, warrior kings and princes of their realms, filled the harbor and soon would fill his halls. A gathering of such magnificence had never taken place in Lacedaemonia. No king before him had commanded such respect.

And no daughter of Sparta had captured the hearts of so many suitors from afar.

He turned to the tall tower along the western wing of the palace. Gossamer curtains billowed out from the balcony of Helen's apartments. He had tried to visit his daughter before the cocks crowed, wishing to see her one last time before his obligations as host superseded all other considerations, but she was gone before first light. He whispered a prayer to Artemis, fervently beseeching the Goddess to protect his child in the hunt of suitors soon to follow.

On the docks, the suitors greeted each other as brothers, a spirit of sportsmanship evident in strong embraces and well placed blows to arms. A spike of resentment festered in

Tyndareus' heart. Which one of them would steal his daughter away?

Orion screeched again, his mournful cry echoing in Tyndareus' ears. "I know." He stroked the bird again, his eyes never leaving the gathering men below. "Woe to any unworthy man who tries to make claim." Tyndareus swore. "Woe to him."

"Princess! Your suitors are arriving!" Astyanassa exclaimed.

Helen spun from her spot beneath the olive grove to look in the direction her handmaiden pointed. Shielding her eyes against the glare of the rising sun, she strained for a glimpse of the men who sought to be her husband. Though the harbor was half a league away, the Grecian longships were easily visible.

"So many—" She tried to hide the fear that lodged itself into her heart, but it was difficult. Astyanassa had spent the last fortnight filling her head with stories about the men who had accepted her father's invitation. Many of those tales described feats of valor that Herakles himself would be hard pressed to match. If her handmaiden's stories were half true, then heroes of a Golden Era had come to seek her hand.

The sight of so many suitors ought to have filled Helen with pride. Sparta had never before played host to such a fine collection of kings and princes. But that knowledge did little to quiet the yammering of her heart. Before such an array of accomplished men, how would she compare? A sixteen-year-old innocent who had never left the rocky slopes of her beloved homeland? She was terrified she'd be an embarrassment to her father and to Sparta as a whole.

"You should be back at the Palace to greet our guests, not laboring in the fields like a slave." Aethra, Helen's elderly matron, chastised her again. "You'll naught win a man looking like a nymph dragged through the heather."

Aethra's arguments fell on deaf ears, as they had in Helen's apartments that morning when she announced her intentions to aid the harvest. It was duty, not fear of the wild men who came to take her from her home, that kept Helen far afield. At least, that's what Helen convinced herself in the predawn darkness of her sleepless night.

The orchards around them were filled with palace workers as every hand available contributed to the early harvest. With so many visitors come to court, the realm was hard pressed to provide, but Grecian hospitality demanded they must.

Helen sighed. This extra burden was her fault, the festivities planned were in her honor. She could not ask her people to suffer the cost on her behalf without contributing her fair share. The woven basket on her arm was nearly filled with plump oranges and dark olives.

She studied her people. Everywhere Helen looked, her gaze was met with excited grins. It spoke of Sparta's character that her citizens did not mind the extra work. They cared only for the success of Helen's impending match and how much glory it would bring to Sparta.

She lifted her chin, forcing a show of bravado. She would not be caught quivering in her skirts on the eve of her engagement. Right or wrong, her suitors would have to wait on her. She ignored Aethra's barb, and turned back to the harbor. "Can you see them?"

"Aye. Large hairy brutes, one and all." Came Aethra's droll reply. "You'll have your pick of the litter, Princess." Aethra's stern manner was to be expected. As head of the royal personal staff, her world centered around pragmatic absolutes. But even Aethra was not immune to the courting fever that had taken over Sparta the past fortnight. There was pride sparkling in her dark aged eyes.

Technically Helen's slave, Aethra was a model of civility, every inch the noble woman she once was. But, over the many years they spent together, she had become more than just a servant to Helen; Aethra was friend and mother.

Helen dropped her basket and grabbed her matron's hands, spinning the older woman around in an impromptu dance. "Golden Aphrodite, Goddess Divine. Find me a Love who's Sweet and Kind." She trilled away in a melodious tone. Her spinning was a tad over vigorous and they both dropped to the ground in a cloud of dust.

"Hurmpf." Aethra's iron-grey hair came loose from her tight bun as she tried to collect herself. "It's a man you're after, not a myth. And I've yet to meet one who was sweet *and* kind. Best you hope for clean, child. The man who washes is rare enough."

Helen collapsed into giggles, her golden tresses fanning out around her in the undergrowth. Small twigs and pebbles poked into her back through the thin fabric of her pleated chiton. She didn't mind the discomfort. The ground was as rough and unyielding as its people, but it was home.

And now I must leave it.

The stray thought creased her brow as she stared up into the pale pink sky, a pang of sorrow washing over her. Soon she'd be mistress of a new land, surrounded by strangers. Would her new people be like Spartans? Strong but honest? Fierce yet fair? She brushed away a traitorous tear that managed to escape her eye.

"Do you think he will love me?" Helen barely dared to speak the question, much less face its answer. Leaving everything and everyone she knew would be bearable if her husband's love matched theirs. In time, she could learn to love him as well, and her new home. But it would never replace what she felt for Sparta.

Astyanassa laid down beside her, the young maid taking Helen's hand into hers. The handmaiden was four years Helen's junior, but spoke with a confidence a Spartan soldier would envy. "Of course he will love you, Princess. You are the beauty of our Age. They will *all* love you."

Helen sighed. She had been hearing that sweet nonsense her whole life. She was not so vain that she actually believed it. A wife must be many things, and pretty was the least of them.

Aethra stepped in front of them, blocking out the light like a disapproving Titan staring down from the heavens. "Pah, *love*. What silly nonsense is this? There are more important things than love. What about respect? Honor? Duty?" she frowned at the handmaiden. "You'll make her sick with your idle ramblings, girl."

Astyanassa winced and looked away, ashamed. A lashing from Aethra's tongue was second only to that of the paddle at her waist. The girl leapt to her feet and resumed her work.

Helen accepted Aethra's hand to rise and dusted off her soiled dress. Her matron was right, of course. Helen was a princess. Her marriage would have little to do with love. Her father would choose the best match for the realm, not the man who would love her most. Still, even knowing how little concerns of her heart mattered, she hoped to share more with her new husband than just his bed.

Aethra was watching her closely as she muddled through her mixed feelings. Helen learned long ago that her matron's gruff manner was to instruct, not to intimidate. One day Helen would be a queen and she must learn to see all sides of an issue, not just the one that pleased her most. "What is respect if not love?" Helen countered, her head held high. "What is duty, if not the ultimate expression of a king's love for his people, or a husband to his wife?" She delighted in the look of approval on Aethra's face.

"Aye, that is love," Aethra conceded. "And the fealty of the people to their ruler is one shade of such affection. But it is *earned*, Princess, not handed out as simply as a 'good morrow'."

So I must earn my husband's affection?

That was the one task that frightened Helen the most. The physical act of love was foreign to her. She had no idea how to please a man. The priestess said a woman gave a piece of her soul in that sacred embrace, a thought that terrified Helen.

She glanced back down to the harbor and the multitude of ships now berthed at their dock. So many men answered her father's call. Could she really give her body *and* soul to one of them?

Or perhaps the right question was—the one that kept Helen awake at night—would she have any choice?

Chapter 2

Courting Helen

AN HOUR before the supper bell would ring, Helen waited outside her father's megaron, the rectangular-shaped throne room set aside for matters of state and ritual. She was not scheduled to be introduced to their guests until the banquet, but her father had sent a messenger to her privately.

"Wait for me outside the hall. There is something I need to show you."

She paced the carpeted antechamber nervously. On the other side of the double oak doors were two score of militant men eagerly awaiting her arrival. They had been in their cups for the past hour and were currently making more noise than a whole herd of wild bulls. Her feet itched to race back to the field and far far away from these halls.

Breathe, Helen. She coached herself while pacing aimlessly.

The narrow entrance to the hall was lined with tapestries displaying scenes from sacred *mythos.* Their coarse woolen fibers were faded from time, but the images were still recognizable, seemingly leaping off the textile with vivid energy. She paused before one showing the Garden of Hesperides and the Tree with the Golden Apples. It was her favorite. The weaver had masterfully entwined golden thread into the tapestry, making the apples look real enough to eat.

She touched a similar pin on her shoulder, tracing its sharp curves with her fingertips. It was an heirloom from her late mother. Leda was a great beauty. It was rumored a dozen men fought for her hand before Tyndareus claimed her. Helen tried to pull forth an image of her mother's face, but could not. She let her hand drop, a sliver of bitterness threatening to undo her stately composure. Self-pity was not worthy of a Spartan. As much as she wished her mother was present to guide her into womanhood, she'd have to get by on her own.

"Hello Daughter," Tyndareus whispered into her ear.

Helen squeaked and immediately blushed at her childish reaction. Her father had snuck up on her again, a feat he had not managed in quite some time. "You scared me!" she batted his arm away playfully.

"You weren't paying attention," he chided, a spark of merriment in his deep blue eyes. "Dangerous things happen when you don't pay attention."

Had it been any other day he would have chased her through the Palace, enjoying their mock game of cat and mouse. Some of the house staff whispered she was too old for such childishness, but Helen didn't mind. It brought happiness to her father, a man of many burdens. For Tyndareus, she would always be his little girl.

"You look lovely, Father." She smiled graciously at her king.

Tyndareus beamed under her praise, exuding an aura of quiet strength. He did look quite splendid. His ornamental shin guards and arm bands showed off his well-sculpted muscles. His shoulder-length brown hair was neatly kept, longer in the back than in the front. Even his beard was trimmed and coiled into tight curls. For Helen, the king was a standard of perfection any suitor would be hard-pressed to match.

Tyndareus stretched out his hand, gently lifting her chin. "Would that I could keep you forever." His voice cracked with emotion as he placed a solid kiss on her forehead.

Helen felt her earlier nerves return with force. Once married, she'd be queen of some distant land, no longer a daughter of Sparta. And it wasn't just the motherland she'd be leaving. What would her father do when she was gone?

"Father?" she asked hesitantly, unsure how to put all her mixed emotions into words. But his moment of sorrow was brief in tenure. He linked his arm with hers and bestowed his most generous smile upon her.

"Come, walk with me," he said, pulling her away from the megaron.

Helen released a deep breath she had not realized she was holding. It appeared she was not to meet her suitors just yet, and she was grateful to put that introduction off for as long as possible.

With a few quick steps Tyndareus led her through the palace proper, choosing the narrow corridors used mainly by the household staff. The servants were in full motion. Maids ran down the halls with arms loaded with linens. Scullions bent under the weight of greasy copper pots as they rushed to the wash stations. Heat from the kitchen fires and the pungent scent of roast mutton foretold of a mighty feast tonight. Tyndareus promised an event men would talk about for years to come. It thrilled Helen that he would go to such lengths in her honor.

"You must prepare yourself, not only for this union, but for the role you will play as a queen." He instructed as they walked. "In that endeavor, it is crucial you approach negotiations with your eyes wide open, that you see the true nature of the men who would treat with you, not just their honeyed promises."

Helen nodded demurely, hanging on his every word. Tyndareus was a great king and she was fortunate he took such efforts to train her. It was a stupid tradition that forbade her from ruling after him. Only a prince could inherit the throne.

They entered the central court, an expansive clearing framed on four sides by elevated walkways that connected the disparate wings of the palace. Spartan quartermasters were busy setting up weapons in the yard where her suitors would later enjoy some sport. But Tyndareus pulled her away from the activity to a small set of stairs—stairs she knew led up to the eastern facing portico of the megaron.

So, we are to enter the hall discreetly.

Tyndareus had chosen a clever route that allowed Helen and him to see their guests before being announced. Her pride in her father surged. He was a peerless tactician.

As they mounted the balcony, the wild shouts she heard earlier grew louder. As a child, Tyndareus let her watch the first-blood ceremony for a new phalanx of Spartan soldiers. The Hoplites fought in mock battle, under the express order to take any killing blow that presented itself. Thus did the Spartan infantry weed out any weak links. But even that bloody mess had no measure on the ruckus sounding from within.

Great Gaia, what is going on in there?

The jarring clatter of breaking pottery was followed with drunken voices screaming in heated anger, a commotion that shocked Helen to her core. Those sounds had no place in the megaron of a noble king. She turned to her father searching for any sign of alarm, but he continued toward the hall untroubled. They stepped around a set of pillars into the hall's shadowy recesses, and there the deafening scene unfolded before them.

This was no battle, but a turbulent sea of man flesh. Helen's eyes flew wide in shock. Of the forty men come to seek her hand, half were stripped to the waist, the sheen of sweat glistening over their hard-packed muscles.

The crowd had separated into an informal ring where her suitors were taking turns pummeling each other into a bloody pulp. Currently two unclad men circled one another, fists held high as they darted forward and back in a boxing match. They were youths, by the look of them. One of golden hair and the other of brilliant red.

Something stirred deep within Helen. She had never seen a naked man in the throes of passion, for that was what battle roused in the Men of the Hellas. Their muscles were taut, ready to pounce on their prey. Their skin, flushed, the intensity of their efforts radiating from their bodies like heat from a kiln. Even their phalluses stood erect, their rock-hard organs another measure of their manliness against their foe. Helen fanned herself, the powerful display igniting a warmth inside her.

Such strength...

The golden giant landed a good blow and blood flew from his opponent's jaw as he was flung into the jeering crowd. Like a wave cresting forward, her suitors tossed the boy back into the ring, accompanied with a string of insults that made Helen blush to her ears. The red-headed youth stumbled on his long legs, woozy from the blow, but unyielding. The circling ensued again.

Helen tried to rationalize what she was seeing. She studied the nearby men, a crowd of mixed ages and builds. Grizzled veterans with silver hair cheered just as loudly as the stately middle-aged rulers beside them. Most were wearing their courtly finest. But finely clad or stripped to loincloths, they all hollered and jeered with a primal urgency.

Their bloodlust was as naked as their bodies, and it frightened Helen. She felt like a tender dove in the presence of fearsome raptors. When the next bone-jarring blow landed, she shrunk behind her father. For the first time in her life, she worried for her safety. These men were here to claim her...

Tyndareus pulled her behind a set of pillars, allowing them some space from the vigorous activities. His eyes seemed to be everywhere, absorbing the movements of each man, even those reclining in corners.

"Are you paying attention now, Dearest?" He clasped her shaking hand tight, inclining his head toward the fray. "The two in the ring are Patroclus of Lokris and his famed cousin, Achilles. Young, but with great promise of stamina and skill."

Helen craned her neck to get a better view. Patroclus, the fire kissed, was on his back by a stiff uppercut from his cousin. Achilles stood triumphantly over him, his arms raised high in victory and pumping to the steady chants of his admiring peers. The clatter of metal exchanging hands rang throughout the room as bets on the match were honored.

Helen tried to imagine the youth as her intended, but it was hard. Achilles could not be more than a few years older than herself, and he still had soft down upon his cheeks. His beauty was hard to deny, but it was a wild beauty, untempered. And the battle lust in his eyes disgusted her. She squeezed her father's hand and frowned. Blessedly, he made no comment.

"Why are they fighting?" she asked, her disapproval leaking through.

"How else are they to determine who's worthy to claim you?"

"But that's barbaric!" Her shocked words carried into the megaron. Thankfully the men were too busy setting up the next match to notice her less than dulcet tone.

"Barbaric?" Tyndareus paused, watching her as shrewdly as he watched the suitors before. "A strange assessment coming from a Spartan."

Helen stiffened at the intended barb, fire flashing in her clear blue eyes, eyes she inherited from the stoic man standing beside her. "They should save their fighting for the battlefield, not the halls of their host. It's disgraceful!" Honor and respect were greater virtues than valor. Whatever quality her suitors wished to prove was lost in the manner in which they proved it. Their behavior was no better than the barbarian tribes that roamed the north.

Tyndareus chuckled softly at her, clearly enjoying her moment of pique. He had raised Helen to voice her opinions, and like a true Spartan, she would not bite her tongue when insulted. But it was for the king to determine what behavior would be tolerated in his court, not a woman, not even a princess.

"The greatest strength is one you need not display." Helen quoted him, her eyes flaring. *"Only a desperate man pulls a sword without intending to truly use it."*

"Good." He gave her a sharp nod, clearly pleased she remembered her lessons. "But don't let your passions cloud your reason, Daughter." He turned again to the crowd. "Gathering en masse encourages the worst sort of behavior, especially from those with weak constitutions, but we are fortunate to witness this crudity. It allows us to—"

"See them as they truly are." Helen finished for him, finally understanding the purpose of this lesson. "Is this what you wanted me to see?"

"Yes." Tyndareus smiled, his pride apparent. "So that this decision will be based on fact, not the convenient fiction your suitor has adopted to impress."

Helen nodded, hearing the wisdom in his words. She hoped he could see past all this nonsense and find her a worthy husband. Still, her sense of propriety was deeply offended. These were noble men, favored by the Gods. They should be held to a higher standard than the vagaries of pack behavior. A Spartan would slit his wrists before abusing the hospitality of his host.

"Do not judge them all by the same stroke." Her father whispered in her ear. "Look, that one is from Ithaka." He pointed to a sandy-haired man conversing quietly in the eaves of the hall. "Odysseus, son of Laertes. He is a cunning man, one of great promise. His weapon is that of wit, not of bronze." Tyndareus nodded, the small motion indicating he approved of this suitor.

Helen soothed her hurt pride and gave the man a second look. He was one Astyanassa spoke of frequently. She claimed he was favored of Athena.

"Beside him is Diomedes, son of Tydeus, King of Argos."

Her father continued. The man in mention was well built with dark curly hair on his head and chest. He greeted Odysseus with an affectionate embrace, refusing the offer to wager on the next match. "He is a well respected man, one who inspires great loyalty."

A man of cunning, and one of respect. And both seemingly participating in the brutish activities, but politely not when pressed. She made note of their inherent skill in politicking. They could be great allies or dangerous adversaries for Sparta.

"Would you have me look favorably on them?" she asked, hoping her father would give some hint towards his decision.

"Perhaps," he frowned, studying the men intently. "And perhaps not. There are many kingdoms, but only few *great kings*. I would see you wed to the greatest." His eyes burned with that promise.

Helen blushed. She knew her father dreamed of rising Sparta to greater prominence. Like all the people who called the Greek isles home, he believed his actions in life would dictate his standing in death. Glory, above all else, was sought. And her marriage could help him achieve it. But what he said next surprised her.

"Most of all, I want to know what *you* hope to find in this match, Dearest. I would see you happy in your union." His forlorn expression pierced her heart, and for a moment the devastation of his imminent loss was laid bare.

Her breath caught. It was uncommon that the bride be given any choice in her bridegroom. A marriage contract was precisely that, a business contract between families. More so for nobility. Her sister was given no choice. Neither had their mother, although Helen suspected Leda's suggestion might have swayed her grandfather's favor. Helen held her father's gaze, hoping he understood how much she treasured him.

"I only hope he is a good man." She told him fervently, blinking back the tears swelling in her eyes. "Like you."

Tyndareus was a man of stone. He once faced down a pack of wolves without an ounce of fear. But standing there, hearing her heartfelt words, the stone cracked. Helen watched in awe as her father cried. Only a few tears strayed down his grizzled cheeks, but for Tyndareus, that was an ocean.

She wished she could stay here forever, to love him dutifully as her father deserved, but as strong as that impulse was, another feeling pulled her forward. There was something waiting for her. Something powerful. She didn't know where it would lead her, she only knew she needed the courage to follow it.

A horn blast shattered their peaceful moment. The resonate note echoed down from the palace walls, bouncing off the stone foundation of the court, demanding one and all to pay heed. Servants froze mid step in response to its shrill call. Even her quarrelsome suitors shushed to a man.

Tyndareus stepped forward onto the balcony, surveying the yard for the cause of the blast. One sounding was meant to call attention, and two were blown for danger. When the second blast did not fall, Tyndareus unclenched his jaw and he flagged down the nearest servant.

"Asclepius," he called out to his royal steward from across the court. "What is the meaning of this?"

The thin man bowed, snapping his heels together with the readiness all Spartan officials effused. "Another ship approaches, Your Grace," he answered curtly. "Bearing the Lion mast of Mycenae."

CHAPTER 3

ALLIANCES OF BLOOD

THERE WAS no king more greatly admired nor greatly feared than Agamemnon, son of Atreus, ruler of Mycenae. A warrior of incredible prowess, he had brought the majority of the Hellas into his fold, either with the promise of friendship or the boot of his heel. Helen's father was right. There were many kings in Greece, but not many *great kings*. Tyndareus might wish Helen the greatest king for her match, but it could never be, for her sister had already married him.

Helen raced down the long halls of the palace toward the eastern gates that faced the harbor. After one look at her eager face, Tyndareus had dismissed her. It had been two years since she'd seen her sister last, far too long for twins to be separated. Helen's feet couldn't carry her fast enough to the dock.

Aethra trailed behind her, the poor matron failing to keep up with her youthful speed. "Dignity, Princess! Dignity!" she shouted as Helen almost ran over a maid.

But Helen did not care of such scruples. Not when Clytemnestra was near. Propriety be damned. Her hair had already come free from Aethra's pins, falling wildly around her ears. She ran through the courtyard, barely heeding the admiring looks of her newly gathered suitors. Each tried to turn her head, their heated calls echoing throughout the courtyard. Those cries of affection turned to shouts of bravado as they turned on one another when she passed. Their crude behavior was a mild annoyance now. She didn't have time for their nonsense.

She continued out the gates and down the cobblestone path toward the harbor, Aethra hopelessly left behind. Several shop workers called out greetings and well-wishes. She knew she should stop and acknowledge them, but she reasoned they'd understand. Many of those citizens shared her grin, her enthusiasm so intense it couldn't help but be infectious.

She leapt onto the weathered dock with a graceful leap just as the giant galley tied off. This longship was larger than any other that made berth in the harbor. Fifty free men pulled at its rigging, furling an ivory sail with the baleful face of a gorgon stitched into its center. Carved into the mast was the head of a lion, the sigil of House Atreus. The ship's sleek hull was curved, like the belly of the great beast, and at the stern a large post rose ten feet above the deck like a rigid tail. Beneath that tail stood the king himself, a massive man thick of chest and hair. And seated demurely by his side was Helen's sister, Clytemnestra, Queen of Mycenae.

Helen didn't wait for Nestra to disembark. She leapt right onto the ship and wrapped her sister in an enthused embrace, showering her face with kisses. The royal attendants cast her shocked looks, and even the king smirked at her behavior, but Helen didn't care. She clung to her sister with a fierceness that shocked even herself. Nestra held her just as tightly, and they dissolved into tears and giggles.

Holding her twin, Helen realized how hollow life had become without her. Now that they were reunited Helen's angst-ridden world seemed much calmer.

"Sweet Sister, how I've missed you!" she exclaimed, pulling back to study Clytemnestra proper. The queen was regal in a thick gold pleated chiton. The shawl draped over her shoulders was intricately embroidered, clearly the work of a craftsman. Her hair was piled atop her head in tight braided coils, a style that lifted her scalp high and angled her eyes. As she gazed back at Helen, those eyes filled with love, and for a moment, the sisters were mirrored images of each other.

"Ahem." Agamemnon cleared his throat, discontent to be ignored any longer.

Nestra immediately pulled back and adopted a more queenly manner. After a slight hesitation, she responded formally, "I am pleased to see you, too, Helen."

The effect was startling. Clytemnestra appeared to age right before Helen's eyes. Her lips pinched together, her brow furrowed, and she seemed altogether tense. Though she was born only 20 minutes before Helen, she seemed half a dozen years her senior. Helen dropped her eyes to the deck, trying to hide her astonishment from her sister.

Agamemnon grunted again and Helen quickly collected herself, forcing her face to adopt a pleasant smile as she turned to the man. "King Agamemnon." She hailed him sweetly, dropping into a graceful curtesy. Only the dark shade of her eyes indicated the emotions simmering beneath her calm surface.

"Princess." He spoke with a heavy drawl, savoring the word as his eyes savored his view of her. "We have come to bear witness to your betrothal. A union Mycenae looks forward to with great interest." She held her head down demurely, her face flushed from the heat of his lustful gaze. Behind her, Nestra stiffened but held her tongue.

"I am honored by your interest." Helen replied with the same formality. Her eyes darted to Nestra, wishing she could erase the hurt on her sister's face. It seemed it was not Mycenae who watched Helen's union with interest, but Agamemnon himself. She tried to hide the spike of hate flaring in her heart. This man took her sister from her, and now he shamed Nestra with little afterthought.

He should not lust for me, she scorned the man for his greed. Clytemnestra was her identical twin.

But one stray glance at Nestra's twisted face belied that fact. It was commonly rumored amongst the palace staff that Aphrodite blessed both of Tyndareus' daughters with her beauty, but only one with her grace. It was an unfair comparison, but one Nestra never fully forgave.

Agamemnon tossed his cape over his shoulder and strode down the dock to the gathering nobles. Tyndareus had arrived accompanied by his advisors and liegemen. The men greeted each other stiffly and set off for the palace. Nestra's eyes followed their father as he left without a single sign of welcome for her.

Helen slid her hand into her sister's, giving it a gentle squeeze. This awkwardness was her fault—she insisted Mycenae be present for her courtship. Matters between the two kingdoms had been tense over the past three years. Agamemnon had demanded a Spartan bride as recompense for some squabble Helen could not recall. As eldest, Clytemnestra was offered. But the greedy king chose not to wait until her sister came of age and married Nestra at the tender age of 13.

A year later, when he needed help quelling an uprising in the north, Agamemnon came courting again, this time for Sparta's fearsome Hoplite soldiers. He thought to soften Tyndareus with an impromptu visit from his daughter. But when Tyndareus saw Clytemnestra was with child, and her barely more than a child herself, Agamemnon's plan backfired. Tyndareus steadfastly refused aid. The Mycenaean king left in a hurry, and the two sisters hadn't seen each other since.

Helen begged her father to make amends, but he refused to relent. Finally, when her courtship was announced, he had no further excuses. Agamemnon was too powerful to insult in such a manner. The invitation was extended and politely accepted.

The sisters watched the Mycenaean entourage disappear into the city, and only then did Nestra's hard exterior melt. "Were that it you who was given to the brute instead of me," she sighed, tucking a loose strand of Helen's hair behind her ear. "But you were always slower than me, even in birth." Her sharp laugh gave lie to the jest. Helen took it in stride. Nestra had few people she could truly talk to, and Helen didn't mind if the words stung.

"Have you ever considered that I waited for your approval first?" Helen asked playfully, her eyes alight as she studied Nestra's face, still in quiet disbelief her sister was actually here. "Or that I'd follow you into this world and the next? Would you mock such loyalty?"

"Oh, Sister," Nestra rolled her eyes, hooking Helen's arm in hers as they started the long trek back up to the palace, "You are *so* dramatic." Her chiming laughter was like music to Helen's ears. "It is good to be home."

Agamemnon warmed himself by the central hearth in Tyndareus' megaron. It was the Hour of the Wolf, that ominous time when the night was at its darkest. Agamemnon should have sought his bed hours ago. But the hall was quiet as it hadn't been since his arrival. And his host, the honorable —and seemingly tireless—King Tyndareus still held vigil over his hall. Only at this late hour could Agamemnon command his full attention.

A week had passed since he landed on Spartan soil and the fighting had only grown worse. Courting games were usually conducted with the sacred spirit of sportsmanship, but every suitor wanted Tyndareus' prize for himself. Blood feuds would soon ensue. And if that happened, the fragile alliance Agamemnon spent the last few years developing would be at risk.

Damn Tyndareus, and his bewitching daughter!

Helen was a great beauty, there was no denying that. She had a sweet innocence his wife lacked. Even the Gods would hunger for a taste from her ruby lips. But these princes and lesser kings hungered for something more than Helen's honey. In a world where the reigns of power shifted more swiftly than the tides, a king's reputation was sacrosanct. He must always exude an aura of strength, and any sign of weakness was an invitation for conquest.

Somehow the princess' union had gotten tied up in that maneuvering of power. Claiming Helen would greatly elevate a new king's standing, and no suitor wanted to walk away from this realm a step further down on that ladder.

Why did he have to invite so many? There's no region that will escape this decision untarnished. The Spartan's pride will bleed our realms.

Agamemnon tightened his cloak around him. The weather was unforgiving in Lacedaemonia, its high elevation forcing even the hardiest men to shiver around a fire at night. The fur lining of his cloak was blessedly warm against that cold. It was a lion's hide from a beast Agamemnon had slain with his own hands. He made sure his servants told the Spartan staff of that hunt. Relations had been strained between Sparta and Mycenae since his last visit. And if he could not earn Tyndareus' favor with friendship, Agamemnon would damn well make sure the Spartans feared him.

A draft wafted down from the oculus in the roof. With the raised hearth in the center of the room, the opening was an unfortunate necessity. Agamemnon eyed the gaping hole with a sneer. Black soot stained its edges, and the overlapping tiles, meant to keep out the elements, restricted ventilation. It was a primitive design. In fact, the entire megaron showed a similar lack of sophistication. The firebrick walls were barren, and the pillars supporting the roof—freshly cut beams of pine— stank of sap. If those beams ever caught fire they'd explode as violently as Vulcano himself.

But it was said imitation was the highest form of flattery. Agamemnon smiled. Already the outlying kingdoms aped his advancements. At Mycenae, his megaron was twice this size, its walls adorned with great works of art. Soon, every king would copy the splendors of Mycenae.

"Make sure to double the guard." Tyndareus instructed as he led his steward to the exit of the megaron. "Stagger the reserves at every junction in the palace. Give no soldier leave until the festivities have ended."

"As you command, my Liege." Asclepius gave the ruler a perfunctory bow and exited into the cold night. When the double doors clambered shut, Tyndareus finally acknowledge his presence.

"You wished to speak with me, Agamemnon?" Tyndareus addressed him, the first specter of weariness cracking through the king's tone. He returned to his throne, electing to speak to his son-in-law from his position of power, a tactic he had not—Agamemnon noted—adopted with his own staff.

"Yes, Father." Agamemnon inclined his head politely, cursing the necessity for the deference. But he was a guest in Tyndareus' house, not the other way around. Only a lesser man insulted his host, and Agamemnon was no lesser man. "I am concerned about the fallout of your imminent decision. By choosing one suitor, you risk offending all others," he warned the king. "And, if you let them fight it out, they might kill each other down to a man."

"I assure you, precautions are being made." Tyndareus responded curtly, his harsh tone affording no argument.

Stubborn to the bone. Such unreasonableness was a failing all Spartan's ingested with their mother's milk.

"Blood will be shed, Tyndareus." Agamemnon paced before the king, his hands clasped tightly behind his back. "I've said it before, and I'll say it again. Times of peace breed restless men, and right now they are fixated on your daughter. If we were to give them another outlet? Perhaps something guaranteed to sap the virile energy they have pent up?"

Tyndareus' eyes narrowed, glaring at him like a mastiff who caught the scent of another predator. "Such as?"

"A quest." Agamemnon spat the word out in eagerness. "Let the men prove their meddle, not by fighting each other, but in some noble pursuit. If the challenge is great enough, no one will deny the victor his right to Helen."

Agamemnon tried to hide the hunger in his voice, but it was hard. He desperately needed this opportunity. When Menelaus refused to travel to Sparta and participate in the courting games, Agamemnon almost sent his little brother to the whipping post. But Menelaus' absence presented Agamemnon with a unique situation. By representing his brother's claim, Agamemnon could compete with the other suitors without the stigma of being *competition*.

Mycenae was the dominant trade force in the region, and Agamemnon already commanded more respect than any other king of the Hellas. But that was the respect of the purse, not of valor in the field. He needed a golden fleece, a divine quest, a regal cause to showcase his superiority. Only then would the headstrong princelings of Greece acknowledge his ascent to Overlord. Only then would he have an Empire to rival those of the Old World.

Tyndareus laughed softly, his eyes never leaving Agamemnon's face. "And who would lead this quest? How would we decide? No, Agamemnon, we would exchange one potential insult for another. I will not delay Helen's wedding so needlessly."

Agamemnon grimaced. The wily old king could see right through him, and he was woefully reminded of the last time the two monarchs had met over similar desires.

The barbarians along Mycenae's border had swelled in number, a danger Agamemnon could no longer ignore. He wanted to ride forth with an army at his back, but no army was complete without Spartan soldiers. He came to Tyndareus seeking aid, and as his father by vow, he should have granted it.

"I will not start a war to avoid a war." Tyndareus had steadfastly refused. *"Ares would never forgive it."* Agamemnon cursed Tyndareus and his superstitions. The Spartan's piety might have gained the king great esteem throughout the

mainland, but his devotion was peasant nonsense. The Gods did not care of the plight of man, however much the priests and priestesses claimed otherwise. It was an inconvenient truth in a world where prophecy and omens held as much influence as facts.

"And what of Helen's safety?" Agamemnon wielded his last weapon. "If there is no clear victor, she will forever be in danger. She will *become* the quest, the prize for proving one's valor against a lesser king. You will doom her to a life of constant war."

Tyndareus mouth hung open, his will to deny betrayed by his love for his daughter. He *had* to see reason. Helen's salvation lay in a union with a house no one would dare offend. A stronger union with Mycenae was Tyndareus' best course.

Agamemnon locked eyes with the Spartan, pouring a command to obey in that gaze. *There is no way out, save through me.*

Tyndareus wilted into his throne. He was on the verge of surrender. The slump of his shoulders declared it louder than any words he could muster to protest. "I... I will consider your suggestion."

Agamemnon's blood sang, thrilling in this hard-fought achievement. While these many suitors fought over Helen's prestige, they did not see her true value. The princess was the key to Lacedaemonia. Tyndareus had no living sons. Helen's husband could make a valid claim to his throne. And though Sparta boasted no great wealth, the king of this land could summon an army of incredible strength and courage. It would be better to display his dominance in a noble quest, but barring that, Agamemnon would take a Spartan army and make the realms pledge fealty by force.

"Your Grace?" a herald called from the apex of the megaron. "King Odysseus is requesting an audience."

Agamemnon froze. What in Great Gaia was that man doing up at this hour? He almost told the herald to tell the

Ithakian to come back at a more reasonable hour when he realized this was not his megaron.

Tyndareus, eager for a respite from his oppressive company, waved the guard on. "Granted."

Odysseus entered the hall and strut toward them with a light step that spoke of a carefree manner. He had doffed his regal attire for a simple woolen tunic favored by the Spartan free men. He seemed a likable fellow, neither too handsome to invite jealousy, nor too homely to incite resentment. He bowed low before Tyndareus, careful to give Agamemnon equal respect.

"Your Majesties," he addressed them both with deference. "I have come to offer counsel, if you wish to accept it."

Tyndareus looked to Agamemnon, the question apparent in his eyes. *Is this his idea or yours?* those eyes asked. But Agamemnon's stormy expression was all the answer Tyndareus needed.

"You should hear him out," Agamemnon muttered reluctantly. "There are many virtues and we cannot be masters of them all. You may recall what Odysseus is renown for?"

Tyndareus nodded, a flicker of understanding settled into his deep blue eyes. Already, the king seemed more in command of his faculties, his brief moment of weakness long forgotten. Agamemnon cursed the Ithakian and his horrible timing.

At two and twenty, Odysseus was quite young to be a ruler. But his father was an Argonaut, and like many of the heroes from that legendary vessel, Laertes did not have the stomach to actually govern his province. Odysseus took on his mantle of kingship when he was barely more than a lad, while Laertes warmed his bones by the fire and recanted tales of his wild youth. Agamemnon scoffed at such idleness, but it seemed Ithaka had benefited from the arrangement. Odysseus held great promise.

Tyndareus came to a similar assessment and waved him on. "Speak, Odysseus. Have no fear of reprisal."

The Ithakian approached the throne and lowered his voice in a confidential manner. "It is no secret that your daughter's beauty has stirred great rivalry amongst your guests, Honorable King. Once your decision is set, you needs must worry about Helen's safety, that the other suitors might seek to steal this prize by conquest even after her vows have been spoken. The blood spilt would be a dark stain on all of our honor."

"You speak truth." Tyndareus acknowledged. Thus far, the man had not spoken one word they hadn't already discussed.

Odysseus leaned forward, emboldened by the warmth in the king's tone. "What if I were to tell you there was a way these men will leave happily of their own accord? A way to announce a betrothal without shedding a single drop of blood? And for a cost you'd scarce notice?"

"Cost?" Agamemnon growled, inserting his bulking frame between his host and the young king. This was one upset too many for his tempered blood. If Odysseus had the audacity to bargain like a crude merchant before the throne, then he had clearly misjudged the quality of this man.

"I ask only for a boon," Odysseus added quickly, retreating half a step. "A token of gratitude I assure you you'll consider fair."

Odysseus quickly divulged his plan, its brilliance matched only by its simplicity. Agamemnon curled his fingers through his oiled beard, studying the worth of the man before them. Odysseus' wits were unmatched in all of Greece. A cunning man could easily use his skills for devious endeavors. But Ithaka was too far from Mycenae for Agamemnon to consider it a serious threat. Nonetheless, he was glad to count the young king his ally.

The advice was sage, and because it came from Odysseus, Tyndareus would not refuse it. Agamemnon almost laughed, deciding instantly that he liked the young man. Odysseus had stones to match a mighty bull. He let his mind wander, considering the benefits this new arrangement provided. With one sacred vow, Tyndareus' dilemma would be solved. The Hellas would be a step closer to unification.

And if they make one vow, it is a short measure to make them swear another.

A lust of a different sort flooded Agamemnon. Mycenae would prosper from this match, by blood or sacred vow. Just like he intended.

CHAPTER 4

THE LOVE THAT BINDS

THE PAST week had flown by in a blur for Helen. She spent every waking moment with her twin, delighting in Clytemnestra's tales of her new life at Mycenae. Dominating the northeastern coast of the mainland, Mycenae was the trading center for the rest of Greece. The capital was a bustling port city that rivaled the wonders of ancient Crete itself, so Nestra said, and it abounded with modern advancements. Agamemnon's palace played host to all manner of exotic guests. To Helen, Nestra's life seemed a glorious adventure filled with exciting people.

"Hardly." Nestra snorted when Helen voiced her thoughts. She bounced her daughter on her knee, alternating her attention between Helen and the chubby toddler. "Most of the visitors are glorified merchants, fat on the riches they collected from cheating lesser lords. They're more likely to make off with the silver than provide company of value."

Helen laughed at the thought, but after the past week there was no behavior of houseguests that would surprise her. The situation with her suitors had grown steadily worse. Every time she tried to appear in public, their competitive nature got the best of them. They'd start with wild boasts of their accomplishments. Whether they meant to impress her or each other, she could not tell. And if the chest puffing wasn't enough to get a fellow suitor to stand down, it would come to blows. Helen tried to avoid their gatherings, certain she had witnessed enough of that barbarity, but Tyndareus insisted she attend every event. He was constantly filling her ears with the virtues and weaknesses of each suitor. It was an exhausting endeavor. Only now that the courtship neared its end, was she given a moment for herself.

Though Clytemnestra's rooms were identical to Helen's own, the royal suite felt cramped. The Mycenaean delegation had twice as many retainers as Helen was used to. Adding a baby into the mix, the walking space became nonexistent.

Helen took Iphigenia from her sister, tickling the baby into giggles. "She's absolutely perfect, Nestra. She hardly cries at all." The babe cast her a toothless grin.

"A blessing, I'm sure of it." Clytemnestra crossed her fingers to the Gods in thanks and leaned back against a pile of cushions. "I've heard most babes are little monsters."

Helen laughed. Only Nestra could look at a baby and call it a monster. "Careful," she warned her twin. "You're asking the Fates to make your next child a beast."

Nestra didn't laugh. She had been under considerable strain for the past week. Agamemnon made constant demands of her. He was grooming her, Nestra confided, to behave in a manner that better reflected her new station, a High queen of the Hellas. She took pride in that lofty title, but the cost was a bombardment of belittling comments and disapproving glares.

"He wants a son." Nestra's voice drained of joy. "He's after me twice a day with the bedding and yet still has an eye for the serving girls. His lust is insatiable."

"Impossible," Helen gasped. "He made a sacred vow!" The king might have a roaming eye, but he wouldn't betray Nestra's honor. Doing so would tarnish his reputation as well.

Clytemnestra's knowing gaze spoke a different truth. "Words are just words, Helen, whether they're sacred or not.

You'll learn soon enough. For the men of the Hellas, women are for breeding. There is no vow they'll honor save the ones they make to each other."

Helen bit her tongue and resisted the urge to challenge her. Clytemnestra couldn't mean what she said. Her tough experiences with a brutish husband had twisted her heart and made her less forgiving. The race of Men could not be so bereft of honor.

But what if they are? Helen swallowed a nervous lump. Thus far, not a single suitor had proven himself anything more than a quarrelsome brigand. She had to trust her father to see more than what she had witnessed, to find her a husband of quality. But if what Nestra said was true, it wouldn't matter which man Tyndareus chose.

Some of Helen's concern must have reflected on her face. Nestra reached out and squeezed her hand in sympathy, a hard look emblazoned on her face. "Pity them, Sister. They know nothing of what you and I share."

Helen squeezed back, returning her sister's affection measure for measure. *This* was real. The love the twins shared was complete, unconditional. Was that such a rare thing?

A timid knock came from the hall and Astyanassa peaked her head in to the room. "Princess? Tryphosa awaits you at the Temple." She bowed her head, letting her dark brown hair hide the flush of excitement on her cheeks.

Helen froze. She had momentarily forgotten about her womanhood ritual. Her betrothal was being announced tomorrow. This was officially her last night of childhood. It was time for the Priestess to anoint her with Aphrodite's blessing as she moved into the next phase of life.

"Come with me." She turned impulsively to her sister.

Clytemnestra's eyes lit up, sharing Helen's excitement. Her own wedding came too fast to observe the old rituals. She missed out on the Blessing.

"Forgive me, Princess," Astyanassa interrupted softly. "But Tryphosa said the ceremony was for maidens only."

Helen turned on her handmaiden, her irritation plain on her face. "That's a stupid tradition. I'm sure the Priestess won't mind."

"But—"

"She can make an exception." Helen insisted. "Clytemnestra is my twin. We entered the world together. She shares my innocence."

The poor girl looked terrified. Her nervous eyes darted to Clytemnestra and the baby Iphigenia in Helen's arms. Helen knew her argument was feeble—Nestra was no innocent—but it was unfair to exclude her from this important ceremony.

"Forget about it, Helen." Nestra snapped bitterly, snatching her daughter from Helen's arms.

Helen froze, torn between her obligations to the temple and her loyalty to her sister. "But I want you to come."

One glance at Nestra's hard face told Helen how little that mattered. There were few women as stubborn as her twin, and becoming a queen had only increased that quality.

"*Go.*" Nestra insisted. "Have your ceremony. Don't let *me* spoil it for you."

It's not you, Helen tried to console herself, stiffening from Nestra's hurtful tone. *She's upset to be left out. She's not angry with you.*

Then Iphigenia began to cry. It was such an unusual occurrence it jarred Helen out of her private thoughts. Clytemnestra was holding the child too tight and was pinching the baby's sensitive skin. Astyanassa wisely stepped into the hall to wait for her, leaving the twins alone.

"Will I see you tonight?" Helen asked, adopting a sweet smile that reflected none of the hurt she was feeling inside.

Nestra spun towards the wall, shielding her face from view. "Perhaps," she answered tersely. "If I have time."

"Then I will wait all night."

Helen curtsied and exited the apartment.

The moon was halfway through the night sky when Helen waited outside Aphrodite's Hall to be collected by temple initiates. She wore a simple white chiton, unadorned like the sort children wear. Her hair hung loose around her shoulders free of any bindings, a symbol of the burden-free life she was soon to leave.

The temple was outside the palace defensive walls, a simple columned building beneath a grove of apple trees. Torches lined the exterior in ornate sconces set on each pillar. Those flames fought valiantly to keep the darkness at bay, the tongues of fire crackling with the slight breeze that threatened to snuff them out.

Helen shivered. Her wardrobe offered no protection against the night chills. But that was not the cause of her discomfort. Left alone for the past hour in the inky blackness of full night without a soul to share her vigil had left Helen plenty of time to dwell on her current predicament. When the Priestess deemed the time was right, she would enter the temple and beseech Aphrodite's help in securing the man of her heart. And Helen had no idea which man that might be.

The chiming of cymbals rang out accompanied by rhythmic clapping and the sweet voices of the Goddess' initiates. In a burst of light, the girls emerged from the temple adorned in garlands of myrtle and white flowing dresses similar to Helen's own. They formed a chain that wove around the princess in an elegant infinity symbol, one end around Helen, the other bending around the temple entrance.

The girls chanted in rhythm to the music, their voices united in a spirit of youthful energy and anticipation. Helen thought she recognized some of the faces that passed her by. Astyanassa was there. As was Clymene, her doe eyed chambermaid, a girl of twelve years. None of the initiates were older than Helen, a fact that reminded the princess she no longer belonged in their company.

The circle broke as Tryphosa emerged from the Temple. Helen's trembling returned, this time from awe at the priestess' lush beauty. A long dress of crimson accentuated Tryphosa's womanly curves. Her sandy locks were pulled high on her head and cascaded down her back in spiral waves. Her plump lips pressed together with a knowing smile, one that invited all manner of speculation of what naughty thoughts it suppressed. She was exquisite. The Goddess had bestowed many favors on her chosen one.

Tryphosa spread her arms wide and the initiates divided into two lines creating a tunnel between Helen and the priestess. With a flick of her delicate hand, she motioned the princess forward.

Helen adopted her father's cool confidence, pacing herself as she walked sedately toward the temple entrance. The girl's giggles followed her as she passed. Reaching into satchels tied to their waist, they tossed blood-red poppy petals over her head. By the dim light of flickering torches, the portico seemed to rain blood.

"Who approaches the Altar of Aphrodite?" the priestess demanded in a deep voice that made her chest heave.

Helen bowed her head. "A humble child who would share in Her secrets of Love." The soft kisses of petals trickled down her neck and gown.

"Such secrets are not for the ears of children," Tryphosa declared, her azure eyes narrowing as she studied her initiates with a frown. "If you step into Her realm, you will be a child no longer, but a woman fully grown. The transformation does not come without a price. Are you prepared to pay the toll?"

Helen straightened herself. Fully erect, she stood eye to eye with the priestess, equal in height and stature. "My heart is pure, my body chaste. I offer my Innocence at Love's burning altar. Do not hide your face from me, Goddess Divine."

According to ritual, she should have been ushered into the

temple immediately, Eros' secrets confided in the newly raised woman's ear. But the priestess blocked the entrance, a strange look crossing over her beautiful features.

Suddenly, Tryphosa threw back her head and cackled like a crone. It was a terrifyingly mocking sound.

Helen froze. Even the initiates tittered nervously behind her. The torch light flared high by some unseen force, and when the last note of the priestess' cry died off, an eerie silence permeated the portico.

"Shoo. Begone!" Tryphosa shouted to the girls, and the initiates scattered like the wind. Once alone, the priestess beckoned Helen forward.

Helen made no move to follow, shocked by the awesome display.

"Don't be shy, Princess." Tryphosa beckoned again. "You asked to see the Goddess' face, and you will soon learn she has many."

But the Goddess was love divine. She was passion, the heat that burned in a maiden's breast. She was erotic energy that stabbed at a person's soul, drawing lovers together with a force that could not be denied. There was nothing sinister or ugly about Aphrodite.

"And what of jealousy, betrayal and rape?" Tryphosa questioned, answering Helen's unspoken question. "These are the shadow faces of Love. You cannot be a woman until you recognize the dangers of the Goddess' power. Now, come." She added more forcibly.

Helen had no choice but to comply, transfixed on the unblinking gaze of the priestess. Tryphosa led them into the temple's inner chamber. A copper brazier sat in the center of the room, the glowing coals inside heating the room almost to the point of sweltering. A heavy incense burned, clouding Helen's vision and thoughts.

"Breathe deeply, Princess." Tryphosa purred in her ear, pressing Helen down onto the embroidered cushions lining the floor. She crossed to the other side of the room and picked up an urn decorated with black figures—maidens dancing beneath the trees, a similar scene to the one replicated outside. Tryphosa tipped the urn, pouring a thick liquid over the coals. Steam erupted, billowing to the sky like the putrid breath of Vulcano, filling the room with an acrid tasting cloud. Helen blinked back tears from her stinging eyes. She could see nothing.

"Priestess?" she coughed. But the only sound came from the sharp hissing of the coals. "*Tryphosa?*"

The warmth had worked its way into her bones. Helen felt her muscles slacken, and she had to resist the urge to crumble into the cushions. It was so soft, so comfortable...

"That's it." The priestess' musical voice floated to her through the void. In the darkness it had grown deeper, rumbling with a hidden power. "Give in to your pleasure. You will find the Goddess there."

Helen's head felt unbelievably heavy. She tried to stay upright, but it was a losing battle. She had neither the will nor the strength to resist. She collapsed onto the floor, her body tingling from head to toe.

It started in her chest, the pulling sensation that caused her heart to race as though the organ was trying to escape her ribs. Her nipples tightened, elongating beneath the rough fabric of her chiton. Helen groaned. Never before had her breasts ached in this manner. Every inch of her skin screamed in exquisite sensitivity.

The pulling travelled down her torso, infusing her body with waves of blistering warmth until she broke out in a sweat. Like a ghostly brush of fingers, the feeling trailed down her abdomen until it latched firmly down on her vulva.

A wave of pure euphoria engulfed her. Helen gasped, her back arched against her will, and she cried out as the strange feeling crested to new heights.

And then the phantom assault was gone. Her body crumbled back to the cushions and she was left in a hazy peace.

"What was *that?*" she whispered huskily, her hands roaming over her still tingling skin. Her pulse was skyrocketing. She had never felt more alive. She sat up slowly, her mind no longer clouded but blessedly clear.

Tryphosa, beside the brazier in the diminishing smoke, sat opposite of her. "That was Aphrodite's touch. You will receive it again with Love's true embrace."

Helen blushed. Receive it again? She didn't trust herself. It was too powerful, she was too weak. The promise of such pleasure would make her a wanton, desperate for more.

"You share it with another?" The prospect of that intimacy was both tantalizing as it was shocking.

"If the soul is your match, yes." The priestess answered. She tossed a tightly bound bushel of herbs into the brazier, a leaf Helen didn't recognize. Thin tendrils of smoke trailed upwards, and the priestess breathed of them deeply, her eyes rolling back in her skull. She seemed utterly at peace until she lurched forward in a violent jerk.

"Ask what you will, Blessed Daughter. I am here."

Helen's eyes shot wide. It was no earthly voice. No living creature could produce such an awesome mixture of melody and vibration. Tryphosa, the mortal, had vanished. The person sitting before Helen was a rigid shell, the mouth for the Goddess who spoke through her lips.

Helen leaned forward, drawn towards that force like a cub to her dame. *Ask,* she had offered. Helen's mind swirled with the many faces of her suitors. But her curiosity, as always, got the best of her. "Is it true-" she hesitated, hating the question but desperately needing its answer, "Is it true that men are ignorant of love, real love?" She didn't want to believe Nestra, but her sister had been married three years. She had seen much of the world. Helen's knowledge of men was nonexistent. What little she'd seen had done nothing to convince her Nestra was wrong.

"There are some, both male and female, who are ignorant of my love." The Goddess intoned. *"But I am not so fickle to deny them*

that bliss. They choose *the cold solitude of a shuttered heart."*

"But why would anyone choose that?" Helen frowned. A world with no compassion, no care, no love...? That gaping chasm opened itself before her. It made her want to cry. What God would be cruel enough to let their people suffer so?

The coals sparked and the priestess lowered her white gaze on Helen, making Helen shiver despite the sweltering heat.

"The love that you receive is equal to the love you give." Her white-lidded eyes bore into her. *"And for those rare souls who give with no thought of receipt, on those I bestow my special favor."* The Goddess' voice rose in volume, cresting in ecstasy. *"Only they are worthy of the eternal love; the force that breaks bonds of brotherhood, that transcends the vagaries of pride and ego, a binding of souls that endures across the Ages."*

"...soul mates." Helen whispered. Was it possible? She had thought such tales were fabrications by the bards who sang for their suppers. The original Man was neither male nor female, the legend went, but a perfect balance of both parts, a creature so whole and happy that the Gods looked down from Olympus with envy. And so Zeus, in his jealousy, struck Man down with a bolt of lightning, severing its soul in two. And thus mankind was doomed to roam the earth, searching in vain for their other half.

Helen's heart skipped a beat. Why was the Goddess telling her this? "Am I...? Are you...?" her feeble tongue choked on the words.

The brazier blazed to life, flames leaping five feet into the air. Tryphosa rose to her feet, her perfect features aglow with a burning power.

"You, Helen of Sparta, will have the greatest love that ever was, is, or is yet to be. Your love will rock the foundations of this earth."

Helen didn't breathe. She didn't even dare move. A clamoring bell of alarm rung loudly in her mind. Her father was choosing her husband on the morrow and none of her suitors invoked the feelings the Goddess described. "How will

I know?"

"It is a power undeniable, a force stronger than the turning of the tide. You cannot mistake it, for the visage of your other half will be as familiar to you as your own. You will know."

Tryphosa lurched forward, her arms flopping at her side as though someone cut the cord that made them function.

"But how!" Helen leapt to her feet, desperation lending her strength.

"Follow your heart." The Goddess' heavy words drifted away as though sucked back into the priestess' quivering throat. *"It never lies."*

An enormous gust of wind rushed through the temple, lifting Helen off her knees. It seemed a living entity, this wind, a ghostly touch of some unseen power. It wove around the priestess, her limp and lifeless body held tight in its embrace. Tryphosa's arms spread wide and back and her head tipped up towards the heavens. In a rushing vortex, the gust crested to the sky and vanished. Unsupported, the priestess collapsed to the ground.

The room was utterly empty. Not a trace of incense remained, and the brazier coals burned low, its heat replaced with a bone chilling cold. The magic woven by the Divine Presence was gone.

Helen rushed to Tryphosa's side, lifting her head as the woman's eyes rolled back into place. Helen soothed her brow as she regained her bearings, the priestess moaning as though she were entangled in a lover's embrace. As an open vessel to the Goddess, Helen supposed she might have been.

Slowly, her breathing calmed and Tryphosa's luscious smile returned. She pulled herself up into a sitting position, her round eyes watching Helen with a naked expression of fear and awe.

"A child no longer." She trembled, pulling away from Helen's touch.

Helen shivered, equally frightened by the Goddess' powerful foretelling. She had come seeking a solution to her marital dilemma and was now more uncertain than ever.

"All things must end." Helen whispered with a touch of remorse, her tremors tripping her voice. And tomorrow they *would* end, soul mate or not.

"They must." Tryphosa agreed, kneeling before her. "But they must also begin." She raised Helen's hand to her lips. "Long may you reign, My Queen."

CHAPTER 5

THE OATH

MORNING CAME all too soon for Helen. She waited outside the megaron, exhausted from her ordeal in the temple. She had hardly slept. What precious moments she claimed prior to dawn were robbed of her as Aethra stormed her apartments with an army of chambermaids. The world would be watching her today, and the princess must look the part.

The matron had outdone herself with her preparations. Helen's hair was gathered up into a pile of small coils draping over her bare right shoulder. A crown of parsley leaves and white blossoms of heliotrope lay atop her brow. Her ivory chiton had sashes of vermillion and rose criss-crossed over her torso and down the pleated folds of the dress. A net of hammered gold links rested on her collar, the adornment chiming ever so softly whenever Helen turned her head. The matron even pressed lavender oil to Helen's lobes and wrists. Helen knew the effect must be dazzling. Still, she feared this armor of grace and beauty would not be enough protection in the battle ahead.

Follow my heart?

Those words played over and over again in her head. It was a simple instruction, but one she could not fathom. Her traitorous heart pulled in several directions, none of which aligned with the suitors gathered on the other side of those double doors. She was drowning in worry that the wrong path would be chosen, that she would prove herself unworthy for Aphrodite's blessing.

"I missed you last night." Clytemnestra spoke softly beside her, a faint hint of hurt in her tone. Nestra had the uncanny ability to walk soundlessly when she wanted, and was equally talented at spotting anyone trying to sneak up on her. Their father could never catch her unawares.

All of Helen's frayed nerves seemed to explode at the sight of her lovely sister. Clytemnestra, looking every inch the queen, was resplendent in a heavy chiton of gold and saffron red. Helen impulsively wrapped her arms around her twin, a small sob escaping her lips.

"Helen?" Nestra's hard facade broke, real concern pouring out of her. "What's wrong? Are you hurt?"

But Helen couldn't find words for what plagued her. The pressure of the imminent betrothal weighed down on her like the burdens of Atlas. She must uphold the honor of her father, of Sparta, of the Goddess, and in some small portion, her own heart. "I'm... *scared.*" She finally admitted out loud.

"Shhhhh." Nestra held her tight, soothing her shaking arms. "There's nothing to worry about. You'll walk inside. Father will make his decision, and it will be over. There's nothing more to say or do."

It sounded so easy when Nestra said it. Helen simply had to accept her fate, and go to whichever future shores the Zephyrs chose to send her. But something inside her rebelled against surrender. Down that path, she was noting but a prize to be handed out by others, not a person worthy of great love.

"It will all be over." Nestra cooed, wiping away Helen's tears. "And you'll find a way to be happy."

"But Tryphosa—"

"The priestess did this to you?" A crease of anger shot across Clytemnestra's face. "Helen, she's nothing but a drug-addled zealot. You can't take her advice to heart. You're going to be queen, not some village house wife."

Clytemnestra's words were harsh, and they cut right through the fog that paralyzed her. "That's blasphemy, Nestra."

"That's *reality,* Sister." Nestra countered. "There's a real world out there, filled with men, and kingdoms, and wars. And you and I have *real* responsibilities in it. You cannot be so easily manipulated."

Was I? Helen played through the events at the temple, looking for any instance where Tryphosa tried to influence her. She shook her head with the effort. There was none.

"You'll have to trust me." Nestra asserted, holding Helen's hand in a death grip. "*'Where you go, I follow'*, remember?"

Nestra was so certain, so strong. With no real guidance from the priestess or her father, such confidence was a relief. Clytemnestra had survived her own betrothal and marriage. She knew, *intimately knew,* the path Helen would soon be forced to walk. Facing that unknown future, Nestra was the only person she could trust.

"I remember." Helen's resolve returned, a warm wave of relief flooding over her. She clung to her twin's hand, a lifeline in the torrent of her fears. Together, she felt strong. Together, she was safe.

A great fanfare of horns trumpeted from inside the megaron. The double doors flew open and a pair of heralds stepped forward, both wearing the colors of Sparta, the same saffron red of the carpets beneath their feet. They carried polished wooden hoplon shields, their surface plated with a thick layer of bronze. In their other hands, the heralds lifted two long ox horns decorated with flags of ochre red and brownish yellow. They pressed the horns to their lips and trumpeted two short blasts, the regal notes hanging in the air, an invitation for Helen's entrance.

Inside, a crowd of dignitaries, both citizens of Sparta and Suitor alike, spread apart, carving a clear path for her to travel to the throne. Their heads bowed forward, each man and woman eager to catch a glimpse of the princess.

Helen steeled herself. A confidence that previously eluded her snuffed out her fears. She lifted her chin, a defiant glint in her eyes. *Fear does not exist. It will not be my master.*

Clytemnestra moved to disengage herself, but Helen held her fast. "Walk with me." She placed a gentle hand on her sister's forearm.

Nestra's smile was unforgettable. Reaching out, she tucked a stray hair out of Helen's face. "I envy the man who lays claim to your heart. He will possess riches beyond the wealth of this world."

If Helen's heart had wings it would have fluttered away. Together, they faced the megaron and began the long walk to her future. She set a stately pace.

A solemn hush fell over the crowd as they passed. Fevered whispers of awe and admiration rose to the rafters. Her suitors could barely contain themselves. For a moment, Helen feared their aggressive behavior would return, but something more powerful held sway in the hall. Some crossover of her regal bearing fused into the men. They held themselves straight, more than one with a touch of embarrassment on his face for past behavior.

Tyndareus faced the gathered men from where he sat upon his throne, his visage akin to engraved stone. Both she and Nestra curtsied low before him, and his stern eyes softened when they fell on her. As Helen straightened, her sister finally released her arm and took her place beside her husband in the front row. Helen waited for the crowd's murmuring to lessen, and then walked up the raised dais to joined her noble father. When she finally settled beside him, he began to speak.

"Honored guests!" His strong voice rang out across the hall. "You have come here, to glorious Sparta, seeking the hand of my daughter, Helen, blessed of Zeus and Aphrodite. Over the past week, you have displayed your prowess in feats of strength. You have impressed this king with your courage and fortitude. But in the end, only one man can claim Helen as his bride."

The crowd shuffled, the nearness of the announcement stirring them like the winds of Aeolus. Helen bristled as the entire room laid eyes on her. It was unsettling to be the center of so much attention. She turned to her sister for support, locking eyes with the queen. That was when she noticed Agamemnon whispering discreetly into the ear of King Odysseus. They were the only people in the room not wholly focused on Tyndareus words.

"Before I continue, if there be any item of concern, I would have my guests speak forthwith. Let each man be at peace before this decision is set."

Helen distrusted the cunning look on Agamemnon's face. She turned to her father to see if he had noticed and was shocked to see the same hard look on Tyndareus' face. She turned back to the crowd just as Odysseus stepped forward.

"Humble Tyndareus," Odysseus began with a bow. "It has been an honor to court your daughter, the beauty of our Age. And while I swell with pride to be considered alongside such noble and honorable men, I must respectfully withdraw my candidacy."

A shocked titter ran through the crowd. Odysseus waved down his fellow suitor's questions. "I beg your forgiveness, dear Princess." He turned to Helen. His insincerity oozed over her, freezing her in place. "In truth, I would be a poor choice for you compared to these great warriors."

Many men harrumphed their agreement. Ajax of Salamis, a giant of a man who towered a good head over Odysseus, quickly puffed up his chest and stepped in front of the Ithakian king, casting Helen an eager grin.

"I appreciate your candor, young Odysseus." Tyndareus acknowledge the request formally. "As consolation for your loss, I will speak with my brother Icarius. I know his daughter Penelope has loved you from afar. May fortune favor you in that match."

Helen turned to her father, puzzled. Penelope had never laid an eye on Odysseus. What was going on here?

But she had no time to question. Tyndareus raised his hands, gathering the attention of the remaining crowd. "And now the time has come." He paused, waiting for each man to hang on his words. "Last night, virtuous Artemis visited me in a dream. As patron Goddess of this city and of all chaste and innocent girls, she warned me of the repercussions of this day. Helen, sweet Helen, was soon to be lost to her. She would not let such a joyous event be soiled by jealousy and anger."

Tyndareus' words chilled Helen. She had always known her father to be devout, a faithful servant to the Gods. Had he been visited the same as she? Or was this all the posturing of kings and kingdoms, as Nestra insisted? Somehow, her fate was woven into this maneuvering, and she was powerless to stop it.

The men muttered in anticipation. This news, whatever Tyndareus was trying to say, sat no better with them than it did with Helen.

"'Goddess,' I swore to Artemis, 'the friends of Sparta would not dishonor *you* with such vile actions.' But she was not assured. She then insisted that any man who thought himself worthy to be wed to such beauty abide by a sacred oath. Only then would she allow the matrimony to commence."

The double doors opened again, this time for a pair of stable hands towing a massive heifer. The poor beast bellowed in fear, sensing her imminent doom. Helen had never heard a more pitiful sound. They led the beast to an altar beside the central hearth.

Tyndareus stepped down from the throne, unsheathing his ornate short sword. "Come all who would be my son. Come and swear this sacred oath. To defend and protect he who is chosen like a brother of your blood. Swear to defend him against any wrong done to him in regard to this union. Swear by the blood of this sacrifice, and share in the protection of

Artemis and Her Almighty Father."

He sliced open the heifer's neck, a crimson tide of blood spilling into a bronze urn at his feet.

"I will swear that oath," Diomedes declared, stepping boldly beside Tyndareus and thrusting his hand into the flowing blood.

"As will I!" Protesilaus joined them. Then Patroclus, and Achilles and Ajax. Even Odysseus, caught up in the moment, joined his peers.

Tyndareus studied them all, counting to ensure there was none unaccounted. And then Agamemnon stepped forward, his mighty fist thrust between the others. Helen turned in alarm to her sister who seemed as shocked as she.

"Don't be greedy, Agamemnon." Diomedes teased. "You already have a wife to warm your bed."

"I assure you brothers, one daughter of Sparta is enough for me." He announced to great laughter while Clytemnestra blushed. "I stand for my brother Menelaus, who, by no fault of his own, was left behind to tend to affairs of state."

There were forty men, Agamemnon included, who so swore. Helen watched in disbelief as they commingled their bloody hands into an enormous fist.

"All hail the Oath of Tyndareus!" Odysseus proclaimed, his voice ringing out the pact with great finality.

"THE OATH OF TYNDAREUS!" the others shouted in unison.

The voice in her head told Helen this was a momentous event. The men of the Hellas had never made an oath of unity. But here they stood, the mightiest warrior kings of the western world, hands locked in purpose. And she was that purpose! Should some ill fate befall her, all of Greece would unite in her defense. Tyndareus had achieved the impossible, and he had done so in her honor.

But that voice also whispered other words, bitter words her sister had confided just one night ago. It was not respect for Sparta that created this moment, but hubris and ego. Sadly, she understood why her father's oath was necessary.

"Helen," Tyndareus startled her from her reflections. "Lay your crown at the foot of your chosen."

"The choice is mine?" She was so stunned she forgot to address him properly. He smiled at her slip.

"Choose wisely."

She removed her crown of flowers with a shaky hand, her eyes darting over the men eagerly awaiting her decision. The hunger was written in their faces. They wanted her body, but there was something more. Violent streaks of crimson blood ran down their arms. Red was the color of conquest, of victory. She was nothing but a prize to them. And her choice would elevate the victor over his brothers.

Again she turned to Clytemnestra. Standing alone now, her sister had a sad look on her face. Helen's heart flooded with remorse, remembering the day Nestra left their home for Mycenae. They were losing each other again as sure as they had three years hence.

But it didn't have to be. The choice was right before her.

Follow your heart.

Clytemnestra locked eyes with her and Helen knew what she must do. She stepped forward boldly and placed her crown at Agamemnon's feet. Menelaus, the man she had never met, would be her husband.

The room erupted in cheers. The Mycenaean king seemed utterly surprised by her choice. Cries of "Huzzah!" rang out while his peers congratulated him. Helen was all but ignored. She worked her way over to her sister, happy to join Nestra in the shadows.

Helen finally understood what the Goddess was trying to tell her. Her great love, the other half of her separated soul was right in front of her. Where Clytemnestra went, Helen knew she must follow. She reached out to her twin, gently wiping away Nestra's tears. "Sisters forever?"

Clytemnestra was so broken with emotion, she could barely speak. She wrapped her arms around Helen in a fierce embrace. "Helen, you crazy fool!" Her face twisted in horror. "You don't know Menelaus. You've made a terrible mistake."

Part 2

Ten Years Later

THE CURSED PRINCE

IN THE LANDS across the sea, in the plains of Anatolia and the twin rivers of the Tigris-Euphrates, the Old Empires clung to their seats of power.

Here, the land was different, crueler. Volcanic eruptions, earthquakes, and floods wiped out entire populations. Both high and lowborn fell victim to plague. Death, in its many manifestations, was a familiar threat that struck indiscriminately.

In these times of chaos, the people turned to their spiritual leaders: Seers, Soothsayers, Priests and Priestesses. They were tasked to make sense of a senseless world. As reason gave way to fear, the cold grip of superstition ruled over the masses, and in many realms the king was at the mercy of the temple's influence. There was no greater example of this phenomenon than in the Royal House of Troy and the sad tale of Paris, second born son of King Priam.

Hecuba, beloved wife to the king, had a vision on the night she gave birth to the prince. She dreamt of a burning torch, the heat from its flame so terrible it burned her very soul. Aesacus, Priest of Apollo and Seer to the Throne, interpreted this dream into a dark omen. The queen, he said, was giving birth to a fire that would consume all of Troy. This child was cursed and must be killed to ensure the safety of the realm.

King Priam refused. He would not give the temple zealots the power of life and death over his son. But Hecuba, blinded by her devotion to the Gods, tried to smother the infant child. Priam stopped her, but it was the first of many attempts on the innocent boy's life.

The influence of the temple was too great, and though the king did his best to protect his son, he could not denounce the omen outright. Paris was an outcast, rejected before he took his first breath. Priam's only option to save him from temple knives was to send Paris away to foster abroad.

At the same time that Helen was wedded in Mycenae, Paris came of age and was named an Ambassador of Troy. Normally a prestigious position, this appointment was not given for honor. Its true purpose was to keep the prince away from his homeland, where his presence would not create more turmoil for the king.

And thus, even Priam, the greatest ruler of mighty Troy, was laid low by forces he could not control.

CHAPTER 6

A PRINCE OF TROY

PARIS STOOD at the prow of his longship as it coasted into the crystal blue waters of Troy. The forlorn cries of a flock of gulls floated across the clear spring sky, a fitting song to herald him home. He took a deep breath, and savored the view of the golden city from afar. It had been too long since he last gazed on the splendors of Troy.

The world was changing. Empire clashed with Empire in feuds that spanned a millennium. And in that chaos, Troy was a shining ray of hope. Nestled along the coast of the Aegean Sea and the river lands of Anatolia, it was the gateway between the aged wisdom of the east, and the youthful vibrance of the west, a perfect blend of the old world and the new. No matter how far afield his duties sent him, no matter what exotic lands he beheld, to Paris, there was no place as special as Troy.

The lowlands that fed into the harbor were densely packed with a thriving market town. Merchants from Cyprus, Babylonia, Crete and the Levant intermingled in the Trojan streets, eager to profit from the bustling commerce of the hub city.

Beyond the plateau and encircled by massive gates of

stone, the inner city bloomed like a desert rose. It was an immense complex of interconnecting buildings of limestone and marble that stretched up to a steep acropolis. And at its peak sat the Royal Palace, an elegant structure that rivaled any court in the ancient world.

Paris savored this beauty. In these few moments before he set foot on Trojan land, he could admire his home. He could pretend that he actually belonged here.

Fifty men pulled at the oars behind him, gliding the elegant ship through the busy harbor, navigating past fat galleys some sixteen meters long sat at anchor. They coasted past the royal shipyard, where the shells of new vessels rested, timber bones left to dry in the afternoon sun. The oars dipped into the water in unison, pulling his vessel onward to the capital and eventually to dock.

The Harbormaster waited along the wooden landing, a roll of sheepskin and quill in hand. "I'll need to see your register —"

Paris leapt off the deck in a giant stride and landed beside the middle-aged man, his crimson cape swirling around him in the gentle breeze.

"My Prince! Forgive me." The harbormaster stammered.

"Good to see you, Eteocles. How fare your daughters?" Paris slapped the man on the back with gusto and stretched out sore muscles cramped from a month at sea.

"Growing, Your Grace. Soon they will tower over me like Amazons." Eteocles grinned, giving Paris a curt bow. "We were not expecting you for several weeks. Is there news from the South?" His voice tightened with concern.

Paris shrugged, feigning a lack of knowledge. Information was the true currency in a town with open borders, and Eteocles often traded gossip for a cup of mulled wine. Paris enjoyed making the man work to ferret his information out.

"I'd say the negotiations were dismal." Paris replied with a wink as his crew began unloading copper ingots from the hold. "Their vassals couldn't hold their drink, and their women were as chaste as a temple initiate. I had to settle for this lot." He waved nonchalant over the heavy mass now lining the dock.

Eteocles' eyes spread wide as he counted the raw material. There were well over 300 oxhide-shaped ingots of copper and half as many of tin: a kingly treasure.

"It should suffice." A fevered glow gleamed in the harbormaster's eyes. "The Court of Smiths will be celebrating tonight."

Paris laughed, tossing Eteocles a nugget of copper he had in his pouch. "I'll meet you there. We'll toast to your daughters' good health." He turned and headed down the dock.

"Shall I marshal the royal guard?" Eteocles called after him, but Paris waved him off. He hated the fanfare that typically accompanied any movement of the royal family. He was not so shallow that he needed trumpets to declare his every footstep.

He made good time despite the growing crowds in the city. When he reached the base of the acropolis, he stopped at the feedlot where visiting shepherds quartered their animals. King Priam would want a report of his expedition right away, but Paris was so rarely at the capital he could not pass up an opportunity to converse with old friends.

"Agelaus! Get out here, old dog!" he hollered to the silver-haired herdsman. With the spring thaw on the horizon, the shepherds would soon take their flocks up Mount Ida. It was fortunate Paris had returned home early, otherwise it would be a full year before he would see his dear friend, and any year might be Agelaus' last.

"Paris? Is that you?" the old man hobbled out of his yurt. Traces of blue film, the telltale signs of blindness, covered his eyes. "How are you, my son?"

Paris engulfed Agelaus in a stout embrace. Normally, it was forbidden for a commoner to address a royal in such a familiar manner. But unlike his highborn kin, Paris did not stand on tradition. He spent the majority of his youth in the wilds of Mount Ida, and this man had saved his life on more than one occasion. He felt more at home here, amongst common sheepherders and tradesmen, than he ever did at court.

"I'm alive, despite the best efforts of the powers that be." He jested, knowing Agelaus would appreciate his talent for evading the knife. Paris had lost count of how many people wished to see him dead, from the common brigand who wanted his purse to some of the most powerful players in the world—people Agelaus had defended him against his whole life.

Paris quelled a pang of sadness as the herdsman steadied himself on Paris' shoulder. It was a shame the blindness had taken such a toll on the man. Soon even simple household tasks would be beyond his ability. Agelaus' hands roamed Paris' chest and face, 'seeing' what his eyes could not.

"You've grown stronger, an ox in his prime. When will you finally settle down and marry?"

Paris expected this question. As the second son of Priam, he was afforded more patience in regards to his duty to replenish the royal line. But that did not absolve him entirely. At eight and twenty, he was long overdue.

"I'll settle down when I find the right woman. These river girls are not pretty enough." His laugh was forced. The excuse was a boldfaced lie. It did not matter if he found the most beautiful woman in the world, he could not marry her. No woman should marry a man who is cursed.

"She is out there, Son." Agelaus sighed. "The Gods spared you for a reason. You will find your mate, and she will fill your days with endless sunshine."

And I will bring her nothing but sorrow.

It was insanity to dwell on matters he could not change. Paris quickly changed the topic, and they conversed of many things: the wool harvest, the spring calving, and the fallout of trade with the lands to the east. He soon said his goodbyes and headed back up the acropolis, taking a moment to marvel at the massive gates of the inner city and the thick defensive walls that had stood for a thousand years. He whispered a prayer to Athena as he passed that they would last another thousand.

By the time he reached the palace, news of his arrival had preceded him. The trumpeters raised their bronze instruments to the sky, the banners of Troy billowing beneath the lead pipes. "Hail, Prince Paris, valiant Son of Troy!" the herald announced with a brass ringed voice.

Paris groaned, brushing past the man and into the palace. He suspected the announcement was meant to alert the courtiers as much as to honor a son of Priam. Sure enough, his reception was a different affair amongst the highborns in the palace than in the city proper. Telltale wisps of colored chitons disappeared down corridors as he strode through the courtyard, the mere mention of his name enough to send the queen's sycophants running. Of the few courtiers who remained, their open sneers of disapproval were enough to quicken his steps.

He turned down a corridor to the columned hall that led to the throne room. Light flooded in from a dozen balconies evenly spaced down the lengthy marble hall. Their long curtains of lavender and rose fluttered from the ocean breeze.

The design of the palace was ingenious. Priam spared no expense when he reconstructed this wing of the acropolis after the last quake. King Rameses II sent architects all the way from Memphis to assist in the renovation, a show of respect from one great king to another. Paris had visited too many satrapies in his travels whose heavy fortresses were built of stone. One could not tell if it was night or day from the inside. In Troy, the buildings were as open as the spirit of its people.

"He's home!" the joyful voice of Prince Troilus announced. Paris quickly found himself tied up in the arms of his five-year-old brother. He lifted Troilus, spinning the child about, and quickly looked for further company. If Troilus was here, his other brothers could not be far.

Sure enough, on a far balcony overlooking the city, Prince Hector conversed quietly with his bride Andromache. Paris set Troilus back to the ground and released his built up tension. Besides Troilus, Hector was his only friend at court. And when the young boy tired of Paris' tales of faraway lands, he would succumb to their mother's dark influence as his other brothers had. Only Hector's favor was certain.

"Did you bring me anything?" Troilus asked, his youthful face flushed with eagerness.

"There was one thing. Oh, where did I put it?" Paris patted down the many pouches lining his belt. Troilus tugged at his leg as he continued to "search".

Hector gave Andromache a tender kiss goodbye and moved to join them. The princess was a stunning beauty and well loved by the commoners. Her soft brown hair fell in waves about her shoulders and her deep blue eyes sparkled like sapphires. Her courtship by Hector had already been spun into song.

She deserves their love, Paris acknowledged, casting her a polite nod as she went. His sister-in-law was uncommonly kind and had shown him compassion when so many of his kin did not. She smiled demurely to him, disappearing down the hall on soundless steps.

"So, the victorious son returns!" Hector hailed him, slapping Paris robustly on the back. "Your reputation grows little brother. Paris of Troy, an arbitrator of fairness that even the Gods would well acknowledge." He announced in lofty tones.

Paris eyed him suspiciously. Hector was terrible at playing coy. Once he came within arms' reach, he shifted his weight and swiftly turned the friendly gesture into a headlock. Paris cursed himself for not paying better attention. But he was committed now, and the brothers tussled like they had when they were boys.

"I'll have you." Paris warned, buried under the weight of

Hector's hold.

"You've been too long in the company of sailors and thieves, little brother. You've forgotten the power of a real soldier." Hector flexed his muscles.

It was not an unfounded boast. Hector was a formidable opponent, easily twice the size of Paris' build. But therein lay his flaw. Reliance on muscle alone was a mistake, a mistake Paris delighted in reminding Hector of on countless occasion.

Paris pivoted using Hector's weight against him. He leaned his shoulder into his brother's torso and shoved hard, easily breaking the headlock and sending Hector tumbling on his back. Hector gasped as the air was knocked from his lungs.

"I warned you." Paris gloated, helping Hector to his feet. "And the Phoenicians are not *thieves*. There's a lot even a solider like you can learn from a seafaring culture." He pushed an unsteady Hector for emphasis. "Like how to stay on your feet?"

"That only matters if I don't pummel you first." Hector cuffed him gently across the cheek. They shared a laugh as Paris danced out of his range.

Olympus help any man who earns his ire. The man was as strong as an ox.

"Seriously, Paris. Six months in Tyre?" Hector's happy grin faded. "A year with the horse traders in Phrygia? Stay put for a while. I miss you."

Hector's sincerity gave him pause. They were the two eldest sons, they trained together, and fought together. Paris always hoped they'd spend their lives at each other's side, watching their children grow old and conquer the world. And now that Hector was happily married, it drew to the forefront all the things missing in Paris' own life.

"What about my present?" Troilus stamped his foot, upset at being forgotten.

"It's here!" Paris turned from Hector, happy to avoid the familiar argument. Hector knew why Paris could not stay. To pretend otherwise was a cruel form of denial.

But still, he cast Paris a stubborn look. If there was a man who could bend the fates to his will, it would be Hector. This conversation was not over.

Paris reached into his pouch and pulled out a parcel of crimson fabric the perfect length for a child-sized cloak. Troilus gasped when he saw the material, the rich color a deeper red than any to be found in the city.

"It's beautiful." Troilus whispered. "However did they make it?"

"That's a secret, Brother." Paris winked, his crooked smile suggesting he withheld the information on purpose.

"I suppose you are full of secrets by now." Hector whispered in his ear, his words a bitter dart meant to shame Paris into staying.

"I've picked up a fair few." Paris shrugged, knowing better than to take the bait. He adopted a familiar grin, his forced gaiety the only weapon he possessed against Hector's insistent demands. "The bath houses in Rhodes were most instructive. I daresay I learned a few things that would make even your hair curl."

Hector coughed, blushing to his roots.

Troilus, however, gave up trying to follow their conversation. He took off, racing to the doors of the throne room. "Mother!" he cried. "Mother, look what Paris has brought me!"

Paris' smile vanished. "She is here?"

He hated the pity lining Hector's face, but it was unavoidable where Hecuba was concerned. The favored son linked arms with the disgraced. "Come," he led Paris to the doors. "She cannot hurt you more than you allow. Face it like a man."

Troilus raced before them as they entered the throne room. The child laughed merrily as he ran, his melodic voice echoing across the cavernous hall and between the hundred pillars that supported its domed ceiling.

Epic scenes of legend lined the throne room in brilliantly colored frescos: Zeus defeating the Titans, Prometheus's gift of fire to Man, and Athena handing the ring of kingship to Ilus, the first of King Priam's line. The heroes towered twenty feet over Paris. He suppressed the surge of awe the artwork inspired, reminded—as the artist intended—of his own petty mortality before the Great Kings of this realm. The greatest king was none other than his father, Priam.

The king was not alone. The Royal Seer, Aesacus, hovered behind the throne whispering into his father's ear. Aesacus' pet monkey, Sosa, was leashed beside his leg. As the princes approached, it began to hop up and down, screeching like mad. Paris clenched his teeth against the piercing sound. Had the Fates been kind, that foul beast would have long since passed from this world to the next.

Hecuba, beloved queen of Troy, stood beside the slick-tongued seer. Her back was washboard straight and stress lines showed along her aged but beautiful face. He wished her eyes would fill with love, as they did for Troilus, but they did not. Instead, he was greeted with eyes harder than stone and colder than ice. He continued forward, trying his best to ignore her chilly reception.

"Troilus, come away from there," she demanded, panic gripping at her high-pitched voice.

The boy skipped up to the throne, ignorant of her concern. "Mother, look at the gift Paris has brought me!" He flourished the fabric, spinning it around for all to see.

Hecuba snatched it from her son, inspecting the material on all sides. "Did you steal it?" she accused him, her eyes darting around nervously for some hidden danger.

Paris knelt before the throne. He raised his head formally to his mother's address. "It is a gift, Your Grace, from the Queen of Tyre. So that your sons will stand out as Prince of Princes and the honor of Priam's house will be undisputed."

"It is not honor this child brings you." Aesacus cut in. "But the ruin of your house. The ruin of Troy."

Hecuba moaned, tapping her brow with the ritual sign to beseech Athena's favor. "Forgive me Goddess, forgive this curse of my loins." Her voice cracked as she prayed.

"What superstitious poison is this?" Hector glared at the graybeard seer with unveiled disgust.

The monkey cackled and raced up his master's back, clinging desperately to Aesacus' head. The seer did not budge, even when Hector—bristling with youthful anger—stood toe to toe with the man.

"You speak of ruin when Paris returns with bounteous tribute?" Hector spun toward the king. "Father?"

Priam shared Hector's look of distaste, but not his boldness. He reclined on his throne, the strain of his rule wearing heavily on his shoulders. It was happening already. Paris sighed, regretting the burden his presence added to his father's troubles. It was far better to keep these meetings brief.

"Leave us, Soothsayer." Priam dismissed the graybeard. "Preach your omens to those with weak wills."

"Even kings must heed the will of the Gods." Aesacus warned.

"GO!" Priam shouted, his powerful voice affording no argument.

Aesacus disappeared down a nearby corridor. Hecuba quickly joined that retreat, gathering her youngest child as she went. She paused at the exit, watching Paris with a mixed look of fear and sorrow. As Paris expected, fear ruled out, and she left with no further comment.

"Rise, Son, and give account of your travels," Priam commanded him. The king ran his hand across his stout jaw, rubbing his fingers through his short-trimmed black beard. There was more grey in that beard than when Paris had left. A result, he suspected, of the ongoing hostilities in the East.

"King Baal-Termeg accepts your offer of friendship and

will stand with you against the Hatti. The tribute I returned with is a sign of his friendship and esteem he bears for your kingship. He pledges another shipment in two weeks time. He is eager as you to rid Anatolia of the rot of their empire."

A wave of relief washed over Priam's face. He descended from the throne and swiftly embraced Paris in a hearty manner that shocked both Paris and Hector. "Ha, ha!" he shouted. "Well done, my son."

Paris straightened under his father's praise. Any sign of favor was a rare event from Priam. He normally adopted a strict neutrality when dealing with his ill-favored son.

"I only wish to honor you, Father." Paris bowed his head.

Hector stepped forward, his face still fuming from the seer's disrespect. "Paris has done everything you have asked of him. Can you please denounce the omens and be done with it?"

Paris stiffened. What Hector asked was an impossibility. As much as he wished his father's love would prevail over politics, Paris understood the problem he represented. How could Priam claim to rule by divine right if he defied the divinities? Even if they denounced his own child.

"Peace, Hector." Paris waved his brother off. "He has his reasons."

"What reasons?" Hector demanded. "That rumor and whispers are more powerful than the king's will? That is not how I would rule."

"BUT YOU DO NOT RULE YET!" Priam towered over his eldest son. "The boy-king of Hatti has called for my head. My bondsmen are falling beneath the fist of his armies, *and you want me to start a battle at home?* Are you mad?"

Hector, shaken, bowed his head. With great effort, he held his tongue.

"Your brother still lives. And he will continue to live under my rule. There is your victory over the power of superstition." Priam grumbled and began to pace. "Now, go. I have business with Paris and I tire of your insolent tongue."

Paris whispered a prayer of relief when Hector ducked into a respectful bow without further comment. They both loved their father dearly, but that love was not the armor Hector mistook it for. Paris did not want his brother to say something he might regret, especially on his behalf.

As he turned to depart, Hector grabbed his arm. "I will see you after?"

Paris nodded, watching his brother leave with a pang of sorrow. He was touched by Hector's concern, but it was a losing battle. He had long ago accepted his role as an outcast of the court. He only wished Hector would one day accept it as well.

Priam resettled on his throne, also watching his eldest child with heavy-lidded eyes. "He was born to rule but does not have half your patience or discernment. Loyalty is a noble trait, but not when it clouds your mind from reason."

Paris joined him on the dais, allowing himself to finally relax and enjoy a moment of peace with Priam. The expectations of the temple hung heavily on the king's head. It was only behind the privacy of closed doors that they could converse as father and son.

"Is it so bad that he says what he means? Or that he will not back down no matter how mighty his foe?" As a young prince, Hector terrified the other noble sons. Paris lost count how many times Hector's righteous wrath scattered Hecuba's minions who sought to do him harm.

"A king must pick his battles wisely. And your brother cannot right all the wrongs of the world with his sword arm. The sooner he realizes that, the safer the realm will be."

Paris could not help but agree. Troy was on the brink of war. Cooler heads needed to prevail in their conflicts, both foreign and domestic. Which was usually the case when Priam asked to speak with him privately.

"What is troubling you, Father?"

The king grimaced, a shadow of remorse on his aged face. "The Hatti have choked off our trade from the east and now some fledgling king in the west seeks to cheat me. I have need of you, Paris."

Paris pushed aside his disappointment. Every visit home was short-lived, but this was exceptionally short. Usually, he'd have at least a fortnight in the golden city before the next mission was set. "What would you have me do?"

"My merchants return from the Greek isles with payment half the value of the wares that they took. This *High King* of Mycenae thinks himself, and his spoils, far grander than they be." Priam scowled at the title. "He refuses the sea tariff that keeps the channel free of pirates, enjoying the free trade my campaigns deliver but believing himself too important to pay for it. He is a pig who wallows in mud but claims it ambrosia. I want you to go and educate him otherwise."

Paris stiffened. Never before had Priam sent him to deliver a threat. He was always the negotiator, the one who broke bread with wary kings and created bonds of fellowship. Priam didn't settle trade disputes by sending an ambassador. Why now? Why him?

"Surely the Trades Master—"

"This is too important to leave to the merchants." Priam interjected. "If it was only a matter of coin, I would not call on you. But the Hatti campaigns have cost us dearly. With every success in battle they weaken my hold over our satraps. I cannot let this barbarian king also defy me with impunity. My vassals will slip through my fingers if they think me so weak. And if I cannot tame the wildlings in my own backyard, I do not deserve their respect."

Paris gazed up into his father's eyes, the mighty monarch an awesome sight enshrined on his golden throne. Few kings deserved the privileged position they inherited, but Priam possessed an aura of authority that could not be denied. He commanded respect from kingdoms from the river lands to the Egyptian delta. He was a giant amongst lesser men. This Mycenaean king was meddling with powers he could not possibly understand. The West would suffer for this insolence.

"And you think I'm best suited to deliver this message?" He had to ask. He would walk into fire for his father, but this quest was an altogether different matter than what he had been trained to do. Surely Hector would have been a better choice.

Priam watched him with an astute eye. He raised his right hand and tapped Paris over his heart. "The man who must threaten force is not one to be feared. It is what is left *unsaid* that strikes a dagger in the hearts of lesser men."

Paris blinked back his surprise, unsure if he understood his father correctly. "You want me to remind these Mycenaeans of the glory of Troy?" he asked, trying to decipher Priam's request. "Of the respect we carry throughout the world and the power we represent?"

Priam nodded. "And how unwise it would be to invoke my wrath. You are my fist in the silk glove. Quell this rebellious king before the sword becomes necessary."

"A delicate affair... " Paris mused, his mind already devising tactics to complete the task.

"That is why it must be you." A hint of pride gleamed in Priam's eyes. "You have never failed me."

And I never will.

Paris gave his father a curt nod, indicating he understood. "I will do as you command. My ship can sail on the morning tide."

Priam stood and reached out for him, placing a sturdy hand on Paris' shoulder. For a moment he showered Paris with the love he withheld for Hector alone.

"Alexandros Paris of House Laomedon, I know I have asked a lot from you, and I promise it has not been for naught. You were named after the bravest man I have ever known—a great king of men. You bear his name, now bear his honor."

Priam's chest swelled as though the shade of his old comrade walked the hall. "Teach Mycenae to respect their elders. Do this, and I swear I will never send you from my side again."

CHAPTER 7

THE COURT OF SMITHS

LATER THAT evening, Paris joined Hector for festivities at the Court of Smiths. Each trade claimed a district in the hub city surrounding the acropolis. The Smiths, whose work was marveled throughout the river lands, had constructed theirs with an eye for opulence.

Massive copper gates, forged with an embossed hammer and anvil on alternating panels, were open to the public. Towering buildings three stories high surrounded the interior court, their ivy-clung walls studded in bronze rosettes. Craftsmen, journeymen and apprentice alike were out of doors swilling grog and hollering requests to a band of minstrels. The hearth fires burned bright, laughter was in the air, and with the promise of wealth from the bounty Paris had secured from Tyre, the Smiths celebrated.

The princes reclined in wicker chairs beneath a canopy of stars. Of the few hours he had left in Troy, Paris preferred to spend it in the company of these honest craftsmen in lieu of the hostile halls of the palace. The libations were flowing and even Hector deeply indulged.

"He swore? By Apollo's honor, you better not be lying to me. You are coming home to stay this time?"

"Zeus strike me down if it's not true." Paris lifted his flagon of ale to toast with his brother. "To home." He forced a smile, though inside his heart was in chaos.

Home...

Paris' restless wanderings could soon be at an end. It was the moment he had always dreamt, and now that it was in sight, he wasn't sure he wanted it. Troy, and all her wonders, was never truly home. And despite Hector's assurances, Paris doubted he'd ever really be welcome here.

"The Western Wilds." A note of longing filtered into Hector's slurs. "You lucky bastard." He drained his cup.

"Slow down." Paris plucked the empty flagon from his hand. "Andromache will never forgive me if I deliver you home drunk as a shore-leave sailor."

Hector's smile slipped into a boyish grin at the mention of his beautiful bride. "Aye, she won't at that." Hector's love for Andromache was as vibrant as his chestnut-colored hair. Paris envied his brother's happiness. The newly-wed couple shared something sacred.

"Seriously Paris, aren't you a teensy bit excited?"

Paris was, despite his cool demeanor. Mycenae was located along the frontier, their lands comprised of the edges of the known world, lands rumored to be home to creatures of legend—wild, like the men who settled there.

"Do you think they are barbarians like Father insists?" Paris mused. The men of the Hellas were mostly unknown to him. Who knew how they'd react to a royal delegation.

"If they are wild, perhaps you can learn some new secrets to share...?"

"Like I'd share it with you." Paris chuckled. Hector had been trying to illicit details from his sojourn at the Cypriot bathhouses for the past half-hour. With a new wife to bed, Hector desperately wanted to impress.

But the question did bear some consideration. If the men of the Hellas lived up to their reputation, would the women be as wild? He wondered if they'd all be hairy femmes covered in untanned leathers as fearsome as the Amazons of legend.

"Watch yourself!" Hector laughed when Paris voiced his thoughts. "That's precisely the sort of woman who could force you to swear your vows."

Paris swirled his cup, watching the amber liquid froth while he considered Hector's jest. *A barbarian wife?*, he laughed to himself. He was enough of an embarrassment to the royal family without adding that sort of nonsense.

"Don't hold your breath." Paris muttered. "I'm going into the lion's den to yank its tail. And everyone knows it's the lioness who has the longer claws."

"More likely the cub's den." Hector snorted. He shared Priam's low esteem for their western neighbors. "It's a daft mission. You have a better chance of slaying the Minotaur than getting this Agamemnon to bend the knee. I swear Father is inventing reasons to send you from the city."

The remark hit closer to Paris' heart than he was sure his brother intended. Priam's pledge to finally let him return to Troy was wholly unexpected, and Paris was unsure if he could accept it. His homecoming would cause more havoc than the king could afford.

He shrugged off those morbid thoughts and turned to Hector with a grin. "You think I can't handle a minor king? Your skill with a sword might have no match, but diplomacy is *my weapon*. You'll swallow those words when I return."

It was not an unfounded boast. Paris had brought Tyre, Millawanda, and Cyprus into Priam's fold, each realm eager to unite against their common enemy. How different could Mycenae be? They might not share Troy's hatred for the Hatti, but they shared a common language. Other similarities must exist. Paris had only to discover what Agamemnon wanted, his secret desires, and exploit them.

But Hector could not be diverted. "Father could have let you stay a week, at least." He grumbled a few choice curses into his empty cup.

"Oh, no. Wipe that sourpuss expression off your face." Paris leapt to his feet. "I only get one night here and you are not going to ruin it." He banged their empty flagons together to garner the attention of the crowd. "The next round is on your princes. DRINK UP!"

His words rippled through the crowd with welcome cheers. The minstrels picked up a lively tune and a busty serving girl quickly replaced their mugs, the ale foaming over the tops. When the libations were all handed out, a hundred smiths raised their drunken voices to toast to Hector and Paris' good health.

"Watch out, little brother," Hector warned playfully as he pulled Paris back to his seat, "or they'll dub you the Prince of Hops."

Paris took a long swig of the yeasty brew, and wiped the foam from his chin with his sleeve. "I've been called worse."

It was a poor choice of words. He knew it the instant he saw Hector's face. "Forget about it."

"I will not." Hector slammed his cup down on their table. "Not until I see Aesacus hung from a gibbet. And that foul monkey, too."

Paris sighed and put down his drink. No amount of spirits was going to save him from this conversation. Hector thought he could deal with any threat with the strength of his arms. But this foe could not be bested with an army, let alone by the passion of one prince.

"You can't save me, Hector." Paris turned to him. "Father can make as many promises as he likes, but it won't save me either. Killing Aesacus will not convince his followers that his prophecy is untrue. You know I am not welcome here."

"How do you know—"

"Because I do." He spoke more firmly than he intended. "I've spent six weeks in Troy in the past two years. *Six weeks.* And every visit felt too long by half. You fighting everyone only makes it worse. I... I just want a moment of peace. Let me enjoy your company without having to dwell on all the other

mess. Please."

Paris watched the fight drain from Hector's muscles. "I... will." His brother sighed, wilting into his chair. "Forgive me, Paris. It's just that I miss you."

"I miss you, too."

It was a surprising moment of candor between them. Paris treasured his brother. The years had steadily pulled their lives in different directions, but not their affection. The summers of their youth playing on the steps of Mt. Ida could not be erased by time and politics.

"I'll only be gone a few weeks this time. We'll talk about Aesacus when I get back, all right?"

Hector reached out and grabbed Paris' hands. "Promise me you won't do anything stupid." There was a strange urgency in Hector's words.

Paris almost fell from his chair. He looked into his brother's earnest face, stunned by Hector's serious pallor. It was tinged with a prophetic aura, like their sister Cassandra's when plagued by her dire visions. Why would he question Paris' return now? On a mission far simpler than any in recent memory?

"I promise." He clasped Hector's hands tight and made his vow. "I won't risk my life needlessly. If the Gods are fair, I will make it back to Troy."

As the night wore on, Paris buried himself in his drink, trying to drown out that ominous feeling. The Gods had never been fair, and to Paris least of all. He knew better than to expect their favor.

Mycenae, the frontier of civilization... what dangers could it hold in store for a prince of Troy?

CHAPTER 8

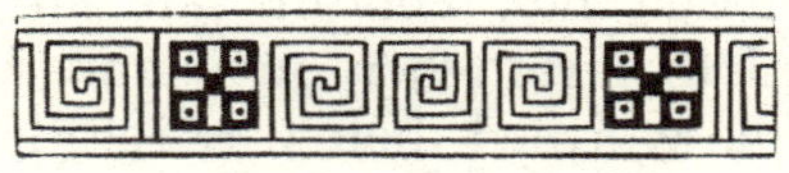

IN MYCENAE

THE BRIGHT afternoon sun stabbed Helen's eyes as she exited Mycenae's royal granary. She dusted her hands on the leather apron Philon had pressed on her for the inspection. The planting season was almost over, and their stores were running low. A concern Philon, as Harvest Master, voiced to her in secret.

"They drained the reserves when the last merchant vessel came through, Your Grace. Won't naught be left if another trader comes before the summer rains."

Helen sighed, stretching out the knot growing in the small of her back. The time she spent at the Mycenaean court had done little to acclimatize her to Agamemnon's capricious rule. Her Spartan sensibilities were constantly challenged. Tyndareus would never demand so much of his people while giving so little in return.

Her heart filled with sorrow at the thought of her father. It had been ten years since she last had spoken with her beloved king, just after they finalized her betrothal. Tyndareus had been explicit—no son of Atreus would rule in Sparta. And since Menelaus was a second son with no land to rule as his own, Helen had cursed herself to a life of irrelevance, a lesser member of an already crowded royal household. If she had known that laying her wedding wreath at Mycenae's door she would be choosing her sister over her father, would she have chosen the same?

One glance at Philon's worried face pulled her from her dark musings. She did not have the luxury of living in hindsight. Helen would not wallow in self-pity while these good people needed her. Lending an ear to the citizen's concerns seemed to lessen her own, and in little time the Mycenaean people wormed their way into her vacated heart. She could do little to change her own situation, but she *could* help them.

Clytemnestra might think mingling with the common folk was beneath her, but Helen didn't. The time away from the palace was a respite from the pressures of court. And the warm regard of commoners like Philon was a welcome change from the chilly affections of her husband.

"And the planting?" Helen pressed. "Can't we expand? Plow farther afield?" She pulled the apron from her waist, careful not to snag her embroidered chiton. The craftsmanship on the garment was lovely, despite the low neckline. It did wonders to show off her youthful curves. The dress was from Agamemnon, a gift to his sister-by-law. Helen knew better than to refuse the Great King's gifts, but wearing the garment made her feel half-naked.

Philon shifted nervously, seemingly embarrassed by her question. A poor planting would mean a poor harvest, and a poor harvest would cost him his job. "We're having troubles, Your Grace. A massive bull has claimed the borders along the western fields. He's a monster ten span long with horns to match a Minotaur. My plow herds say he is Poseidon incarnate. They won't go near him."

She sighed. This news would not bode well in the Master's Council. Only yesterday, Nestra threatened to cancel the *Mounichia* Festival if more supplies could not be found. The queen detested the religious superstitions of the common folk.

And if they cost the crown a prized festival...? Helen frowned, not wanting to envision how her sister would respond.

"A hungry child is a far greater danger than that of a wild bull." She chastised Philon lightly. "I will ask the king to dispatch his huntsmen. But see that you increase the crop accordingly. No excuses."

"Thank you, Princess." The harvest master effused, ducking his head in deference.

A ghost of a smile graced her lips. She tried her best to make amends for Agamemnon's careless rule, but an increased harvest couldn't answer all the problems plaguing the growing nation. A larger bounty would only inspire the power-hungry king to continue his expanded trade. And while his royal arsenal grew, the people sacrificed one meal at a time. At least with Helen's visits, the common folk felt their needs were being addressed. She was their conduit to the throne.

She headed up to the palace along a steep inclining ramp. The granary was located at the base of the rising acropolis, surrounded by the enormous defense walls that separated palatial land from the communal. The Grand Walkway, as the ramp had come to be known, was the widest road of Mycenae. Small indents carved from the ruts of chariot wheels were the only blemish on the otherwise smooth limestone surface.

Helen continued westward, following the ramp ever higher. It was a long hike, but finally, at a natural curve in the bedrock, the inner wall gave way to a massive staircase that revealed a palace that out-marveled any in Greece. Despite all the hardships Agamemnon pressed on his people, Mycenae had grown under his rule. The capital was twice the size from when Helen first arrived.

Her smile turned bittersweet remembering those first few days on the foreign soil—of her first glimpse of the towering fortress and how it had filled her with wonder. Her heart had swelled with hope and dreams of love on meeting her husband-to-be. What a lovelorn fool she had been.

It hadn't taken long for Clytemnestra's dark warnings to

prove true. The men of Mycenae dreamed of battle and swords not of love. Too soon she realized the absence of Menelaus from her courtship was not a matter of duty, but a lack of care. Her husband sought nothing in this life more than spiting his older brother, an unfortunate familial grudge that manifested in all manner of petty acts—acts that Helen now found herself an unfortunate pawn.

From the courtyard, she climbed another staircase to the megaron above. Nestra was hiding behind the pillars of the portico, spying on the king and his audience. She waved Helen over, her nervous manner warning Helen to keep quiet.

"I am not some lackey you can command. I am king in my own right!" Menelaus' baritone voice pierced the air about them.

Helen stiffened, knowing now why Nestra hid. Her husband was in a temper again. She peaked her head around the pillar and watched the drama unfold.

Fire and fury, those were the elements that graced her mighty lord. Fire of hair, of tongue, of temper. And fury for any man stupid enough to provoke him—a pastime Agamemnon loved to indulge.

"You are no king yet, *Brother.*" The High King sneered. "Tyndareus is not dead. Only when his flesh feeds the worms will Sparta be yours."

"A favor I have you to thank for." Menelaus spat. "It's you he despises, not me!"

Agamemnon leapt to his feet, grabbing his jeweled scepter like a club. "You *should* thank me. You should bow down and kiss my feet! Had I not pressed your suit, you would not even be married and next in line to rule. A throne afforded you by contract, not divine right as I hold here. *So you will obey me.*"

Helen sighed. Direct demands meant this confrontation would not end well. Nestra was shaking like a leaf. If their husbands did not settle their differences, the wives would bear the burden of their displeasure. Nestra bore too many scars from Agamemnon's fearsome temper.

But there was no reason for them both to suffer. Helen lifted her shoulders back and walked into the throne room at a regal pace.

"Are you crazy?" Nestra whispered after her. Helen's heart fluttered, secretly agreeing with her sister. But crazed or not, she would not let Nestra suffer. Not when she could do something to help. She entered the megaron behind her husband, quiet as a mouse.

"I will not go." Menelaus glared at the king, his foot on the raised dais that led to the throne. He taunted Agamemnon, standing just outside the king's striking distance. "The foaling season is about to begin. I won't abandon the herd to collect your tribute. Send someone else."

Agamemnon's eyes blazed with anger, raising his scepter threateningly. But when Helen crossed his line of sight, those eyes turned to unveiled hunger. She bowed low, sure to accentuate her near exposed bosom. He had designed the dress with a purpose. Agamemnon could not claim her outright—especially in public—but his eyes had no qualms marking her as prey.

"Sire." She lowered her head and voice respectfully. "If I may be of service?"

Agamemnon relaxed immediately. He retook his seat, casting his brother a mocking grin. "You spend too much time with your ponies, Menelaus, and not enough with your own mare. Be careful another stallion does not tend to your flock."

Helen blushed furiously. She tried to shield her face from her husband in her golden tresses. The audacity of the man... he knew well enough what other "stallions" were braying at her door.

"Rise, Sweet Sister. What would you have from your king." He said the words as though they were an invitation. Menelaus stiffened, his evil glare equally for her as for his brother.

"The farmhands complain of a great bull harassing the wheat fields." She rose to her feet, adopting a mask of indifference. "I told them I would petition you for a hunt."

"Bah." He spat. "I have no time to dispatch every animal that ranges near our fields. Not when we have so many outstanding debts to collect." He cast another glare at Menelaus, his potent ire simmering again.

"Of course, My King." She added quickly, trying to draw his attention back to her. "If it is conflict of circumstance, perhaps I can tend to the foals and free my husband to the task?"

Menelaus grabbed her arm roughly, spinning her to look at him directly. "And what would a woman know of horse husbandry? You presume much, Wife."

She grit her teeth, knowing she was crossing into danger. "I know nothing, My Lord, save the troubles of giving birth. That, it seems, is a province of women." She planted the barb with just enough defiance that Menelaus would redirect his anger and stop this futile fight with his brother.

"Some women, perhaps." He responded, taking her bait. "But not you, Wife. In that regard you are just as useless as a crone."

Agamemnon's cruel laugh mocked them both. It struck a sliver of fear in Helen's heart as it shamed her husband. "I will consider your offer, Sister. Now go. Both of you. I sense my brother is keen to give you a lesson in husbandry."

Menelaus didn't bother to respond but towed her roughly out the hall. She barely caught Clytemnestra's eye before she was tossed into the outer chamber. Her sacrifice was not lost on the queen.

"You need to learn your place, woman." Menelaus growled in her ear as they neared their apartments.

"Yes, My Lord." Helen's reply was automatic now, devoid of emotion. He would hit her if she ignored him, he would hit her if she shouted back. There was no reason to fight back, not when it only made her situation worse.

He tossed the doors to their apartments open, scaring the chambermaids near to death. "Out!" he shouted as they scattered.

He tossed Helen down on the bed, pushing the skirt of her chiton over her back. He lifted her hips, spreading her legs roughly as he fumbled at his breeches.

"I am your lord." He growled into her ear. "And You. Will. Mind. Me." With each word he shoved himself violently into her, mounting her from behind. His engorged phallus was a sword that ripped her apart.

She grasped the furs on her bed, trying to stabilize herself. It was difficult to stay balanced. Menelaus was a powerful man and he never held back when he took her. She thanked the gods how rare those events were.

When he had spent himself, he collapsed on top of her, the weight of his body crushing the air from her lungs. "I will put a son in your belly. That should teach you to mind your mouth."

"Yes, My Lord." She struggled to breathe. He rolled off her, and she pulled her legs up onto the bed, tucking into a small ball. She wished she had the fortitude to sit up, to shout her defiance at him from the rooftops. But everything inside her hurt. It took all her strength to not cry.

"Get back to your duties." He sneered, lacing himself back up and storming out of the room.

The room was eerily quiet when he left. Helen sat unmoving for a time beyond her counting. The silence flooded through her, allowing her a brief moment where nothing existed. Not Menelaus, not Mycenae, and not her broken dreams.

You should not provoke him, a little voice inside her warned. *Agamemnon treats him like a child. How should he react when his wife affords him no respect either?*

She propped herself up onto the embroidered pillows covering her bed, but that only served to give her a better view to the door of the adjoining servant's quarters. She glared at it, pouring all her hurt into that mournful stare.

If you loved him better, he would not seek comfort in the arms of another.

That room had never housed a servant. She learned quickly why Menelaus spent all his time in the stables. He liked to keep his lover close. He spent their wedding night in that room, rutting another man. Even now, ten years later, he preferred to sleep in Sabineus' bed than in hers.

She moved in a daze. Her dress was torn. It would never do to be seen in court in such a state. She let the garment drop to the ground and selected another. Without conscious thought, she grabbed her wedding robes, the soft linen caressing her skin as she tied her belt in place. Her hair came next. She began to pleat her golden locks, but when she was half done she caught a glimpse of herself in the bronze mirror by her bed. Her hands dropped uselessly at her side.

What was the point of it all? Why replace the damage Menelaus caused? Her beauty only caused her more troubles. If it was not her brute husband, then it was Agamemnon who visited her bed, eager to possess his brother's prize. She could not believe Nestra said coupling could be pleasurable. It only filled her with pain and loathing.

She tore at her braids, a wild cry escaping her lips. Her hair fell loose around her shoulders.

"Princess?" A timid knock came from the door. Aethra had returned. Helen ignored her, staring at her reflection in a daze. The woman in the mirror was a wild thing, not a princess at all. When the knocking became more insistent, she grabbed her crimson cloak and fled through the back door.

The wind had picked up, ushering in a great mist from the sea. She raced into it, running down the steep hillside, past the royal gardens and out to the easternmost precipice of the palace walls. It was an isolated vista, a rocky outcrop that hung above the crashing waves of the Argolian Gulf. She ran to its very edge, completely enshrouded in mist. Finally, with this cloak of solitude, the tears came. They flooded her cheeks, spilling down to the thundering waves below.

"Why?" She demanded of the Gods. "I've done all you

asked of me. I cannot take it any longer." How had her life gone so terribly wrong? Bound to a husband that neither needed nor wanted her, and with no home to return to... where was her great destiny now?

Her slippered foot traced the edge of the precipice, sending loose limestone tumbling down to the jagged rocks below. It would be so easy to step over the ledge. With one step, she'd no longer be anyone's disappointment. She'd lost count how many times she considered it.

"Please," she begged the Gods. "Make it stop. End my torment." The desperate prayer gripped at her heart. "Blessed Hera, Gentle Aphrodite, please... just give me a sign."

A loud horn reverberated off the cliffs, cutting through the fog. At first she thought she dreamt it, but it blasted again, gaining in volume with each peal. Like the hand of Zeus, the sun broke through the clouds. The mist parted.

And then she saw him.

He stood at the prow of a ship, a phantom encased in silver fog. He was unlike any man she had ever seen: tall, like the Thracians from the north, but svelte like the strapping island men of Crete. When he turned to her, lowering the horn from his lips and reaching a hand in her direction, she had the uncanny feeling he was important.

The mist reclaimed him and the moment was broken.

Helen shook off her vapid thoughts and pulled her cloak securely around her shoulders to ward off the chill. The Gods had never answered her prayers before, and Helen knew better than to trust to hope. No divine intervention was coming to save her. She was alone.

She walked back to the Palace, the hole in her heart growing larger with each step.

The oars of the Trojan longship dipped into the frothy waters of the Aegean. Paris' crew had left Troy's golden shores ten days hence. What should have been a simple journey erupted into chaos as the rough winds and unpredictable currents tossed his ship in circles. But, if their maps were correct, they were nearing their destination.

The coastline of the Greek isles should have been visible on the horizon. But when the sun stirred from her nightly rest, a sea-born mist, heavy like the breath of a dragon, obscured their line of sight.

"Bring out the sounding horn!" Glaucus shouted to his bosun. The captain was a venerated sea dog. He often boasted there was no squall strong enough to keel a vessel in his charge, but even Glaucus took notice when they sailed into the western Aegean. He swore any man who braved these waters must have the courage of Herakles and Poseidon combined. Paris heartily agreed.

Paris grabbed the instrument and took a vantage position at the bow of the ship. Any manner of danger could be hidden in a fog. They could run aground on jagged rock, or crash unknowingly into a cliff. He blasted a note into the sky and waited for its echo to return if solid mass lay before them. If there was danger ahead, he'd be the first to hear it.

Paris inhaled deeply as he waited. The tang of salt air filled his nostrils and the crisp bite of the western winds numbed his bones. The great expanse of unknown lands lay before him. He lived for moments like these.

Glaucus joined him at the bow, the captain's pale-grey eyes narrowed as he searched for hidden dangers. "Give me a feisty squall or maelstrom any day, but the Gods curse this bloody fog."

Most sailors were a superstitious lot, but Paris' captain delighted in finding ways to thumb his nose at the Immortals. The priests called it blasphemy, but thus far Glaucus had never lost a ship.

"Don't fret, old friend." Paris laughed, slapping him on the back. "We'll land in one piece. Your reputation is well deserved."

"As is yours." Glaucus eyed the short staff tightly secured at Paris' belt. Twin serpents encircled a rod capped with winged tips. Only diplomats of the highest order were given the *kerykeion*. It afforded the bearer protection in hostile lands, assuming of course, that the visiting realm was civilized enough to honor it.

Wearing the *kerykeion* reminded Paris of the unpleasantness he was walking into. Priam was trusting him to quell this rebellious king. Failure was not an option. "I hope you know what you signed on for." Paris sighed, feeling the weight of that scepter as heavily as the duty that lay ahead of him.

The captain grinned, and ran his hand through his salt-crusted hair. "I've sailed rough waters with you before, Paris. I eagerly sail for the next. Better a life filled with adventure than a quiet death of old age." With a curt bow, he turned to his crew, barking orders to trim the sail. Paris was left to his musing.

A quiet death of old age... Paris had never considered that an option. The majority of his youth had been spent on ships like this one, his life carried in the winds never finding a port to call home. As he sent out another horn blast, his last conversation with Hector haunted his thoughts. If he returned to Troy as he promised, what happened next? He imagined taking a wife, settling down in Troy, and he and his brother watching their children grow up.

But some force pulled at his veins, denying that future. He was meant for something different. For what, he could not say, and that unknown fate was playing havoc with his head. He found himself in an existential crisis, questioning everything he thought he wanted.

As the zephyrs pushed him closer to his destination, one thing became clear: this would be his last journey in service to the realm. War was brewing in the east, and a clash of empires was on the horizon that could very well determine the fate of the world. If Paris wasn't careful he'd end his life a pawn in that power tug-of-war, and he wasn't ready to die before allowing himself to first live. He had this last task to complete for his father, and then he'd be free to live and love as he saw fit. The Gods owed him that much.

Paris sent out a third blast on the horn, and then a fourth, the mist swallowing the booming notes whole, hiding what dangers lay beyond. A timid breath of air stirred the fog, raising the hairs on Paris' arms. The clouds parted, and a golden ray of sunshine burned through the darkness, illuminating a rocky outcrop not a hundred feet off the bow.

And on that cliff stood a Goddess.

Paris could not breathe. Thought fled him. He was struck by a beauty that had no parallel on this earth. Long tresses of gold billowed around her like a veil of sunlight. She was dressed all in white, a bride enshrined in mist. He reached for her—

And then the mist took her. She disappeared as suddenly as she appeared.

"LAND HO!" the bosun hollered, finding the words Paris could not. The deck became a fury of men desperately redirecting the ship. In the madness none save Glaucus noticed Paris' lax response.

"Paris? Are you all right?" Glaucus rushed to the bow, shaking him roughly.

Had he dreamt it? "Did you see? On the ridge?" He stuttered like a sun-sick sailor. "There was a woman...."

Glaucus shook with a hefty laugh. "More apt you saw a siren. If it happens again, I'll have to bind you to the mast."

Paris knew the captain did not believe him, but he didn't care. The vision of that beauty held firmly in his mind. Was it an omen? A warning? He shook his befuddled head.

The only thing he knew for certain was to be wary. This quest had hidden dangers. If he was not careful, it might truly be his last.

CHAPTER 9

THE TROJAN AMBASSADOR

"HE'S A *Prince of Troy.*" Clytemnestra announced in the antechamber of Agamemnon's megaron. The royal family and council waited for Mycenae's nobility to gather in the adjacent hall. With the assembly almost filled, the Trojan delegation would soon be presented to the throne.

Helen was too alarmed to speak. She had thought her mysterious visitor on the high seas to be a sailor or a merchant, or even a figment of her imagination. But a prince? All thought fled her mind as a new panic took root.

Who is he and what is he doing here?

"What is he doing here?" Clytemnestra grumbled, echoing Helen's inner thoughts. "Since when have the Trojans ever sent anyone other than an oily merchant? I mistrust this, Husband."

But Agamemnon wore an expression of sick eagerness, looking anything but displeased. "It's about time they graced us with a royal visit. Priam could not ignore Mycenae forever!"

Helen shied away from the heat in his voice. Agamemnon was forever harping on about his standing amongst other rulers. His lust for power was almost as great as his lust for women. And a conquest in one usually led to the other.

Her sudden movement must have caught his attention. His heated gaze lingered on her. She pulled her shawl over her bared shoulders, doing her best to cover up. Thankfully, Nestra stepped in-between them, dominating Agamemnon's view.

"You have his attention now." Nestra shot back at the king. "The question is whether or not that is good for Mycenae." She refused to move away and slowly Agamemnon's eager grin turned sour.

"I will make it good." Agamemnon growled, then turned to his *lawagetas* counselors, the military leaders that followed his every step. "All of you! Keep your eyes open. My wife is worried I let a wolf into the house." He addressed them with a mocking smile.

They laughed crudely, none more so than Rhopalus, a bear of a commander with a wicked scar running down his face from scalp to jaw. "A wolf will always be bested by a lion. Have no fear, Your Grace," he scoffed.

The others echoed Rhopalus' derisive comments, claiming Nestra's fears as paranoia while continuing to fawn over the king with praises of his growing import. Helen scorned them all. They told Agamemnon precisely what he wanted to hear. They should not mock her sister for having the stones they lacked.

Nestra, also disgusted, turned to her, and upon seeing a similar look on Helen's face, let loose a merry laugh. "Do not be bothered by fools, Sister. They are nothing but toadies and yes-men. A gadfly could demand greater attention than this lot. Their fondest dream is to have an ounce of Spartan courage."

Helen took a deep breath and soothed her ruffled feelings, amazed as always by Clytemnestra's courage. Her sister never feared to speak her mind, even after all the "lessons" Agamemnon bestowed upon her. In some ways it encouraged Nestra. The greater the king's reaction, the more likely her opinion would prove true. And thus did the queen's reputation grow: strict, insightful, and one to be feared. Agamemnon had trained his pupil well.

Both women had apparently been forgotten as the council continued with their mindless chatter. Nestra led Helen away to an unoccupied corner of the chamber. "You look lovely, Helen. Why the special efforts?" Nestra kissed her lightly on her cheeks.

Helen smoothed the folds of her lavender chiton, searching for a reasonable answer. But nothing about this afternoon had been reasonable. She had begged the Gods for a sign, and they had granted her one in the form of a man. When she learned he was flesh and blood, and not some phantom of her imagination, she knew—inexplicably knew—she had to make her finest impression. As Aethra dressed her in the elegant gown— a classical cut chiton pinned on her left shoulder with an eagle-headed fibula—she felt like a soldier preparing for battle, her beauty the only armor she possessed against the Gods and worldly powers that threatened to engulf her.

But she couldn't tell her sister that. Visions and omens? Nestra would mock her behavior as superstitious peasant nonsense.

"It's so rare we get royal visitors." Helen blushed. "I didn't want to embarrass you or your court."

"I will never be embarrassed by you." Nestra swore fervently. But her eyes turned inward as she smoothed the folds of her own dress, a regal but faded garment of woadish blue. The birthing malaise had struck Nestra hard, and she had great difficulty dressing at all most days. Orestes fought hard to enter this world. After two daughters, Agamemnon finally had the heir he always wanted, but Clytemnestra was drained to a point of ruin.

"I... I wanted to thank you for what you did earlier, distracting Menelaus." Nestra stammered, her queenly composure gone. "It couldn't have been easy—" her words died off as she struggled to broach the delicate topic.

"It was nothing." Helen brushed off her sister's concern. Nestra frowned, perhaps sensing the lie for what it was, but she let the matter lay. The twins were no strangers to quietly enduring what could not be changed.

"Why do you think he's come?" Helen pivoted back to their royal visitor. She didn't want to waste another second on their stubborn husbands.

"Why do any of them come?" came Nestra's terse reply. "To honor themselves and increase their status amongst other men." She seemed preoccupied, lost in her earlier dark thoughts.

Helen frowned. "I suppose you're right." Certainly every other ambassador had proven himself shallow, filled with hubris and love of their own position. Most were so exotic in appearance that they frightened the serving girls. "Did you get a good look at their men?"

Clytemnestra paused, eyeing her suspiciously. "Why so interested?"

"This is a *prince*, not some fat merchant. Aren't you even curious about where he came from?" Helen chided her twin. As girls they dreamed of meeting mysterious princes from foreign lands. Helen refused to let Nestra sulk through this encounter.

"Something's different," Nestra muttered. She reached out and tucked a stray wisp of Helen's hair behind her ear. "You seem like your old self."

"Isn't that a good thing?" she smiled generously.

It was impossible for her twin to stay sullen in the warmth of that smile. Nestra's lips curled softly, infected by Helen's gaiety. "Not good... *wonderful*." she admitted and they shared a short laugh. For a moment the two women were almost identical.

"We are ready to begin, Your Grace." A herald announced from the inner chamber door.

"Sound the horns." Agamemnon ordered the herald out, and the rank and file began their march into the megaron.

The king and royal household held back to enter last. Agamemnon gestured imperiously, waving them over to his side. He scrutinized Clytemnestra and Helen both, a slight sneer on his face as he regarded his wife. "Wipe that smile from your face, Wife. You're a queen, not a doe-eyed maiden. I don't want you walking in there like a prized idiot."

Nestra straightened herself, a dispassionate mask hiding the flush of anger behind her eyes. Helen took her place beside her sister and tried to mimic her regal stance. Together, they marched into the hall.

Paris shifted anxiously in the dimly lit antechamber outside the Mycenaean megaron. A dozen Trojan men-at-arms stood in formation around him, an impressive honor guard resplendent in their ceremonial armor. They held thin spears ten feet long with tassels of gold tied around the head. Their helms were made of hammered bronze with an elegant crest of black horsehair. Leather pleats encircled their waist, each fold studded with copper pellets. Shin guards covered their legs from ankle to kneecap, and arm guards from wrist to elbow. It was an impressive sight, both ornamental and intimidating.

In contrast, Paris chose simplicity for his own garments. He wore a plain ivory tunic cinched at the waist with a thin golden belt. His Phoenician cape flowed from his shoulders, the deep crimson color vibrant against his tunic's pale canvas. His sandals were made of unembellished leather and he held a simple rounded helm in his left hand. Altogether, he projected a modest demeanor, a man who did not need to impress—just as Priam had instructed.

"Make sure your men look disciplined but disinterested," Paris instructed Glaucus again. "These visits are routine, these Mycenaeans pose no threat." The captain nodded. This portion of their ruse had been Glaucus' idea. It was not Paris alone who would convince Agamemnon of Trojan superiority, but a collective effort of their entire delegation. Fortunately, Glaucus' men would walk over burning coals for their captain.

They had been waiting in the entry hall for far longer than would seem necessary. It had been the same at the harbor. Either these Greeks were stalling for time to prepare for his arrival, or they intentionally meant to keep him waiting. Neither boded well for his mission. The longer they waited, the more repetitive his instructions became.

"Dismissal, but not laxity." Paris added.

"My men are ready." Glaucus grunted, his tone a firm but gentle reminder for Paris to do the same.

Am I ready? He had never felt so agitated before greeting a new ruler. Every nerve in his body was taut. He kept looking over his shoulder expecting to find someone watching him. It was an unnerving feeling of being exposed in the wake of a battle.

Whoever he expected to see was never there. Nevertheless, Paris studiously watched every shadow. The castle was more fortress than palace, and it boasted enough hidden alcoves to house an army of assassins.

Or one mysterious beauty...

Try as he might, he could not get that woman's face out of his mind. He had an overwhelming urge to seek her out. If she was really flesh and blood, and not a siren like Glaucus insisted, he needed to find her. And that desire was distracting him to no end. His duty to his king could not afford such deviations.

Paris straightened himself, determined to stay focused on the task at hand. A good ambassador was an observant one. He sorted through the information he had gleaned about the Mycenaean king from his short duration thus far. From the towering Lion Gates at the base of the acropolis, to the monumental walkway to the palace, Agamemnon had designed his keep to strike fear and awe into his guests. The thick cyclopean masonry, with stones twice the size of men, would have impressed Paris had he not seen its like before.

And found here, so far on the frontier, it smarted of pretentiousness.

The holding chamber he was waiting in was brightly painted in alternating squares of red, yellow and blue stucco, a delightful pattern that formed a series of zig-zags down the long hall. He counted each square twice, the familiar rhythm of counting numbers calming his agitated mind.

Finally, a short horn blast echoed from within the hall. Paris' soldiers formed ranks in front of him, and Glaucus gave him a curt nod before stepping forward to lead his troops.

Paris took a deep breath, calming himself like the mountain-dwelling Amorites taught him. Agamemnon was what mattered now. He let his mind drain of all else, letting his racing thoughts trickle out of him with each measured exhalation.

The double doors opened wide and light flooded out, momentarily blinding him. The megaron was packed. Highborns, from the look of their fine clothes, lined its walls, each noble craning their necks to get a better look at the Trojan men. A short herald stepped forward, bridging the gap between the entryway and the main hall.

"THE DELEGATION OF TROY NOW APPROACHES!"

Paris motioned to Glaucus that he was ready and the captain relayed the command. Glaucus used small almost unnoticeable hand signals, and the unit responded as one. They joined together in block formation, shielding Paris from view. Another wave from Glaucus brought forth two of their own heralds, each with a rounded trumpet in hand. They lifted the metal instruments to their lips and filled the air with a brazen blast.

The crowd erupted in whispers, murmuring to themselves over the magical quality of the brassy note, a sound so crisp it seemed almost godly. When the final reverberation died off, the Trojan delegation marched forward, the heavy fall of their boots drumming a staccato beat on the stone floor.

Directly before them, in the center of the room, stood a

round ceremonial hearth twelve feet in diameter. It was bordered in decorated plaster with an extravagant design of flames and spirals. Surrounding it were four wooden columns sheathed in plates of bronze, resting atop carved base stones shaped to resemble lion paws. Upon reaching it his troops halted and, moving in unison with knees locked, they parted lengthwise, revealing Paris at the aft of the room.

The Mycenaean herald stepped beside him and raised his baritone voice again. "Paris, Son of Priam, Son of Laomedon, Prince of Troy approaches the Throne."

Paris' heralds resumed their trumpeting, trilling out a clarion song for his entry. He clenched the *kerykeion* in his right hand, letting the encrusted gemstones bite into the flesh of his palm. The impressive item was the one object of finery on him. He lifted it higher so it would be the first detail his host would see, then strode forward at a stately pace, allowing the throng to satisfy their curiosity of him.

Behind the pressing throng, the walls of the megaron were decorated in a massive frieze, showing an epic battle of the Mycenaean people. Horse-drawn chariots raced across a stylized landscape where Mycenaean warriors dressed in short white kilts fought in hand-to-hand combat with strange enemies: barbarians coarse of feature with wild shaggy hair. A retelling of the taming of the wild lands, Paris surmised.

As he passed his troops, the squad closed ranks behind him, pounding the butts of their spears in tempo with the renewed trumpeting. Once he reached the hearth, he took a sharp right turn, facing the throne for the first time since entering.

Agamemnon sat atop a backless throne, its rectangular legs plated with ivory tusks carved to resemble the haunches of a lion. The man himself wore a pelt of the regal cat, its reddish-orange mane lining the cape and imbuing the large king with the creature's fierce aura. Paris marched forward, keeping his eyes locked on the massive man before him. And Agamemnon studied Paris as Paris studied him. There was a distinctively smug twist to the king's broad face.

Paris heard his father's voice whispering in his ear, *"This Agamemnon thinks himself far grander than he be... Go, educate him otherwise."* Paris stiffened his back, pausing before the throne, and lowered himself into a respectful bow—a mark of respect but not of reverence.

The Mycenaean herald returned. He bellowed a solid note from the bone horn strapped to his waist, a brutish sound following the elegant instrument from Troy. A flash of irritation creased the face of the king.

"You approach the throne of Agamemnon, Son of Atreus, Son of Pelops, Sacker of Lydia, Slayer of False Brothers, favored Son of the Hellas, Ruler of the Argive and High King of Mycenae. All Hail the King!" The herald was nearly out of breath by the time he finished.

"ALL HAIL THE KING!" the assembled Mycenaeans repeated.

Paris righted himself, prepared to launch into his prearranged speech, but the tingling sensation had returned. His eyes darted to the left of the throne.

And he saw her. A vision of elegance and grace. Their eyes locked and breath escaped him. He would not have been more stunned if Zeus had struck him with a thunderbolt.

Gods save me. I'm Ate's fool.

For the moment the Trojan delegation entered the room, reality shifted for Helen and she felt like she had slipped into a dream. The Trojan guard reminded her so forcibly of her father's Spartan Hoplites, with their crested helms and rigid formations, that a small cry escaped her lips, earning her a stern glare of disapproval from her husband.

And the prince himself!

She soaked in every detail. His skin was a tanned olive with the healthy glow of a man who spent a good deal of time beneath the sun. His eyes were almond in shape and framed by dark lashes. His hair was a dark brown, the color of rich earth, and it fell in thick waves about his wide-set shoulders. His muscles rippled beneath the tight linen of his cream colored tunic.

Helen had never seen a more handsome man. He lacked whiskers on his chin, a style uncommon in Mycenae. And though his features seem youthful, only a fool would say he was less man than the hairy warriors of Mycenae. His beauty was exotic, strange and undeniable. She was woozy by the time he bowed before the king. He was so close she could almost smell the scent of his oiled hair. She could not keep her eyes off him.

And then he turned to her, his dark penetrating eyes seeming to see *into* her. Helen's heart hammered against her ribs like a war drum, she had never felt so exposed. She was paralyzed in that gaze. It was fortuitous the prince tore his eyes away to turn back to the king. She doubted she had the fortitude.

She cast the king a furtive look, careful to not look in the prince's direction. Agamemnon was not pleased. Helen recognized the hard expression he reserved for dealing with men whose loyalty he questioned. The silence lasted longer than would seem proper, both men studying one another, waiting for the other man to speak first.

Agamemnon finally relented, albeit with a note of irritation. "Rise, Son of Troy, and state your business with Mycenae."

Helen shifted nervously. It was no accident their visitor's titles were so brief, and Agamemnon's so long. He meant to intimidate this prince.

Paris recognized the clumsy tactic as well. He adopted a mask of pleasant indifference, neither responding nor acknowledging Agamemnon's slight. He kept his focus on the king, refusing to look towards the mysterious beauty on his left. But now that he knew she was near, his senses were heightened, as if he could feel her movements instinctively.

"Noble Agamemnon," he steadied himself. "It is with great joy that I travel to Mycenae to cement the bonds of friendship between your realm and that of my father, King Priam of Troy. The prosperity of that friendship is one Priam treasures. Mycenae's influence grows in the Old World as your trade passes through our borders. The kingdoms of the East clamor to know you. And as neighbors who share a common tongue and ancestry, we have been amiss to not visit you sooner and greet you as brothers."

He watched Agamemnon's face closely, searching for any hint of his desires. Was it pride that would move this man? Greed? A mixture of both? It was Paris' task to discover the Mycenaean's weakness, and his every word, his every movement was designed to unveil it.

Agamemnon seemed mollified by his declaration of friendship, but there was still a question in his hawkish eyes. *Am I friend or foe?* Paris cast him a benign smile that gave no indication either way.

Helen knew the prince's elegant words were meant to soothe Agamemnon. And while the king seemed pleased from what he was hearing, her sister appeared less convinced. Clytemnestra's face was pinched as though she caught the scent of insult.

"You are welcome here, Paris, Son of Priam." Agamemnon straightened on his throne. "We *are* past due acquainting our two kingdoms. But may I assume this is a visit of profit and pleasure?"

Helen almost choked. The hint was obvious. It was no secret that Agamemnon hungered for riches. And the bards delighted in singing tales about the golden wealth of Troy.

Paris also picked up on the slip. So it was greed that unlocked this man. "Our ship holds are full. I will leave the details of our barter to my Trade Master. But I do have one item to impart, a small token of Priam's regard." He turned to Glaucus. The captain pulled a long dagger stowed at the small of his back, handing it to the prince.

The weapon was sheathed in a decorative cover, depicting a great hero in the act of slaying a Minotaur. The hilt ended in a golden head of a bull, its horns encircling the holder's hand. Agamemnon took it from Paris' hands eagerly, pulling the bronze blade free with a ringing chime.

Helen pressed forward to get a better view just as the prince pulled back from his offering. His furtive eyes darted past her again, and being so close, she could hear his sharp intake of breath. He took an involuntary step back, stumbling to regain his balance. It was the first break in his elegant poise.

Agamemnon, however, paid little attention to the prince, his razor-sharp focus on the tribute before him. "Excellent." The king crowed, sheathing the blade and tucking the weapon into his belt. "My Steward will see you are housed." He waved Nextus forward. The thin man gave a curt nod and quickly disappeared down the hall.

"Menelaus!" Agamemnon called out sharply behind him.

Her husband stepped forward. He shared a similar glare of disapproval as Clytemnestra, whether for the prince or his brother's curt summons, Helen could not tell. "My brother will arrange entertainment for your visit." Agamemnon continued. "Something involving sport and horse should suffice. You can manage that, can't you Little Brother?"

Menelaus stiffened, trying unsuccessfully not to register the barb. "Perhaps a hunt?" he grimaced. "If we can rouse the banner men, we can put the chariots to field as well."

"Done!" Agamemnon announced. "And a feast for the *Mounichia*. Let it not be said that Agamemnon broke the bonds of *xenia*."

The prince bowed again, his hand over his heart. "You honor me, Great King. I look forward to the festivities. But if I may ask one more boon?"

A small crease of irritation crossed the king's face. Helen knew what Agamemnon was thinking. *What more could he want after feasting and games?* The prince could ask for anything right now and the king would be honor pressed to provide.

She recognized Agamemnon's conflicting interests immediately. Their silos were running low. They could scarcely afford such festivities as it was, and this unexpected visit would bring additional hardship to his already beleaguered people. But a chance to display the might of Mycenae? She feared this request would not bode well for their people.

"Ask and I will do as I can," Agamemnon conceded.

Paris smiled, knowing he was playing his part superbly. He waited a few moments longer to allow the king to fret over what greater cost Paris could extract, then spoke. "My father requested I make efforts to know the customs and cultures of this land. Long have we heard of the wild spirit of the Hellas and the independent men and women who tamed its shores. I would be honored to see your city and meet its inhabitants."

It was a simple request, one Agamemnon should have no trouble meeting. But the king groaned irritably. "That's women's work." He rolled his eyes dismissively. "But if you insist, I will put my queen at your disposal."

Helen studied the Trojan as he frowned. The man was unsettled by Agamemnon's suggestion. After a slight hesitation he turned to her and bowed deeply, far deeper than he had for Agamemnon. "Your Grace, I would be honored by your assistance."

Helen looked over the assembled court nervously. A stunned silence followed the prince's words. No one knew how to respond. But her sister registered the insult. Clytemnestra glared at the Trojan, her teeth clenched tight.

The prince, however, was blissfully unaware, his head bowed before her.

"Get up." She whispered fervently, hoping he didn't shame himself too long.

Agamemnon's mocking laughed filled the hall. It was a bitter laugh, one that insulted his guest and his wife alike. "That is my brother's wife you address, Trojan. But I understand how you might be fooled since the women shared a womb."

Paris stood quickly, completely off-guard. He did a double take between the princess and queen. Identical twins? They couldn't be more different in his eyes. He collected himself, and turned to the queen, bowing even deeper. "Forgive me, Your Grace."

"Don't concern yourself with the foibles of feminine feeling." Agamemnon chided, thoroughly enjoying Trojan's mistake. "We know you are weary from your travels. Rest. We will rejoin in the morning." He clapped his hands together, signaling the end of the audience. The crowd erupted in chatter as Paris and his retinue excused themselves.

As he turned to go, Paris glanced one last time to the mysterious princess. His body ignited at the sight of her. He felt inexplicably connected to the woman.

A married woman, he reminded himself. Somewhere in the heavens the Gods were having a fantastic jest on his behalf. With great effort, he turned away and disappeared down the corridor.

CHAPTER 10

A GAME OF STONES

AGAMEMNON WAITED for the hall to empty out before retiring to his private antechamber. He quickly dismissed his staff, leaving only his family behind. Once alone, he pulled the Trojan dagger from his belt and inspected the weapon again. The craftsmanship was superb. The gold filigree on the sheath must have taken weeks to complete. It was a kingly gift, one he could bequeath to his son, and his son's son thereafter.

This was one item from Troy's treasure trove. One example of the wealth they possessed, wealth he hungered for. Agamemnon's subjects excelled in works of clay and bone, but metal was the province of Old World smiths. He had amassed an arsenal of bronze weaponry, traded every scrap he could to gain more. He knew, in his heart of hearts, that whichever kingdom mastered the manipulation of metal would rule the world. There was no reason it couldn't be Mycenae.

"I do not trust him, My Lord." His queen continued her harping. "Every word he spoke was veiled in double meaning and innuendo. He is here for a purpose he does not state."

Agamemnon studied his wife. She was intelligent for a woman, a fact he would only admit when they were in private. "So what if he is? I hardly see the danger in letting him converse with peasants and travel the countryside."

He had already deduced the Trojan's presence signified something greater than mere trade relations. The young prince played a game of wills. He was quite good at it, in fact, with a few minor exceptions. But his skills paled in comparison with Agamemnon's own. Agamemnon was content to let the game play out and see if the Trojan had more to give than just decorative swords.

He settled back in an armchair, and watched his family come to their own conclusions. Menelaus paced by the door, frowning irritably. His aloof behavior here, and in the megaron before, broadcasted Menelaus' resentment loud and clear. He hated politics, preferring instead the thrill of battle and sport.

Agamemnon sneered. His brother claimed the rights of a king but behaved like a petulant child. "Is there somewhere else you'd rather be, Menelaus? Or do you have something to contribute to the conversation?"

Menelaus grimaced, swallowing the insult like a bitter tonic. "I agree with the queen. The Trojan could be spying on us, scouting our perimeters, checking for weaknesses."

"For certain," Agamemnon mocked his brother. "Priam sends a beardless boy to scout out our defenses. The perfect ruse."

Menelaus scowled and turned away, continuing his antsy pacing beside the door. Agamemnon disliked this ill-mood. First Clytemnestra, and now his own brother. They were jumping at shadows. This prince was no threat. He could not even be an accomplished ambassador. Mistaking a queen was the mark of an amateur. No true ambassador would have been so clumsy.

Agamemnon frowned. Was that a message Priam made? That Mycenae was important enough to treat with but not enough to send their best? Or did he think Agamemnon would be wooed by a visit from a pampered prince and a set of pretty soldiers?

Only Helen seemed immune to the invading paranoia of

his council, her gentle eyes lost in thought. "And what say you, Sweet Sister?" She startled as he addressed her. "Do you preach caution as well? Do you believe the prince is all that he seems?"

"No..." she stammered, drawing the ire of his queen and her husband. "What man can be known after such a short audience?" Her confidence grew as she steadied herself beneath their judgmental stares. "But one thing I am certain of, My King—if he is looking for weaknesses, he will not find any."

Agamemnon laughed. What a spirit she possessed. Such sweet innocence mixed with unquestionable loyalty. It was a pity she was not born the elder. His poor brother had no idea how to savor this treasure.

"Well said, Sister. He can't find weakness if none exists. The only tales this Trojan will spread will be of our courage and strength. Mycenae is as powerful as the Empires of Old."

And my kingship rivals any they hold.

"Be wary, Husband." Clytemnestra warned again. "No king willingly gives away prestige. The prince said, 'through Troy does our influence grow'. King Priam would make you his vassal."

"I would die first!" Menelaus spat. "We bow to no foreign power."

"You will if he brings an army to our shores!" she fired back. "Or blocks our trade? We'd wither away if that happened. He is a danger!"

"Settle down, both of you!" Agamemnon shouted at his brother and wife alike, pushing Clytemnestra behind him. "I will not respond to a royal messenger like a paranoid barbarian."

"My Lord?" Clytemnestra continued, unfazed by his stern glare. "There is something false about this man. I can sense it."

Agamemnon groaned. Clytemnestra would always advise to strike first. It was a Spartan frailty. She lacked the patience to be subtle. But not so her sister....

"And what if he speaks the truth?" Helen countered, staring her sister down. "What do we lose by acting in good faith? What have we to fear?"

Helen crossed the room and addressed him directly. "Let him see Mycenae. And in return we are afforded the same opportunity to study him. We should seize this moment so we might better understand Troy and her intentions."

Agamemnon stroked his beard, considering the move. To let the watched become the watcher? It had a devious flare that would make men whisper of his cunning. This foreign knowledge might be exactly what he needed to convince the other Greek kingdoms to unite behind him.

"You are wise, My King, to not overreact." Helen lowered her head demurely, though there was no retreat in her eyes. "If we are not servants to a distant land, than we should not cower like one."

A fire burned in his belly with her words, her challenge laid bare. *Are you a king worthy of great glory, or a pretender clamoring for attention at the edge of the world?* One look to Menelaus was all the reminder he needed of how much he detested that comparison.

"Welcome him," Agamemnon decided. "Show him the glory of Mycenae. He has full immunity."

"Brother!" Menelaus protested.

"Do it!" he glowered at the puerile man. It was one thing to advise, but Agamemnon would not take outright rebellion in his own house. "Whatever he asks, whatever he requires, you give it."

"No." Clytemnestra's cold refusal shocked him to his core.

"*What did you say?*" He felt the rage building up inside him. Defiance? From his woman?

Clytemnestra stuck out her jaw, refusing to back down. "You want to show him our greatness? Do not put your queen, and by proxy our king, at the beck and call of this ambassador. We do not kowtow to a visitor who lands on our shores unannounced. Send Helen instead."

Menelaus choked. "Absolutely not. You saw the way he looked at her. I don't want that Trojan within ten yards of my wife."

Agamemnon took a closer look at Helen. Her cheeks were flushed a rosy red, her beauty undeniable. What better an envoy to strike jealousy into a rival's heart?

Yes. Let Troy envy Mycenae's might *and* her beauty.

"You worry too much brother." He pushed Menelaus back. "Only a boy-sick fool would not be touched by your wife's grace. We can use this to our advantage."

Helen blinked, sweet confusion on her face. "My King?"

"Get to know him, Helen. Make him fall in love with the city and our people. Get him to confide in you. And when he does, you report back to me. Can you do this?" It was fitting that she challenged him before. He could now return the favor.

Are you a daughter of Tyndareus? Does the fierce spirit of Sparta still run in your veins?

There was cold fire in Helen's lovely blue eyes. Her barely contained anger made his cock grow hard. Nothing could provoke Helen more than questioning her honor, and that obsessive virtue made her easy to manipulate. She was different from his queen in so many ways.

Helen raised her chin. "As you wish, My King."

CHAPTER 11

THE FAMILIAR STRANGER

AGAMEMNON'S STEWARD, Nextus, showed Paris to his guest quarters shortly after they exited the throne room. The stoic man barely said a word, even when given a direct question. After a few failed attempts at conversation, Paris fell silent. Thus far, the Mycenaeans seemed as chilly as their cold stone halls.

After a short walk down several narrow corridors, they arrived in the eastern wing of the palace where the royal apartments were housed. His chambers were accommodating but snug, its walls built in the same thick defensive style as the rest of the palace. Paris was given a main room with two connected sleeping chambers. The suite had an open-air balcony that looked over the inner courtyard one story below. By the lack of adornment, he suspected the rooms typically housed non-royal visitors or vassal leaders. Definitely a strange choice for an ambassador who was usually afforded a ruler's best.

A small repast was set for him in the apartments, a haunch of roast mutton and a decanter of mulled wine. Sparse, but satisfying. After his cool reception in the harbor, he wondered if Agamemnon was purposely restricting his hospitality, or if

Paris' visit had really taken the Mycenaean by surprise. If the king was truly motivated by greed, it was logical he would not waste his finery on others. But if the snub persisted, Paris would have to take counter measures. Priam had been explicit —this wayward king would not disrespect Troy with impunity, and that included disrespecting Paris, himself.

He hoped Agamemnon didn't make his last excursion more painful than it needed to be, but only time would tell. Paris needed to be wary, but not overtly sensitive. In his experience, if you went searching for insult you will eventually find it, whether intentional or not.

Don't make snap judgements. What feels like disregard is usually a cultural misunderstanding.

It was quite possible these apartments actually *were* the king's finest, and the hot meal a courtesy an unexpected guest should be grateful to receive. It was too early to be jumping at shadows or losing sleep on this assignment.

Paris decided to keep Glaucus nearby, giving the captain one of the sleeping chambers for his own, while the rest of the Trojan guard took housing down the hill in the royal barracks. Glaucus joined him for the meal. They both ate heartily, reclining on the thick pillows lining the sitting area of the main chamber.

"What do you think of the Hellas thus far?" Paris stretched, feeling the ache of his travels catching up to him. He took a long pull from their skin of wine, savoring the faint taste of nutmeg and elderberry.

"I like the scenery." Glaucus snorted, the sound of a man who'd seen too many distant shores.

Paris frowned. "And which scenery is that?"

"The same one you've been admiring. Gold spun hay, clear blue skies, rolling contours of hill and vale. The Gods couldn't paint a prettier vista."

Paris stiffened. Glaucus wasn't talking about landscape. The princess' beauty wasn't far from Paris' mind either, try as he might to distract himself with his father's task. Every line of her perfect face was forever etched into his mind: the arc of her high cheekbones, the delicate button-chin on her heart shaped face, her jewel eyes a deeper-than-lapis blue framed by coal black lashes. She was breathtaking. In all his travels, Paris had never seen her like.

"We aren't here to moon over the view." Paris tried to clear his mind. "We have a big day ahead of us tomorrow. We can't afford to make any more mistakes." Glaucus gave him a wolfish grin, the captain more than aware who needed that advice.

They had discussed their duties in great detail on the trip across the Aegean. While all eyes were on Paris, his retinue was free to infiltrate the market town and learn the truth of Mycenaean capabilities. Paris need only distract the queen, glean what information he could about Agamemnon that could be used to unsettle the man, and present an impeachable regal presence of Troy. A simple, albeit boring, task. He would suffer through the grand tour when he'd rather be swapping tales in the taverns.

"You're coming with me." Paris informed his captain and stifled a yawn. "If I have to be miserable, so do you."

"How considerate of you, My Prince." Glaucus snorted again. "But say it plain. You can't bear to be without me. I know I'm a charmer." He winked at Paris.

Paris' laugh came out more as a gag. He decided it was time for bed. "Rest well, Glaucus. In a week, good or ill, this will all be over."

It was a mantra in his head. *One more week, one more week.* He had only to survive the next few days, complete this mission and his duty to Troy would be over. A new chapter of his life would begin.

How much trouble could he possibly stir up in just one week?

"I am no spy." Helen bemoaned to Aethra as her matron busily prepared her for touring duties the following morning. "I haven't the faintest idea how to get a foreigner to confide in me."

"Gracious child, don't let your mind take flight with fancies. Observing a man and spying are not the same thing." Aethra tugged the horsehair brush through Helen's hair harder than would seem necessary. "Now what were the king's words? His *exact* words?"

"He said to make the prince fall in love with Mycenae and her many splendors." She shivered, remembering the heat in the king's voice. The tour was a ruse to lower the ambassador's defenses, make him comfortable, and in his laxity she should seek to exploit a cordial relationship. Falsehoods and lies when Helen prided herself on truthfulness and candor. The whole enterprise made her feel dirty.

Aethra cupped her chin, forcing Helen to meet her motherly gaze. "That does not sound so hard, does it? Now stop your fretting. A face like yours is meant for smiles." She tucked a red saffron flower into Helen's brow, a red blossom to match her elegant chiton. The fabric was no match for the prince's fine cloak, but its design was the best in the Hellas. Tyndareus had given her that dress, and its colors reminded Helen she was still a Princess of Sparta.

Why me? Helen groaned again. *I am no diplomat. And Nestra says I'm a hopeless hostess. Why send me?* But knowing Agamemnon, there was some twisted reason behind her selection. "What do you think he wants me to do?" She tightened her shawl around her chest.

"Peace, child. You'll do nothing you aren't willing to do. A king cannot command a man's dignity." Aethra grumbled, rubbing a drop of rouge onto Helen's cheeks. "Or a lady's!" She pulled Helen to her feet and inspected her nose to toe. "That'll do. At least you look the part, so long as you don't betray yourself by running through the fields."

Helen attempted a grin at the lighthearted remark, but

failed miserably. It wasn't only Agamemnon's odd request twisting her stomach in knots, but the prospect of spending an entire day in the prince's presence. She wanted very much to get to know the man better, and that desire frightened her. A fire ignited in her breast the moment she saw him, a fire she could barely contain. She felt like a young maiden dancing in the orchards waiting for a festival to begin. She could scarcely focus on the matters before her. Blessedly, she wouldn't be alone. Aethra was more than capable of keeping her from making too much a fool of herself.

"Let's go. The cock's already crowed twice." Helen headed to the door.

"But you must eat!" Aethra urged her toward the untouched tray of steaming oats.

Helen waved her off and was halfway down the hall by the time her matron caught up. She could no more eat than calm her racing heart. In short order, they arrived in the guest wing of the palace and Aethra rapped on the prince's door with her hard knuckles.

The door immediately swung open. The Trojan guard at the entrance was similar in age to Aethra, the grey in his whiskers dominating the brown. He had a quiet presence about him, like that of the wildcats which roamed the mountains of Sparta, seemingly relaxed but ready to pounce in a moment's notice. His eyes widened in recognition when he saw her, but other than that small gesture, he was a rock.

"Your Highness," he opened the door wide, stepping aside to grant her access.

The prince stood by the balcony, his back to her, overlooking the court and numerous household staff busily completing their duties. He had forsaken his simple clothing for garments more suiting his station. A band of multicolored embroidery ran along the edge of his tunic. A matching sash was draped over his shoulder and tied along his waist. The cape was the same, the crimson material tied across his neck with golden rope. It was an item he clearly favored.

Aethra stepped forward to announce her, but Helen held her maid back with a wary hand, taking the extra moments to study the stranger. The prince clasped his hands behind his back. He wore a heavy signet ring on his left hand that he twisted unconsciously as he watched the activities below. The curve of his shoulders lacked the bulky muscular frame of a Mycenaean soldier. His build was lean, like the Spartan men who finished the *Agoge* and went on to join the ranks of the royal army. He was incredibly handsome.

Paris waited impatiently for the queen to be introduced. His shoulders itched, knowing she was near. He had carefully placed himself at the balcony so he would not be seen waiting submissively. Now that she was in the room, he couldn't be the first to turn. In the delicate game of politics, whoever moved first lost.

What is taking her so long?

Then Glaucus cleared his throat. Loudly. Paris sighed, and spun to meet his host. He wasn't going to win this first contest of wills.

He made it half-way through his turn before jerking upright in alarm, his greeting frozen on his lips. He knew he was staring openly, but it couldn't be helped. Of all the people Paris was prepared to see walk through his door, his mystery princess was not among them. His dignified poise vanished as he failed to find words.

Helen curtsied gracefully as Aethra rattled off her titles, doing her best to ignore the confusion playing out on the prince's face. "Your Grace." She addressed him respectfully, keeping her eyes steady on his olive face as she righted herself.

The soldier cleared his throat again, stirring the prince from his silence. "Princess, to what do I owe the pleasure?"

Helen blushed, preparing herself for her first lie. "The Queen, my sister, finds herself preoccupied this day. I volunteered to act as your guide in her stead, if you so desire." She watched his cheeks flush, whether from her words or the obvious insult, she could not tell. The lie was necessary, she reminded herself, if the prince was what Clytemnestra feared.

Paris' mind raced. So he was to be shuffled off to a lesser house member? Was Agamemnon trying to provoke him? One stray glance at Glaucus told him the captain's opinion. The first jab was meant to see how many you would take before striking back. "Am I to assume the queen will be similarly preoccupied on the morrow?" the tension in his shoulders leaked into his words. "And for the duration of my visit?"

Helen stiffened. He had every right to be upset. She knew he might take her replacement badly. It was stupid to take his anger personally, but strangely his response felt like a rejection of her. "I do not know the affairs of the queen," she tore her eyes away from his handsome face, "but if you'd rather have another guide—" she turned to the door.

"No." Paris stopped her quickly, grabbing her hands and pulling her back. "On the contrary, Princess. Nothing would please me more."

The second the prince touched her, Helen's pulse began to race. His hands were rough, calloused from working rope or leather. It was a heady contrast to the scented oil in his hair and the fine clothes that he wore. Could he really be her enemy? Everything about the man seemed refined and genteel.

"Please," Paris added more gently. "I would be honored to share your company."

Relief flooded her and she smiled. It was one of her rare smiles, one she shared only when truly happy. His hands tightened in response and he lost himself in studying her face.

Aethra cleared her throat. "My Lady?" Her tart voice cut right through the fog in Helen's brain. "Should we start at the workshops?"

Helen blushed, yanking her hands away. She was behaving like a brazen harlot. They were not alone. The last thing she needed was for idle whispers to reach her husband.

"Yes, thank you Aethra. Your Grace?" She stepped aside to

allow him to pass into the hall.

"Paris." The prince straightened his perfectly smoothed tunic. "Please, call me Paris. And this is Glaucus, my Captain at Arms." He waved the guard forward, motioning the man to exit first.

"Paris." The word rolled easily off her tongue, familiar and smooth. She savored it like a rare foreign fruit. "And you must call me Helen."

They strolled through the palace grounds chatting amicably about nothing of consequence. Helen kept their conversation light, maintaining a steady pace toward the royal stables. She was determined to conduct herself regally and kept a proper distance between her and Paris, a prospect much easier in public than it had been in his chambers. And should she fail, there was always loyal Aethra, trailing a few paces behind them. The matron conversed quietly with the Trojan Captain, her eyes never far from Helen and her virtue.

Helen asked on his travels, and Paris responded with generic details. They cast furtive glances at one another as they walked, and every few seconds their eyes would lock. A jolt of energy shot through her body each time that happened.

"The city seemed a bit overcrowded when we travelled from the harbor yesterday." Paris commented after a particularly tense silence. "Is that common?"

"Yes," she tore her eyes away from his, grateful for the change of topic. "There are many visitors for the upcoming *Mounchia* festival, but most are residents. The city has grown under Agamemnon's rule. The land is fertile, and its rivers clear. Mycenae is the most influential state on the mainland."

Paris nodded appreciatively. "With so much land to spread to, I'm sure that trend will continue." He glanced at her from the corner of his eye. "I noticed you say 'the city' not 'our city'. Is this place not also your home?"

"I am from Sparta." Her chest swelled with pride. "It's farther south from here and inland. In mountain country." It had been too long since she last visited her homeland. The western steppes would be covered in lilac now. And Tyndareus would soon be sending the young recruits into the wilds to hunt their first blood. She sighed wistfully, lost in her memories.

When she did not elaborate further, he prodded, "And is Sparta equally rich and fertile?"

A stray image of legionnaires working the field crossed her mind. It was so preposterous she laughed out loud. "We do not grow crops in Sparta."

Paris raised his eyebrow, confused. "Then what do you grow?"

A wicked smile crossed her face as she answered him point-of-fact. "Warriors, of course." She walked a few paces before realizing he had stopped. It was clearly not the answer he expected to hear. "Are you coming?"

"You lived along the western border?" Paris jogged to her side, trying to fit this new piece of information into the puzzle the princess represented. "Is it true what they say? Do the mythos live on the outskirts?"

Helen stopped in her tracks. "What? Dragons and chimeras and hydras?" Those were rumors for young boys to whisper about when their mothers weren't close enough to box their ears. "You have been spending too much time with sailors."

"Probably." He grinned. "But if they do exist, it would have to be in the *terra incognita*. The western wilds are some of the last places unmapped. It's bound to hold some secrets." Paris' eyes lit up with the prospect. "I'd give anything to walk those lands."

"And that land would grind a soft prince to mincemeat if he tried," she added playfully, enjoying the banter. There was something irresistible in his excitement. How many frontiers had Paris travelled? How many new cultures had he explored?

As an ambassador, the prince lived a life of adventure that she could only imagine.

"Were the Spartans the first to conquer the wilds?"

"Some of the first." She stated proudly. "But certainly the best. The barbarian hordes fought harder in our region than in any other." She tried not to boast, but she was proud of her ancestors' achievements. They deserved the respect of Troy.

"So Sparta claimed those lands, but not Mycenae?" Thus far, Paris was having trouble understanding the complex alliances of the Helladic peoples. If they were back in the Old World, and Sparta was the premier military force, it would hold suzerainty over the other kingdoms.

"Well, no..." Helen stumbled, realizing her mistake. Agamemnon was his host, not Tyndareus. "Mycenae is a port city. Her strength comes from trade." But her explanation only made her adopted home sound weak.

"Ah, traders." Paris laughed. "Merchants have taken hold of Troy as well. One day I swear they will rule the world."

"*Traders* ruling instead of kings?" It took her a moment to realize he was joking, and she joined his hearty laugh. "I did not take you for a comedian."

"My brothers say I am more a fool than a diplomat." He readily agreed, only his self-assured smile belying the comment.

They were forced to wait at the royal stockyard while a shepherd crossed his herd of goats. It was an abnormally large flock, and the shepherd shot her an apologetic glance as they waited. Helen counted the dams, each with a pair of billies. The kidding had been a great success this year.

"How many brothers do you have?" she asked, trying to imagine what a brood of Trojan princes would be like.

"Too many." His brow creased. "There are five of us legitimate, another twenty that are not, and equally so for my sisters."

Helen's eyes shot wide. "*Fifty?*" It was hard to imagine.

She always dreamed of having brothers. In her nocturnal imagination, they were twins, like her and Clytemnestra, and they lived to protect the girls from harm. But to have fifty brothers and sisters? "How do you tell them all apart?"

"You don't." Paris grimaced. "At least not the ones who don't matter." He didn't bother to add that he spent so little time at the capital he didn't find that lack of familiarity inconvenient. He could only wish for that same anonymity from his siblings. But it was a vain wish. Everyone knew his name.

The herd finished crossing, a young kid bleating as it raced to catch up to its dam. Helen watched as the doe nicked the babe's heels and they disappeared into the thick of the herd. "Every child matters," she calmly disagreed, "to their mother if no one else."

The effect on the prince was startling. A haunted look crossed over Paris' face and he turned away from her. "Yes, I suppose that's true." When he did not turn back, Helen gingerly started back on the path, hoping she had not inadvertently said something to upset him.

A waft of manure and fresh hay greeted them as they approached the royal stables. The braying of expectant mares echoed through the rafters. The sound was deafening and Helen had to cover her ears as she called out for the stable master.

"I don't mind walking." Paris offered as groomsmen rushed to tackle two chariots for them. He always found it impossible to get the feel of a new city from on high. It was better to walk amongst the citizens and engage in conversation where possible, a prospect much easier when you met them on eye level.

Haemon, the slightly hunched Horse Master, led over two chestnut mares and cast him a puzzled look at the unusual request. Even Helen frowned. "We could, if you insist," she began, "but there is a lot of ground to cover."

He was about to when Glaucus leaned forward and

whispered in his ear. "Princes don't *walk*."

Paris quickly took the reigns from Haemon, trying to hide his slip. "No, this is fine." He swept his cape aside and tried for a dignified half-bow to allow Helen to mount the chariot first.

He had one duty to complete today: to represent Troy with dignity. And instead he was acting like a wide-eyed farmhand catching his first glimpse of a city. Paris cursed at himself. He had travelled across the civilized world on behalf of Troy, and not once had he met someone who could put him at ease as easily as this princess. Conversing with her was as calming as spending an evening with Hector, as heartwarming as Troilus' hugs. She felt like family. He couldn't shake the feeling that he knew her somehow.

He watched as Helen stepped to the front of the cab. A glance over his shoulder alerted him that Glaucus and Aethra had done the same, his captain waiting stoically for Paris to lead. Paris murmured a quick thanks to Haemon and leapt up into the cab, taking his place beside the princess.

The cab was designed small, forcing him to stand sideways to avoid touching Helen in a too familiar manner. It was an awkward position. He was about to signal the horse when he realized he had no idea where they were headed. He turned to the princess, offering her the reigns instead. "Perhaps you'd like to drive?"

Helen gingerly reached for his hand. That was twice in the space of a few breaths that Paris had surprised her. No highborn man of the Hellas would let himself be chauffeured in public by a woman. Save her father, that was. Tyndareus supervised her equestrian training himself. But a decade of following Mycenaean rules gave her pause.

"You might want to hold on to something." She warned him, taking the point position in the cab. "It's been a while since I've managed a horse."

"Don't worry, it comes right back to you." He coached. "Once learned, you never really forget."

She eyed him suspiciously. "And how would you know?"

"I spend a lot of time at sea." Paris confessed, still grabbing a handrail, nonetheless. "Sometimes it's months before I travel by horse. It takes a moment to get used to the rhythms, but provided you're not battling a headstrong filly, you should be fine." He leaned across her to take a better look at their mare. "This one seems docile enough."

Helen waited for a frown of disapproval, or some sign of mock. But Paris wasn't playing her a fool. He waited patiently for her to set off, a pleasant smile on his face. If he thought to challenge her, he was in for a surprise. She whipped the reigns down sharp and the chariot leapt forward.

She had forgotten the feel of air brushing past her cheeks, of how it lifted her hair and made her feel like she was flying. In Sparta, Helen would roam the countryside, the remote ravines begging for long rides taken bareback. But in Mycenae, she was grounded, her duties forbidding her the time to take any sort of selfish joyride. Unfettered, she forgot to play host and simply luxuriated in the brisk ride down into the western holdings.

Paris instantly regretted handing over the reigns. Not that Helen was a bad driver—quite the contrary—she handled the chariot over roughly shod roads and loose gravel, leading them expertly down the steep rampart and away from the palace grounds. But placing the princess at the head of the cab forced Paris to stand behind her. Every jolt of the cab pressed her into his pelvis—and there were many jolts in their ride down the hillside. The constant rubbing kindled a fire in his loins. He put a death grip on the rail and tried desperately to regain his focus.

Just outside the palatial wall, Helen pulled the chariot to a stop beside a series of residences surrounding a central courtyard. Paris stiffly stepped off the cab just as a group of workers spread out into the court to greet them. It was a mixed lot, perhaps a dozen men and women in well-kept homespun tunics of wool. One man, clearly an overseer, wore an off-white linen robe. He bowed low to Helen, showing a bald spot on the crown of his skull.

"Princess, what an honor it is to see you again." His smile was genuine, even though his eyes continually darted Paris' way. In fact, all the workers were staring at him, a nervous titter spreading amongst the crowd, each worker equally curious about his foreign presence in their shop.

"The honor is mine, Bacis." Helen greeted the man, taking his rough hands in a familial grip. "Bacis is the head of the Potter's Guild in Mycenae. Examples of his skill have been traded as far south as Egypt, and east to your homelands." She turned back to the blushing artisan. "And this is Prince Paris of the royal house of Troy, a favored son of King Priam." The honorifics rolled melodically off her tongue.

Paris forced a grin. Her words were innocent, but she could not understand the irony of their choice. He gave the man a curt nod, and inspected his surroundings in an appreciative manner. "You are the master of this shop?"

"Yes, Your Highness. I was formally trained at Knossos before King Agamemnon hired me. Now the best potters come here to train." Bacis nodded proudly. His workers parroted his movements, as proud as their master of his esteemed background. "Would you like to see inside?"

"I'd be delighted."

Bacis waved his craftsmen into motion with a sharp cry, and they fled back to their stations. Each building had two stories, the bottom dedicated to varying workshops, the upper level set aside as living quarters for privileged artisans and palace officials. Paris followed Bacis inside the largest.

The expansive room had two dozen potter's stations, each with a stone wheel the artisan could kick counter-clockwise while shaping their pieces. Helen moved between them, greeting many artisans by name, and inspecting several pieces that caught her eye. She stopped beside a four-foot amphora, where a middle-aged woman with careworn wrinkles around her eyes put the finishing touches on the black-figure vase.

"Melete! What are you doing here? You should be at home resting." Helen swooped down on the worker.

"Princess!" Melete set down her wooden stylus and quickly dropped into a respectful curtsey. Either age or hours spent at the wheel made the move as stiff as a two-day corpse, and she nearly fell over.

Helen pulled Melete up immediately, forcing the woman to retake her seat. "You were so ill the last I saw you. I thought you'd never recover."

Melete smiled graciously, rubbing her clay-coated hands on the small of her back. "Delia brought back the syrup you gave her, Your Grace. It worked miracles. The cough is almost completely gone."

As the two women conversed, Paris took a moment to get a better look at the workshop. Every station was in use, and the back wall was lined with completed amphorae and stir-up jars ready for the kiln. The whirling of the potters wheels gave the room a light hum that welcomed quiet conversations to be indulged without fear of disrupting any worker's concentration. The senior artisans, like Melete, had assistants who collected discarded clay, refilled dipping bowls, and attended to any need the artist might have.

Melete's work was by far the finest in the shop. The rich red clay of her amphora was coated with a veneer of black in which the artist scraped off layers to create silhouetted characters. A geometric pattern ran along the top and bottom of the vase's oval swell. In the center, Melete had carved out a regal head of the eagle owl of Ares. It was masterful work. Paris could easily imagine it displayed in many palaces he had visited across the world.

"Do you like it?" Melete asked softly, a slight hesitation in her voice as she addressed him directly. There was so much hope in her eyes as she spun the piece around to show the opposite face. It was Ares again, this time in his human form, astride a chariot led by twin griffins. The beasts reared in fury, their eyes and nostrils wide. The God was fierce and divine all at once. The detail was exquisite.

Paris sighed. It was a delicate business negotiating power relations. He could not appear to be wooed by Mycenae. "It is a decent example." He used his reserved tone, careful to not show his admiration visibly.

Melete frowned, the disappointment written on her careworn face. She turned to Helen, "I meant it as a gift for you, Princess. To show my appreciation for the medicine, and all the care you've shown."

"It's lovely." Helen praised the woman while watching Paris closely, puzzled by his reaction. She had hoped for more, as well. Agamemnon instructed her to impress him, and she thought there was no finer example than Mycenaean pottery. Perhaps if he understood the passion that went into the work? "Melete is a *damos,* a free worker who splits her time between her shop in the town proper and here at the royal workshop." Helen told him, hoping to pique Paris' interest.

It worked, and he gave the woman a second appraisal. "You are not bound to the Palace?"

Melete blushed, "No, Sir. I mean, Your Grace." Her eyes darted away sheepishly from the prince's direct gaze.

"We don't have bondsmen here." Helen intercepted. "All of our workers are free, save for the few captives taken in battle. And both free worker and slave has the right to own and sell their own work." Melete nodded beside her, pleased to have Helen explain her situation.

"It is an honor to work in the royal workshop," Melete finally found her voice. "Bacis is the best of his craft. Plus my work here lessens the amount I must contribute to the tax collectors."

Paris was modestly surprised. He had rarely seen such pride in the lay folk. The sense of greatness that was usually restricted to the palace seemed a badge of honor for the workers, both high and low born. And that pride was evident in their craft. These Mycenaeans were not at all what Priam had led him to believe.

But something Melete had said nagged at his ear. *Lessens her tribute...* Paris inspected the workshop again. Every station *was* filled, their quotas well met. The potters worked diligently on their pieces, their hands cracked from the effort, and in some cases, their blood mingled with the thick clay.

"It's certainly a creative way to collect taxes," he murmured to himself, then turned back to Melete. "Good fortune in your endeavors, Mistress. I am certain you deserve it." He gave her a courtly bow, deep enough to show his respect, then rushed to join Glaucus outside.

Helen was fast at his side, his stray comment clearly not gone unnoticed. "I'm sure our ways seem strange to you..."

"Not at all." He responded offhanded. "I've visited dozens of kingdoms, and each king has a different method of rule. But strip away the titles and religious customs, they all share the same basic principles. Commerce is sacrosanct. Each land works out a system that works best for them."

And Agamemnon has learned what system works best for the king. Paris cast a cursory glance to Glaucus, questioning if the captain had noticed the poor condition of the workers. Glaucus raised a single dark brow in response. Nothing escaped the keen man's notice.

Helen blinked back her surprise from Paris' academic response. He sounded so much like Tyndareus, she had an overwhelming feeling of reclining around the central hearth of her father's megaron receiving another lesson. She studied the prince with renewed interest. It was rare to meet someone who instinctively understood the heart of matters.

"Oh." She stuttered, that moronic response winning out over a million others that sprang too late to mind. She felt like a prized idiot conversing with a scholar.

The prince waved Glaucus forward to retrieve their chariots. Helen kicked a pebble around with her slippered toe as they waited, using any excuse to keep from looking at her guest. "It is a relief to know we meet the Old World standards," she began, feeling anything but relief. "We're a young realm, but given time, we might surprise you with what we can accomplish."

She hadn't meant to sound defensive, but she found herself desperately wanting Paris' approval. Not for Mycenae, not for the king, but for herself. She forced her chin up, daring herself to meet his gaze.

Paris paused, jarred from his thoughts by Helen's impulsive declaration. "I'll tell you what surprises me." He leaned down and whispered in her ear. "Your people love you. Truly love you."

She was paralyzed by his penetrating gaze, the one that felt like he looked straight into her soul. "Is that so odd?"

Perhaps she imagined it, but a ghost of sorrow crossed his eyes. "More than you know."

They rode down to the village in silence, Helen humbled by his kind words. So much of her time in Mycenae she had felt like an outsider, a person neither wanted nor needed. She often toyed with the idea of slipping quietly off the southern precipice and into a watery grave. She had little doubt she'd be missed. To hear that the commonwealth held some affection for her was a ray of light in her usually overcast days.

But was it enough? A whole lifetime of public service spread out before her, constantly giving to the people only to return home to a cold bedchamber. It was a loneliness that had no resolution. Honor forbade her to even speak of it.

As they exited the acropolis, they left the rock-hewn streets for wider ones of hard-packed earth. The city spread out in pockets of settlements, the boundaries of Mycenae amorphous, shifting as the city continued to grow.

The villagers were out in numbers, busily preparing for the upcoming festival. Flags of red and orange adorned workshop doors and sounds of industry filled the air. The smiths worked their bellows, the bakers pounded their dough, and merchants lined the streets barking prices to any potential customer. One and all they paused as Helen and Paris passed, eager to catch a glimpse of the foreign prince.

She looked over her shoulder at Paris. He seemed lost in thought as well. His eyes were furrowed as he stared off into the horizon at some distant point. The man was such a mystery. He wasn't like any man she had ever met. He was thoughtful, forthright, but guarded just the same.

They visited the goldsmiths, the ivory carvers and finally the shipyard. Each time, Paris was respectful but aloof, showing no great interest in any one industry. She found herself stretching her memory to pull out facts that would dazzle the man. But no number would impress, no detail was unique. He was far more interested in the people themselves, asking them questions about their life and livelihood. If the man was a spy she'd swallow her slipper.

Towards sunset they walked along the wharf, the prince deep in conversation with the harbor master, when she spotted a ship she hadn't seen in several months. Heedless of the scolding she was sure Aethra would administer, she raced to the dock, greeting the captain as he tied off at the pier.

"Lukos!" Helen shouted, wrapping her arms around the stern faced man. The captain's scowl melted to joy, and he spun her around in a circle.

"The Golden Girl returns! Mark my words boys, our fortune's favored this tide." He tousled Helen's hair.

She grinned at the man, making a playful attempt to bat his hands away. Lukos was of an age with her father, a grizzled veteran of many Spartan campaigns. As he approached his silver years, he opted for the "quiet" life of the sea. It was a paltry excuse. No Spartan dreamed of a dying of old age in their beds. Lukos defied the odds by surviving so long. He hoped one day the capricious sea would remedy that poor luck.

"You are looking fit." He grunted after a sour-faced inspection. "I expected a soft life in Mycenae would have fattened you up by now."

"Do you think so little of me?" Helen pouted, soothing her chiton down over her round hips to further prove him wrong.

He laughed heartily. "True blood will always rule out. *Spartana Aeterna.*"

She kissed her fingers and lifted them towards Olympus. "Sparta Eternal." She repeated.

Lukos' galley was a small vessel. When the trade winds blew, he boasted there was no ship as swift. A quick glance confirmed he had a light crew of six sailors, none of which Helen recognized. "Did you come from the homeland?"

"Aye. I've got four talents of olives to unload before we sail to the southern continent."

She almost didn't have the courage to ask, but the man before her would never shy away from the truth, no matter how unpleasant. Besides, she was *not* soft. She could handle the answer like a Spartan.

"Any messages from the palace?"

His dour expression returned. "I'm sorry, Princess. Tyndareus did not send any."

"Oh." She buried the hurt deep inside. For the past ten years she had asked after her father and was always met with silence. With every new tide, she hoped the passage of time would soften his heart. But Tyndareus was a man of stone, and Helen was too far away to crack the shell that protected him.

"Will you send him my love when next you see him?" She forced a tender smile.

"I can do that," he promised.

Paris, having finished his discussion with the harbor master, strode toward them. Lukos' eyes widened with recognition as the prince stepped onto the dock.

"Trojan." He grunted the word, the Spartan equivalent of a gasp of surprise.

Paris also studied the captain, a perplexed expression on his face.

"Lukos, this is Prince Paris of the royal house of Troy, a guest of Mycenae." But the men already shook hands, ignoring her words.

"Jaffa, right?" Paris asked with a pleasantly surprised grin. "The Boar's Tusk tavern?"

Lukos grunted again, a slight shade of embarrassment on his face. "What little I remember of it, aye. You should never offer a sailor a bottomless cup."

Paris turned to her. "If you are wondering where my outlandish ideas about the frontier came from, Princess, you have to look no further. Lukos is quite adept at spinning a yarn."

"Only when it buys me trading rights along the Sidonian coast." He nodded to the prince. "Many thanks for that, Your Grace."

Helen watched in amazement. Lukos was not a man who warmed to a person lightly. Yet here he was, addressing her mysterious prince like an old comrade in arms.

"Perhaps you can return the favor?" Paris suggested. "My Trade Master is in the market. I'm sure he'd be interested to know the current rates you've encountered in your travels, both near and far. If you don't mind?"

"Done." Lukos readily accepted. "Forgive me, Princess. But I best see about my cargo."

"Of course." She stepped out of Lukos' way.

"I will deliver your message." He promised again, then picked up his register and marched into town.

Helen watched him go, a pang of homesickness flooding her heart. She envied Lukos, that he could board a ship and sail wherever he pleased. If she had that luxury, she'd be back on Spartan soil.

"Were you expecting some news?" Paris asked her softly.

"No, but I was hoping."

"From your father?" The question popped out of Paris' mouth before he could censor himself. "I'm sorry, that's none of my business." But something inside him told him he was right. Helen had seemed so happy a moment ago. To watch the sorrow creep over her joyful face was daunting. He wanted to help her, if he could. That urge was almost overpowering.

Helen tensed. So many conflicting emotions battled inside her. It had been too long since anyone asked her about her father. Even Nestra, who shared her estranged status, never spoke of him. Giving these emotions voice would stir a pot of resentment that would only fester, Nestra said. But it *was* festering. Unable to share, those unspoken feelings boiled within Helen, unable to escape. Paris was a foreigner. He had no stake in her current predicament. She felt an overwhelming urge to confide in him.

"I made a mistake, a long time ago. I'm waiting for him to forgive me." She tried to smile through the tears swelling in her eyes, but her traitorous mouth wouldn't cooperate. A moment of respectful silence followed her words.

"I don't know if this helps," the prince finally spoke after a weighted hesitation, "but you should know you can't change him, or how he feels about you. You can only be the best person you know how. The rest is up to the Gods."

So many times during the day, she had seen a dark presence take hold of the prince, as though he were haunted by some dire purpose or secret too terrible to bear. As she stared up into his almond eyes, she saw it again, this time recognizing the darkness for what it was: the same abandonment she felt ripping her heart in pieces.

"Thank you." She wiped away her tears, finally finding the will to smile. The one she received in turn made all her previous heartache vanish.

"I guess we should head back to the palace." Paris added reluctantly, never taking his eyes from hers. The sun was dipping low on the horizon.

Helen turned to the fortress towering high on the acropolis. Reality, and the crushing weight of all the things she could not change, returned in force. She wished she could stay in the village and enjoy a simple life like the common folk she so loved. But she was a princess. The Fates had a different future in store for her.

Paris held out his arm for her and she readily accepted it. It wasn't until they had left the village behind and rode up the Grand Walkway that she realized he no longer pulled away from her touch. She leaned back against him as they continued up the ramp, feeling comforted for the first time since she left her homeland behind.

CHAPTER 12

A CONFLICT OF INTERESTS

"HE IS well travelled." Helen reported back to Agamemnon and her sister later that evening. "He has treated with a half dozen of our southeastern allies, and some of those unknown to us as well."

"I knew that already." Agamemnon shouted testily at her. "Details! Give me details, Helen." He paced the space of his private antechamber completing the circuit in three giant strides. It made the room feel more cramped than usual. Helen couldn't take two steps without the tall man glowering down on her.

At Clytemnestra's insistence, they held this meeting behind closed doors. There were too many toadies at court who couldn't be trusted, she said. And right now discretion was their biggest asset. Against what, Helen couldn't fathom.

She dug into her memory, trying to unearth some detail that would satisfy the king. But, after several hours in the company of the prince, she had surprisingly little information to share that Agamemnon deemed appropriate. She could not find a fault where none existed.

Paris was nothing like her family suspected him to be. He was dignified and refined, showing her respect in ways she hadn't experienced since leaving Sparta. Yes, there was a darkness to him, but it was nothing to be feared. When she looked into his almond eyes, she saw elements of herself reflecting back. He was simply a man performing his duty to his king, a position she intimately understood.

Clytemnestra sat behind the king on a bench lining the wall. Periodically she would glare at Helen and roll her eyes. Helen didn't need to hear her thoughts to know her sister was disappointed in the lack of salacious news.

"There are dozens of royal children," Helen added. "He is second born, but I sensed from his manner he was not in line for succession."

Clytemnestra looked sharply to the king, this last detail spiking her interest. "A matter of legitimacy, perhaps?"

Agamemnon paused, giving the possibility some thought. "A bastard ambassador? I doubt it." He scoffed. "Either he lied to you, Helen, or Priam considers his children disposable. Neither answer inspires confidence in me."

"I told you his presence here was a message." Clytemnestra's voice cut through the room. "Priam won't honor you with his heir, Husband. We can gather little lasting favor from this prince. You should refuse to treat with him until Priam sends a real ambassador."

Helen swallowed a ball of guilt forming in her throat. The atmosphere of the chamber was fast resembling the frenzied craze of a witch hunt. Clytemnestra was usually cautious, but this behavior bordered on paranoia. She hardly knew the man. And Agamemnon did not care about the truth unless it uncovered some weakness he could exploit.

"He *is* a real ambassador." Helen grit her teeth. "The traders in the market knew him."

"What traders?" Clytemnestra turned on her. "He could have paid them to throw you off."

"Are you saying Lukos can be bought?" Helen shot back. "You might question my judgement, Nestra, but do you question *his*?"

But her twin was intractable. "Don't be blinded by his charms, Sister. You know he's up to no good."

"Quiet down, both of you!" Agamemnon shouted, the violent edge to his voice silencing them instantly. He turned to Helen, his coal-black eyes darker pools than the pits of Hades. "You promised you would study this stranger, Helen. You said you would help me see the truth of his intentions. Do you still plan to honor that promise?"

Years facing Agamemnon's displeasure and free-flying fists had taught Helen to proceed with caution. She shivered, but held her ground. "I took him to the workshops and down to the market, like you requested." She answered through clenched teeth. "He seemed genuinely interested in trade. If he has some hidden agenda, he has yet to show his hand."

Yet. She saw the word settle into his mind. Only too late did she realize Agamemnon would not be satisfied until he found some nugget to discredit the Trojan. He would not see strength in their guest in fear it might lessen his own.

"And what of the man himself." Agamemnon spoke after some consideration. "What are your personal feelings?"

Helen lowered her gaze, guilt overwhelming her. Paris had shown her nothing but kindness today, and she repaid him by betraying his confidence. What type of honorable person behaved in such a cowardly manner? When she looked up, she wiped her face blank, a clear canvas that reflected none of what transpired beneath. She had become expert in hiding her feelings.

Helen reclaimed her noble bearing and answered with a clear voice. "In my opinion-and this is based on very little information—the prince is here on errand from his king, a duty he is not pleased to conduct. His travels have made him arrogant, and he is numb to the splendors of Mycenae. I doubt there is anything we possess that would impress the man." She hated the lie, but it seemed to mollify the king. Perhaps, if they thought Paris a vainglorious fop, they wouldn't be so hell-bent on creating a reason to fear him.

Agamemnon turned to his queen. Clytemnestra left her perch on the bench, pressing her lips together tightly the way she always did when puzzling out information. Helen's sister had the mind of a commander when she wished to indulge it.

"If he is nothing but a messenger, than perhaps we can send one back with him." Nestra suggested, her cold blue eyes never blinking.

"What message?" Helen asked, a shiver of foreboding constricting her face.

Agamemnon brightened under the prospect, grasping immediately what Helen did not.

"What message?" she asked again, her eyes darting nervously between her sister and the king. He shrugged and waved Clytemnestra on, letting his queen do the honors.

"Take him to the armory tomorrow." Clytemnestra instructed her. "Show him the practice fields and soldiers in training. We'll see then if the Trojan remains indifferent."

Helen froze. The armory... they intended to see the prince cowed. She cursed the Fates that bade she be this messenger. Helen gave Nestra a curt nod acknowledging the assignment and turned to the door, claiming the need to refresh herself before the dinner bell.

"Helen? One more thing." Agamemnon called out to her. "The groomsmen said that you drove the chariot today?" His chill of disapproval struck a nerve of fear in her.

"Yes." She swallowed the word, the blood draining from her cheeks. Helen tried to sneak rides in the field when she first arrived at Mycenae. The king quickly disabused her of the idea. Royal women did not cavort in public. "The prince was uncomfortable behind the reigns. Too much time at sea, he claimed. I thought it unwise to decline his offer since it seemed to put him at ease."

Agamemnon's eyes narrowed, and she feared he saw right through her bluff. Helen enjoyed her time with the prince, and that enjoyment was bleeding into indecent behavior. Any moment Agamemnon was going to toss her to the ground and remind her what happened to family members who reflected poorly on his kingship.

But Agamemnon's lips spread in a lewd smile. He enjoyed watching her distress. "Thank you, Sister. You may go. And if you see your husband later, please express my displeasure that he was not present."

Helen quickly took her leave, racing down the hall, as far away from the king's plots and deceits as possible. She needed a bath. A hot one. And all the soap in the world might not be enough to scrub away the shame of what her family was forcing her to do.

Menelaus was not in their chambers, nor was he at the dining hall when the dinner bell rang. Helen entered the near-empty hall and took a seat several spaces down from the head table, her nerves frayed. She hoped it was enough to ensure she didn't have to converse with Paris. After her interrogation by the king, she was terrified she would betray her growing affection for the prince.

She was torn between two duties. One to Agamemnon who commanded her loyalty, and the other to her honor that demanded she act on behalf of truth. Helen couldn't let any harm befall Paris, not when she knew it was in her power to stop it. He was a blameless victim of Agamemnon's quest for power.

Paris entered the room, crossing the hall with a light step. His hair was wet from the baths. Glaucus, as always, was a shadow step behind him. He cast her a friendly smile then proceeded forward to the king, taking a place on his right hand side.

She lowered her gaze to her empty plate, guilt overwhelming her. She couldn't bear look at him.

"Helen."

She turned, surprised to see Clytemnestra take a seat

beside her. Nestra had also taken the time to freshen up. She wore a fresh chiton the color of a clear sky, offsetting her lovely eyes. It folded along her torso, belted at the waist, hiding what little pregnancy fat that still clung to her.

"Nestra." Helen inclined her head to her sister, still smarting from their earlier encounter. She could not help but place blame at her sister's feet. Nestra should have played guide today. It should have been the queen forced to choose between her duty and her honor.

Nestra fidgeted with her utensils, her eyes also downcast. "I regret some of the things I said today." she blurted out. "Will you forgive me?"

The admission took Helen by surprise. Nestra hardly ever admitted when she was wrong. "There's nothing to forgive." She squeezed Nestra's hand. "You were acting out of love for your king."

But the fierce look on Nestra's face belied that statement. "I don't trust the Trojan." She snapped. "And I dislike having you so close to the man. We... *I* sent you off with a stranger with no protection at all. I'm sorry, Helen. I won't let my fears cloud my reason again."

Helen sighed. Her sister's concerns were well meant, but wholly unnecessary. "He's harmless, Nestra. He's a pampered prince who probably thinks I'm a spoiled royal. He can't hurt me." She reiterated, hating to perpetuate the lie she began in the king's antechamber. But Clytemnestra *did* seem mollified.

Helen dared a glance up the table towards Paris and the king. She hoped she was right about him. The Gods save him —save them both—should he prove to be false.

The kitchen maids laid out a course of roast pheasant spiced with sage and goat cream just as Paris took his seat. Glaucus needed persuasion, but at the request of the king, Paris' captain took a seat beside him.

"I hope you have been enjoying your time in town." Agamemnon offered, raising a rhyton filled with spiced wine to his lips.

Paris dug into the meal with appetite, taking a juicy bite of the meat. "Yes, I have. It was unfortunate the queen could not join us. I hope her pressing concerns were not serious?" He pretended to be absorbed into his meal, but secretly watched the king from the corner of his eye.

Agamemnon, to his credit, did not gloat. He rolled his rhyton in his hand, letting the perfumed wine swirl dangerously to the lip of the vessel. "No woman's duty is truly serious," the king scoffed. "But unfortunately her responsibilities will keep her occupied for the remainder of the week."

Paris took another vigorous bite of the fowl, letting his relaxed manner translate to the king. *You cannot provoke me. An insult is not an insult if I do not acknowledge it.*

"I must thank you for sending the princess in her stead. The horse master said I could not have a better guide. She is quite knowledgeable." He made sure to thicken his voice enough to be misinterpreted.

There was a crack in the king's armor at the remark. Was it pride? Or irritation? Paris had been trained to read the tiny reactions in a person's face, to determine the subtext that the slightest fold at the eye, or the crease of a brow would indicate. Many of his missions sent him to realms without a common tongue. Body language was often the major form of communication.

But when he mentioned Helen, Paris swore the king's eyes flashed with jealousy. The moment passed almost fast enough to not be called a moment. In its place, the king leered back, the eager smile of a man about to hook a fish. "She is at that."

Of course, Paris meant what he said. An afternoon of drudgery had been replaced with something wholly unexpected. And though he let little of what he felt show externally, he was surprisingly impressed with the candor of the Mycenaean people, and with Helen in particular. The princess forced Paris to reevaluate everything he previously believed about the men of the West. She *inspired* her people, and yet had no idea the depths of their affection. It was an intoxicating mix of greatness and humility.

That was all, he told himself. He respected the princess. His esteem would never go beyond that. He had a job to do here, and he would not let his nascent feelings get in the way. To ensure that, he steadfastly refused to look down the table in her direction.

"Is your brother not present? I had hoped to establish a better acquaintance with the prince." Paris asked. His words couldn't be further from the truth. He had no desire to meet the man Helen wedded, but it was suspicious that Menelaus was absent. Was it another intended slight?

"He is busy rousing the banner men." Agamemnon's creased brow broadcast his irritation. "Your arrival caught us off-guard, I'm afraid. Every noble in the region would be distraught if we did not invite them hence to meet you. We seldom have royals grace our distant shores."

"A pity for those other royals," Paris added. The heavy aroma of roast peppers filled his nostrils as another servant deposited a tureen of barley stew before him.

Say what you will of this king, the man knows how to set a table.

He inhaled deeply, letting his appetite bleed into his words. "I have to admit, you haven't lived until you've seen the frontier. There is a vibrancy in the West unfound in the Old World."

Agamemnon brightened under the praise, as Paris knew he would. However, he mistook approval for his people as approval for his rule. His craftsmen were overworked beyond acceptable levels for even slaves, and if what Hyllos, Paris' trade master, told him was true, then Agamemnon had brought his kingdom near to starvation in his quest for greatness.

But greed could be persuasive, and Paris would not

condemn the man. At least not openly. He ripped into a drum bone, taking his frustration out on the poor dead bird. It was amazing how many rulers shared the same frailties. Just once, he wished he would be surprised, that he would find a leader worthy of being followed. Thus far only Priam had earned that distinction.

"Vibrancy, how aptly stated." The king laughed, motioning his cupbearer over to fill Paris' rhyton. "You've had but a small taste of that vibrancy. Wait till you see the games we have in store. There is no sport yet devised that a Greek cannot master." He winked, and took another large swill of his cup.

Paris forced a grin, taking the opportunity to tap Glaucus' foot with his own.

"Forgive me, Your Grace," The captain waited for the king to dispense with his drink before speaking, "I could not help but notice the new vessels in your shipyard. Is that Cypriot planks you're using for the hull?"

There were twelve ships under construction by Paris' counting, the ribs of their substructure lying open to the elements like the carcass of sea bird. The shipwrights were easy enough to engage in conversation since they had no more wood to complete their projects. The dozen ships were one order of many. The king was building an armada.

Agamemnon did not answer Glaucus. Perhaps he detested being addressed by a non-royal, or perhaps the question offended him. It was hard to tell. The king was unerringly cagey. Paris suspected every word he uttered was being weighed for double meaning.

"Glaucus has the honor of being the captain of my guard as well as captain of his ship." Paris added. "Sailing is a passion to him."

Agamemnon cast a shrewd eye over Glaucus like a Master of Coin weighing the measure of a man. "Yes, the wood is from Cyprus. The best vessels are made from Cypriot wood." He answered in a condescending tone. "Mycenae has long been friends with Ibiranu of Cyprus."

And thus it began, the dropping of names and alliances. Unfortunately for Agamemnon, that was a game he would inevitably lose. Troy was far better established.

"I'm sorry to inform you, Your Grace," Paris adopted a mock expression of concern, "but Ibiranu might not be long on his throne. The boy-king of the Hatti threatens his borders."

He waited for the news to settle on Agamemnon, for him to acknowledge a blow to his dwindling circle of influence, but the large king merely shrugged. "That concerns me little." He grunted, holding his cup out for another refill. "What should Mycenae care for the struggles in the Old World?"

Paris stiffened. Was the man willfully this ignorant? "You shouldn't." He hastily lied to the king. "I only meant to warn you that your crafts may suffer. If the Hittite king takes over Cyprus, trade would cease with the region. He would keep the tribute for himself."

Agamemnon leaned forward, a shrewd narrowing to his eyes. "Your father opposes this boy-king?"

"He has." Paris adopted the same aloof manner as Agamemnon. "Many times. It has earned him the support of all the kingdoms fighting Tudhaliyas' oppressive rule. Cyprus included."

"And I suppose that support has made him rich, no?"

Paris tried not to show his scorn. The man was as clumsy as he was obvious. Had Priam enabled him to bribe Agamemnon, Paris was sure this audience was enough to satisfy both monarchs. As it was, Paris felt his cheeks blush with heat.

"Yes, Agamemnon, Troy has many riches. I am happy we have so much to share with one another."

He was grateful when the staff brought out the cleansing dish of clotted cream and berries. He busied himself in the treat while the king called for more wine. The maneuvering was over for the evening as Agamemnon lost himself in the liquor. He pressed for examples of Troy's riches, delighting in tales of gold and tribute.

By the end of the evening Paris was exhausted. But the king was primed. Agamemnon was a man starved for influence and power, and Paris had laid out the table with the golden victuals Troy could produce.

Temptation was the easy part of Priam's plan. Next came something far trickier. For every meal, there was a price to pay. And this price was something a gluttonous king like Agamemnon would have a hard time swallowing.

Paris returned to his apartments, eager to get some rest before facing the second stage of his father's plan. If this dinner was any indication, he was going to have his work cut out for him.

CHAPTER 13

FIELDS OF WHEAT

"HE COMMANDS 5,000 men, a sizable host for a principality this small." Hyllos reported to Paris and Glaucus in his guest chambers the following morning. The trade master had not seen his bed, spending the dark hours before dawn in the common rooms of Mycenae's inns plucking information from locals too deep in their cups to be circumspect. "I've asked several different free soldiers, and they all say the same. Each realm is independent. They cannot agree on a collective name for their people, let alone a cause to march to war. Any action made by Mycenae is an act alone."

Paris suspected as much. As great as Agamemnon thought his realm, it was a flea bite compared to the territory Priam commanded. This king might dream of greatness, but he had never actually seen it. Unfortunately that made Paris' job more difficult. It was hard to prove something to a man that he had never seen and was disinclined to believe.

Paris twirled the *kerykeion* in his hands. Holding the heavy scepter helped him to think, as though the authority the object bestowed buoyed his spirit as well. "Are you sure about the price fixing?" They had only one shot to get this right, and there was no room for mistake.

"Absolutely," Hyllos swore. "I checked with the harbor logs three times. Agamemnon is selling Trojan goods at market price, not at the rates he strong-armed from our merchants. The profit goes directly to the crown."

He cheats his own people.

It made Paris sick. It was a wonder these Mycenaeans put up with their king's antics. But their national pride was astounding. They might not love their ruler, but they loved their land. And whatever exceptionalism Agamemnon claimed trickled down to them.

There was one royal who did deserve that loyalty. Helen was a treasure Paris had no right to expect on this wayward mission. She was unlike any woman he had ever met, drastically different than even the members of her own house. Her every word, her every action was dictated by honor. It seemed incredible to find such a person on the edge of the civilized world.

An image of her graceful smile lulled him away from the drudgery of Priam's plots and intrigue. Paris felt powerfully drawn to her in a way he could not explain, a dangerous folly considering who they both were.

"Paris?" Glaucus shook his arm.

It had happened again. Paris had tried, unsuccessfully, to keep the princess out of his mind the night before. He had been up late strategizing with Glaucus and would get halfway through a chain of thoughts only to have his words drift off. He cleared his throat, hoping the vigorous cough would clear his head as well.

"What where you saying?"

"I said, if the common folk knew the truth of their king's policy, their fealty might break." Glaucus added, a crinkle of concern around his eyes.

Paris quickly nodded his agreement. "Tell the others to keep spreading their tales along with the ale. I want any man who crosses our path to be overwhelmed by Trojan generosity." It was a simple plan, honey for the people, the stick for the ruler. With each new friend his troops made, Paris subtly undermined the king's harsh trade policy with Troy. It was harder to cheat a man you considered your friend. "Pricing should be mentioned only in passing. We don't want these whispers being followed back to us." And with that small push, the legs of Agamemnon's seat of power would wobble.

"Yes, My Prince." Hyllos bowed sharply and collected his reports.

"And what of you, Paris?" Glaucus pressed. "We need you with the king, not traipsing about the countryside."

There was a river of unspoken warnings behind that simple sentence. Paris tightened his grip on the *kerykeion*. Glaucus was a soldier, pure and simple. He met his adversaries head on. What Paris was tasked with was far more complicated.

"I know what I'm doing, Glaucus."

The severe frown his captain returned very much put that in question. "Winning hearts and minds of the people? It's honorable, but hardly necessary. We should be spending our time among the courtiers. Let them see what you, and Troy, are capable of. I could arrange a demonstration in the practice yard—"

But his words were cut off as Hyllos flung open the apartment door and froze with a sharp yelp of surprise. Helen was on the other side, her hand half raised to knock.

She lowered her arm, a demure blush gracing her cheeks as she nervously looked past his man. Her eyes widened softly when she found him, those jewel blue orbs more dazzling that the finest lapis lazuli. She was a vision.

"Paris?" Glaucus prodded again.

"It can wait, Captain. You both have your orders. See to it." Paris dismissed them coolly, his focus solely for the princess.

Was it possible for a person to grow more beautiful overnight? It seemed his nocturnal visions paled in comparison to the intoxicating presence of the woman before him. He wondered, not for the first time, did she think at all of him?

"Helen." He bowed low before her, forcing himself to not openly gape. "What wonders do you have in store today?"

She graced him with one of her stunning smiles. "We saw much of the city yesterday, I thought we could begin with the royal holdings."

"That sounds delightful." He tossed his cape over his shoulder and exited his apartments.

With some prodding, Hyllos disappeared down the hall, the trade master equally enamored with Paris' royal guest. Surprisingly, Glaucus stayed glued to his side.

"I thought you were through with sightseeing?" Paris whispered to his captain.

"I swore to protect you, My Prince." Glaucus glowered, his baritone voice too low to reach Helen's ears. "Even from yourself."

The armory, Nestra had commanded. Helen hated the cold dank space, the fortress that was more tomb than a storage room. But her queen had been insistent. Agamemnon meant to strike fear and awe into the prince, and there was no better way than visiting Mycenae's stronghold.

But as Helen walked out of the palace grounds into the brilliant morning sun, she didn't have the heart. Paris' enthusiasm to see her was infectious. She wanted nothing more than to spend the afternoon in his charismatic company. Agamemnon be damned.

"Aren't we going to get the horses?" Paris asked, turning towards the stables.

Helen blushed, remembering the feel of his strong arms surrounding her as they rode the other day. It was unfair the innocent act reflected poorly on Paris. She didn't want to give Agamemnon another opportunity to disparage their guest, no matter how much she enjoyed their ride.

"I thought we would walk." She suggested. "It's such a lovely day. And some of the best views from the acropolis can only be reached on foot." She turned to the southern precipice away from the bustling palace grounds.

Aethra walked stately beside her holding aloft a small standard to provide shade. "My Lady? Shouldn't we go—" Aethra croaked in Helen's ear as she tried to redirect them toward the Lion Gates. Aethra knew the queen's commands—Helen had fretted her concerns to the cantankerous woman all night with little sympathy in return. Aethra was unforgiving about matters of duty. In her opinion, Helen's task was clear. She must do as she was told.

A spike of rebellion festered in Helen's heart. She promised she would go to the armory, but she didn't say *when* she'd go. "Let's start with the temples. They aren't far." She pressed past her frowning matron.

They travelled down a meandering staircase hewn from the bedrock of the palace summit. The staircase was steep, dropping quickly down the terraced hillside. Whenever the rock looked unstable, Paris would dart ahead and hold his arm out in support for her. She laughed on several occasions.

"Do you think me so fragile?" she jested, refusing his arm and picking her own path. "I know this path better than the halls of the palace." It wasn't a boast. She could find her way in the dark to the southern summit if need be.

Paris tucked his hands behind his back, a mock show of withdrawing his unneeded aid. "Ah, are you very religious, then?" His jaw clenched as he asked the question.

It was an innocent question, but one that stumped her nonetheless. Her trust in the Gods led her to the biggest mistake of her life. She honored them, as all mortals must, but no longer trusted in their protection. A guarded respect was the best course when dealing with capricious immortals.

"I'm no more religious than any other person." She replied truthfully, watching the tension drain from Paris' shoulders.

She wondered why the answer seemed to ease him.

"The Princess is favored of Aphrodite." Aethra interjected with a sniff, her devout sensibilities offended. The mere hint of blasphemy and Helen's maid would harangue her for hours.

"I do not doubt it, Mistress." Paris gave the woman a respectful nod.

Aethra patted down her dress like a bird ruffling her feathers. Helen could tell the prince's manners had yet to pass the matron's strict standards.

They turned south on the frontage road leading up to the temple plateau. The road was empty save for the few guards patrolling the perimeter wall. Helen delighted in the solitude. There was a peaceful quiet in this corner of the palatial grounds. It was a welcome change from the prying eyes of the court.

Paris seemed to enjoy the privacy as well. He lacked the strained focus that dominated his behavior in the megaron and at supper. He looked truly at ease.

"And what of you, Trojan? Do you have a patron God?" Helen asked pleasantly as a lone egret took flight from the brush beside her.

It was Paris' turn to flush. "None that I am aware of. But Troy is protected by Athena, and our Apollian temple has more prophets than any I've ever visited."

"You have the same Gods as us?" Helen brightened from the news. For some reason she thought Troy would be more foreign, the divides between their cultures as vast as the distance that separated them.

"And the same language," he added with a nod. "I can't tell you how relieved I am to converse in my native tongue. Learning a new dialect can take years."

Years? She couldn't fathom spending so much time away from her home and the people she loved. But some part of that prospect thrilled her. What adventures he must have had!

"How many do you speak?" she asked eagerly.

Paris shot Glaucus an inquisitive look. The captain had been with him on many of those trips. "Seven?"

"That sounds about right." Glaucus agreed.

"Now you're teasing me." No one could possibly learn so many. But Paris looked insistent. "All right, name them." She tucked her arms on her hips, refusing to walk another step.

Her petulant glare was delightful. Paris considered dancing around an answer just to prolong that glare, but he recognized the stubborn glint in Helen's eyes. Hector would stand just so when he would not be denied. She would get her way eventually. He decided to spare himself the struggle.

"Phrygian, Assyrian, Babylonian, Egyptian, Hebrew, Amorite and Hittite. Oh, and Phoenician if you count their alphabet. It's similar to the Amorite dialect with subtle variations."

"That would be eight." Glaucus corrected him, earning another harrumph from the matron.

Of course, Helen didn't believe him. He wouldn't believe him either, if he hadn't lived those long journeys. Apparently she needed a demonstration. On impulse, he lifted her hand to his lips, breathing in deep her perfume of rose and lilac.

The words came instantly to him, rolling off his tongue with a husky guttural accent. "ז. כֻּלָּךְ יָפָה רַעְיָתִי וּמוּם אֵין בָּךְ:"

Both Glaucus and Aethra gasped, the latter for his impropriety, the former because the captain knew what he said.

Why those words?

But staring into Helen's radiant smile, Paris knew why. Ever since he saw her on that rocky cliff, it was all he could think about.

Helen was stunned, her hand forgotten in his. "What does it mean?" she asked, breathless.

"It's from a song, from the pastoral tribes in Canaan." He swooped her hand onto his arm, covering his slip with a nervous cough as they trekked up the remainder of the hill. "It means, 'You are flawless'."

"Oh." Helen tried to still her beating heart. She had spent her entire childhood hearing nonsensical flattery of her beauty. She learned long ago to turn a deaf ear to that praise. But when Paris spoke, his words vibrated something deep inside her. For the first time in her life, a man complimented her, and she whole-heartedly believed him. She felt undeniably beautiful.

Another snort from Aethra jolted her back to the earth. She yanked her hand away from Paris like a person touching burning coals. "...Thank you." She cleared her clenched throat. "The temple... uh, is this way." She spun and began a hurried walk to the plateau, her maid closing ranks behind her protectively.

Glaucus grunted. Paris refused to look in his direction. He didn't need a lecture. Besides, he had told her the truth. 'Flawless' was the gist of the lyric; the actual words were *'You are all fair, my beloved, and there is no blemish in you.'*

Helen refused to meet Aethra's disapproving glare as she walked and shielded her face with a veil of loose hair. She raced past a cluster of buildings grouped together along the perimeter wall without stopping, a sweet confusion building inside her. His lips on her hand... it was an act a thousand courtiers had done before, but when Paris touched her, time stood still. Every nerve in her body came to life and she wanted nothing more than to explore his touch with some of her own.

She cursed herself and her lewd behavior. She was a married woman and a princess! She could not give in to these feelings. These... urges... were fleeting, a moment of weakness in her traitorous heart. She was tasked with showing him the capital, and that was all. She picked up her pace.

A handful of goldsmiths worked along the porticos, taking advantage of the soft light of the mid-morning sun while they hammered plates of the precious metal into intricate designs. Some of the artisans waved to her, but Helen rushed past them, too agitated to stop for a friendly hello. She climbed further up the summit, increasing her speed as if she meant to outpace her unfaithful thoughts. It wasn't until she reached the top of the acropolis that she realized where her feet had unconsciously taken them.

A hundred feet ahead the hillside came to an abrupt end, the rocky precipice jutting dangerously over the vast Khavos Ravine to the south and the violent Argolic Gulf waters to the east. It was the place she found solace when her thoughts grew dark, when she needed to escape the pressures of the life she had chosen... the place she had first seen Paris.

Helen spun back toward the prince, a sudden realization flooding her. She had prayed that night, begged in fact, for the Goddess to grant her some reprieve from her life. Was it mere coincidence that Paris arrived at that precise moment? Was *he* the answer she asked for?

"Princess?" He approached her, a puzzled look on Paris' face as he waited for her to pick their path.

She chided her foolishness. Nestra would mock her if she gave ear to this superstitious nonsense. But still, Helen couldn't shake the uncanny connection she felt with this man.

"This way." She turned away from the precipice and back toward the temple plateau.

Paris frowned, certain he had said something to upset her. He hadn't meant to act so familiar before. He prided himself on his reserve, his discipline, but Helen had a bewitching way of putting him at ease. He scarcely felt himself in her presence.

And when she pulled away... he was instantly reminded of his life back in Troy, the cursed child whose presence was to be avoided at all cost. His clumsy attempts to impress her only seemed to make her more uncomfortable.

Paris shook his head. The princess had no use for his friendship. And, as much as he wanted it, his mission did not require earning hers. He needed to stay focused on the task at hand.

The plateau comprised over a furlong of flat open space.

At the southern edge an enormous temple dominated the vista. It towered three stories high and was open to the air, a dozen fluted columns stretching to the heavens like fingers of the earth goddess reaching for her mate in the clouds.

"The House of Columns, sacred to Hera." Helen spoke as four priestesses exited the inner sanctum. They held clay censers filled with smoking incense that they swung from side to side as they sang a light hymn. It was a pleasant tune, one that spoke of the Goddess' birth waters fertilizing the plains.

Helen paused, watching Paris closely for any sign of awe. Most pilgrims dropped to their knees when they first spied the sacred temple. But Paris was not looking at the House of Columns. Instead, he faced a solitary building sheltered on the corner of the plateau.

"Now there's a sight," he whispered.

Helen turned to the direction he was looking. A modest-sized temple sat beneath an orchard of blooming apple trees, its limestone walls covered in ivy and a narrow stream trickled across its portal door. She was glad he noticed the small treasure.

"It's a shrine to Aphrodite. A gift from Agamemnon to my sister and me. Would you like to see it?" When he nodded, she led him across the plateau.

Once they stepped beneath the shade of the sacred grove, Helen could not help but smile. This small parcel of land, so similar to the temple in Sparta, always made her feel at home. She raised her hand, trailing her fingers across the low-hanging branches, its pink blossoms floated into the air like butterflies on wing.

Helen closed her eyes and let the flowers shower over her, spinning with delight. The clear water from the stream licked at her ankles as she stepped over to the portal door. Pausing at the entrance, she turned to find her guest. Surprisingly, Paris was not at her side. He hung back a safe distance, watching her play.

"Come on." She beckoned him to the door.

But he balked at the stream. "I shouldn't. I feel like a trespasser."

"It's all right," she insisted. "Men are allowed."

"*Noble men,*" Aethra placed a firm hand on Glaucus' chest as he moved to join the prince. "Not the likes of you." Her sharp tone brokered no argument. "We'll wait for you outside, Princess."

The shrine was not large, no more than ten paces wide. Skylights allowed sunbeams to dapple into the small room. Helen walked into the familiar space and past the stone altar covered in wild flowers. A bust of the Goddess rested in a nook, Her serene gaze smiling down on Her offerings.

Helen lit a candle from the other burning votives lining the wall. "At the full moon, they say Artemis guards the grove with a silver bow, keeping away the unwanted eyes of men." She spoke softly, the quiet nature of the shrine adding to her pensive mood. "Young virgins will dance beneath the trees and beseech the Goddess for her favor. If the girl is pure of heart, Aphrodite will bless her with a life of love and happiness."

Paris watched her, feeling the sorrow he was not sure she intended to impart. There was something achingly sad about Helen's tale, as though she said the words but did not believe them. "Now I know I am trespassing." He forced a laugh, a nervous tremor marring his regal composure. "Didn't your maid say you were chosen by the Goddess?"

"Yes, or so they tell me." Helen made efforts to keep her tone light. Chosen of Aphrodite... Her father had sworn it was an honor. His conviction had given Helen faith, and she trusted the temple as naively as a little child. Only Nestra had the wisdom to warn her against such blindness.

"Did you dance once? In a grove like this?"

A vision of her womanhood ritual flooded over Helen, and of all the wonders Tryphosa had promised. "I did." She clenched her jaw, fighting the bitterness that had become a constant companion once those promises had proven hollow.

She shook off her dark thoughts and managed a bittersweet smile for the prince. Plucking a poppy off the altar, she tucked the blossom into the binding of his cape. "You said no God has claimed you?"

"Not to my knowledge." Paris tensed as she pressed the stem against his skin.

"Then perhaps you are meant for Aphrodite. Maybe you are one of her chosen ones, too."

Her chosen fool, perhaps... Paris' heart pounded beneath Helen's gentle touch. Propriety screamed at him to go. He knew he shouldn't be alone with this intoxicating, *married,* woman. But when she gazed up at him, her jewel-blue eyes framed by black-as-night lashes, he was utterly powerless. He could not take his eyes off her; her rosy lips parted ever-so-slightly as if begging to be kissed. His tongue grew heavy in his mouth.

"I... um, doubt the Goddess would want me." His muscles finally unclenched, and he backed away from her nervously. He raised his fingers to his lips and pressed them to the altar. Whispering a prayer for self-restraint, he hastily backed out of the temple like an awkward boy.

The hot sun hit him with the force of a tidal wave. He soaked it in, the roar of his heated blood clouding his vision to all but the image of Helen's breathtaking face. He was within inches of pressing her down on that altar and ravishing her.

What am I doing?

"Paris!" Glaucus hailed him from along the drop-off facing the ravine. Helen's dour maid was at his side, glaring at Paris as he exited the temple.

Not that Paris blamed her. For all his rigorous discipline and training, he felt control slipping from his fingers. Paris tried to shake off his bewilderment, and sloshed through the stream in Glaucus' direction.

Helen quickly followed after him, her face flushed with embarrassment. Had she upset him? He moved away so quickly. And then her words struck her. The Goddess was a patron of youth and innocence. She could not claim the prince if he was already claimed...

"Is your wife very beautiful?" Helen swallowed a small lump in her throat as she followed him to the ridge.

"I... don't have one."

Helen nearly tripped, she was so stunned. As handsome as Paris was, she suspected he'd have been married ages ago. "Why?"

"That's... complicated." He picked up his pace.

Complicated? How could it be complicated? Especially for a royal? Most matches were prearranged before a prince or princess came of age. She pressed him for an answer, mindless of fact that she was prying.

"I haven't gotten around to it yet." The words fell like stones from Paris' mouth. He had no desire to tell her his reasons for bachelorhood, of the burdens of being a man shadowed by a dark fate. That truth would only result in the warmth of her kind affections to grow cold.

But to Helen, his reluctance to speak spoke volumes nonetheless. His reticence in the temple, the pained longing that occasionally tensed his face—she recognized the loneliness that haunted her days. Whether by choice or by fortune, she was certain he was denied the love of the person he sought. Her heart twisted as she imagined a woman of stunning beauty standing along a seashore whispering a prayer for Paris' safe and swift return.

"...is she waiting for you? This woman that you love?" Helen spoke after a slight hesitation. She had no idea why she asked, but the question felt important, like a missing piece in the puzzle of the man before her.

Paris glanced nervously toward the nearing ridge. Glaucus and Aethra were almost within earshot. "There is no other woman," he swore, and the haunted shadow returned to his face.

Helen gasped, finally understanding what he meant by "complicated."

"It is a man, then?"

The prince stumbled, nearly tripping over himself. Apparently Glaucus had excellent hearing. The soldier was beside himself with laughter. Only Aethra wore her same dignified frown.

"That has never been my appetite, Princess," he asserted as soon as he could speak. "I have been an ambassador for Troy for the past eight years. That lifestyle is not conducive to finding a bride." He spared an evil glare for Glaucus who had yet to settle down. "Although I know a few men who could use a good buggering."

"Forgive me, My Prince." The captain wheezed, still waving them up to the overlook. "But I think there is something you would like to see."

Aethra immediately stepped between them, hoisting her standard over Helen's head. "Having an engaging conversation, are you?"

Helen flushed. Ignoring her matron's glare, she joined the men on the overlook. The ridge rose a hundred feet over the Khavos Ravine where fields of wheat extended far into the horizon. A gentle breeze picked up from the west and set the stalks in motion. The land rolled like a golden sea, an ocean that could feed a nation.

Helen sighed. It *would* feed a nation, but not theirs. Agamemnon had already promised this yield to Crete on the summer tide. Philon was right to be concerned.

"I have to go down there." Paris declared with surprising urgency.

Helen cast him a puzzled look. *This* gave him pause? No piece of art, no palatial structure could spike his interest, but a wheat field inspired awe? "There is a meadow on the far side of the crop. We can have our afternoon meal down there, if you'd like."

"Yes, please." he answered eagerly, his face lit up with childlike glee.

Helen turned to Aethra, a similar eagerness dominating

her own face. She could use this distraction to her benefit and rid herself of her disapproving chaperone. "Go back to the palace and gather some refreshments. We'll be by the laurel tree on the west side."

Aethra hesitated, her hands twisting with concern. She looked at Glaucus and the prince suspiciously. "I shouldn't leave you, Princess. It wouldn't be proper."

Anger flashed in Helen's eyes. She was tired of Aethra's peevish concerns. Helen was not a child any longer; her matron should not question her judgement.

"Fetch the meal, Aethra," she repeated firmly. The elder woman, albeit reluctant, ducked into a curt bow and retreated without another word.

Helen led the Trojans down a narrow series of switchbacks that cut into the rock face and down to the valley below. It was a dusty affair, this road was normally reserved for beasts of burden, but they reached the valley in a matter of minutes.

It was hotter in the valley. A light sheen of perspiration broke out on Helen's forehead as she pressed through the crops. She mentally cursed herself for her pride. If Aethra were near, she'd at least have some shade.

After what seemed like an eternity, they entered the far meadow. Helen took off her sandals and cooled her feet in the nearby brook, not caring if the behavior was unbecoming of a princess. The sun was shining, the day was young, and she was enjoying herself far too much for such scruples.

Paris and Glaucus entered behind her, deeply engrossed in conversation. "It must be a hybrid strand. Look how robust the stalks are." Paris twirled a piece of wheat in his fingers.

The curiosity was killing her. "Wheat?" she laughed. "Truly? Are you that enamored by a silly plant?"

Paris crossed to her rock, amused by her playful ignorance. He attempted a serious tone as he spoke. "When kingdoms go to war, they salt their enemy's fields. Nothing will grow for seasons and people starve." A haunted memory pulled at him. It was a cruel fate that the people suffered the sins of their rulers. He had seen too many children dying of starvation, images he could never forget. "But a hardy plant," he continued, twirling the stalk in front of Helen's face, "like this one here, might have a better chance to survive. It could save lives." He tapped her on the nose with the stalk. "Now what where you saying about silly plants?"

"Silly?" she feigned innocence. "Did I say silly? I meant special, of course."

It was special. Helen had never seen a ruler show concern for the commonwealth the way Paris espoused. Agamemnon cared only for his own greatness, the plight of his subjects be damned. But Helen knew it was the people who made a land great, and the might of a king was only a reflection of theirs.

Glaucus circled around the clearing, his eyes darting over the tall crop. "There's too much cover here, Paris." he grimaced, gripping his spear tight. "I'm going to scout the perimeter." Paris waved him on, but the captain hesitated at the edge of the clearing. "I'll just be gone a moment."

Paris suppressed the urge to toss a rock at the man. It was one thing for Glaucus to watch his back, but he didn't want the man's prudish nature alarm the princess. He turned back to Helen, relieved to see she paid the guard no attention. She was splashing her feet in the stream, her chiton gathered about her knees exposing two perfect ivory-toned legs. Her hair was unpinned, and the golden tresses dangled loosely around her breasts.

A small wave of panic gripped Paris as he realized they were completely alone. But even knowing that, he could not help but ask, "May I join you?"

"Of course." She scooted over on her rock.

Paris unlaced his sandals and dipped his feet alongside hers. The water was refreshingly crisp, the product of spring thaws on the mountain rages above. "That feels blessedly good." he groaned. Closing his eyes, he leaned back on the ground, soaking in the warm sunlight.

Helen leaned over Paris, watching him breathe. His chest

fell in even rhythms. It was a muscular chest, not brawny like the Greek men she was accustomed to, but lean. As he exhaled, a tiny smile crept over his face. He looked absolutely content laying in the dirt.

A pang of guilt twisted in her heart. She could not imagine sharing a day like this with Menelaus. He would never allow her to speak as freely as she did with Paris. He would never surprise her with an act of kindness or compassion.

Paris' eyes shot open, and he gasped, utterly surprised to find her so near.

"I..." Helen stammered, an inexplicable guilt washing over her. She hadn't meant to sit so close... she was only curious. But that was a lie, and she knew it. She was drawn to this prince as powerfully as two magnets pulled by some inexplicable force.

Paris swallowed nervously, trying hard to reclaim his composure. But at this proximity, he couldn't think straight. He wanted this mysterious beauty with a desperation that burned out reason. His pupils constricted as he stared hopelessly into her eyes. No wall of propriety, no mask of humor barred its way. His look was one of pure unadulterated adoration.

Helen could scarcely breathe, mesmerized by his powerful gaze. Her head felt woozy. She felt herself sinking towards him and planted a hand on his chest to steady herself. But that touch only intensified the feeling.

"I am a twice-damned fool." Paris moaned, and reaching up he pulled her lips to his.

Shock waves ran through Helen's body. Paris' kiss ignited her in ways she couldn't describe. The hot steam of his breath, the rough stubble on his jaw, the salty taste of his tongue... she reeled from it. She opened her mouth for more, inviting him to continue.

But when he reached his other hand to cradle her neck, the moment snapped. She pulled back sharply, eyes wild, panic flooding her.

What am I doing?

Paris sat up, reaching for her. "Wait, Helen..."

But she leapt to her feet, shame lending her strength. She couldn't stay here, she had to get away. She turned and ran into the field.

"Helen!" his panicked voice followed after her.

The thick stalks slapped at her face, the bristles scratching at her bare skin. In her mad rush, she had left her sandals at the brook, and the dried husks littering the ground bit into her soft feet. Helen ignored the pain, and continued to run as fast as she could.

She was outside the main field at the edges of the tilled land when a root snagged her foot and she fell heavily to the ground. The fall knocked the air from her lungs. She lay on the ground gasping, too ashamed to pull herself to her feet.

Guilt riddled her. She was a married woman, and yet she knowingly, willingly, placed herself in this situation. Her wicked mind tried to make an excuse. It was an accident. It wouldn't happen again. Not if she was careful. But her mind was a liar. Her traitor heart knew better. She asked Aphrodite for this man, and the fickle Goddess didn't care what misery Eros' arrow wrought.

Paris continued to call her name. He was making a terrible racket searching for her. Helen knew she should call to him, let him know she was all right, but she was too scared. Instead, she lay in the turf, crying softly to herself.

A deep grunt jolted Helen from her misery. That sound was too near to be Paris, too brute to be human. She raised her head and found herself staring into the malevolent glare of a massive bull.

You stupid reckless girl.

Philon had warned her the beast was about, and she ran right into its territory. Helen had never seen such a baleful creature. Enormous horns, each five feet long, protruded from its skull. The bull snorted. Its eyes gleamed red as it kicked dirt behind it with thick hooves the size of mallets. The monstrosity bellowed angrily and charged at her.

Helen screamed.

Suddenly, Paris was there. He leapt over her fallen body and dropped to the ground in a roll right into the path of the charging beast. The bull reared, falling sideways into a patch of wheat.

Paris leapt to his feet, pulling his cape up high in front of him. He had no sword, no weapon at all, but still stood protectively between her and the animal with nothing but that deep red fabric. Helen knew she should move, run for help, but her muscles wouldn't work. She clung to the ground, helpless.

The bull strained to get back up, rolling over and taking out a bushel of wheat in the process. Now back on its hooves, it shied away from the prince's cape, balking at the bright foreign object.

Paris pressed his advantage, using his cape to wave the animal back. "Tut, Tut, Tut." he shouted, flapping the material with each cry.

The bull was clearly confused, unsure of what to make of the strange man who barred its path. It pivoted, trying to find a way around Paris, a way back at her.

But Paris refused to give ground. When the bull shifted, he grabbed its horns, yanking its head back to him. "NO." he shouted. "Not her. Me."

It bellowed again, kicking up sod as the prince held it in place.

Tears flooded down Helen's face. Any moment that bull was going to swipe its head and impale Paris on those vicious horns. He was going to die, and it was all her fault.

"*No,*" she gasped, her arm reaching for Paris, certain she was about to watch his end.

But then Paris did something unexpected. He lowered his cape and held his hands out in front of him in a nonthreatening manner. He started making soft noises, cooing like a baby calf. His imitation was superb. The bull stopped moving, its eyes darting to and fro in confusion.

Then Paris spoke in a tongue she did not recognize, different than the poetry he quoted before. The words had a melodic soothing tone. Slowly, the beast began to calm and Paris stepped in closer, his hands within inches of the bull's wide snout.

"Tut, Tut, Tut." He soothed the creature, gently stroking its muzzle.

Helen stared in shock. That wild beast would have needed a dozen hunters to bring it down. Yet Paris had tamed the monster with nothing but his hands and voice. He patted the bull again, gently pushing it towards the perimeter.

"Go," he said forcibly, slapping the bull's hide. It reared and took off in a gallop.

Precious air rushed back into her lungs. She gulped it in, staring at her savior with tear-streaked eyes.

"Helen?" Paris rushed to her side, sinking to his knees. "Are you hurt? Are you all right?" Fear constricted his face as he held her trembling arms.

She couldn't stop crying, those last terrifying moments still held her heart in a vice grip. She clung to his arms in disbelief. He was alright. He was unhurt. Why couldn't she stop crying?

"I'm so sorry." The words tumbled out of him. "I was weak, I didn't mean to. Please, don't run from me." He was wrought with fear, desperate for her forgiveness. Was this the same man who just stared down a mighty taurus?

She didn't think. She was beyond coherent thought. She rose to her knees and pulled him into her arms, kissing him passionately. Paris melted into that embrace, his eager lips pressing fiercely into hers. In a sweeping move he lifted her off the ground, pressing her tightly to him.

She could feel every curve of his body. Her hands roamed his taut back, they wove into his thick hair. His heart hammered against hers. She kissed him hungrily, a woman starved for love's embrace. She couldn't control herself, she didn't want to.

Paris pressed his lips against her throat, his mind ablaze. Hearing Helen cry out in fear had struck a dagger into his heart. He had never been more afraid in his entire life than in that single moment when he though she was harmed. What followed next was a blur. Instinct took over, guiding him with the bull. It held sway over him still as he kissed her, filling him with a desperate need.

She overpowered his senses: the floral scent of her, the silken touch of her skin—so soft and yielding. He was mad with desire. He shifted his hold, his right hand moving down her back and sliding under her dress.

Helen leaned into him with a moan, her legs parting ever-so-slightly. Paris nearly lost himself as the heat from her mound rolled over his palm. He knew this was wrong—she was forbidden fruit, the nectar of another man's flower—but he couldn't control himself. Having come so near to death, a primal instinct took over.

He renewed his kisses down her neck, his lips circling her breast, pushing aside the loose fabric of her chiton and exposing a taut pink nipple. She arched her back, pressing her breast into his eager mouth as his hand probed farther down, stroking her.

All of Helen's nerves were on fire, his touch igniting her. She wanted him, she wanted *all of him*. She pressed herself against him harder and felt his erection dig into her thigh.

The second she touched his phallus, reality doused over her like a powerful tonic. She gasped, releasing Paris and backing off with a slight tremor.

"I... I *can't*," she cried, her wide eyes reflecting all the fears consuming her. "I'm married. And you're a guest in our house. *This is wrong*."

Paris' chest heaved in ragged gasps as he panted for control. "I know," he groaned, sharing her awful remorse. He reached out to wipe away her tears. When he touched her, his tender expression changed to utter longing. "But the Gods know I want to. I've never wanted anything more in my entire life."

She pulled his hand away from her face, squeezing it in a tight grip. "We can't do this. Think about our families. We can't dishonor them. This can't happen again."

Paris dropped to his knees, clinging to her hands. "Tell me what to do. Should I go to the king and ask for a different guide?"

"NO!" Panic gripped her. "Agamemnon would suspect, he'd want to know why."

"Then I'll lie. I'll tell him I've seen enough."

Helen groaned. If Paris went back to the king less than pleased with his visit and not eager to see more, the blame would fall on her shoulders. And Agamemnon's anger made Menelaus seem tame by comparison. The fear set into her bones, and she shivered uncontrollably.

"Helen?" Paris cupped her face, forcing her to look at him. "Tell me what you want."

Tears spilled down her cheeks. "Don't say anything to him," she begged. "*Please*."

Concern constricted his face. He gently wiped her tears away, and then knelt before her. "On my father's honor. I'll do whatever you ask."

CHAPTER 14

FEINT AND PARRY

THE REMAINDER of the day had proven quite difficult for Paris. After the incident with the bull, he insisted on ending their tour for the day. Helen was still in the throes of shock from her near death encounter. Adding in their... indiscretions, and the poor princess was as fragile as spun glass.

Aethra vanished the girl into her apartments as soon as they returned to the palace, and Paris was left to entertain himself until supper. He tried to check in with Hyllos, but was too distracted to absorb the details of his trade master's negotiations.

Paris was furious with himself. His feelings for Helen had grown to the point where they could not be denied. But to actually act upon them? To let those desires take flight and damage Helen's honor? He felt like a vile Sidonian spice merchant, famished for his next taste. He had to restrain himself. The danger to both their necks was too great for him to fail.

After a not-so-subtle suggestion from Glaucus, Paris retreated to the training yard for a little exercise. He hoped the strenuous activity would quell his boiling emotions. The yard was sparsely occupied, only two of the six roped off arenas were in use where a handful of recruits trained with their arms master. Agamemnon had the majority of his regiment in the field far from the prying eyes at the palace. Paris was sure it was no coincidence. The rural king was as cagey as a badger defending its den.

"Again!" Paris shouted to the squad of Trojan soldiers circling around him. He lifted his bronze sword high, ready to parry their attack. The blade was tapered from haft to point in the shape of a flat leaf and was over a foot in length—a long weapon compared to the stabbing blades the Greeks favored. Unlike a spear, the sword forced a warrior to battle in close proximity to his enemy, and up close Paris' dexterity evened the odds against any muscular adversary.

Paris held his sword "on-guard", the curved metal "horns" along the haft parallel to his eye line. He had been sparring with his men for over an hour now, and signs of strain were beginning to show on their sweat soaked faces. They were stripped down to their waists, but the heat of their exertions was still oppressive.

Brygos came first, his feint was easy to parry, the bulky man broadcast his movements by the way he twisted his body before the strike. Paris deflected his sword and spun to meet Dexios' blade on its downward strike. The two men strained against each other, swords locked, until Paris was able to push the young man back. They were too similar in build, their sword reach near identical. Paris danced a few steps back, giving himself some breathing room. But that lent space for his mind to wander again.

Stupid, lecherous fool, he cursed himself. Of all the idiotic things he could have done, he had to fall for a princess who would one day be a queen herself. As the royal emissary to an emerging and potentially hostile kingdom, he couldn't afford this mistake. Priam's alliance would be destroyed, and Paris' hopes of returning home, gone. This... infatuation would cost him everything.

Ariston spun and delivered a flash attack from Paris' left

flank. He barely managed to whip his sword around in time to parry the thrust. "Hades Ghost!" Paris cursed. He had let his concentration slip, a dangerous misstep when sparring with Trojan soldiers.

"Don't go soft on him, Ariston!" Glaucus taunted from the sidelines. "He can take it."

Paris grimaced, wishing the captain had the nerve to enter the practice ring himself. He tried to center himself, to find that perfect balance of physical conditioning with mindset, but the second he closed his eyes, his mind filled with images of her.

She danced beneath the apple blossoms, the pink flowers showering down on her like blushing kisses. She waved invitingly to him, beckoning him forward, her smile radiating brighter than the sun. Her deep soulful eyes captivated him, commanding him to love her. He was powerless in her presence. There was no creature like her in the heavens or on earth.

"Paris!" Glaucus' shout pulled him from his revere.

Ariston's blade was falling toward his neck with alarming speed. Paris raised his sword, taking the brunt of its force along the haft. Glaucus' timely warning had helped, but Paris was still at a disadvantage. Ariston reversed his swing, conducting a barrage of counter strikes that sent Paris across the yard defending himself. Backed into a corner, he was forced onto one knee. The final blow fell on his shoulder, the practice blade stopping short of true damage. Paris would carry a bruise for the next few days, but in real combat it was a killing blow.

"Forgive me, My Prince." Ariston apologized, dropping his sword and offering Paris his hand. "Are you wounded?"

"Only my pride." Paris grumbled, accepting the soldier's help.

"TROJANS. AMASS!" Glaucus snatched Ariston's sword from his grasp. The other soldiers snapped into formation, watching the captain attentively with a touch of hero-worship.

"That's enough exercise for one day. Regroup with the others. And tell Iamus I better not see him in his cups tonight." When the soldiers were gone his gruff manner evaporated. He pulled Paris aside, away from the watching Mycenae Arms Masters and recruits.

"What are you doing, Paris?" he asked in a guarded whisper.

"I... I don't know." Paris covered awkwardly. "It's just some ill humor affecting my concentration. I'm sure it will pass."

Glaucus was no fool. He had found Paris and Helen in the aftermath of the bull attack. He knew what was happening between them even though he was gentleman enough not to voice it.

"We have work to do. You need to stay focused."

Paris nodded, grateful for his captain's concern. He knew he was playing with a fire that could burn them all. The prudent thing would be to distance himself from Helen and stick to the task he was bid. But in Paris' many travels, he had learned to trust his instincts, and every fiber of his being told him the princess was important.

As if his stray thought drew her near, he looked up to the second level walkway and spotted the princess. Her hair was damp from the bath and she wore a new chiton. Her eyes were on him as she walked hurriedly down the hall.

"Have you ever been tempted, Glaucus?" he asked as Helen disappeared into the south corridor. "Is there anything that would make you question all the decisions you've made in your life and wish you chose another path?"

Glaucus turned to where Paris looked and shook his head. "If temptation came to me with a face as fair, and if she looked at me with similar longing? Aye. I might fall under her spell." He seemed embarrassed to admit it. He collected the discarded swords, muttering to himself about the vagaries of the Gods, a few choice curses spotting his colorful language.

Paris sighed. He trusted Glaucus like a brother, but the

captain didn't have the same responsibilities that Paris bore. Paris had to be stronger than the temptations the world threw at him. Duty demanded it.

She begged him to not act on these feelings. She begged him, even though he saw the selfsame desire in Helen's eyes. He hoped by all his honor, and those that he loved, he had the willpower to do as she asked.

A group of courtiers trailed after the princess, tittering amongst themselves like chicks in a flock. One look down at him and they erupted into loud whispers. Paris took the towel Glaucus offered and mopped the sweat from his exertions, pulling his tunic on before he was half-dry. News of his encounter with the bull had spread like wild fire. Thus far, he'd been spared retelling that climatic encounter. But that reprieve wouldn't last for long. He shuddered to think what supper would be like.

A small page ran into the courtyard. The lad was no taller than Paris' hip, and he placed the boy at around eight years of age. "Your Grace!" the page hustled to the alcove Glaucus and Paris had taken over. "My master wishes a word with you."

"Your Master?" Paris didn't have time to finish his question before the hulking form of Prince Menelaus stalked into the courtyard. He was trailed by a band of equally burly men, hunters by the look of their spears and leather armor.

Paris forced his face to blankness. Menelaus was an intimidating sight. He had the stature of Agamemnon, a giant amongst men. His copper tinged hair was unkempt, lending the prince an aura of fire. His thick beard would make a bear envious, and the scowl on his face was set on Paris.

He can't possibly know...

Glaucus stepped protectively behind him, helping Paris to relax a notch. This was not a man he wanted to face unarmed.

"Your Highness." He gave Menelaus a sharp nod of his head. They were technically equals after all.

The Mycenaean grimaced uncomfortably. "I hear you saved my woman." He grunted, disbelief written all over him.

"I owe you a debt."

Paris was taken aback. Of all the things he expected this man to say to him, thank you was at the bottom of the list. "Think nothing of it. I did nothing any other man wouldn't have done."

Menelaus snorted. "Doubtful. I've been tracking that bull. Half the villagers have lost their stones at its mere mention." There was a ripple of agreement in his men.

"Then I was fortunate," Paris added. "The bull was not used to human confrontation. I had the element of surprise working in my favor." He hated debasing himself, especially to this man, but if Menelaus was anything like his brother, he wouldn't stomach a powerful rival at arms.

But Paris' modesty only made Menelaus more cross. "Stop that nanny nonsense. You bested the beast. Take the compliment as it's given."

It was no wonder Agamemnon kept his brother away from court affairs. He was as blunt as a rusty blade. Paris had to shut his jaw.

A raven-haired hunter cleared his throat. Menelaus cast the man an irritated glare, but then corrected himself. "What I meant to say is, it was impressive, taking on a bull with your bare hands. I'd like to see what you are capable of with a spear in your hand."

Paris blinked, "I beg your pardon?"

Menelaus chewed his lip, his attempt at court decorum puckering him like a sour grape. "A hunt!" he bellowed. "Tomorrow. The spears are gathering in the stables at the hour of the wolf. Come enjoy some real sport." He hefted the sword holstered at his hip, a thick broadsword that could cleave Paris in two.

An entire day alone with this brute? Paris hesitated, shooting a quick glance to Glaucus. The captain looked similarly undecided.

"That is, unless, you prefer the company of women..." A wicked grin spread across Menelaus' broad face. He shared a crude laugh with his hunters.

It was a familiar laugh for Paris. Their mocking tone cut right to his core. They saw his smaller frame, his preference for civility and respect, as a source of weakness. With one glance they presumed to know the measure of his worth. And like Hecuba and her minions, they found him lacking.

Glaucus gave a tiny shake of his head. *Don't let them bait you,* that motion warned. But Paris didn't care. He felt the slap of that challenge. He didn't want to back down anymore. This crude man had *no idea* the world of hurt Paris could inflict.

"I *could* use some good sport." Paris slapped Menelaus on his thick arm, meeting the prince glare for glare. "Count me in."

Clytemnestra jostled Orestes on her lap, trying to find a comfortable position on her throne as she nursed her infant son. The stiff replica of Agamemnon's lofty chair cut into her tender hips. She longed for the cushions of her apartments, at least until she healed from the birthing, but such laxity was forbidden to her. A queen of Mycenae did not show that sort of weakness.

The hall was filled with various courtiers and administrative toadies, whispering in shadowed corners. *The Buzzard's Bay,* she'd dubbed them. Those cowardly men who waited till their betters showed some sign of frailty, and then they'd descend with their vicious gossip, pecking apart their beleaguered prey until there was nothing but bones and a shattered reputation.

And today they waited for Helen to arrive, to hear her tale of danger and rescue. Not because they were concerned for the princess. No, they only cared how these new events would affect their standing. They waited, hoping for some slip of honor or duty, something they could exploit for their own benefit.

Clytemnestra sneered. Ever since she arrived on Argive soil, a child bride alone and untrusted, they had tried to find a way to challenge her authority, desperate to discover a hole in her armor. They found none, and never would. So now they tried to strike at her through her sister.

Pigs. She jostled her babe again, trying to still his constant kicking. Orestes bit down on her nipple, latching on with manic strength.

"Hades Hounds!" she cursed, pulling the writhing babe from her breast. He wailed with powerful lungs, filling the megaron with his racket. "Take him." She shoved the child to his wet-nurse.

Orestes was becoming impossible to handle. He cried night and day. Cursed with the colic, her midwives informed her. Flesh of her flesh, she should have greater patience with the babe, but a growing resentment was festering in her heart. When she saw his swollen face red from crying, or his chubby hands grasping for her breasts, she wanted no part of him. He was his father's son. Bit by bit, she left Orestes care to his nurses.

Helen entered the hall trailed, as usual, by a flock of noble maidens. The women were as bad as the men, but instead of grasping for power, they traded in secrets. Fortunately, they were easier to manipulate, and this flock belonged to the queen.

Nestra caught the eye of one of Helen's handmaidens, Astyanassa. The girl had fleshed out into an alluring vixen in her time at Mycenae, her long black hair a veil to hide a naughty nature that would make even Aphrodite blush.

Astyanassa smiled seductively, a telling sign to Clytemnestra that her mission was a success. These Trojans were no different than other men. Spill their seed and their secrets would follow.

Nestra descended from the throne and rushed to her sister's side. Helen's sudden arrival this afternoon, trembling like a leaf and pale as a ghost, had taken the palace by surprise. Her matron refused to let anyone near her. Clytemnestra almost had the Trojan prince seized, certain her condition was somehow Paris' fault. But Aethra and the unflinching Trojan captain immediately revealed the circumstance of Helen's shock. And their tales spread like wildfire throughout the palace.

The heroic Prince Paris... Nestra hated when events moved beyond her control. This information should have come to the king first, and then revealed to the court in the manner he deemed fit. Now every noble wanted a piece of this foreign prince, the girls to woo him and the men to garner favor. It could all be lies for all Clytemnestra knew.

But a well told lie was as good as truth for these toadies. *Let them suck up to the prince. He'll probably enjoy it. What do I care so long as Helen is safe*?

"Sister." Nestra wrapped her warm arms around her twin and pressed her lips to Helen's cheeks.

This is flesh of my flesh. She clung to Helen tightly, her twin's love fulfilling her in ways Agamemnon, and even Orestes, never could. She pulled back from the embrace, and inspected her sister. The color had returned to Helen's cheeks. Nestra insisted she soak away her trauma in a hot bath before presenting herself to the throne. It appeared to have done wonders.

"Leave us. All of you." Nestra glowered at the court. "My sister has endured enough today without you buzzing around like harpies."

The hall emptied, but that hardly meant there weren't lurkers in the eaves. Nestra took Helen's arm in hers, and led her to the private antechamber behind the throne. It was the only place she was modestly sure they wouldn't be overheard.

"Where is Agamemnon?" Helen asked.

"Finishing his afternoon repast." Nestra answered with a sniff.

Helen watched her with a concerned eye. The sisters showed the world a brave face; their Spartan dignity demanded it. But to each other, those defenses were unnecessary. They shared their hurts freely. "Which one?"

"Chimera, a kitchen wench. He's been favoring that one lately."

There was no illusion what her husband was up to. He began taking his meals alone in their apartments as soon as she grew too round to be mounted. Normally Agamemnon would cast off his harlots by this stage in her recovery, but not this time. Not that Clytemnestra minded. Severing the physical side of their relationship had strengthened their ability to work together as King and Queen.

Mistresses were an unfortunate reality of palace life. Clytemnestra was too smart to acknowledge the dishonor publicly. But she had ways of making the lives of those brazen bitches miserable. Catching the eye of the king was not the honor they thought.

Helen curled her lip, as disgusted with the king's behavior as she was. It was a shame Agamemnon had not learned the art of discretion as Menelaus had. There were only a handful of people who knew of the prince's particular appetites.

Helen crossed the antechamber to warm herself by the hearth, a distant look in her eyes as she stared into the glowing coals. Nestra made sure the chamber door was secure before joining her. "What happened, Helen? Tell me everything."

"I... I lost my way." Helen wrung her hands, her knuckles turning white under the pressure. "I got too far ahead of Paris and his guard. I thought the sounds up ahead belonged to them and I walked right into the bull's territory."

Nestra sucked her breath between clenched teeth. Helen was *lying*. She could always tell. There was a slight tremor to her voice, and her eyes would shift nervously. Why would she lie?

"Is that all?" Nestra pressed. "You weren't trying to escape the Trojans? Paris didn't do anything to upset you?"

Her sister went frigid, her eyes as round as saucers. "Of course not!"

But there *was* something hidden behind her terse reply. Clytemnestra grabbed Helen's icy hands, forcing her sister to meet her gaze. "Whatever it is, I won't breathe a word to Agamemnon, I swear. You can trust me."

Helen's silence slammed into Nestra with the force of a hammer. There were no secrets between them.

"What happened?" she demanded again.

The change was subtle, invisible to someone who did not know this woman as intimately as she. Helen softened. A wave of relief flooded over Nestra. She could suffer terrible insult and injury, but the thought of estrangement from her twin was beyond agony.

"I— " Helen began.

That was when her idiot husband chose to join them. Helen clenched her jaw shut and instantly regained her armor of disaffected coolness.

"Ah, there are my ladies." Agamemnon strode across the chamber to place a lusty kiss on her. He had the decency to make Helen's more chaste. "Now what is this nonsense I hear about a bull?"

Clytemnestra retreated beyond the hearth, tightening her shawl around her shoulders as Helen recounted her story. It was a terse description, action with no embellishment, a retelling so colorless it would make a number-loving scribe envious. Agamemnon listened intently, missing the salient fact that Helen gave no indication of her personal feelings in the encounter.

"He wove a spell over the creature with his words." Helen finished her tale. "I would not believe it had I not witnessed the event with my own eyes."

Agamemnon slapped his knee and let fly a harsh laugh. "He is no wizard, Little Sister. He's a tauromancer."

Nestra looked sharply to her husband. *A what?*

"I forget how stunted your Spartan upbringing was." His laugh died off derisively. "Bull fighting. In Crete, the practice is common. I was first introduced to the sport when visiting my grandsire's court. But its origin is further east, from Cyprus and beyond."

"Sport?" Helen recoiled, a flash of annoyance in her hard stance. "I hardly think the bull was playing."

Her annoyance amused the king. He always lorded his superior knowledge over Helen's innocence—schooling her, he said. Nestra stepped protectively between them and watched her husband's lusty grin morph into a leer.

"You're supposed to kill the bull, not tame it. Only the acrobats confront the beasts unarmed." He pulled his fingers through his thick beard. "It's a devilishly tricky sport to master, leaping bulls. Perhaps I've underestimated our little princeling."

Nestra sniffed. *A prince leaping bulls!* That was behavior for jesters and entertainers, hardly the province of royalty. This piece of information did little to impress her. But Agamemnon laughed again, clearly of a different opinion.

"This should make tomorrow interesting." He muttered.

She felt Helen tense behind her. "Tomorrow?" Nestra turned to her husband. "What's happening tomorrow?"

"Menelaus has arranged a hunt." Agamemnon's expression turned sour as it always did when his little brother was mentioned.

Nestra studied her twin from the corner of her eye. Helen was trembling. Was she *worried* for this prince? A spike of jealousy lodged itself in Nestra's heart.

The Trojan is not worthy of her concern.

Clytemnestra took a deep breath, burrowing that spike away. She reminded herself that Helen had just been saved by the man. Some leniency was merited. And considering Menelaus' fierce temper, perhaps concern was in order, tauromancer or not.

"We should accompany them." she declared to the surprise of her husband and Helen alike. "The court could use a demonstration of their leader's prowess. They've been holed up in the palace all winter like rats in a den."

Agamemnon seemed eager for the excursion, too. Her fool husband was probably intending to join the hunt, regardless. *Serve him right if he gets pelted by a stray arrow.*

"A brilliant suggestion, Wife." Agamemnon leapt to his feet. "But keep the list small. Some of those sycophants are more apt to scare game away than chase it out."

Nestra smirked. Restricting the invitation had the added benefit of making the ones left behind fret over why they were left out. "As you wish, Husband."

"And let's keep this information about the prince to ourselves." Agamemnon decided with a wicked grin. "Why bother Menelaus with little details?"

Nestra rolled her eyes. The games those brothers tormented each other with were beyond her. She often wondered what was the source of their mutual hatred.

"May I take my leave, Your Grace?" Helen asked.

Nestra had thought Helen would be more relieved at her suggestion, but her twin was as twitchy as a flea-ridden mongrel. She could hardly stand still. Something odd was happening with her sister, and Clytemnestra did not like it.

Agamemnon waved her off, and Clytemnestra followed after her. Helen was not going to escape their conversation that easily. But the second Nestra exited into the megaron, a dozen courtiers surrounded her. Helen was already disappearing out the portico.

"Your Grace?"

Nestra turned to Astyanassa's sultry voice.

"A moment of your time?"

Clytemnestra balked. Helen would have to wait. It was disturbing that her sister would try to lie to her, but she decided it was more important to root out the source of that betrayal, and that meant uncovering every dark detail about this foreign prince.

And if the Trojan hurt her precious sister in any way, Nestra would hold nothing back.

CHAPTER 15

THE HUNT

THE ANNOUNCEMENT that the court was joining the hunt reached Paris shortly after his brief meeting with Menelaus. Since the gathering was so early, the dinner meal was cancelled. The kitchen staff brought trays to their rooms, which meant he had to suffer through dinner with no one but Glaucus for company.

The captain had gone hoarse preaching caution. Paris murmured the occasional "of course" and "certainly" during the diatribe, but Glaucus' dire warnings fell on deaf ears. Paris hungered for this opportunity. Men like Menelaus had pushed him around from his infancy. They attacked him with impunity knowing the temple approved of their measures, and that the crown would not defend him. But not here, not now. All of Paris' hopeless desires for Helen channeled itself into a single, overwhelming urge to prove his worth to Agamemnon, to Menelaus, to the world itself.

He woke the next morning bristling with energy, and was down to the stables before the rest of the house had awakened. Haemon greeted him at the barn doors, his limp more pronounced in the frigid pre-dawn air.

"We weren't expecting you for another hour, Your Grace."

Paris took the proffered torch, craning his neck to get a good look at the stock. "I don't like to ride out on an animal I haven't acquainted myself with," he told Haemon while inspecting the horseflesh from stall to stall.

The majority of the animals were stocky, bred for charging. Paris passed them by. They were too much like their Greek masters, muscular and inflexible. He wanted an animal that could respond quickly and adapt to a changing terrain. "Is this the entire royal stock?"

"Half the mares are thick with foal." Haemon answered with a nod of apology. "But the best bloodlines are here."

Paris was about to give up hope when a loud braying erupted from a dark corner of the stables. He lifted his torch high banishing the shadows to the rafters, and a magnificent red-gold stallion reared from the flame.

He was young, barely over a two-year. The horse whinnied like a bellows, trumpeting his frustration at being imprisoned. Paris approached the animal, his hand outstretched to allow his scent to precede him. "Why is this one separated from the others?"

"What, Kronos?" Haemon spat in the hay. "He has a temper as foul as his breeding. He's a runt, Your Grace."

Kronos reared again, shaking his black mane with fury. Paris reached out and pulled his snout down, forcing the stallion to meet him eye to eye. "He's perfect. Bring out some tackle."

Haemon shuffled off, grumbling to himself, *"Don't listen to me, I'm just the Horse Master..."*

"He doesn't think much of you." Paris told the horse in Phrygian. Kronos' ears perked up at the foreign tongue. The Phrygians boasted they were the first to tame an equine, that they shared a kinship with the noble creatures. It was moments like this that Paris almost believed it true. *"Would you like to prove him wrong?"*

Kronos watched the horse master hobble away and brayed again. Once the outburst was finished, he turned to Paris, an inquisitive look behind his wide liquid eyes. Paris fished an apple out of his tunic and took a bite. The horse nudged closer, his nostrils flared until Paris handed over the morsel.

"You know, tough guys don't beg for treats." He rustled the stallion's mane, keeping his hand close to Kronos' muzzle. Paris could tell the beast was calming; his tail stopped swishing and his ears relaxed.

"That runt's not broken, Trojan." Menelaus shouted from across the stable. "My brother won't be pleased when the beast throws you and you break that pretty neck." The Mycenaean crossed into the stall of the largest stallion in the barn, tossing a padded saddlecloth over the giant's back.

Kronos brayed nervously, shuffling back into his stall and away from Greek prince. Paris stepped protectively in front of him. If Menelaus' voice could create that panic, Paris wondered what other abuse the horse had received.

"I doubt you have an animal here that could unseat me." Paris shot back. It wasn't a boast. He and Hector had been placed in a saddle as soon as they could walk. But Menelaus eyed him doubtfully, a lifetime of false truths making him overconfident. Size did not make a man harder to toss. It only made them land harder when they fell.

In a single move, Paris grabbed Kronos' mane and leaped up onto the stallion bareback. Once up, Menelaus could no longer sneer down on him. He grinned at the Mycenaean, kicking Kronos into motion. "But I am touched by your concern, Your Highness."

"I hope you brought your sword this time, Trojan." Menelaus' bitter laugh followed him out of the stable. "That sweet tongue of yours won't save you in the king's Wood."

The stockyard was filling with huntsmen and courtiers when Helen arrived in the pre-dawn darkness. The hounds raced underfoot, feeding off the energy of their human counterparts.

Blood would be shed this day, and both hunter and hound lived for that opportunity.

Wrapping her furs around her tightly, Helen took a seat on a hay bale and waited for the others to gather. A maid scurried between the courtiers offering steaming cups of hot tea. Helen took a cup, holding the warm crockery with both hands. The bitter brew helped to clear the fog from her weary mind.

The past twelve hours had been the most difficult of her life. She couldn't lie to herself any longer. She had fallen in love with Paris, as impossible and unlikely as that was. She barely knew the Trojan, but five minutes in his presence and she knew she belonged with him. And when he kissed her... she was transported somewhere between this world and the next.

But she had made her vows to Menelaus, before Gods and Men. She was bound to Mycenae. She had made an awful, terrible mistake in that choice, and now the Gods were tormenting her. They dangled happiness before her eyes, showing her what she could never have.

Nestra entered the yard looking every inch the queen. Her hair was wrapped up into a severe bun with a delicate golden diadem woven through it. The thick cloak around her shoulders was cut from a wolf's hide, its grey black fur nestled tightly against her neck. She spotted Helen readily and took a seat beside her.

"Helen," Nestra kissed her on both cheeks, "will you ride with me today?" She seemed overtly pleased with herself, like a cat left alone with the cream.

Helen eyed her suspiciously. "Have you been in the spirits?" Nestra's chipper attitude was beyond what Helen would expect for irritating a few courtiers.

Nestra was not offended, if anything, her grin grew an inch. "Can't I be pleased without you thinking I'm soaked in spirits?" she pouted in play. "A day outside the palace walls, the *Mounichia* festival and feast tomorrow... there are ample reasons to be excited."

Helen sighed, releasing the tension in her shoulders. She was jumping at shadows while her sister smiled gaily. It was as though she and Nestra had switched bodies. She massaged her aching temples. Ever since Paris arrived she had lost her usual patience, sensitive to any slight. It was exhausting.

But Nestra's gay smile twisted maliciously as the Trojan hunters entered the yard. A spike of alarm rushed through Helen's cold blood. Her sister was up to something. "Are you —"

But she lost the words as Paris led his horse into the yard. The courtiers' loud conversations died off into hushed whispers as he passed. Tales of his heroic rescue had only grown overnight, and every noble, both man and woman alike, was fascinated by her mysterious prince.

He did not openly look in her direction, but she was sure Paris was aware she was near. It was in his bearing, the turn of his shoulders and shift of his stance that kept her in his peripheral line of sight.

Helen's heart leapt up into her throat, fluttering as madly as a hummingbird's wings. Even half a court away his presence magnetized her. Wearing tan leathers suitable for riding and defense, and standing amongst his elite soldiers, Paris looked so much like a man from Sparta. Her heart ached with that sweet pain.

"He is handsome, isn't he?" A girlish giggle pulled Helen back to herself. Iphigenia stood beside them. The princess, a blossoming girl of eleven, was a perfect mixture of Nestra and Agamemnon. Her flowing hair was a mousy shade of brown with honeyed highlights. Her round eyes were brown as well. She was surrounded by a coterie of friends, all between the ages of eight and thirteen, every one of them sighing like sops over the prince.

"What makes you think him so special?" Nestra snapped at her daughter. "What battle has he won? What city has he ruled?"

Iphigenia blushed. Helen felt sorry for the poor girl. She

was a sweet thing and normally would back down to her imperial mother, but she was surrounded by her peers and at the tender age where the opinions of others mattered as much as proper manners.

"He saved Aunt Helen." A small voice called out from behind the princess. While Iphigenia was a mixture of the king and queen, Nestra's youngest daughter was the spitting image of her father. Electra's raven-colored hair was pulled back into a tight braid, and she planted her arms on her hips, glaring at her mother with eight-year-old superiority.

Iphigenia, pulling courage from her sister, stuck her delicate chin out and responded to their regal mother, a slight wobble the only indicator that her conviction wavered. "He faced a mighty taurus with nothing but his bare hands. That makes him brave!" Her friends tittered their agreement behind her.

"Or it makes him stupid." Nestra grumbled.

Helen groaned, and the unfortunate sound drew her niece's attention to her, despite Helen's best intentions to stay out of the matter. Iphigenia immediately latched on to a source of aid.

"Aunt Helen? What was it like, him saving you?" Her eyes lit up with hope.

"I bet it was very romantic." One of Iphigenia's maids cooed.

They were only girls, but the idiotic chatter combined with her sleepless night had caught up to Helen. She put a staying hand on her sister—Nestra's cross expression a forewarning of an imminent rebuke—and addressed the girls herself.

"Oh, yes. It was very romantic. Lying there in the dirt, knowing death was staring me in the face, and worse, that the man who was forced to save me was just as certainly dead. I near *swooned* from the romance." She rolled her eyes as the droll words dripped off her tongue.

Iphigenia's face puckered when she realized Helen was not going to indulge her fantasies. She gathered Electra and her friends and quickly departed.

"Did you see their faces?" Clytemnestra laughed merrily as they went. "Ah, we shouldn't be so hard on her. Do you remember how heartsick we were at that age? Dreaming of foreign princes and demanding one more heroic tale from the bards at supper?" She pressed her elbow into Helen's ribs.

The huntsmen, now mounted, began the caravan out of the palace grounds. Helen watched Paris mount. He leapt gracefully, like a man born to the saddle. As he spun his horse around, she caught his eyes momentarily, and again her heart hammered against her ribs. Like Iphigenia, she did dream of a foreign prince, and Paris was the perfect embodiment of those dreams.

"Fool's dreams." Helen snapped, pulling her eyes away from the Trojan. She pressed off the hay bale, anxious to get moving. As spectators, they'd travel with the rear guard. "We shouldn't fill her head with that romantic drivel. It'll only hurt worse when she learns the truth."

Nestra studied her with a worried frown. "And what truth is that?"

"Love is for minstrels." Helen spun away from her sister. "Her life will be dictated by duty. For a queen, there is no room for love."

Nestra stood silently beside her as Haemon and another groomsmen led a chariot their way. The groom did not hand over the reigns, but mounted himself. It seemed the unfettered freedom of her last ride was not to be repeated. Agamemnon would not tolerate such unseemly behavior twice.

Once mounted, their driver cracked his bullwhip, jolting their horses into motion. The hard leather sandals nailed to the animals' hooves tossed up chunks of mud, the flat surface keeping the horses from sinking too deep in the muck. The mud slapped against the cab like the whips of a cattail, and the yoke chains creaked like bone rubbing bone. It was fitting the ride sounded like a torture chamber. Helen felt like a prisoner.

"It's not true." Nestra murmured.

"What's that?" Her sister's words were spoken so softly Helen almost missed the admission over the commotion of the cab.

"There's no man who is all he claims to be. And a wise queen knows to never trust them, anyway." Nestra turned to Helen, a fierce look emblazoned on her face. "But that does not mean we live without love." She grabbed Helen's hand, squeezing it tight to the point of forcing Helen to wince. "I have your love, Helen. Sisters forever, remember?"

All the sounds of the world dropped out as Nestra's words washed over her. The jostling of the chariot over ruts in the road seemed distant. The hint of frost—spring's last grasp to the winter gone by—vaporized. Helen saw her life behind her like a giant vortex drawing her relentlessly to this point. All the dangers that threatened her swirled harmlessly on the outside. But on the *inside* there was Clytemnestra. There had always been Clytemnestra. There was no future uncertain, no danger so vast that seemed insurmountable so long as her twin was at her side.

She squeezed Nestra's hand back, just as fierce. The Gods would toy with her, the Fates wrecked havoc on her soul, but she would always have her twin.

"Sisters forever," Helen fervently agreed.

But for the first time in Helen's life, a tiny portion of her heart remained empty. It was a hidden part, buried deep in her core, a place her twin's love could not fill. And now that she was aware it existed, Helen doubted she'd ever feel whole again.

Agamemnon and the hunting party had departed from the assembly over an hour past once the game trail had been confirmed. There were many animals to hunt in the king's Wood: buck, bull, pheasant and the occasional cat, but it was a wild boar that crossed their path.

Menelaus rode at the vanguard, confidently leading them toward their quarry. Agamemnon half-suspected his brother planned to hunt the cantankerous pig. It was rutting season, and the over-sexed males were particularly dangerous this time of year.

The Trojan prince rode a few paces behind Menelaus, seemingly nonchalant. Agamemnon was not fooled. Paris' eyes were wary, and his back was as taut as a feline ready to pounce at the slightest hint of danger.

The Trojan delegation turning up at his door had been an unexpected present. His wife might fret herself into panics about the intentions of the delegation, but Agamemnon was beyond such pettiness. Friend or foe, this princeling did not matter. He was a spark, one a clever king could use to push his people in either direction. All he had to do was wait and see which reaction was necessary. If events did not move fast enough, he had only to stir up the pot, something Menelaus made all too easy.

Menelaus nickered his horse, dominating the path ahead and cutting off the Trojan's steed. His brother rode Perses, a blood tested warhorse that towered two hand taller than the Trojan's young stallion. But Kronos, like his rider, refused to admit when he was outmatched. He reared up high, kicking his forelegs wildly, pressing Perses out of his way. The Trojan, to his credit, did not slip. He gripped the beast tight with his thighs and pressed his weight forward.

"Whoa, Kronos. Easy." Paris stroked the nervous animal's neck. The horse, though agitated, did listen to his rider. Perhaps there was some merit to Helen's wild tales of the bull encounter. Tricking a beast was different than outmaneuvering one. This day held lots of promise for Agamemnon's entertainment.

With the horse's hooves back down on solid ground, Paris reined it aside, giving the lead hunter his due space. But the princes were both keenly aware of one another, like cocks ready to let the spurs fly. Yes, today held lots of promise...

Agamemnon, in contrast, was thoroughly relaxed. He reclined on his massive steed, enjoying the extra padding of embroidered blankets. The adornment not only made his steed look regal, but it made his ride more enjoyable. There were creature comforts to being king.

He also didn't give two shits who brought down the prey today, so long as he was there to witness the act. He had long stopped trying to best younger, more hale men on the field of sport. When he fought, it was for blood, not sport. The rage of battle filled him like the terror of Ares. It was better to unleash that rage only when necessary.

Menelaus waved forward his favored huntsman. Each man in his company would lay on his sword for the prince, but none more so than Sabineus. The raven-haired hunter held the tethers on a dozen large mastiffs, the best hunting dogs in Agamemnon's kennels. At Menelaus' command, he unleashed them, and the dogs sprinted through the underbrush in giant strides, howling like the hounds of Hades.

"LET FLY TO CHASE!" Menelaus bellowed, raising his sword arm high. A dozen huntsmen leaned forward on their charges, and the hunt began.

Agamemnon kept good pace. He was surrounded by loyal Mycenaean guards and a few Trojans as well. But it was the princes who took the lead. Even their horses seemed to be in fierce competition.

They caught a first glimpse of their quarry as they crossed over a rushing stream swollen almost to flooding from the heavy snow runoff. The beast disappeared into the brush ahead of them, while the horses had to slow to pick a safer foothold. Agamemnon got a good look at the beast. The boar was at least five feet long and four feet high. Its grey hide was dotted over with coarse black hair only visible in small patches. Massive tusks protruded from its lower jaw, a great wealth of ivory.

Menelaus, impatient as ever, growled and forced Perses through the slick riverbed in three reckless leaps.

"Wait you fool!" Agamemnon shouted, but the man was already gone. One slippery rock or bad footing, and the horse would break an ankle. Menelaus risked hobbling one of Agamemnon's finest warhorses.

Stupid, impulsive child. What would push him to be so reckless? But then the Trojan followed after him, Kronos taking a slightly different path where the riverbed was easier to discern. In a matter of seconds both princes were gone from sight.

Agamemnon nickered his horse to greater speed. His brother was a braggart with more love for himself than anything that truly mattered. Agamemnon usually left him to his ways, despite the frustrations Menelaus caused him on a regular basis. But if he harmed the Trojan, they would all suffer. And Agamemnon was not going to let his simple-minded brother blow this opportunity.

A deep mastiff howl echoed amongst the trees. It was a resonate howl, a lusty call of satisfaction and longing.

They had cornered their prey.

Paris urged Kronos to top speed as they emerged on the far side of the riverbank. The ride out from the palace had been filled with a never-ending stream of baited comments. Menelaus delighted in mocking him, first his horsemanship, then his dress, and even the Trojan longbow he had stowed on his back. There was no artistry in the prince's attempts to unsettle Paris; he simply chose whatever item his eye fell upon and crafted an air of superiority for himself.

Paris let the insults wash over him like the harmless air they were. Stronger, more adept men had conditioned him with their heckles and hate. Menelaus' efforts seemed pathetic by comparison. If you really wanted to unsettle a man, you need to discover what they cared about, and that required more effort on behalf of the heckler.

It was easy to see what was important to the Mycenaean. His cavalier attitude towards manners and his monarch spoke of a resentment of authority. Menelaus could not tolerate being beholden to anyone; he had to assert his independence. And that meant second place was not an option to the Greek prince. Which was why Paris was going to enjoy killing this pig so much the more.

Kronos was gaining on the leader. Sweat poured down his chest as the lithe horse heaved with the effort. Warhorses were irreplaceable animals when leading a cavalry charge, but in dense cover like in the woods, their heavy structure limited their ability to maneuver. It was akin to having a ship with a wide berth while navigating a narrow stream.

They hit a small clearing almost neck and neck just as the boar doubled back towards them. On the opposite side, the pack of mastiffs had created a perimeter. Both Menelaus' and Paris' horses reared as the beast charged toward them, its long tusks dangerously level with their tender bellies.

The boar, facing four flailing hooves, screamed in frustration and bolted to the side, trying to find escape. But the dogs penned it in, their jaws snapping viciously close when the pig tried to force a break in their defenses. Its fear-streaked squeals turned to grunts of rage as it realized it was trapped.

Screaming defiance, it turned back to the them and heaved its tusks violently in the underbrush. Fallen tree limbs, rocks, and dirt flung into the air in the awesome display of fury.

A heavy thud by Paris' side drew his attention away from his prey. Menelaus had dismounted.

"Are you crazy?" he shouted at the prince. But Menelaus' husky laugh belied the danger. He spun his short spear in his hand, banging the wooden end against his shield.

"Watch and see how a real man claims a beast, Trojan." He hammered out a taunting rhythm on his shield.

The boar narrowed its eyes. It tossed up dirt with its forelegs, preparing itself to charge.

"*COME ON!*" Menelaus bellowed, and the pig raced for

him.

Paris danced Kronos out of range of the boar's sweeping tusks, and loaded an arrow, the taut bowstring rubbing against his cheek. This was madness. Menelaus was going to get skewered all to prove his manliness to a foreigner who couldn't care less. Paris had a clean shot. No one needed to get hurt today.

But he hesitated. And the boar continued its charge.

Menelaus had planted himself in the soft earth, his legs spread wide to absorb the shock. When the boar came within striking distance, he pivoted on his left leg, sidestepping. And as the beast ran past, his spear came down, sinking in deep into the boar's haunch.

It wasn't a killing blow, but the pig screamed in pain as the thick shaft tore through its flesh. It spun, taking out a dense fern as it struggled to make the turn. Loss of blood fueling its rage, it took another bearing on the Greek prince.

Menelaus pulled a dagger from his boot, reversing his hold on the haft, and tossed it right at the boar's head. But the pig was thrashing its tusks again, and the blade was deflected away. Menelaus, unarmed save for his shield now, planted his feet and held the wooden barrier before him like a battering ram.

The prince was blocking Paris' shot. He could not take aim without risk of hitting Menelaus. "Move!" Paris shouted to him, but Menelaus refused to budge. The Mycenaean roared at the boar, a cry the beast matched rage for rage. It charged again, slamming into Menelaus' shield, shoving the prince back two feet with the force.

Menelaus tried to reach a fist over his shield to hit his prey, but the tusks were too long. The boar's vulnerable head was just out of reach.

Paris took aim again. If he didn't shoot now, then he was committed to letting this animal take a piece of the prince. He let his arrow fly just as Kronos shifted nervously away from the action. His arrow, meant to distract the pig by striking its flank, sailed dangerously close to Menelaus' head and sank just below the pig's ear.

Paris cursed, leaping off the horse and narrowing the space between him and the animal. "He's mine!" Menelaus screamed, his fury unabated. "Back off!"

But the boar had made no such promise. It spotted Paris, a smaller obstacle and lacking the wide shield Menelaus carried. It decided these odds were much better. Paris loaded another arrow as it raced towards him.

Aim. Draw. Loose. This time his arrow flew true, sinking into the beast's baleful eye. But its momentum was too great; it still charged at Paris, unaware that death was grabbing hold of its tail. Paris dropped his bow and held his hands out before him, grabbing the boar's tusks as they thrust at his chest. He launched himself over the beast, his heel kicking the butt end of his arrow deeper into the boar's brain. It dropped instantly to the ground.

"NO!" Menelaus scrambled through the loamy soil towards him. He ripped his spear from the carcass and advanced on Paris, puffing as wildly as the wounded pig. "That was my beast, Trojan. I had him dead to rights."

Paris froze. Nothing in his training had prepared him for an encounter like this. Menelaus advanced on him, his haft dripping blood, his eyes wild with battle rage. Paris itched to unsheathe the sword at his hip, but a deeper voice screamed inside his head for restraint. He could not, under any circumstance, bear a weapon against his host. It was a line he would not be the first to cross.

Paris stood his ground. He let his arms drop uselessly to his side. He was far from helpless, his body was as much a weapon as the metal he carried, but Menelaus didn't know that. By sheer size, the advantage was still in the Mycenaean's favor, if he chose to press it by attacking an unarmed man. Menelaus raised his spear, and—

"HOLD!" Agamemnon's heavy voice boomed through the clearing. The king and remaining huntsmen stared down on them from the tree line. He spurred his horse forward, forcing Menelaus back a pace. Agamemnon lowered his voice, but Paris was still close enough to hear their heated exchange.

"You fucking braggart, he's my guest!"

"That was my pig!" Menelaus growled back. "He stole my kill. Only a worm hunts with a bow."

Agamemnon dismounted, landing hard beside Menelaus. Shoulder to shoulder, the king dominated his little brother. *"Only a worm harms a houseguest. You. Will. Back. Off."*

Menelaus cursed. He tossed his spear at the dead boar, crushing in the top of its skull. He stalked back to his horse and mounted, spinning one last time to Paris, the struggle for control playing out on his face. "That was my pig. The next time you steal what's mine, I'll slit your fucking throat." He reared his horse and tore off into the brush. Half the huntsmen followed with him.

Paris could feel Agamemnon's eyes on him, carefully watching his reaction. He had none. He wouldn't give the blowhard his anger or fear. He gave him nothing, just like he deserved.

But that didn't mean he felt nothing. Paris' rage simmered just beneath the surface, stretching every nerve in his body taut. He felt like a coiled asp, ready to strike, yet utterly still until that last decisive moment.

Menelaus was an animal. And he was Helen's lord. Paris remembered the fear in her voice, the terror when she spoke of her duty to her husband. Paris had to still the shaking in his arms. Of all the cruel injustices...

"Please forgive my brother." Agamemnon stood beside him, his eyes also following the retreating form of the prince. "The Gods were wise when they made him second born. The prospect of him commanding an army is terrifying."

Paris turned sharply to the king. There was no apology in his voice, he meant for Paris to consider that prospect. Menelaus was married to Helen, and Helen was a Princess of Sparta—a land, by her own admission, that bred warriors.

Paris swallowed the bile creeping up his throat and looked down at his kill. The boar was bloodied, its flesh torn, its skull cracked. Yes, Paris had landed the killing blow, his arrow sunken into the pig's brain with only the feathered fletching protruded from its eye. But Menelaus had exacted a heavy toll.

And perhaps that was the lesson of this hunt after all.

CHAPTER 16

EROS' ARROWS

HELEN AND the courtiers returned from the hunt shortly after her husband charged through the assembly covered in blood and cursing like a sailor. It took over an hour to sort out what had happened, an hour she waited in near panic, too afraid to ask after Paris. The Trojan prince had also disappeared back to the palace with his delegation, but without the dramatic exit of her husband. Fortunately there were enough gossip hungry courtiers to do her asking for her.

Neither Paris nor Menelaus made an appearance at the dining hall, further adding to the rumors spreading through the court that there was some sort of altercation between them. Did Menelaus know of her transgression? Did he try to kill Paris? Would she be next? She dreaded facing her husband, and even though she could barely eat, she spent an hour longer at the table rolling her untouched meat around with a fork. The hall had nearly emptied out when Agamemnon dragged a chair over to her side and took a seat.

"You are looking pale, Sister. Are you ill?"

The note of concern surprised her. Agamemnon was only sweet when he wanted something from her. She closed her eyes, and prayed whatever he wanted was small. She couldn't bear a night visit from the king.

"Just my moon cramps." She winced to make the lie more believable. Agamemnon scooted back a foot in his chair, clearly uncomfortable at the thought of her bleeding. Most men stayed away from women during their blood phase, believing spirits battled within them. A physical foe was easy to face, but the intangible? A wise man knew not to tempt that evil.

"Ah, well I hope it passes." He grimaced. "I've been meaning to ask, but why didn't you take the prince to the armory like I requested?" His dark eyes bore into her, never once blinking.

"I... I wanted to save the armory for the end of our tour—so it would have a lasting impression." She fumbled.

Agamemnon nodded thoughtfully and she breathed a bit easier. On occasion she could surprise her king. It didn't happen often, but the reprieve from his anger was worth the effort.

"Take him there tomorrow. Early. He needs to be aware of our resources." He nodded again, making some mental decision she was not privy to share.

"As you wish." She dropped her gaze. Unfortunately, she could still see the lecherous smile on his face.

"Wear the chiton I had made for you."

She flushed. "But it's soiled, My King. There is no time to launder it." Was it not enough that she was forced to do his bidding? Did he have to flaunt her flesh like some cheap harlot?

Agamemnon leaned toward her, his lips so close to her ear she felt his hot breath against her neck. "Wear it, Helen. Or I will dress you myself."

She didn't trust her voice, but nodded her agreement. Agamemnon pressed his lips to her neck and left. She waited until she was sure he was fully gone before pressing back from the table and rushing to her quarters.

The torches were burning low in her private chambers, casting the room in a sultry darkness. Incense smoked in their burners and a half eaten meal lay scattered on the small table. Roast fowl, grapes off the vine and an empty flagon of wine. Menelaus' absence from the dining hall was no longer a mystery.

He had left the door open again. She hated when he did that. With the servant door shut, Helen could ignore his indiscretions and pretend the grunts and moans belonged to someone else. With it open, she felt like an unwilling participant.

She decided to risk his displeasure and shut the door herself. She crept to the portal, trying hard not to make a sound, but before she could lay her hand on the latch she caught sight of their rutting.

Menelaus was on top in his favored position. He cried wildly as he stabbed Sabineus with his sword of flesh. It seemed a violent act to Helen, each thrust going deeper and harder. How could the man bear it?

But Sabineus cried out in ecstasy, welcoming the embrace. He wasn't fighting Menelaus' thrust, but yielding to it, his groans of pleasure matching that of her husband.

Helen watched, enthralled. Coitus had never been an act of pleasure for her. She'd never felt the rapture that other women spoke of, the utter bliss Sabineus enjoyed with the man that should be hers. She had long resigned to the fact that she never would.

Menelaus climaxed with a heavy cry, collapsing into Sabineus' arms. The men locked lips, tearing at each other with a deep-seated hunger.

Her hand faltered and she backed away, leaving the door untouched. The way they touched... Her fingertips grazed her own lips. She could still feel Paris' mouth on hers, his tongue probing hers. Just remembering it caused that passion to reignite and dampness to seep between her legs. What would it be like to lay with him? Would she still feel pain? Or would she find joy, like Sabineus?

It was a foolish question. It could never be. She was not free to follow her heart. She was an object, a pawn for kings to maneuver as they pleased.

Resentment boiled within her as she watched Menelaus cradle his lover. How was this fair, that her husband could lie with whomever he chose and have no fault in the eyes of Gods and Man? But if it where she? They'd stone her as an adulterer, and any man she lay with would be hunted as a thief.

Was it so evil? Sabineus was an honorable man. He never spoke crudely to her. In fact, he hardly spoke to her at all. A pervasive guilt kept them a good distance apart.

She bore the man no ill will. Menelaus' lack of affection for her wasn't his fault. Sabineus and Menelaus had been children together. They trained together and fought by each other's side. Neither man would be alive if the other had not defended him with sword and shield. They had history. It was Helen who was the intruder in their unfortunate trio.

She often wondered if that was the source of Menelaus' cruelty towards her. He could never openly be with the man he loved. Society kept them apart, but so did she. Helen never understood what that felt like until now.

They had grown quiet now. Only the soft vesper of kisses could be heard from the adjoining room. Helen backed away, leaving her husband to whatever happiness he could find and retired to their big empty bed.

Glaucus insisted the entire delegation lay low after Menelaus' outburst. The prince was a loose arrow, one that Agamemnon could not, or chose to not, rein in. It was better to let the heated man's blood cool. Accidents happened when passions ran high, and an accident on this mission could lead to war, a pastime Agamemnon seemed all too eager to engage.

Paris didn't mind the time away from court. His own

blood was boiled near explosion. An evening spent with his troops was exactly what he needed to reestablish his priorities. They sat around a bonfire in the courtyard outside where the troops were housed and passed a skin of mead between them, swapping tales of the absurdities they encountered in their travels.

"Where was that elephant hunt?" Brygos slurred, lurching for the skin, the dancing light of the fire making the thick man look more wild than usual.

Ariston groaned, knowing where this story was headed. As the youngest member of their crew, the jibes of his naivety were almost as common as those regarding the fuzz on his cheeks. Fortunately for Ariston, he had a natural talent for the sword and usually made his tormentors suffer in the practice ring.

"The Kassite lands, on the Euphrates." Iamus shouted helpfully. After a stern glare from Glaucus, he passed the skin by without partaking. The sandy-haired sailor was on notice for his love of drink. Glaucus had a strict regime for any of his men who over imbibed that involved ice baths and salt water flushes. Iamus was the only warrior Paris had met who suffered through that regime over ten times. From the green-tinged cast to Iamus' face, he was probably going to add to that record number.

"Yes, in Babylon!" Brygos continued on with his story. "Our prince was the guest of that puppet king... Kad... Uh, Kur..."

"Kudur-Enlil." Paris helped the poor man out. Brygos was already red of face. He was likely to have a stroke if he forced his brain to work any harder.

"Yes, His Grace Kudur-Enlil, thick of gut and skull! How could I forget?"

"Is that a real question?" Dexios laughed, shielding himself from the spray of dirt Brygos kicked in his direction in response.

"I was saying... The elephant hunt." Brygos' grin spread

another two inches. "The entire court had taken to the king's reserve, and this bugger—" he pointed a wavy finger at Ariston to a round of heavy laughter, "had a fancy to impress a pretty little skirt in the king's harem."

Ariston suffered through a round of kissey-faces from his brothers-at-arms. "Oh, piss off, Brygos. Shurusha was no 'pretty skirt'. She had eyes the color of a sunset at sea, and hair more fine than spun silk." He sighed wistfully, all to another chorus of laughter.

"SO," Brygos raised his voice to cut off the din, "he thought it was the Fates shining down on him, blessing his quest, when he stumbled across the albino pachyderm, the beast so miniature he could trap and net it himself."

"Wait, *albino elephant*?" Dexios questioned. "Isn't that—"

"Aye." Brygos winked. "Our little lover bagged the king's royal pet. Which he found out quick enough when he proudly displayed his prize to the court."

Ariston blushed. "It's not funny, Brygos. They almost took my head for that."

"If you had your way with that woman, Kudur would have chopped off more than your head." Brygos chortled between gasps. "You're lucky our prince has a silver tongue and saved your neck."

Paris inclined his head, acknowledging the round of thanks each man sent his way. They might tease the lad, but he was a sworn member of the royal guard, and that fraternity was bound with ties of love and duty.

"Don't be so hard on him, Brygos." Paris tossed a handful of hay into the bonfire, watching the strands spark and lift into the night sky as they caught fire. "What man here hasn't fallen victim to Eros' arrows? You'd act the fool if the right girl crossed your path."

That, of course, set up a challenge amongst his troops, each man revealing his biggest love, both won and lost. For Dexios, it was a raven-haired beauty in Ugarit. Iamus had a strawberry kissed lass in Troy, a brunette in Aleppo, and a fisherman's wife in Thebes. He would have continued the list if Brygos hadn't cut him off. When it was his turn to share, Paris decided he had enough of story time.

"I'm off. Get some rest, boys. The festival starts tomorrow. With the crowds inside the palace grounds, the opportunity to get a knife in the ribs triples."

A loud chorus of groans followed his announcement. Brygos in particular, was not happy with being put off his quest for embarrassing information. "A name, My Prince! Surely there is one bright-eyed beauty who's put your heart in a flutter."

Six sets of eager eyes watched him, begging for an answer. Most of these men had travelled with Paris to the far reaches of empire. They knew there was no lover he left behind. But sailors lived for their stories, and they'd make one up for him if he did not satisfy their curiosity.

"You want a name?" he toyed with his men, waiting for their renewed chants to reach a boisterous level. He waved down the ruckus and, ignoring the worried look on Glaucus' face, he whispered, "*Aphrodite.* If you are going to lose your heart to a dame, you might as well aim high."

Amidst a new level of lustful cheers, he retired to his rooms.

CHAPTER 17

THE HOUSE OF ATREUS

PARIS LAY awake most the night. It was not Helen's lovely face that banished sleep from his grasp, but the knowledge that Agamemnon was manipulating him, and that Helen was certainly part of his plan. Hyllos had informed him about Tyndareus' Oath last night, a commonly told tale in the taverns of Mycenae. Any threat to her marriage could unite the Hellas. Agamemnon used her as bait, a delectable treat to tempt Paris and enrage his berserker brother. And now that Paris knew the trap was set, he could not willingly walk into it.

He gave a brave face to his men the night before, but he was no luckier in love than young Ariston. For Helen, he had played the fool, and he could not afford to play that role any longer. This impulse, this *infatuation,* would destroy them both. And surrendering to it meant betraying their families, a stigma Paris had defied his entire life. He had to banish her from his heart and mind.

The grey dawn came with storm clouds in the eastern horizon, a stone colored sky to match the stony resolve in his heart. "We'll need to give a donation to the temple. A few amphorae of our best wine should suffice," he told Glaucus shortly after the kitchen staff cleared their chambers of the morning meal. He tied his sword belt over his fresh tunic, determined to not go without a weapon for the remainder of his visit. "But wait until the plateau fills with pilgrims."

"A gift is not a gift if no one sees the giving." Glaucus nodded appreciatively. "And what of you, today? Many of the courtiers have been sending invitations to luncheon with them."

Paris pulled a hand through his hair, trying to get his weary brain to function. "Have we determined which house is Agamemnon's chief adversary? I don't want to waste my time dining with sycophants."

"I'll have to check with Hyllos. He was keeping track of the court maneuvering." Glaucus rose to his feet as though he meant to see to the matter immediately when a sharp knock came from their door. He cast a wary eye to Paris. "Are you expecting anyone?"

Paris shook his head, but composed himself for any contingency. He leaned against one of the tall-backed chairs in the greeting room, a casual hand on his sword hip. He had a good view of the hall as Glaucus opened the door.

Helen stood on the other side, her grey-haired matron behind her. There were dark circles beneath her eyes, and her lovely gold-spun hair was limp, falling loose around her shoulders. Despite her unkempt appearance, she was still the most beautiful woman Paris had ever seen. Glaucus took a step back, allowing her into their chambers.

"Your Grace," she curtsied low, the move giving him an uncomfortable view of her bulging bosom. The chiton she wore criss-crossed in vibrant colors, but the neckline was immodestly low, even for Paris' liberal tastes.

"Princess." He forced any trace of emotion from his tone. "What do I owe the pleasure?"

She saw where his eyes landed and blushed furiously, pulling her shawl closer for a modicum of cover. "The king wishes for me to finish our tour. There are a few items of interest he does not want you to miss."

Paris shot a wary glance to Glaucus. If Agamemnon had sent her, any manner of surprise could lie in wait at their destination. "I'd be obliged, Princess, but I have so much to do today. For the festival..." It was a lame excuse, but he couldn't put himself at the king's beck and call. Not after that gauntlet was dropped yesterday. The man who blinked first would lose. And Paris was far from ready to surrender.

But Helen's face creased with panic. She forced a timid smile as she turned to Glaucus. "Captain? I need a word alone with the prince. Do you mind waiting in the hall with my matron?"

"Of course." Glaucus bowed stiffly. He was out the chamber with the door shut behind him in a matter of seconds.

"What are you doing here, Helen?" Paris turned to her, hating the cold edge that laced his words.

As the latch clicked shut, Helen's shoulders sagged, the life drained from her bones. She gazed up at him, her sad eyes lidded with thick coal-black lashes. She didn't speak, her mouth seemingly unable to work. After two failed attempts, she rushed into his arms and buried her head into his chest.

"Helen?" His stately reserve was burned away in worry for her. She clung to him fiercely, her small body wracked with sobs.

"I'm so sorry," she cried. "You don't deserve how they are treating you. And yesterday, with Menelaus... I was so worried he would hurt you."

Paris pulled her off his chest, trying to soothe her shaking arms. She was near beside herself with worry.

For me? It seemed impossible. No one had ever shown such concern over his welfare. Even Hector only protested his poor treatment—it never unmade him.

But that was exactly what was happening to Helen. He wrapped his arm around her shoulders, helping to support her. "He didn't hurt me. He *can't* hurt me. Look for yourself. I'm fine." He placed her hands on his chest.

Her shaky hands roamed his uninjured frame, a look of relief overtaking her. "Thank the Goddess," she whispered, her hand coming to a rest over his heart.

She was so close. He could see the rosy stain to her cheeks, the wet pool of tears caught in her lashes. More so, the floral scent of her perfume filled his nostrils. Her lips parted, welcoming him.

It took all the effort he could muster to pull away from her. He had made the decision to put these feelings aside. He would not act the fool before Agamemnon and his court. The decision stung all the more, because—with Helen before him, so soft and caring—he didn't care if a thousand Agamemnons tormented him. She was worth every barbed injury. She was worth death itself.

Helen seemed as affected as he. She wiped her tears away with the corner of her fringed shawl, a haunted shadow still hovering over her face. Then it dawned on him. She asked if Menelaus had harmed him, but she was the one who shared his bedchamber.

"Did he hurt you?" The words ripped out of his lungs like an avalanche.

"N-n-no." she stammered, unable to meet his gaze.

"But he has before." He completed her unfinished thought. He should have recognized it. He had met many women whose lords beat them. In some countries it was commonplace to punish the woman for the crimes of the lover.

I should have let the pig skewer him.

Her eyes did not refute him. There was a sad resignation in their deep blue depths. "Agamemnon is far worse when he does not get his way." Paris' blood ran cold with her dispassionate words. "Please do not refuse me today. There is something you have to see."

And therein lay the danger. He could refuse her nothing. "Lead on." He finally acquiesced. "Wherever you go, I will follow."

After a quick stop at the stables to pick up their chariot, Helen instructed Paris which direction to head. They took off down the Grand Walkway and out the Lion Gates, Glaucus and Aethra trailing behind them like before. Helen insisted he drive, and Paris thought better than to ask her the reason why. Her melancholy demeanor seeped into him, and they travelled mostly in silence, save when she guided him towards the correct path.

They turned down a new road, one that lead away from the flat lowlands of the city proper. This road was wide, made of rubble smoothed over with a white plaster. It showed very little wear and Paris judged its construction no later than five years hence.

"It leads to Corinth." Helen answered his unasked question. "One of Mycenae's ancillary cities. The roads ensure Agamemnon's tribute is collected on a regular schedule."

When they had travelled over 500 meters into the utter seclusion of empty road and hillside, he had to ask, "And why are we going there?"

"We're not." Helen shook her head, pointing to a small nearly invisible side road on their right. Paris led their chariot over it, the carriage bouncing roughly on the thick underbrush. He pulled the horses to a stop as they reached the eastern facing slope of a slow rising hill.

The hill seemed like any other in the region, the chalky brown dirt was patched with tuffs of dead grass, the hint of green shoots peaking through here and there. There were no trees, only the occasional granite boulder, and the summit was no more than fifty feet high. But Helen dismounted and began to hike along its base, seemingly out for a walk in the wild lands in an ill-suited court dress.

The design was clever. Paris would have missed the entrance had Helen not known exactly where she was headed.

But some twenty paces out from the road, a horizontal avenue cut right into the rocky hillside as though dug from above. Paris paused and marveled at the ingenuity.

"This is a *dromos,*" Helen spoke, showing little of the enthusiasm she had displayed in their previous explorations. "It is a processional walk, bringing petitioners to the House of the Dead."

She began that walk now, the *dromos* some twenty feet wide and over a hundred feet long. Each side of the passage was retrofitted with massive ashlar masonry, one of the bricks measuring the lengths of four men lined head to toe. It would have taken a Cyclops to construct such an undertaking.

Helen marched on, leaving Paris, Glaucus and Aethra to hurry along after her. At the end of the *dromos,* an imposing vertical facade stretched up to the hilltop forty-six feet above. A thick stone door was cut into its surface. The massive door, nine feet across and eighteen feet high, was swung open, framed on the outside by two semi-columns made of grey alabaster, each richly carved in zigzags and spirals. Above the lintel of the door, a triangular cavity was filled with red porphyry, the crystal studded stone glittering like a moonlit sky. It was as fine an entrance as any royal sepulcher Paris had ever visited.

Helen paused before entering, speaking quietly to the two guards holding vigil. When she waved him forward, Paris cast Glaucus a staying hand, motioning his guard to wait outside.

"No, let him come," Helen insisted. "He should see this, too."

And so they all entered into the hillside, the towering doorway opening into a subterranean brick-lined passage. The blinding sunlight behind them cast the tunnel in shadow. But Paris didn't need light to know a gaping darkness awaited them inside. The dank air was thick with the earthy smell of death. He waited as Helen acquired a torch from the guards and continued down the path.

The walls surrounding them were decorated with beautiful

squares of bronze rosettes. Between the rosettes, frescoes of Grecian women carried urns and grave goods into the inner chamber. At Helen's urging, Paris took the torch and walked the final steps into the massive tomb inside the hill.

The space was enormous. Paris had to lift his torch high to see the upper reaches of the beehive shaped chamber, and even still the final bricks remained in shadow. A family of bats that had taken up residence in the upper reaches shuffled their wings in agitation at his unwelcome light.

The tomb was circular in design with each successive row of bricks tapering in, gradually converging to a singular capstone at the very top, a hollow mountain within a mountain. Each brick was perfectly hewn, not a speck of dirt or hint of root poked through its smooth facade.

Paris paced out the chamber's width, counting forty-eight feet across. He surmised it was equally the same in height. It was a monumental structure, rival to even those built by the God-Kings of Egypt.

But it was not the masonry that held Paris' breath. It was the contents of the tomb itself. It appeared, while the chamber awaited its ruler's far-distant demise, it was now host to his many treasures. And for Agamemnon, there was only one thing he truly valued.

The room was overflowing with bronze swords, spears, shields, and armor. By Paris' rough count, there were tens of thousands instruments of death, far outnumbering the people the monarch ruled. It was clear where the profits Agamemnon squeezed from Troy and his people had been invested.

"Does he need this many weapons to fight the legions of the afterlife?" Paris swallowed the bile burning in his throat. "Does he fear death so greatly?" But he already knew that answer. The greedy king would not wait for death to wet these blades with the blood of his enemies. One glance at Glaucus, and he could tell the captain felt the same. This was an arsenal with one purpose... *war*.

"Agamemnon does not fear anything." Helen answered,

the sharp edge of disgust coloring her words. "He needs these weapons for the army he plans to raise and the war he dreams of leading."

"*Princess!*" Aethra exclaimed in utter shock.

"He bade me show him this room. He never said I shouldn't speak my mind." Helen snapped at her matron. "And if he is too stupid to care if the world knows his intentions, then he should suffer the consequences."

Aethra clamped her mouth shut, a firm line forming from her pressed lips. It was enough to satisfy Helen and she turned back to him. "Are you impressed, Your Grace? Do you understand now, the power of Mycenae, of the resources Agamemnon commands?"

Paris was as stunned as Aethra of the change come over the princess. He heard the words leave her lips, her formal detachment worthy of a queen facing her foe. But it was not Helen, not the respectful compassionate person he had come to know.

"I understand, Helen. This is the message that duty demands you share with me." He lowered his torch, and shook his head sadly. "But I am not your enemy."

Helen shut her eyes, pressing down her frustration with great effort. She should not have shouted at Aethra, but it was easier to vent on her matron than keep her boiling emotions bottle up inside. She was a poisoned dart Agamemnon was throwing at Paris, meant to provoke and spy, perhaps even to seduce. What other reason would Agamemnon insist she dress so brazenly? She wanted to expose her king, but even deeper was a fear that Paris would take the bait, that he would prove no better than the men that dominated her life.

When she opened her eyes, Paris had crossed the tomb to stand beside her. He made no move to touch her, but watched her closely, his eyes caressing her as his hands could not. "I'm not your enemy," he repeated softly.

"I... I know." As the words escaped her lips, she knew they were true. She felt safer with Paris than a lifetime of experience would deem wise. And despite her instincts to fall into his arms, she swallowed her guilt, and proceeded as instructed. "But you didn't answer my question. Do you understand the might of Mycenae and of my king?"

Behind the torch light, a twinkle of understanding danced in Paris' eyes. He paused, taking his time to consider her question. "May I speak as frankly as you? Without fear you will repeat my words verbatim to the king? That you will keep my confidence as I keep yours?"

The remark could not help but soften her resolve. It was a question of her feelings for him. *Can I trust you?* he asked. *Is what's between us strong enough for truth?*

"Absolutely," she promised.

He tipped his torch into a brazier along the wall. The flames leapt high, giving more definition to the room. He then handed the torch to Glaucus, indicating to the soldier to continue around the room and light the others. They had a quiet but heated exchange before Glaucus did as he was bid. Aethra remained a respectful distance from Helen, far enough to not eavesdrop, but near enough for her hawkish eyes to watch their every move.

When Paris returned to her, a serious pallor dominated his face. "All of this," he waved to the now brightly lit tomb, "this grandeur to honor the royal dead? That is how we should honor the Gods. It is a small man that feels the need to display his deeds loudly. I do not fear small men."

Helen caught her breath. Did he mean it? He did not fear Agamemnon? "You should fear this man," she spoke with utter conviction.

"Why?" he challenged. "Because he has killed lots of men? He has bathed in their blood? Are those deeds worthy of my fear and respect?"

"No, but that does not mean—"

But Paris, now unleashed, would not stop until he had said his piece. "It's a perverse tradition we honor. Kings adorn their halls with images of battles they won, the people they've conquered." He paced as he vented, a lifetime of frustration pent up in that twisted truth. "I have brought kingdoms on the brink of war to peace, and my deeds will never be deemed as heroic as those who kill."

He spun to her, Helen the Honest, the woman who valued honor so much she would quietly accept all the misery that duty demanded. "If I bent my knee to whomever was the most powerful, what would you think of me? Be honest."

She squirmed under his direct gaze, but silence was not an option. "I'd say you were a coward!" she shot back loud enough to carry to their two chaperones. A hushed silence followed her admission.

"Then I'd say we finally understand each other."

"No," Helen moaned. There was no hint of retreat or bowed spirit in Paris. She could not let him walk away secure in his ignorance. He had to know! "You understand me, but you still don't understand *him*."

Something in Helen's plea gave Paris pause. This was not the desperation of a battered wife, but the open terror of a person who had experienced the black depths of Hades and lived to tell of it.

"Get out. Both of you," he order Glaucus, including Aethra in the command. She was not his to order about, but the matron had been a servant long enough to know when a lord should not be challenged. Glaucus led her by the arm, the swishing of her heavy skirts the only sound in the hollow chamber as they exited.

For long moments neither Paris nor Helen spoke, their ragged breaths echoing throughout the chamber. He studied her forlorn face. He heard the alarm in her voice. Did she fear for her life? Would provoking Agamemnon put her in danger? "What did he do to you, Helen? Please, tell me."

Helen did not answer him. Her eyes fell to the floor and she turned her head away, hiding behind a veil of her golden hair. As she turned, the torch light glinted off the brightly colored embroidery on her chiton, that scandalous dress that left little to the imagination. Suddenly Paris knew – the shame in her bearing and the unbidden sob on her lips announced the king's debauchery as loud as a herald. He understood, finally, why she feared her king so deeply.

"I'll kill him." Paris bristled with anger. Agamemnon would pay for what he had done to her. He swore it on all he called holy.

"You can't," she forced the words through clenched teeth. "Don't you understand? It's what he wants. If you attack him, he wins."

She was right, of course. He couldn't attack the king. Paris was an ambassador, bound by the sacred oaths of ancient tradition. His duty forbade him from lifting a finger against his host.

A wave of shame clenched Paris' gut. For years, he had dutifully completed the missions his father had trusted to him. But it was different this time. He wasn't building alliances. He was Priam's 'fist within the silken glove'. Agamemnon needed to be taught his lesson...

And Helen would be caught in the crossfire.

Can I do it? Knowing the danger I'm putting her in?

He already knew the answer. He valued her life more than his own. He grabbed her hands, pressing them to his heart. "Let me help you." He begged, desperate for a way out of the quagmire the Fates had immersed them in. "Please, you don't have to live like this."

Helen was moved by Paris' earnest plea. This proud prince would not bow to Agamemnon, a man who terrified her, but would prostrated himself before *her*? Whatever loyalty her king could claim from her evaporated. She tightened her grip on Paris' hands and met his earnest plea with one of her own.

"There is something I need to show you."

She pulled him toward a darkened corner of the tomb. What looked like a sunken recess turned out to be a doorway leading into a small side-chamber. Helen grabbed an unused torch hanging in a golden sconce and lit it from the brazier.

She motioned Paris forward, the small light pushing back the veil of darkness in the inner room.

The wall was lined with precious objects: polished faience, crystal goblets, gold studded weapons. In the center of the room was a raised sepulcher. There was room for many more, but the room was currently host to only one dearly departed. The former king was stretched out, his decayed body covered in a cloth of spun gold. A mask of the same fine metal lay over his face, hammered to showcase the features he had in this life throughout the next.

"This is Atreus, father of Agamemnon and Menelaus." Helen stepped into the room gingerly, careful to avoid disturbing the sacrificial bones scattered along the floor. "Once a year, Agamemnon visits the crypt to add tribute to his sire's legacy. There is a fortune buried in this chamber."

A fortune to honor the dead while his people near starve. Helen shuddered. Tyndareus would never seek such extravagance.

"Atreus," she continued, clearing her dry throat with a cough, "after discovering his brother Thyestes had laid with his wife, slaughtered his brother's sons and tricked Thyestes into eating their flesh in a stew." She spoke point-of-fact, hoping he understood the true lesson of this tragic history. "Atreus held the throne for twenty years afterward until Thyestes' new son, born to him by his own daughter, came to Mycenae and killed him, exiling Agamemnon and my husband in the process. When Agamemnon reclaimed Mycenae, he butchered his uncle and cousin, tossing their bodies to the fields to let the carrion birds pick at their bones. He then built this crypt, 'far from the evil ghosts of the rulers who came before' and thus giving his father the proper burial a regal king deserves."

Helen tried not to be dramatic, but there was so much Paris needed to understand before he defied a man like Agamemnon. The sons of Atreus were not typical men. They hailed from a long line of abuse and cruelty. It flowed through their veins as powerfully as the blood they claimed gave them divine rule.

"So you are saying there is madness in the line of Atreus."

She nodded.

"If he attacks Troy, it will end badly for him."

Helen groaned. "It will end badly for *all of us*. There has to be another way."

But Paris was slowly coming to the conclusion that there wasn't. Agamemnon had proven that he was unyielding and more than eager for a fight. He was like a mad dog that when outnumbered wouldn't run away, but would fight to the death infecting any other mongrel he engaged.

Priam had been mistaken. Mycenae was not a hovel on the western frontier. There was great power here—in the land and in the people. If Agamemnon could harness it, he would be a force to be reckoned with. Priam had instructed Paris to teach this Mad King a lesson, but the lesson was for Troy to heed. Yank this lion's tail at your own peril...

A familiar emptiness washed over Paris, squelching any thoughts he had of disobedience. He had no right to defy Priam's command. Priam saved him, when all the Fates screamed for the king to end his son's life. Paris had to believe he was spared for a reason. He might not always agree with Priam's orders, but he had to follow them. He owed his father that.

Agamemnon was not all-powerful yet. He wasn't stupid enough to fight alone. That horde of weapons was meant for an army, and he didn't command one yet. Paris turned to Helen, a dire thought freezing his blood. "Is it true your husband can marshal and army of Spartans?" Was that the message Agamemnon wished for him to deliver? A united West?

But Helen shook her head violently no. "Father would *never* give over his Hoplites. It would take a miracle of epic proportions."

"But when he dies—"

Helen pressed her fingers to her lips and lifted them to the sky, a prayer to ward off such an event. "He will name his successor. It will not be Menelaus."

Paris gasped, the final piece of her tragic life finally falling into place. "Menelaus was the mistake, wasn't he? The one your father can't forgive?" Knowing what little he did of Helen's upbringing, he couldn't imagine her father choosing that brute for his daughter. Not if the esteem Helen held for him was deserved.

But she seemed surprised. "Menelaus? No. If I loved him, my father would have let me go to Hades himself. I chose Nestra. Menelaus was... an unfortunate side effect."

It was Paris' turn to be surprised. "You gave up a crown to follow your sister?" It seemed impossible. To be loved so selflessly... Would he blindly follow Hector into danger? Would any of his siblings follow him?

When he said it, Helen understood how ridiculous the prospect seemed. "Yes... *no*! I was sixteen. I thought I was supposed to come to Mycenae. That the Gods wanted me to come. Ah—it's stupid." She spun from him, her cheeks flushed with embarrassment. How could she explain? She was young and drunk on dreams of love. If he didn't think her a naive little girl, that would confirm it.

Paris stretched a hand to her huddled back, rubbing the tension away. She leaned into his touch, allowing herself to be comforted, and he wrapped his arms around her, holding her tenderly.

She saw a million little crossroads in her life, each choice leading her inexplicably to this point, *to him*. Were the Gods cruel? Did they seek to test her spirit with temptation? But as she looked up into Paris' eyes, she wondered, was this something else? If only the Goddess would give her a sign, some way of knowing what was expected of her. But She gave no such guidance.

Reaching out, Helen grabbed Paris' hand, lacing her fingers through his. He squeezed back, a similar sense of resignation in the tender hold. His touch sent tingles through her body, but it was calmer now, like the warmth of a banked fire, not the raging inferno that possessed her soul in the wheat fields. Every moment they spent together kindled that flame.

A myriad of emotions played out on Paris' face. He was struggling to control himself, as conflicted by these overwhelming desires as she. "I'm sorry your life didn't turn out the way you hoped." He cupped her face gently in his hand. "But I'm not sorry you came to Mycenae. If you hadn't, I would never have met you."

They stood inches from one another, both desperately wanting what they could not have, an ocean of duty and honor holding them apart. She tried to imagine a world where she never met her Trojan prince, where each day blended into the next, a lackluster life devoid of happiness. Even if she couldn't have him, life was better knowing Paris existed.

"Then I made no mistake after all."

She raised Paris' hand to her lips for a tender kiss. It was all she dared give him.

CHAPTER 18

FESTIVAL OF LIFE AND DEATH

BY THE time they returned to the Palace, the *Mounichia* Festival was well underway. The central court was teeming with nobles and town officials important enough to warrant a royal invitation. Minstrels played indoor and outdoor alike, their lively tunes accompanied by the stamping of feet and the cheers of their audience. People danced in the hall, flowing gracefully in choreographed steps, while others enjoyed bottomless cups of wine and mead.

The *Mounichia* was a celebration of renewal, spring's promise of new life defeating the cold grip of winter. It was a time of abundance, of indulgence, of hope.

Helen wove her way through the court, a new gaiety giving spring to her step. She felt like an enormous weight had been lifted from her shoulders. There were no secrets between her and Paris now, no stigma of spying lingering over her. Agamemnon commanded her obedience, but he could not command her heart, and she was free to share it with whomever she pleased.

And so she did. With everyone. She danced with anyone who asked her. She made special efforts to shower her people with affection, taking the time to greet them by name, laughing at their jokes, and sharing a brief moment of candor. They soaked it in. She had never seen so many beaming faces.

The celebratory mood was infectious. Even Agamemnon had a leg tossed over his throne, his cheeks bright red from drink. His mountainous laugh carried over the entire hall.

The Trojans lost their rigid discipline and joined in the festivities. She was sure Paris warned them to be wary after he returned from the armory, but they were safe inside the palace grounds, protected by tradition and the hospitality laws of *xenia*. The music was too inviting, and one by one, they joined the dance. Helen danced with them all, the last one, Hyllos, was so red-faced with embarrassment he continuously stepped on her toes.

"Forgive me, Your Highness," he blubbered manically. She was near beside herself with laughter when Paris finally saved her.

The prince had switched out his wardrobe for the elegant garments he wore when he was introduced to the court. His shoulder length hair was oiled back, the faint scent of musk clinging to his curls. He wore his crimson cape, the rich fabric making him the brightest object in the plaza. Wherever he walked, a dozen maidens followed. He was irresistible.

"Stick with numbers, Hyllos. Dancing will never be your talent." He cut in, taking her hand away from the trade master and bowed. "May I?"

Helen was breathless from her previous dancing efforts, but she could not refuse him. "Are you sure you know the steps?" she teased, raising her hands before her.

"I think I can manage." He pressed his palms to hers.

It was a simple folk dance, each partner held apart by an arm's length. A few steps to the right, a short spin, a step away, then back together. It repeated itself until the couple ran out of room, where they would then spin around and find a new partner to complete the dance again in reverse order.

The crowd instantly gave them space, as they hadn't for Helen alone. A royal couple on the dance floor afforded double the respect. Paris began stately, completing the first cycle with rigid formality. The feigned intensity on his face almost pushed her over into a laughing fit.

"Why so serious?" she mocked, adopting a similar frown of concentration and raising an eyebrow so he could see just how ridiculous he looked.

"I thought I should do it proper first before switching things up."

"Before wh—" but the words were ripped from her lungs as he spun her around. He was *improvising,* adding in more steps. The minstrels took up the cue and sped up their tempo. Soon the crowd was clapping along, keeping pace.

"Follow my lead," he whispered in her ear as he spun her around, his arm and hers raised over their heads as she twirled. The spin flowed seamlessly into the next few steps, Paris spinning around *her,* his cape creating a rippling flash of red, like a flag unfurling in the wind.

With each pass, they picked up speed, the music building along with them. She threw herself into the dance, surprised at her own ability to keep pace. Her heart raced, and she was near panting for breath, but it was *exhilarating*. When they reached the end of the dance floor, Paris had to grab hold of her hand to keep her from flying into the steps again. She reeled, dizzy from the effort.

The crowd exploded with applause. Helen joined them, clapping merrily as she was surrounded by a giggling cadre of courtiers. "That was delightful!" she gushed. "Where did you learn to dance like that?" She was happy to see Paris was out of breath as well. His stamina seemed limitless.

"The Phrygosias!" Agamemnon shouted.

The crowd parted for the king as he joined them on the dance floor. Paris gave him a respectful bow. "You recognized it, Your Grace?"

Agamemnon sauntered across the hall, the drink lengthening his stride. "A Phrygian rain dance." He called out to the curious faces in the crowd. A distant clap of thunder followed his words, lending the king a prophetic aura. "I thought only their Seers were taught those steps."

Paris watched him closely. Agamemnon slurred his words, but he was not as drunk as he pretended to be. His eyes were not dilated, and he held his focus too easily. "I fostered there. When you live in close proximity, it's easy to pick things up."

"Ha!" Agamemnon swung an arm around Paris' shoulders, nearly causing his knees to buckle under the weight. "A man of many surprises! Your visit has been most entertaining, Trojan. Allow me to return the favor."

Paris tensed, instantly distrusting the man. Was he mad enough to attack him in front of so many witnesses?

Agamemnon smiled, clearly aware of the distress he was causing. "Do the Phrygians honor the God of the Grape?"

Paris nodded. "Of course."

The king slapped his hands together with a loud clap. "Let's have a song! *The Seduction of Ariadne.*" A ripple of anticipation ran through the assembly. "Sister, if you will do the honors?"

Helen froze. *The Seduction*, a retelling of Dionysus's wooing of the Cretan princess, was a popular song, one commonly called for late night in taverns when the maids had enough spirits in their blood to be easy prey. "A moment, Your Grace?" she scrambled for an excuse. "I've yet to catch my breath."

But the baleful glare Agamemnon returned made her reconsider. She steeled her nerves and dipped into a curtsey. "As you command." She cut through the crowd toward the minstrels. She knew better than to sing from the masses. If Agamemnon wanted to put her on a pedestal, so be it.

Paris craned his neck to get a better view. The palace guests crowded around the musicians, filling in every gap of open space. He was not familiar with the song and assumed the myth must have been western in origin. Only Helen's reluctance gave him reason to be concerned.

The minstrels struck a minor chord, the darker tone

dominating their melody. An instant hush fell over the crowd and Helen began to sing.

"Far across the distance now, hear their ancient cries.
Searching for the kindred blood, finding you and I."

Her voice was sultry and deep, matching the somber mood she evoked from the crowd.

"She has a lovely voice."

Paris turned, surprised to see the queen standing beside him. He recoiled from Clytemnestra's unexpected presence. It was strange to see another person walking around with Helen's face, yet looking absolutely nothing like her. While he felt drawn to Helen, the queen repelled.

"She does," he agreed politely, trying to catch the following lyrics.

"Come with me and you will see pleasures 'yond reality.
Close your eyes and visualize,
Just a little sin, nothing to forgive."

Paris blushed, realizing now why Agamemnon chose this song.

"Do you like the song?" The queen smirked, enjoying his discomfort.

Paris cleared his throat, and commanded his faculties to order. "It seems a bit bawdry. Is this really appropriate material for the court?"

"For the Ancients indulged in these simple debaucheries.
And then, who are we, to ignore their pleas?
Come and be with me..."

"It's more appropriate than you realize. Do you know that

men have been lusting after my sister since she was born? Our father had to fight a war to keep a greedy king from her. And she was only eight." The queen flung the information as if it were mere trifles.

"Why are you telling me this?" he stiffened.

Clytemnestra cast him an insolent smirk, her hawkish eyes boring right through him, eyes so eerily similar to Helen's. "I wanted to give you fair warning, lest you think you're special. Her beauty is a curse. Don't get caught in its spell."

The music died off, and the crowd erupted into applause. Paris took his eyes off Clytemnestra for a second, but it was enough for the queen to quietly melt away into the crowd. He turned back to Helen, her face aglow with the praise and affection she was receiving from her people.

Was she really cursed, the same as he?

Paris pressed through the throng, trying to get to her side, but it was for naught. A richly dressed herald entered the hall and announced that the banquet was ready. Paris lost Helen in the crowd as everyone marched to the dining hall.

Helen took a seat beside her sister at the head table, eager for a chance to rest. She was more tired than she cared to admit, the day having taken so many twists and turns. She lifted her rhyton, a golden stag-shaped horn used only for special occasions, and quenched her dry throat. The spiced wine tasted marvelous. And it was only the beginning of the treats to come. The kitchen staff loved to over-perform for festival days.

"You were amazing, Aunt Helen." Iphigenia gushed. The princess fidgeted nervously with her gossamer gown. She had stopped wearing the simple tunic all children wore only this past autumn and the finery was still foreign to her. "How did you learn to dance so quick?"

Helen held her rhyton out for the cupbearer to fill, and

gave her niece a sultry wink. "I didn't. I was just too scared to fall over and make a fool of myself. My feet did the rest." The girl giggled, a sweet tinkling sound that snuffed out the second she caught her mother's austere glare.

Clytemnestra wasn't pleased. Helen buried herself in her cup, hoping to avoid drawing her sister's ire. Unfortunately, she had a better chance of growing wings and flying to Olympus.

"You should pace yourself." Nestra snipped as Helen took another sip of her wine. "Wine loosens your virtue. You wouldn't want to do anything you might regret."

Helen turned to her sister, stunned. She had some conceit questioning Helen's drinking habits. Nestra often had wine with her morning meal. "It was your husband who requested that song. You should question his virtue, not mine."

Nestra eyed her daughter darkly. The girl gave a small yelp and disappeared down the table. "I'm not an idiot." She hissed at Helen once they were moderately alone. "You hunger for that prince."

"I do not!" Helen gasped, her heart hammering against her chest.

"You can't lie to me, Sister. I know you better than you know yourself. You want him. Admit it."

She was trapped. There was no escaping Clytemnestra when she was on the prowl for information. A lifetime of giving in to her older sister compelled Helen to tell the truth. But even still, she couldn't betray Paris.

"It's... nothing. An infatuation. Nothing will come of it." She shrunk into her chair.

"You're right, nothing will come of it." Nestra glowered over her. "Whatever 'it' is, you're going to end it. Now." Clytemnestra was furious. Helen had seldom seen her in such a state.

A spike of anger wedged itself into Helen's heart. Agamemnon forced her to his will. Menelaus beat her to it. But Nestra? She was her sister, the one source of friendship she had in this love-forsaken land. Clytemnestra was supposed to be understanding.

"*No.*" Helen slammed her rhyton down on the table. "I will not."

Nestra grabbed her wrist and squeezed. "You *will* end it, or I will end it for you."

"How?" Helen shook off her sister's grip. "Are you going to run to Menelaus? Tell him I've had impure thoughts? Do you want to see me dead? Or perhaps Agamemnon? He'd probably cheer and try to further my education."

Nestra went pale, that last barb hitting too close to unpleasantness they swore to never speak about. Helen sighed, instantly regretting the hurt her words caused her twin. She dropped her head in her hands. "I'm sorry," she moaned, "but don't ask this of me. Please, leave me this small happiness."

"Do you love him?" Nestra's body, her very voice, frosted over with the question.

"I..." Helen couldn't answer. This was no mere infatuation like she pretended. The more time she spent with Paris, the stronger her sense of familiarity grew. *She knew Paris.* In a way that went beyond words or experience. The comfort and ease in their company was uncanny. And he felt the same for her, she was sure of it.

"He doesn't deserve you," her sister growled. "None of them do. I'll prove it to you if I have to."

Nestra could not understand the irony of her words. You did not earn love. Helen had done nothing so terrible as to 'earn' Menelaus' love. Love was a gift, a blessing from the Goddess. Deserve had nothing to do with it. She cast her sister a pitiful look, "There is nothing you can say that will make me change my mind."

That was the line in the sand. Nestra tossed her hand away and stood up, her back rigid. She waited until the conversation paused at the other end of the table, the section where their husbands dined with their Trojan guest.

Panic gripped Helen. "What are you doing?"

All she received in return was Nestra's wicked grin.

Paris followed Agamemnon to the head table. The kitchen staff rushed around them in the dining hall carrying large platters of freshly baked bread, fruits, and cheeses. Any empty cup was immediately filled. The king seemed in a jovial mood, but after his morning in the armory, Paris new better than to relax. Agamemnon was baiting him, and Paris' lack of response was only encouraging the king to try harder. Sooner or later, Agamemnon would expose his hand.

The men and women sat at separate portions of the table. Paris took his seat beside the king and Menelaus sat opposite him. Other royal officials and nobles filled in the remaining seats, proximity to the king determined by some internal ranking. Paris found himself surrounded by sycophants and madmen, his Trojan delegation placed at a separate table within sight but not privy to their conversations.

But Paris was boxed in by more than courtly seating arrangements. The queen's words haunted him. He wasn't a jealous man, and he had no claim to Helen's affections, but the thought of another man touching her against her will filled him with rage. And if it were many men, like the queen implied, his rage burned white.

The princess entered at the back of the hall, her cheeks flushed from her earlier performance. Everywhere Helen walked she was greeted with warmth; she was so well loved by her people. Paris could scarcely believe she was real—a compassionate, thoughtful Royal. A born leader who did not seek power for herself—someone who would refuse a crown out of love and duty. Centuries came and went without the birth of such a person.

But more than her potential as a queen, she was by far the most beautiful woman who graced this earth. Paris had travelled enough to make that claim with confidence. A hundred eyes followed her path to the head table, her charm undeniable. It was a power she seemed wholly unaware of, but one her king was more than happy to wield on her behalf.

"Lest you think you're special..." the queen had warned. *"Her beauty is a curse."*

Clytemnestra's words were the poison he had been hearing his entire life. Cursed and discarded as the least amongst his noble siblings. Unwanted at home, and a stranger abroad, he had no place where he belonged. And until he met Helen, he was content with the lie he told himself, that he neither wanted nor sought that comfort.

But basking in the shine of her radiant smile? One word of her admiration could buoy his spirits against a thousand Hecubas. If she loved him, he needed no others.

Lest you think you're special...

It was eating at him. He tried to focus on the conversation of the table, but it was hard. His eyes would stray, searching for her. For anyone watching closely, he was sure his behavior was obvious.

"—a half dozen liege men have arrived."

Paris turned his attention back to the head table, missing the last few words of Menelaus' report.

"What say you, Trojan? You man enough to face me on the list tomorrow?" The Mycenaean prince seemed eager for that opportunity.

Paris turned to Agamemnon with a stern frown of disapproval for his host. Agamemnon truly was a Mad King if he expected an ambassador to participate in war games.

"Chariots." Agamemnon added, his smug smile showcasing his delight in Paris' discomfort. "It's quite safe, assuming you can handle a horse."

A derisive laugh rippled through Menelaus and his men. "Or do you need a woman to drive it for you?" the Greek prince added.

"I'm sure I can manage." Paris joined their laugh, refusing to let Menelaus mock him. "After boars and bulls, I expect a bit of horseplay will be fun."

Menelaus' cocky grin faded at the mention of the boar. The prince was in for another surprise if he took the field against Paris in a chariot. Dancing wasn't the only skill he picked up from his sojourn in Phrygia.

"I hear you visited our strongholds this morning." Rhopalus, a grizzled advisor who introduced himself as the Master of Arms, spoke. "Did you like what you saw?"

Paris painstakingly adopted an aloof expression. "An impressive structure. I'm sure you spared no expense in its construction."

"For certain." Agamemnon plucked a cluster of grapes from the table, pulling each morsel off with his teeth one by one. "It will house Mycenae's greatest treasure when I depart this world. It is only fitting it holds my treasure now while I still breathe."

Paris almost laughed. It was not enough to intimidate him, Agamemnon wanted to hear Troy whimper before his might. But cowering a diplomat was far easier than cowering the crown, and in Paris' case, he represented both.

"A wise decision, Your Grace. And the stockpile as well. It is best to be prepared for any contingency." Paris tore a chunk off a nearby loaf of bread and busied himself chewing while the officials considered just what he meant.

"If you learn nothing else of me, Trojan, you will know I am *always* prepared." Agamemnon leaned back, a smug certitude in his bearing.

"I'm always relieved to know our allies are well defended." Paris continued with his air of indifference. "Do you know the Assyrians conduct military campaigns every summer? They send their army out in force, expanding their territory year by year. Tukulti-Ninurta claims it keeps his warriors sharp, lest they let their muscles go as soft as their bellies do in winter. He got as far west as Aleppo last year, and was only turned back by the king's prudent preparations." He picked up the sharp table knife and used it to pick seeds from his teeth.

"Has this Assyrian horde ever struck at Troy?" Agamemnon's eyes lit up as Paris spoke. Did he imagine himself in the field against such a worthy foe? Or did he envy the Assyrian rule by conquest? It was impossible to tell.

"Once." Paris paused, keenly aware every ear hung on his words. "The Assyrians tried to cross over the Taurus Mountain range. Priam and his allies sent them packing back to the river lands. That was before I was born. They haven't rode north since." He planted the knife point first in the table. "Outlanders don't fare well in Anatolia. They say our rivers run red from the blood of our enemies."

Agamemnon's wicked grin spread to one of appreciation, a smile Paris shared with him. *Whatever stone you place on the board, I can match. Poke me for weakness all you like, Troy will show no frailty.*

"That's why your stronghold is a good precaution, but an unnecessary one." Paris continued. "The kings who would try to invade this far west will never make it past Troy's borders."

Rhopalus and his fellow toadies choked on Paris' brazen words. Menelaus glared at him with his narrow hate-filled eyes, a low growl escaping his lips. Only Agamemnon had the appropriate response. His deep barrel laugh filled the awkward spaces between them, mocking any man too uptight to be offended. He lifted his rhyton in a toast and bellowed, "To our battle ready allies! May they always defend our interests." The cheer was repeated throughout the hall, many of the men present believing the king honored them personally.

When the cheers died off, a new silence filled the table. Clytemnestra stood formally, staring directly at him.

"What is it, my Queen?" Agamemnon waved to his wife, irritated at the interruption.

"I am curious about our guest." She smiled sweetly, her

twisted lips an aberration on Helen's graceful expression. "Paris is such an unusual name. Can you tell us what it means?"

Paris swallowed a lump of relief. For some reason this woman worried him more than Agamemnon and Menelaus combined. "Paris is my middle name, Your Grace." He raised his voice to carry down the table. "I was named Alexandros Paris after a fierce ally and friend of my father, Aleksandu, the King of Wilusa, whose throne Priam helped him to reclaim."

"Oh," the queen batted her long lashes at him, a show of fake confusion. "I must have heard false information. I was told that the Gods cursed you in your mother's womb, and your father added the king's name to yours after she tried to kill you. That he hoped to invoke protection from a powerful patron against the many people who wished you dead."

Utter silence followed her words. Paris' mind went blank. He felt the bite of metal into his palm and realized he was clenching the handle of his table knife in a death grip.

"Is that not true?" Clytemnestra almost purred. "Aren't you an ambassador for Troy only because you are not welcome at home?"

They were all watching him, head table and hall alike, a sea of dark eyes questioning who he was and what he would do, just like in Troy. He couldn't stay silent, not without bringing more injury to his homeland than his birth already had.

"I... How?" he struggled to find words. But the damage was done. His feeble attempts to answer only confirmed the queen's words as true. A hundred hushed conversations broke out across the hall.

Paris looked into the crowd and found Glaucus' face, the stoic captain's frown the only sign of his deep offense. The queen meant to wound Paris, and through him, the loyal men who followed him. She thought him weak, that knowledge of his curse could lay him low. Paris' shame was fast replaced with anger.

How dare she?

Paris released his knife, pressing his palms flat on the table. "I am shocked, Your Grace, to hear such vile slander. Even idle tongues in Troy would not utter these lies, especially to a queen. Please tell me your source and I would be happy to slice his throat for you."

But the queen was in no mood to share. She spread her hands with a shrug, the false apology stinging worse than none at all.

"Woman!" Agamemnon bellowed, half-rising from his chair. The move upset the entire table, fruit rolled and cups were spilt. "Keep your mouth shut. We have no time for your mindless gossip."

It was as though a spell were broken. The hall erupted into conversation as soon as the king spoke. More than a few suspicious eyes darted in Paris' direction. "Pay her no attention, Trojan." Agamemnon soothed, his eyes still lit up with amusement. "Women are capricious creatures." That earned him a round of laughs from his advisors.

The king grimaced at his empty plate and hollered behind him. "Is this a banquet or not? Where's our meat!"

Menelaus signaled the nearby staff, an eager grin of his own replacing his usual scowl. "I had something special cooked up for our guest, Brother. We gave the pig to the lowborn."

The cooks rushed into the hall carrying covered trays steaming with sizzling meat, the savory aroma making more than one man groan. They planted the trays at key positions along the table, the first directly before Paris and the king. At Menelaus' command, the cook removed the lid, the steam momentarily obscuring its contents. When the air cleared, the source of Menelaus' amusement became clear.

It was the head of Paris' bull.

Helen pressed her way through the hall after Paris. When he disappeared onto the far portico, she finally saw her opportunity to talk to him.

Dinner had been a short affair. After Menelaus gleefully revealed his kill, she lost her appetite. That bull was a noble creature, his offspring could have sired a new breed of cattle, one mighty Zeus would welcome at the steps of Olympus. But Menelaus never thought of the future, delighting only in the feel of his sword through flesh.

When Nestra stood, Helen feared what her sister would say, that she would reveal Helen's indiscretions. Menelaus' sword would not be piercing a bull's hide if that were the case. But Helen never dreamed her sister would attack the prince personally. Her vile accusation... she saw the damage it wrecked on Paris. It was cruel, even for Nestra's standards.

"Princess!" Philon hailed her eagerly, waving her over to a small group of city officials. More than a few people called for her attention, no doubt wishing to pick her mind about the Trojan ambassador. She ignored them all, pressing further past the crowd.

He was alone on the portico, his back to the hall, his hands gripping the rail with white knuckles. She didn't say a word or make a sound to alert him to her presence, but he turned the second she stepped out on the balcony.

"Is it true?"

He nodded.

Her heart bled for him. She wanted to wrap her arms around him and hold him close, but the rumbling crowd behind her—*her sister, her husband, her king*—would never let that be.

"Why?"

Paris struggled to find his words. His mouth moved, but no sound came forth. "There was an omen." He finally spoke. "When I was born, my mother had a vision so powerful in clarity that it terrified her. She dreamt she had given birth to a burning torch, the flames so strong they ignited her very soul.

The Seers interpreted the dream, claiming it signaled the ruin of Priam's house. That this flame, *my flame*, would destroy Troy." He took a deep shuddering breath. "I've lost track how many times Hecuba, or her followers, have tried to kill me. When I was old enough, I volunteered to treat with our distant allies. I was little missed at home, and over time, the feeling became mutual."

Paris felt like a great weight had been lifted from his shoulders. He had never spoken of those events before. Those who knew were gracious enough to not speak of it, and those who didn't had no business in knowing. He had no wish to see the shocked looks that accompanied such news, on Helen least of all. But there was no avoiding it now.

She stood before him, her hands clamped tightly over her mouth, holding back the cry of disgust in which he was all too familiar.

"They're wrong!" she gasped.

"No. The omen is real, I assure you." Hector had once thought as she, trying desperately to disprove the vision. He questioned Hecuba a hundred times, and each time she spoke the same detail. A burning torch igniting her breast.

"Not the omen." Helen stumbled forward, reaching out for him and pulling back at the same time. "Their interpretation. A burning torch does not represent ruin. It is the light that keeps the darkness at bay. It is the candle of hope within the void. The stronger the flame, the greater the courage that fuels it. Paris... it's what I was named after."

Breath escaped him. Paris could not have been more shocked if the Gods reversed the path of the stars and the sun set in the east. It was impossible. He had lived under a death omen his entire life. For it to be wrong? For that dire vision to lead him to Helen?

Helen was utterly convinced. "In the old tongue, my name —Helen—means 'the fiery brand'." Her chest heaved with this new awareness, finally understanding her connection to the woe-begotten prince. "*I am your torch.* You were born for me.

And Aphrodite sent me to Mycenae to wait for you."

A bolt of lightning forked through the sky, the brilliant purple afterglow leaving stars in her eyes. Paris was surrounded by those stars, a million pinpoints of chance, drawing him from a distant shore into her world. He still hadn't moved, his muscles frozen in disbelief. Even when it began to rain, the thick drops turning swiftly into a deluge, he remained locked in place.

"Paris?" She took a hesitant step forward, her chiton already plastered to her skin.

It was in his eyes. His body might refuse to work, but his eyes were windows to his soul, and they belonged to her. She no longer cared for propriety. She took a strident step forward to her prince—

And was yanked back by another one. Menelaus held her arm, his merciless grip bruising her tender skin. "What are you doing out here, Wife?"

She struggled to release herself from him. "I..."

Menelaus turned and instantly spotted Paris, the Trojan enshrouded in the heavy downfall. Paris made no effort to move and Menelaus, after glancing upward at the torrent, decided against following him out.

"We're still racing in the hippodrome tomorrow, Trojan. This rain won't save you." He yanked on Helen's arm, pushing her into the hall before him. "*Nor you, woman*. It's time I taught you to respect your Lord."

Helen struggled to escape Menelaus' grasp, to get back to Paris, but her husband was too strong. A heavy clap of thunder drowned out the din in the hall as he towed her away.

She had one last glimpse of her Trojan from afar.

He was fury incarnate.

CHAPTER 19

APHRODITE'S PRICE

MENELAUS SHOVED her down the private halls of the palace, a sting of curses accompanying every step as he led them toward their apartments. His fingers bit into her skin. He was moving so quickly he was half-dragging her, her wet slippers failing to find purchase on the stone floor.

"Menelaus, please. You're hurting me." But her cries fell on deaf ears. Her husband was in a temper and he stank of spirits, the worst combination for her continued health.

He kicked the door of their chambers open and tossed her to the rugs. The fall pulled the skin from her shins and she gasped from the pain. But there was little time to worry about such trifles. Menelaus was fast upon her, grabbing her legs.

"No!" she kicked at him, trying desperately to crawl away. But Menelaus had strength and leverage over her. With a sharp pull, he slid her under his bulky frame.

"Stop it! Leave me be!" she screamed as loud as her lungs would permit, balling up her fists and pounding on his chest and face.

He reared above her and backhanded her. *Hard*. She saw stars again, and the room went out of focus. The blurred image of her husband raised his fist again, readying for another blow.

But that hand never flew. There was a crash in the room and she was suddenly free. Helen pressed herself up, suppressing a wave of nausea as she moved.

Menelaus was on the floor, the small table in their foyer crushed beneath his back. Sabineus stood above him, his arms held wide like an athlete in the midst of a wrestling match.

"Point to me," he teased her husband. "You're losing your edge, 'Laus."

Menelaus groaned, his arm darting out faster than she could blink, ripping Sabineus' leg out from underneath him. The raven-haired man landed on the ground hard, an odd laugh following his fall.

"Stay out of this." Menelaus growled at his lover. "She needs to be taught a lesson." He lurched towards her, his thick arms swiping wildly toward her legs.

But Sabineus was fast on his feet, tackling Menelaus to the ground. The two men rolled until Sabineus pinned her husband to the floor. "She's a woman." He sneered at Menelaus.

"She's *my* woman." Menelaus growled back, bucking against Sabineus restraining grip.

But Sabineus was too strong, and he was clearly not drunk, a disadvantage to which Menelaus was fast succumbing. It was like watching a cat toying with a mouse. A very large cat with a very large mouse.

"There's no sport in besting her," Sabineus purred. "I have a better use for that energy." And he pulled Menelaus' lower lip taut with his teeth.

The fight fled her husband, sparking something primal instead. He pressed himself to his lover in a violent embrace.

Helen was too afraid to move, too afraid to make a sound. But when Sabineus released Menelaus' wrist, his loose hand waving at her to go, she leapt to her feet. She whispered the man a heartfelt 'thank you' as she raced for the back exit, fleeing into the raging storm.

Paris watched the brute drag Helen from the hall, a burning rage clouding out his reason. He did not care if Menelaus was Helen's husband, or that he had no right to intercede between them. The woman he loved was in danger—serious danger—and he had to come to her aid. He rushed into the hall after them.

No sooner had he stepped one foot off the portico than a thick arm barred his way. Sabineus, the raven-haired huntsman, pushed him back onto the balcony. Paris shifted, his hand slipping to the sword at his waist.

But the hunter held his hands out before him in a nonthreatening manner. "Don't. I beg you."

Paris was through taking the blows that Agamemnon cast at him. He narrowed his eyes, mapping out the series of moves that would take the large man down. "Get out of my way," he growled one last warning.

Sabineus did not budge. "I promise you, no harm will come to her. I won't let it happen. But if *you* go, blood will be shed. You won't be able to protect her then."

His sober words doused the flame in Paris' blood. Could he trust this man?

"Please," Sabineus begged. "Stay away. Let me go to them."

Slowly, against his overwhelming desire to rip the Mycenaean prince in pieces, Paris nodded. Sabineus backed into the hall and took off at a run.

Paris stayed on the balcony letting the storm pour over him. He had no desire to retreat into the palace. His dark mood had no place in the halls of warmth and revelry. Instead he chose solitude and fled down the grand staircase to the court below.

He walked aimlessly, tracing the perimeter of the palace until he became hopelessly lost. The sodden ground covered his legs with mud that even the heavy rain could not sluice away.

Paris' entire life had just been uprooted. He had no idea which direction he was meant to take. Priam, Agamemnon, Troy, the rest of the world... it no longer held any meaning for him. There was only the gaping question, that unknown purpose of his life, the maelstrom of dark omens and unexpected mercy that somehow all led to Helen.

He had strayed from the western wall, his new path bogged down in underbrush and unkempt foliage. Yanking his sword from its sheath, Paris cut through the thin branches that tried to bar his way. He slashed and hacked, cursing the Gods, Menelaus, his mother, Aesacus and his host of temple cronies—he cursed them all and the cruel injustice they had made of his life.

It felt good to strike back, even at an inanimate object. He had suffered in silence for too long, accepting their hellish treatment stoically, believing deep inside that he somehow deserved it. But if what Helen said was true, he had been deeply wronged. Paris wanted to scream. He wanted to kill. He wanted what he could never have.

Curse you Fates. Why would you bring me to her only to give her to another man?

It was one injustice too many. He lifted his sword and hacked through another thick tendril. By the time he cut through the growth, the rain had lightened to a soft drizzle and he finally could make sense of his location. He had hiked up the northern rise of the temple plateau and now stood beneath the apple grove, the shrine to Aphrodite directly before him.

Paris stumbled to the temple, a man mesmerized. Was it only two days hence when he saw Helen dancing beneath the apple blossoms? Her sweet innocence beckoning him onwards, daring him to pay homage to the Goddess. He had thought her a temptation, a challenge to his duty, one he tried and failed to overcome. Paris had spent so many sleepless nights steeling his resolve, trying to deny his feelings for the princess. Never once did he stop and ask if he shouldn't.

He entered the shrine. A steady stream of runoff cascaded from a leak in the roof tiles. The water dripped down to the bust of Aphrodite, tears on the effigy made of stone. He knelt before Her, pressing his forehead to the altar.

"Is this why I was sent here?" His throat clenched in the unfamiliar task of prayer. "Are we meant to be together?"

A thunderclap broke above the temple and rain began to fall again. Softly at first, in small patters against the tiled roof, then heavier, more insistent, the steady drum of the Goddess' heart.

The pounding was too loud to alert him to Helen's presence, but somehow he could feel her. He could always feel when she approached. The hair on his arms rose, and his chest constricted. If Helen did not display the same bewitchment, he would swear he was ensorcelled. He turned to the temple door and found her in the doorstep, soaked to the bone from the rain, her chest heaving as she watched him pray.

Helen had fled her chambers in a panic. Her feet carried her, as they always did, to the temple summit. Perhaps it was the rain, perhaps it was the Fates, but she deviated, heading away from her rocky precipice for the sanctuary of the shrine. And when she found Paris there, she knew it was no coincidence.

He knelt before the altar, a humble man beseeching the Goddess for guidance. Helen's heart ached for him. Menelaus tried to hurt him, Agamemnon to manipulate him. Even his own mother had rejected him from her bosom. Paris was a man who had never known love. When she saw him kneeling there, she saw herself.

Then he turned abruptly to her, his eyes staring deeply into hers, laying her soul bare. She shuddered, her body registering the deep shock of his nearness.

"The Gods never answer my prayers," his husky voice rumbled with the gathering storm, "but I swear they have this night."

She raced to his side and Paris swept her into his embrace, his lips pressing hungrily for hers. Her touch was like lightning, igniting a fire within him. He twined his hands through her wet hair, crushing her body to his. He felt hers do the same. There was no room for coherent thought, only passion existed, and it would bear no resistance.

They pulled at each other, hands roaming everywhere, each of them ravenous to take their fill of the other's embrace. Helen attacked him with a ferocity she never knew she possessed, her lips savaging Paris' jaw, his neck and back to his eager mouth. She attacked him with the desperation of a woman dying of thirst, a thirst only this forbidden man could slacken.

Paris lifted her on the altar, sliding his hands under her chiton and pulling the sodden fabric over her head. A beam of moonlight showered down from the skylight, bathing her perfect curves in its silvery glow. He got his first glimpse of her naked body and groaned heavily, his loins constricting tight.

Twin breasts, perky with rosebud nipples, stood erect. Her skin was the color of fresh milk, and a soft mound of tawny hair hid her sacred flower. She was breathtaking. He ran his hands up her chest, cupping each breast, pinching her nipples between his thumb and forefingers.

Helen arched her back and pulled herself up to kiss him again. She tore at the laces of his tunic, releasing his cape and then the shirt, her hands desperate to remove any barrier between them. His chest was amazingly smooth, his lean muscles rippled beneath tan skin. She trailed kisses down his chest moving inch-by-inch closer to his loincloth.

Paris' hands wove into her hair, stopping her at his navel. "Wait," he whispered, his voice heavy with desire.

But she didn't want to wait. She wanted him, *needed him*, her desire lending her strength. She pressed her face to Paris' groin, breathing in deep his musky scent. She could feel the hard length of his phallus beneath and she nuzzled in closer, covering its shaft in soft kisses through the fabric.

Paris almost lost himself. His entire body was on the razor's edge of ecstasy. Panting, he pulled himself away from that ledge, stepping back from Helen and shuffling out of his undergarment. He pressed her gently back onto the altar and crawled up onto the stone table above her, his hands greedily pulling her close, reluctant to leave her body for even those few short seconds.

He kissed her neck, savoring the soft groan that vibrated her throat. Lowering his head, he circled his lips over her breast to her nipple, flicking it in his mouth with his rough tongue. She gasped, a mewling plea escaping her lips. She pressed her hips against his, digging his stiff erection into her thigh.

He had dreamed of this moment from the first time he saw her in the mist. A Goddess of incredible beauty and grace. And now she was here in his arms, yielding to his touch. He could scarcely believe this was actually happening. He wanted to savor it, and make her feel the exquisite pleasure she gave to him.

He moved down her body with his mouth, trailing sensuous kisses around her navel, his tongue moving to her pelvis, to her thighs and further down. Grabbing her round buttocks in both hands, he lifted her up to meet his hungry mouth. She cried his name as he buried his face between her legs, his tongue spreading the soft lips of her sacred font, probing deeper into her hard nub.

"Paris, please..." Helen begged him over and over again. For what, she did not know. She only knew there was something more, something beyond the wild sensations that had laid claim to her very being. Her loins were on fire, an aching emptiness inside her desperate to be filled.

Paris felt the same urgency, the throbbing of his phallus demanding release. She pressed her pelvis into his face, her thighs squeezing his head as he continued pleasuring her. Her deep moans, heavy and filled with longing, urged him on to new efforts. He shifted his hand beneath her, parting her legs, and plunged his fingers inside, stroking savagely back and forth.

A wild instinct took hold of Helen and she pressed herself harder on him, welcoming his touch, begging for more. His touch was magic, sending ripples of nerve-shattering pleasure throughout her entire body. A pressure was building deep within, the steam of his hot breath and the stroke of his rough tongue was pulling it out. She melted into his touch as wave after wave of pleasure rolled over her. It was the Goddess' touch, but far stronger than she had previously experienced. She cried out in sharp gasps as the pleasure rose.

Paris could not hold off any longer. He was desperate with need. He mounted her, sinking deep into her silk folds as she cried out. There was a magical sensation as his naked flesh penetrated hers, a melding, a blending. He could not tell where his body left off and hers began. In all his previous sexual experiences, the effect was the opposite. His body adapted to the unknown partner and the external pleasure of a foreign touch.

But with Helen, the pleasure was internal. He rocked in unison with her arching thrusts, riding the waves of her orgasm. Her legs, her arms, her very font itself, tightened around him in a perfect fit. His body anticipated her every move, matching each of her thrusts as if it were his own. They moved as one, pushing harder, thrusting further, trying desperately to press into each other's soul. Her pleasure was his pleasure. Any other memory of lovemaking was a pale shadow in comparison.

The fiery touch inside her would not subside, and Helen felt herself growing weak from its strong grip. With every thrust, the ecstasy crested higher until she was sure she would shatter. She felt like a young girl innocent to the world of love. And Paris, her handsome prince, was awakening her to that new world.

He lost his fragile grip of restraint and went wild, thrusting deeper and harder into her, until at long last, his body tensed and he cried out with a violent shudder. The sudden spasm pushed her over the edge of her mounting waves of passion. Helen cried out with him, and he pressed his lips to hers, sharing her gasping breath.

They remained there for a long breathtaking moment, their bodies still entwined, simply savoring the intimate embrace. Paris kissed her tenderly, staring deep into her eyes, his own filled with adoration.

Helen trembled. She had never felt more satisfied—more complete—in her entire life. Her fingers trailed over his sweat soaked skin, tracing his chiseled jaw, and over his arched brow. He was perfection. *This* was perfection. How could anything so wonderful be wrong?

He dropped down beside her and she locked her feet around his, trying to delay the moment when he would have to pull free from her body. "Are you all right?" He kissed her forehead, pulling her in closer to his chest.

Helen nuzzled into the crook of his arm, the steady drum of rain lulling her into sleep. "I'm perfect," she whispered in his ear. "I belong here. Never let me go."

CHAPTER 20

QUESTIONABLE CONDUCT

PARIS DID not return to his chambers until the witching hour when he was sure the palace household would all be asleep. He and Helen stayed in the holy sanctuary for as long as they dared. They rested, they laughed, and they made love, both of them drunk on the affection of the other. But the moon sank beneath the horizon and soon a new day would dawn filled with all the responsibilities they'd rather forget.

It was Helen's sober declaration that Agamemnon would kill them both if he found them together that finally forced Paris into action. As much as he regretted leaving her side, he returned to the palace alone, persuaded by Helen's solemn promise that she could find her way back safely. Her nocturnal wanderings were well documented, but a missing prince...?

It turned out her concerns were well earned. The moment he stepped into his darkened chambers, Glaucus tossed him against the wall, his right hand around Paris' throat and his left holding a dagger at eye level.

"You bloody bastards, what have you done with him!"

"Glaucus! It's me." Paris held his hands up in a non-threatening manner.

Glaucus was a temperate man, humble and well respected.

But he once took down an entire crew of Dorian pirates when he thought Paris' life was in danger. There was nothing more fearsome than the wrath of a man protecting his family, and over the years and their many travels, the captain had become something more than just the leader of Paris' guard.

Glaucus released him, little of his anger abated. "Where the hell have you been? I've had the guard out all night looking for you. We were beginning to suspect the worst."

Paris straightened his tunic, avoiding Glaucus' scrutinizing eyes. "I... I wanted some privacy. I needed to clear my head."

"Privacy? Are you mad? I'm half-certain these Greeks want you dead. Or close enough to it." He followed Paris into the sitting area, his eyes narrowed. "Where were you really?"

Paris sped around Glaucus, walking to the balcony. "What does it matter? I am here now. You should call off the guard before they rouse any suspicion." But he could not escape Glaucus for long. He followed Paris out, as swift footed as a jungle cat in the dark.

"Look at me, Paris." A cold edge of reprimand laced his words. Glaucus' loyalty went without question, and so too did his steadfast adherence to speak the truth. Paris reluctantly turned to him.

"You were with her, weren't you?"

"That's none of your business—"

"Wrong!" Glaucus snapped. "I was tasked with keeping you safe. What do you think will happen to you—to all of us—if this Mad King found you with his treasure?"

"He will do as he pleases, as he already has planned to do!" Paris stormed past him, kicking the small table out of his way as he went. "He doesn't care about Helen. He doesn't care about anybody save himself, and no act of mine will sway his course. This was a bullshit mission from the start, Glaucus. Don't deny it."

The captain squared his shoulders, a man prepared for a fight. "She is married, Paris. Before Gods and Men."

"To a brutal pig who resents his vows as much as she." Paris spat. But his argument sounded petty, even to his own ears. It didn't matter if Helen regretted her vows to Menelaus, or if Menelaus preferred the company of his huntsman, as Helen said. The only thing that could break the laws of man was divine intervention. And who would believe him if he swore Aphrodite intended Helen for him?

Glaucus eyed the scattered furniture with a deep scowl of disapproval. "I have known you for many years, My Prince. Not once have you conducted yourself in a manner unworthy of a king. Don't let this *infatuation* be the start."

Infatuation? Was that what Glaucus thought was happening between him and Helen? That Paris would jeopardize their mission, their very lives, over an *infatuation*?

"You *do* known me, Glaucus. For many years." Paris turned away from his captain's scornful glare to face the wall, the will to fight draining from him. "We've seen the behavior of kings. They are cruel and lack common decency. Do you truly think I should conduct myself like one? I have always striven to be better than that."

"But the princess—"

"You don't understand." Paris spun. He had spent a lifetime carefully guarding his thoughts and feelings. He could stand in the midst of ridicule and defamation without blinking an eye. But the torrent of emotions boiling inside him was something all his years at Hecuba's court had not prepared him for. He was no longer in control of himself.

He held Glaucus' gaze, striving to drive in the depths of how he felt. "I'm not flouting the will of the Gods, I'm trying to *listen to them*. My entire life I've dwelt in darkness, living in the shadow of an omen. But when I'm with Helen, there is no dark future. She *is* the torch burning the darkness away." He struggled for words, desperate to give voice for what could only be felt. "I can't go back to that void. Not after feeling her warmth. For the first time in my life, someone accepts me for exactly who I am."

A prolonged silence followed his declaration. Glaucus stood in the doorway silhouetted by the dim light of the fading stars, a man struck by revelation.

"You love her."

It wasn't a question. It wasn't an accusation. It was the simple truth stated by a simple man.

Love. It felt like a tiny, infinitesimal word compared to what Paris felt. "There is no world for me without her in it. When I'm with Helen, I'm already home."

Glaucus was a hard man, but he was not all made of stone. What tenderness resided in him was reserved for Paris. He knew the enormity of what Paris was saying. "That... complicates things."

"Unbelievably so." Paris gripped the back of a tall chair, feeling the weight of his conflicting duties pressing down on him.

Glaucus walked silently to his side, and placed a comforting hand on his shoulder. They had spent most of their lives at sea, the captain and his prince. And for true salt-tested sailors, tales of sirens and merfolk were as commonplace as news of the harvest. The Impossible was not a vague concept for those who risked their life every time they set sail. It was a familiar wind that rose when least expected. And in that wind, even a cursed and discarded prince deserved some small measure of happiness.

"When we left on this mission, I knew it would be dangerous." Glaucus spoke softly. "I agreed to come because at the end there was a promise of home, that you wouldn't be an outcast any longer. Every man on our crew would die to see that day. But if you have already found it, we will fight to help you keep it, My Prince."

Paris clasped Glaucus by the shoulder, overcome by the man's loyalty. He knew he did not deserve it. He could only hope one day he might. "Thank you."

"Do we abort the mission?"

Paris shook his head, still uncertain which course of action he should take. If the Gods were kind, they'd give him a sign. "Give me a day to work this out."

Glaucus shifted nervously. If their mission was perilous before, Paris had just steered them into uncharted territory. "A word of precaution?" he offered. "This king is picking at you piece by piece, trying to find some weakness. We don't benefit from giving him more opportunities than necessary. Deliver your father's message, and deliver it fast. Or Agamemnon might send one of his own."

Like my head in a box...

Paris felt the events cascading around him like the sands of an hourglass steadily draining out. The might of a kingdom was determined by three factors: the size of its lands, the strength of its arms and the treasures of its craftsmen. Agamemnon already had two of the three. And Paris knew where he would try to acquire the third.

"I'll consider it."

It was sage advice. Glaucus always gave sage advice. Paris suspected he was going to need all he could get in the days to follow. He turned to his bedchambers, hopeful to get an hour of rest before facing whatever Agamemnon had in store. His hand barely touched the latch before Glaucus called out one last time.

"Would you die for her?"

How many nights had they sat around the fire chastising men for that foolishness? How many times was Paris forced to step in and save a poor countryman from throwing his life away in some hopeless cause? Paris never understood what would impel a man to act in such a manner. When he answered, it was not without a touch of irony.

"A thousand times over, yes."

Glaucus grunted. "Better for her if you live. Remember that in how you proceed." He ducked his head in deference and disappeared out of their chambers.

CHAPTER 21

THE OFFER

HELEN HAD scarcely slept for fear she would wake and find this new happiness was only in her dreams. She kept waiting for shame to cripple her, for the heavens to rain lightning on her wicked soul, but there was a spring to her step, and the only thing reigning in her soul was unabashed joy. She felt like dancing.

She entered the megaron the following morning with a radiant smile on her face, a smile she saw reflected on every servant who crossed her path. Even Aethra put aside her dour frowns and joined in Helen's festive mood.

"The sun's burnt through the clouds, My Lady." Aethra took a deep breath, inhaling the crisp scent of wet earth. "There's nothing like a spring squall to wash away the rot. There'll be wild flowers in the fields soon."

"It's amazing, isn't it." Helen inhaled deeply herself, the bouquet of myrrh and juniper mingled with the smoky remnants of festival bonfires. "When all the world appears dead, a new spark of life is found."

A spark is all that's needed to ignite a flame. She blushed, vividly remembering that blaze ripping through her body. Just the thought of Paris was enough to cause her heart to race and her body to ache with longing.

Few people stirred in the throne room. Most of the palace guests slept as heavily this morning as they had drank the night before. Of the few courtiers lining the hall, five huddled together over a smoldering brazier, quietly placing bets on the chariot races of the afternoon. Menelaus was the leading favorite. But if his heavy snoring this morning was any indication, he would hardly be at his best performance.

"Princess!" Nextus waved her over to the brazier, a fond smile gracing his angular face. The steward was one of the few Mycenaean officials who did not curry favor with Agamemnon by snubbing the royal women. "Perhaps you can clarify a matter for us."

Aethra cast her an amused glance. They had both been hounded non-stop for information about the Trojan delegation. Helen had been luckier than her poor matron in escaping their attentions. She stepped up to the fire and warmed her hands. "And what matter would that be?" She smiled innocently at the steward, amused.

Nextus had difficulty sustaining his focus under her direct gaze. He pulled his hands away from the flames, an awkward titter to his voice. "I... uh, *we* were not sure what odds to place on the Trojan prince. You have seen him handle a horse. Do you think he will provide fair competition?"

Helen laughed. She had expected gossip and warmongering. She should have known these men cared only for the metal in their purse. "He is certainly full of surprises. I'd challenge the judgement of any man who bet against him."

"But against your husband..." Nextus prodded.

Helen sighed, deciding it was not as fun as she hoped provoking the nobles. "Menelaus... is a special case. There are few men who could challenge him," she ruefully admitted. "But if there is one, I wouldn't be surprised if it were the Trojan."

She took her leave, Nextus' doubt infesting her happy mood. Paris would take the field with Menelaus again today.

She trusted he could defend himself should her husband lose his temper, but it was a danger she rather he avoided. She rushed across the hall to a refreshment table and poured herself a cup of mulled wine. It was early for the spicy drink, but she needed something to steady her nerves.

"Will he?" Aethra asked, watching her with an arched brow as she downed the entire cup.

"What?"

"Be challenging your husband?"

Helen froze, a new danger paralyzing her. "Am I so obvious?"

Aethra took the cup from her trembling hand. "To others? No. But I raised you child. I can tell when a woman has been properly bedded. She glows, the essence of Aphrodite flowing through her veins. It is not a thing men can see."

Aethra led her down the hall to a secluded alcove, forcing Helen down on a bench. She all but collapsed, her knees were so weak. "I am a dead woman," Helen moaned. "Menelaus will kill us both."

But Aethra snorted, a distinctly unfeminine sound. "You don't know that. Maybe your Trojan will kill Menelaus. Have you ever thought of that possibility?"

Helen gasped, shocked by her blunt words. "*That's treason.* I'd never—"

"You wouldn't have to." Aethra interjected. "Kingdoms change hands as easily as water flows down the riverbank. Men have always killed each other for land and spoils. It is a woman's lot to wait and see who rises the victor. Better you be prepared for when that river changes direction."

More nobles were entering the megaron, lulled in by the fresh aroma of hot buns laced with honey that the kitchen staff carried in. Helen watched them all nervously, her stomach dipping, any trace of appetite gone. Open war? Was this what she started by giving herself to Paris?

Helen lowered her voice, speaking barely over a whisper.

"I don't want to hurt anyone. Not even Menelaus... I... I just want to be happy." Tears leaked down her cheeks.

Aethra raised a gentle hand and soothed them away, her back held rigid, protecting Helen from any courtier who'd dare to come too close. "My poor, sweet, naive little princess. The world does not care how good your intentions are," her calm voice belying the harshness of her words. "You are a royal. Your actions determine the lives of thousands. You cannot afford to walk this gauntlet with your eyes shut."

Helen pulled back sharply, shoving her hand away. "Aethra! You dare—"

"Yes, I dare!" Aethra silenced her with a harsh whisper. "I was a queen once before your father killed my son and took me for a slave. Do you remember none of that?"

Helen gasped, her matron's confession tugging at the hidden corners of her memory. Something lay in those dark recesses, but she could not access it, a formidable wall blocking her.

"No?" Aethra sighed, straightening her skirts fastidiously though they showed no sign of wear. "It's for the best, then. Some horrors are too terrible to carry in our hearts and minds."

A murmur ran through the megaron as Paris stepped into the hall. His eyes quickly found her. He had the uncanny ability to sense when she was near. He was troubled, she could tell by the bend of his shoulders and the heavy furrow of his brow. But when he saw her, he brightened. Paris did his best to be circumspect, greeting the few courtiers who crossed his path, but he was steadily making his way in her direction.

Aethra watched the prince like a lioness protecting her cub. "You lost your mother when you were too young, but the Gods saw fit to send you another one." She turned to Helen, her knowing eyes filled with sorrow. "Trust me, as you would the woman who bore you. Your fate can change in a heartbeat. Grasp what happiness you can while it is still in your power to take it."

Helen's eyes widened in surprise. Was Aethra giving her *blessing*?

The matron spun and raised a hand toward Paris's guard. "Trojan. A word with you?" she waved Glaucus over, and, by default, Paris. Once in reach, she grabbed the tall captain by the arm and steered him away, whispering fiercely in his ear.

Aethra's warnings were but a buzzing in Helen's ears now that Paris stood before her. She had no ability to mask her feelings. Her heart leapt into her eyes. She wanted nothing more than to throw herself into Paris' arms. It took all her willpower to lower herself into a formal curtsey, the dutiful respect of a princess to a prince.

"I can't stop thinking of you." She adopted an innocent smile, seemingly—for the rest of the court—talking of pleasantries. "I need to see you again, *soon*."

Paris flushed, an inner heat threatening to burn out his reason. He clenched his sword pommel to keep his hands from reaching for her. "I know. We need to talk. Before... this... gets out of hand."

But it was already out of hand. One look at Helen, and he could barely control himself. His nerves were taut, like a soldier on the eve of a battle, his whole body aware he was surrounded by danger.

A herald blasted out a note on his horn, announcing the king to the court. Agamemnon rushed past the man and traversed down the hall with long forceful steps. Menelaus and his horsemen surrounded the king, the brothers thick in argument. Menelaus raised his head ever so slightly as he passed them, the unveiled hatred in his eyes making Paris' blood run cold. That baleful gaze was for Paris and Helen alike, and potentially the king as well. The whole world could burn under the rage of that man.

"What are we going to do?" Helen quivered. In her moment of terror she had grabbed hold of Paris' arm. She quickly dropped it like it was a poisonous snake.

Paris craned his neck, straining to hear Agamemnon's

heated words. "Just relax." He tried to soothe her. "I'll think of something." But one warning glance from Glaucus and Paris knew his options were limited. They were running out of time.

He looked down at Helen, a wave of protectiveness for his love stronger than his own self-preservation. He couldn't let her spend another day in this uncertainty. They were both in danger so long as Agamemnon held all the cards. Paris had to act now, and swift, before anything more could happen to her. It was time to teach Agamemnon Priam's lesson.

"Do you remember when I told you I was not your enemy?" Paris swallowed a lump of dread, steeling himself to become the "Fist in the Silk Glove".

"Yes..." Helen wrapped her arms around herself, feeling a chill that did not come from the air.

"I spoke the truth. I'm not your enemy. But my father might be depending on how Agamemnon chooses to act. I'm sorry, Helen. But I came here for a reason. I have to do as my father commanded me." He started off toward the throne.

"*Paris.*" Helen gasped as loud as she dared, the note of finality in Paris' words frightening her.

"If anything should happen to me, go to Glaucus." Paris told her without turning. If he looked back now, he might never leave. "He will help you, if he can."

"Can I not have a day without you pestering me with your petty squabbles, Brother? You whine like a mule." Agamemnon was ready to toss Menelaus out in the fields and teach him a lesson with his sword. "Do as you are bid!"

"There is no reason to delay the games. The best horseman will still rule the field." Menelaus protested.

The storm had deluged the hippodrome. The runoff had made the racecourse unusable. But Menelaus did not care about conditions. He fancied himself another victory, and would not put off the race for better weather. It was hubris gone sour.

"You would ruin my best race track in your mindless pursuit of self glory!" Agamemnon slammed his fist on his throne, letting his irritation get the best of him. "Get back in the stables. Leave ruling the kingdom to me."

"A win for the House of Atreus is a win for Mycenae." Menelaus pressed on, as ignorant of a lost cause as a turtle struggling in vain when flipped on its back. "I will fix your pretty field if you are so worried about it."

Paris approached the throne, his eyes glued on Menelaus. The Trojan's appearance could not have been more timely. The two princes glared at each other like cocks set loose in a hen house.

"You should tend your own fields, Menelaus." Agamemnon smirked, enjoying the crease of outrage on his brother's face. "Lest another man plant them for you."

The Trojan raised his brow, and Agamemnon savored the confusion his barb imparted on the prince. It was always a good lesson for a petitioner to see how he dealt with his insubordinate brother. If the king was willing to punish his own family, what might he do to those not afforded the same protection of blood?

"Trojan." Agamemnon nodded at the man. "It seems the Gods have decided we've had our fill of play. You've tickled my cock with hints and stories long enough. Foreplay is dull. Let's attend to business."

His crude words seemed to embolden the prince, and a shrewd grin spread across the foreigner's face as he ducked into a short bow. "Stories are for children and old men," the Trojan agreed. "Is there a place where we can have a word in private?"

"Of course." Agamemnon waved away his attendants, happy for the excuse to shut off their constant demands. But, when Menelaus stayed, the Trojan refused to speak and stared at Agamemnon's unruly brother with a blank expression.

"Oh, for the love of Gaia. Follow me." Agamemnon leapt

off his throne and headed for his private antechamber, Paris swiftly following after.

Agamemnon crossed the cramped room in three quick strides. Tossing his cape down on a padded bench, he plucked his gloves off finger by finger and warmed himself beside the central hearth as the door closed shut behind them with a solid boom.

"I hope you aren't here to protest your treatment last night," he grimaced. "I can no more understand the wiles of women than the secrets of the Gods. They say and do as they please."

The effeminate prince had been suspiciously put off by his wife's careless words. It surprised Agamemnon that a familial death threat could offend the Trojan so deeply. Any Greek worthy of their title knew to sleep with a dagger by his side for brother and uncle alike. If half the kingdom did not want you dead, then you were too weak to rule.

The prince hadn't moved from the door. He watched as Agamemnon settled down in his seat, taking his sweet time to answer. "The time for pretenses between us has past, Agamemnon. I know what you are doing here, and it's time you knew why Priam sent me."

Agamemnon grinned, pleasantly surprised by the prince's candor. He was as sick of the court maneuvering as Menelaus. "Have I offended the perfumed lords of the east?" he mocked. "Is this where you chastise me for poor behavior? Or insist I pay taxes to a man whom I've never met?"

The affect on the Trojan was powerful. He froze in mid step, his eyes wide with surprise. The prince, like many men before him, underestimated Agamemnon, believing his wits were as thick as his muscular frame. But Agamemnon was no dullard. He had a talent for strategy and command, and he pressed his advantage.

"You wouldn't have come to Mycenae over a matter as petty as that, Trojan. I have something Priam wants. And I'm prepared to give it to him... for a price."

"You have an offer for Priam?" Disbelief was plastered over Paris' face.

"Troy is bogged down in a war with the Hatti." Agamemnon set his boots on the hearth and reclined on his cushioned bench, conversations of war as commonplace for the king as talk of the harvest. "Priam's vassals fall like leaves before the blades from the East. Your enemy does not fear you. But they would fear *me*. You've seen my armory. I can lead a legion of Greek warriors and give these Hatti a bloodletting they'll soon not forget. One taste of Grecian Rage and those horse lords will never trouble you again."

The lust was heavy in his voice. Since he had heard of the campaigns in the east, Agamemnon had dreamt nightly of riding forth with an army at his back.

But the prince was a blank slate, his face devoid of emotion. When he spoke it was through clenched teeth. "And the price...?"

Agamemnon plucked a dagger from his belt and started to shave his nails. The next part of his offer was genius. His fellow kings of the Hellas would never agree to fight a foreign war. But for *familia*, they would cross the black sea and sail down the River Styx itself. "Seal our alliance with a marriage. Tell Priam I would wed my daughter to his heir. Do this and my men are his."

"Priam's heir is already wed." Paris stared at him, speaking again without a trace of emotion. "To a princess of Phrygia, a kingdom both ancient and powerful. My father will not accept your offer."

Agamemnon cursed his foul luck. He needed to find a way to seize this opportunity without losing stature, and a royal match was the best solution. The prestige of uniting Mycenae with an ancient line would cement his rise to Overlord. But if he could not have Priam's heir, he'd settle for the next best thing. "Then it will be you. No exceptions. My men for a royal wedding. Carry that message to your king."

"Iphigenia is a child!" Paris choked, his delicate

sensibilities deliciously offended.

Agamemnon knew he had the beardless boy by the stones, and delighted in watching him squirm. This... arrangement... was a twist for which the prince had not been prepared, and he shook with barely contained anger.

"Wed her now, bed her later, I do not care." Agamemnon laughed at the prince's foibles. "Her mother bled early, this one will as well. I assure you, she is bred from fine stock."

Paris felt sick. If he had bothered breaking his fast this morning he would have emptied his stomach. The king offered insult when he should be giving thanks. Blinded by hubris, Agamemnon demanded a royal wedding with a child-bride, believing Paris would be honored instead of horrified. He was a vile creature, a carrion sucking vulture preying on his own people. He had to be stopped.

"Are you finished?" Paris grimaced.

Agamemnon nodded, a smug grin broadcasting his unfounded confidence in their negotiations.

Had Priam been present, he would have taken Agamemnon's head from his shoulders. A handful of soldiers for the heir to his kingdom? Yes, there was greatness in Mycenae, but it was nascent, not fully formed. In a few hundred years, who knew of what they might be capable? But now? They were a fledgling society, and Agamemnon a pretender grasping at greatness.

Paris walked toward him, pacing around the edge of the hearth. The angry-red glow of the flames lit up his eyes as he stared down on the lecherous king.

"I will *never* marry your daughter. Not in a thousand years would King Priam consider the terms of your conceit. You are mad to even suggest it."

Agamemnon leapt to his feet. His eyes darted wildly from side to side, the man's tenuous grip on sanity clearly in the balance. Paris suspected no one in his entire life had spoken to him with such disrespect.

"You puny little runt..."

But Paris was through sitting by quietly while Agamemnon insulted him—*insulted Troy*—with impunity. "You have never seen Troy. You have no idea of her vastness or the sizable army Priam commands. He has vassals from the plains of Anatolia to the delta marshlands of the Nile. Some are much larger than the lands you now rule." Paris felt his control slipping, the silk glove Priam bade him don ripped from his fist. "You have five thousand men... Troy has *one hundred thousand*. You command a force a fraction of Priam's own. You have nothing Troy needs or wants. Except your obedience."

The muscles on Agamemnon's neck constricted. The king was fast changing color, his robust glow taking on the sick grey of a man not breathing. His eyes were like black fire, staring an inferno into Paris. But Paris was not done.

"I have an offer for you, Agamemnon. For you alone. End your Draconian trade war with Troy. Pay the taxes you owe to my father's campaigns that protect the free-trade, *campaigns that benefit all of Greece*. Do this, and give thanks that Troy is your powerful ally. Do it not, and the next visitor on your shores will not be an ambassador, but the cold grip of Hades as we choke off your trade and sink your ships on the high seas."

The attack happened quickly. Agamemnon sprang on him with the speed of a cheetah. Had the king not shifted his weight to prepare for the move, Paris would have been wholly unprepared. He barely moved out of the way as two hundred and fifty pounds of Grecian rage rushed past him.

"I'm an ambassador!" Paris shouted, allowing his disgust to fully show on his face. "You'd dare offend the Gods by attacking me?"

But Agamemnon more than dared. He spun around, his arm flailing wide, forcing Paris to leap back to avoid getting crushed. The move almost tipped over the fire.

"Stand still and face me, you mewling brat." The giant king growled. "I'll teach you to show proper respect to a king!" Again, Agamemnon launched himself at him, his fist flying at Paris' head.

Paris ducked, grabbing Agamemnon's arm as he passed. He spun and pinned Agamemnon's arm behind his back, shoving the king up against the wall. "Do not mistake my patience for weakness," he hissed in Agamemnon's ear. "Calm yourself."

"I'll have your head on a pike, you braggart."

The king tensed his muscles, preparing to break Paris' lock, but Paris was prepared. He kicked Agamemnon's feet wide, unbalancing the man and forcing his head against the stone in a jarring blow.

"If you kill me, you're dreams of empire will bleed out with me."

Agamemnon stiffened beneath his hold. The king's secret desires were blatantly obvious to Paris. His arsenal wasn't meant for enemies in the east, but a target much closer to home. Agamemnon was not as subtle as he believed.

"The free cities of the Hellas will never unite behind a man who broke the bonds of *xenia*. If you murder an ambassador, they will revile you and call you as mad as your dead father."

That cold truth stifled Agamemnon's wrath as reason could not. Paris felt the fight drain out of the king's muscles. He released Agamemnon and took a giant stride back, sure to stay out of striking distance.

Agamemnon was brutally strong. Paris wondered, not for the first time, if this were the brother he should consider the greater danger. Menelaus' rage was obvious, as naked as a spring shorn-lamb. But Agamemnon was a simmering cauldron, the coiled asp waiting to strike, his danger hidden until you were already dead.

The king turned to face him, the baleful glare in his eyes the only break in a face devoid of expression. He wiped his lip where it had split against the stone, the dark red of his blood staining the back of his hand. He ran that hand across his tongue, tasting his own blood, while casing Paris from head to toe. He flexed his muscles in a threatening manner.

Paris watched him carefully. This was the moment that decided everything. Would Agamemnon listen to reason? Or was he more animal than king? Paris shifted his stance, prepared for both. He readied his palm, knowing he had only to strike once—across the nose, up and back. If Agamemnon attacked, he would dispatch the king to the netherworld. He could do that much for Helen and all the others Agamemnon wronged.

But the the king did not move. Instead, he laughed. It was a bitter laugh, mocking Paris and the real danger this meeting foreshadowed. "You have stones, Trojan. But you fight like a woman. If you stopped that dancing, I would crush you."

Paris leveled a flat look on the king. "Probably. You outweigh me by half a talent. I might not like it, but I can admit when I am outmatched. Can you?"

Agamemnon's cruel smile faded to a grimace. The danger had not passed. Paris shifted behind the hearth, putting more space between them while a mix of pride and greed played out on the king's face.

"There is no match for a man of Greece, Trojan. You're a fool if you do not see it." Agamemnon lowered his voice dangerously. "I will not bend the knee."

"No one is asking you to."

"I will not suffer extortion." His narrowed eyes hinted this was the heart of Agamemnon's defiance.

"The High Seas Tax isn't extortion, it's good policy. And contributing to the public safety will only help you garner esteem." Paris added, an answer ready for any of the king's concerns.

"And the other matter...?"

Paris shook his head. Priam did not care if Agamemnon filled his days attacking his brothers, as detestable a pastime as that was. As much as Paris wished to advise against that folly, it wasn't his role to do so. "Create your empire; Troy will not try to stop you. But you won't keep it long if you make us your enemy."

Agamemnon tensed from the barb, a minor break in his cold demeanor before he adopted a sneer. "Other men have tried to take things from me before, Trojan. Other *dead* men." The king's hand strayed to the dagger at his belt, his fingers tightening around the hilt.

"Whatever you may have heard, I assure you my father values my life." He held his hand before him in warning. Paris knew he was placing his life on the scales when he walked into the room, and he was probably dead, regardless. He had only one last weapon in his arsenal. "You can send Priam my head, and war will be on your shores before my body rots. Or you can send him another message. *A smarter message.*" He folded his arms across his chest. "I have nothing more to say. The choice is yours."

Paris waited, staring into the hate-fueled eyes of Agamemnon, unapologetic. Minutes passed with neither of them moving. They were both paralyzed by the finality of their actions. Whatever next was said, or done, would affect both their countries.

A loud knock pounded on the antechamber door, breaking the ominous spell.

"Go away, or the Gods help me, I will boil the eyes out of your skull!" Agamemnon shouted at the disturbance.

But the door cracked open and a shaking guard peaked his head in. "Y-y-y... Your Grace. There is a messenger ship from Knossos at port. It's flying a black flag..."

There was only a slight moment of hesitation before Agamemnon tore his eyes away from him and stormed out of the room. He shoved the guard so roughly the man slid halfway toward the throne. Paris had no choice but to follow him out.

"What of the offer, Agamemnon?" he pressed, but the king

refused to answer. Paris made to follow him up the dais, but two guards grabbed him from behind, holding him back. *"Agamemnon."*

A gathering of nobles watched their encounter in shocked silence. Paris looked over the crowd and spotted Helen instantly, her round eyes filled with concern. He shook his head, warning her to keep quiet.

As soon as the king took his seat, the doors of the megaron flew open and a young man ran toward the throne. He was dressed in the lively colors of the royal house of Crete, a vibrant yellow and burnt orange. He crashed into a few courtiers before he could steady his trembling legs.

"YOUR GRACE!" the messenger shouted with a hoarse voice. "An urgent message from Knossos!" He almost fell at the steps to the throne, the poor boy heaving from his long run up the acropolis.

Agamemnon climbed down from his dais and lifted the boy to his feet. "What is it?" he shook the lad.

"King Catreus of Crete is dead." The messenger cried, his words followed by an audible gasp from the crowd. "Your grandsire is dead, Your Grace."

Agamemnon was visibly shaken. He dropped the boy and fell back on his throne. "*How*?"

"His ship was attacked on the Aegean. By pirates, some say. The reports are confusing."

Clytemnestra rushed up to Agamemnon, kneeling before him, her words too soft to carry far. But Paris was within earshot and heard her every word, perhaps as she intended. "Pirates would never attack a royal flagship. This is a message, my love. You know who patrols the seas of the East." She twisted just enough to lay two eyes of judgement upon him.

"Someone will bleed for this!" Agamemnon shouted, his grief making his hulking presence more intimidating. *"MENELAUS!"*

The king's cry echoed across the silent megaron. He launched to his feet, scanning the hall for his brother. Courtiers looked amongst themselves, but the prince was not present.

"FIND HIM!" Agamemnon shouted to Nextus, the steward disappearing down the hall at his command. "I leave on the next tide. My brother is coming with me, or so help me, I will banish him from this realm." He turned to Clytemnestra, his fury matching the simmering anger of the queen. "I will find the foul men responsible for this atrocity and flay the flesh from their bones. The Gods as my witness, it will be done!"

He was in a rage now, storming down the megaron. In a moment, that hairy brute would be gone, and Paris would be well and goodly trapped. He raced after the king. "Agamemnon, what of my offer?"

Agamemnon rounded on him, a fearsome sight in his righteous anger. "I'll hear no more of your vile slander, Trojan. You utter another word and I'll cut your tongue off. You know my mind. Bring *my offer* to your king and begone! I have traitors to kill." He fled the megaron, a storm of attendants in his wake.

Paris turned about in the steadily emptying hall, Helen not ten paces from where he stood. She watched him, the unanswered question in her eyes.

What do we do now?

He had no answer. He backed up toward the exiting courtiers, and followed them to the harbor.

CHAPTER 22

THE HONORABLE THING

AGAMEMNON WAS a man of his word. He sailed on the next tide, not four hours after he received the dire news of his grandsire's death. Half the court gathered on the docks of the harbor to see him off. As members of the royal household, both Helen and Clytemnestra should have travelled with their husbands. But Agamemnon was insistent, with a household filled with guests, the queen was needed to see to affairs at home. And Menelaus could care less if Helen accompanied him anywhere. It was Sabineus at his side, not she.

"Make sure he leaves with the next trade winds." Agamemnon instructed his wife, taking her into his arms in a chaste embrace.

"Gladly, My Lord."

He turned to Helen next, embracing her as he did his wife. She cringed. His grip was too tight, his lips lingering on her cheek too long. "Don't look so worried, Sweet Sister. I will be back in a fortnight."

Helen pulled away, hiding her disgust. "Be careful, My King. Your grandsire was lost to us at sea. I pray you do not encounter the same dangers."

Unless the Gods are kind...

"I pray we do." Agamemnon growled, showing his usual display of cocksure pomposity. "These ruffians will not find me as easy prey."

Menelaus stepped forward and planted a chaste kiss on her lips, enough to satisfy the watching courtiers that their marriage was real. They spoke no words. On impulse, Helen reached out for Sabineus, using the opportunity to whisper a farewell to him as she kissed his cheeks.

"Take care of him."

The dark-haired man blinked with surprise. "I... I will, Princess," he promised, his words heartfelt.

And then they were gone. Twenty-five sets of oars carried the longship out of the harbor where they released the mainsail, the linen billowing in the northwestern winds. In a few short minutes, the ship was nothing but a speck on the horizon.

Helen almost cried with joy. It was a rare event when both brothers were gone from the capital, when she was spared the constant anxiety of navigating their violent moods. It should have been a moment of blissful freedom, an unexpected respite granted from the Gods. But when Agamemnon's ship sailed, so too would the Trojan's. She was losing her prince as surely as the turning of the tides, and they had only just found one another.

Helen readily spotted Paris in the retreating crowds heading up the acropolis. She turned to follow him.

"Wait." Clytemnestra grabbed her arm. "We need to talk."

Helen pushed her sister away from her. "I think you've done enough talking. What you did last night was cruel, Nestra. Even for you."

Clytemnestra's face wrinkled in a mixture of anger and deep concern. The sisters hardly ever fought. Any lingering anger was like a poison slowly eating away at Helen's soul. She was usually the one to make peace, more sensitive then Nestra by far. But not this time. Helen didn't want to find solace in her sister's arms.

"I did what I had to." Nestra insisted, still holding on to Helen tightly. "He is no different than all the other men, spouting lies and keeping secrets. You needed to see."

"Consider me educated, then." Helen pulled away again, this time successfully. "You really don't care who you hurt, do you? For shame, Nestra." She motioned for Aethra to join her, and they quickly retreated to the palace.

Helen did not turn to see the crushed look of pain and anger on her sister's face. She knew Clytemnestra would still be standing on the dock watching her depart, regal as a queen.

And so Helen missed when the queen finally made up her mind to follow after her.

Paris and Glaucus returned to the palace at a leisurely pace. Paris opted against the proffered chariot, taking the time traveling on foot to fill in his captain of the king's demand.

"You're lucky he didn't kill you."

"He had his reasons to keep me alive." Paris grumbled, his stomach turning at the king's perversity.

Paris wanted to believe Priam would refuse Agamemnon's ridiculous offer, but how many of his council would whisper in his ear for him to accept? In one move, his father could quell the bickering in the west and rid himself of Paris, the major source of conflict in his house.

Until he met Helen, Paris had resigned himself to a life in service to the crown. He knew he was nothing more than a playing chit in the never-ending game of politics and power. He accepted that duty with a sense of pride, knowing his actions helped to increase the greatness of Troy. But this... *offer*... was a slap in his face. The girl was barely eleven.

He suspected the Gods toyed with his feelings for their own sick pleasure. To deny him home and happiness his whole life, then offer a taste of what he was missing only to keep it frustratingly out of his reach—their cruelty was beyond enduring.

They entered the private quarters of the palace, finally getting a bit of privacy from the milling crowds. Only a few chambermaids were allowed in this wing, and they were busy running about their duties.

"So do we stay or do we depart? With the king gone, we have no formal excuse to linger."

And that was the question that was tearing Paris apart. To stay with Helen, however brief their time might be, was to stay true to his heart. To leave, as duty demanded, would honor his promise to his king. If Paris failed in his duty now, his death omen might as well be truth. Troy would suffer the consequences.

"Ready the men," he decided. "You will carry this message personally to the king. Not to Aesacus, not Hecuba, not even Hector. Priam himself." His father needed to know what was happening in Mycenae. Troy needed to prepare itself for the good and the ill if they chose an alliance with this Mad King.

Glaucus balked. "You aren't coming with us?" They had not discussed this possibility. Paris knew his captain was loath to leave him in danger.

"I need to talk to Helen." Paris frowned, wondering again how she would take this news. "This decision is not mine alone to make. But by moon tide, you set sail. With or without me."

They turned the corner into the guest hall and Paris halted, surprised to see they were not alone. Helen's maid stood outside his quarters. He swore they had left her down at the docks with her mistress. But he and Glaucus had taken the long walk to the palace, and Paris was sure Helen knew every shortcut on the royal grounds.

He quickened his steps. If Aethra was here, Helen would not be far.

"Your Grace." Aethra bowed deep in an elegant curtsey.

Paris rushed past her, tossing his door open.

"Should I stay out here—" Glaucus asked as Paris slammed the door in his face.

"Helen?" Paris rushed through the foyer. There was no sign of her. "*Helen!*" He searched Glaucus' room and then his own before she stepped out from the balcony, cleverly hidden by the long curtains.

"I'm here." She reached for him as he passed by.

The anxiety of the past few hours rolled over him with that touch. He swept her up in his arms, kissing her passionately, fearful it might be his last chance.

She responded in kind, melting into his arms. "Paris, what did the king say? What's happening?" A sharp edge of panic laced into her words.

Paris froze, his arms squeezing her to him. He had no idea where to begin. She must have sensed the dire news in his hesitation. It seemed impossible, but her thin arms pressed him even tighter.

"You can't leave me!" she sobbed into his ear. He could hear her heart breaking with that cry.

She was right. He *couldn't* leave her. Helen had bound his heart to hers as securely as if it were wrapped in chains. If she commanded it, he'd stay. He'd face down Agamemnon and Menelaus both to spend his last days in her presence.

Paris pulled back, tucking strands of Helen's golden hair away from her face. He had spent so much of his life wandering, always the lonely ship at a distant shore. Here, on the outskirts of civilization, he had finally found someone worthy of his sacred oath. He dropped to his knees and gathered her hands in his.

"I love you, Helen. More than life, than duty, than honor itself. I love you beyond the oaths I've sworn to King and Country, beyond reason, and I will spend the rest of my life protecting you from anyone who wishes to do you harm."

She was speechless, her shimmering jewel-blue eyes teaming with unshed tears. A fear-tinged joy beamed out of her radiant face. Paris swallowed the hope blossoming in his heart. Helen deserved to hear it all, to make the right decision not swayed by his emotions. He laced his fingers through hers, raising their entwined hands to his lips.

"I will stay if you ask it of me and face whatever repercussions that follow. Until the axe falls on my neck." He clung to her hands, seeing the inevitable path that would follow if he stayed, the shame and the spectacle. "But everything you stand for, the honor you so cherish, would be wiped away in the stigma of an adulterer. All that you are—*all that you could ever be*—will be ruined."

That bitter truth leeched Paris of his strength. He was willing to sacrifice his life for her love, but not hers. And though it tore him apart inside, he continued on. "Regardless if the omens aren't true, I *am* a cursed man. I will bring you nothing but misery and death. You... you should discard me." He buried his head into her stomach, too ashamed to witness the pain he surely caused her.

Helen wrung her hands, feeling the same helplessness as Paris. He was struggling, trying desperately to do the honorable thing. But there was no easy answer, no right path where no one suffered. If she let him, Paris would suffer the brunt of this pain himself, forsaking his own happiness in deference for others. As he had always done. She saw him, a lonely child rejected by his mother, hated by those who should have treasured him, all for no fault of his own.

"I will *never* discard you." She wrapped her arms around his head, cradling him closer to her womb.

His shoulders shook with emotion, his hot breath warming her stomach. "I do not deserve you."

It amazed her that Paris—who had consistently surprised her with his intellect and insight—would fail to see himself with the same clarity. It was though a lifetime of being denied love stunted his ability to receive it. She thought of her own journey, of all the terrible twists and turns Fate had sent her way. She had almost given up hope, falling into the despair that Nestra preached as wisdom. But even in her darkest moments, she clung to the faith that the Goddess would grant her the love that was promised. And, as she held Paris in her arms, Helen knew that faith was rewarded.

She pulled his head back, staring deep into his eyes with all the passion that threatened to unmake her. "Alexandros Paris, Son of Troy. You more than deserve me... You are the mate of my soul."

The words, once spoken, were like magic, unlocking an inner awareness between them. Paris stared at her as if discovering her for the first time. Their inexplicable connection, the uncontrollable desires, deciphered. Soul mates. Two halves of a single soul cursed to search for each other the world over, yearning for unification. He had been searching for Helen his entire life.

She caressed his face, her touch a conduit linking them body and soul. But that soft touch was the barest fragment of what could be. It was the light fall of snow hiding an avalanche of passion beneath. He rose to his feet, tearing at the sash around her waist.

Helen reached for his belt, ripping at the coarse leather with the same urgency. She needed to feel him, be with him, she'd destroy anything that stood in their way. She ripped the tunic from his back, the fabric tearing into useless rags. His loincloth fell next and she shoved his naked chest, tossing him roughly down on his bed.

She stood before him, unable to take her eyes away from his, their chests rising and falling in unison. She plucked the fibula from her shoulder and the fabric of her chiton unfolded like petals opening on a morning flower. Stepping out of the cloth, she climbed up on top of him, straddling his waist between her legs.

He didn't say a word—it wasn't necessary. There was only the rediscovery of his other half, now acknowledged, impossible to deny. They didn't even kiss. Helen rose above him and lowered herself on his engorged phallus, the soft folds of her silken canal perfectly molded to his flesh. They stayed motionless, both in deep shock at the swirling sensations flooding between them. He *felt* her, every quiver, every tiny breath, laying bare a surge of love pouring from her into him. When he could bear it no longer, he bucked, rolling on top of her, and thrusted as far as her tender body would allow him to reach.

It was a wild, often violent, ride. Helen clung to him, raking her nails down his back with every thrust, trying to pull away the layers and get deeper inside him. His hips bruised her pelvis, his phallus stretched her womb, filling her entirely, and still she hungered for more.

He felt her begin to spasm, the muscles of her font tightening around him as she cried out in orgasm. He came instantly, climaxing in unison with her mewling cries. The pairing was over too quickly, a tantalizing promise of more to come. As he finally pressed his lips to hers, he was utterly certain there would be more.

Helen was trembling. Paris was surprised to realize that he was, too. It was though his body had no experience, no road map, on how to deal with the passion surging within him.

"Are you all right?" he pressed his quivering lips to hers again, her touch helping to abate the shaking.

Helen had no idea if she was all right. Her entire world had been utterly undone. Nothing would ever, *could ever*, be the same again. She studied Paris, her heart swelling painfully, the thought of losing him terrifying her beyond endurance.

"I'm scared."

"I am, too." Paris understood the danger of attachment now. Of having something too precious to lose. Helen's love was a treasure so rare he'd spend the rest of his life defending it. The Gods would have to rip her from his cold dead hands. He cupped her beautiful face in his hands, knowing it might yet come to that.

"Finding you was a blessing, one I don't want to squander or needlessly sacrifice." He kissed her tenderly. "I will die for you if you ask it." He took a deep breath, knowing now the real option that the Fates had left to them, a path with as many dangers as staying.

"But I would rather we live. Please, Helen. Come back with me to Troy."

CHAPTER 23

THE RUIN OF OUR HOUSE

CLYTEMNESTRA STOOD on the dock, the wooden planks lurching forwards and back beneath her with the swell of the ocean. She pressed a hand to her forehead, the wave of nausea crawling up her stomach laced with the bitter taste of bile. She reached out, needing something—anything—to hold on to while the panic attack ran through her body.

But Helen was gone. Nestra watched her twin disappear into the crowds, leaving her alone on the shore.

"My Queen," Nestra's maid grabbed her arm to keep her from falling. "Are you ill?"

It was happening again. She was loosing Helen, the gulf of silence between them growing daily. A man had come and snatched her away, as had happened in their youth, and would happen over and over again.

Her breathing came in ragged gasps. The harbor went in and out of focus, the crashing of the waves morphing into a roar in her ears. She couldn't lose Helen. Not again. Nestra was powerless when they were children, but not now. She was a queen. And she could protect her own.

"You should sit, Your Grace." Her maid tried to urge her toward a pile of grain sacks sitting on the dock.

Clytemnestra shoved her back hard. "Don't touch me!" The young girl cringed away from her. "Get back to the Palace. All of you." she commanded, then spun on her heel and raced down the dock after her sister.

Helen was taking shortcuts, weaving through the city to avoid the slow pace of the procession. Her sister favored these cramped avenues and the crude people who populated them. It was a quirk unique to Helen from the royal family. She cared for the lowest flea-bitten mongrels, showering affection on the disaffected, never seeing the danger her tender heart placed her in. It was one of many reasons why Helen needed protection and a strong hand to guide her. She was too innocent to understand why it was necessary.

Clytemnestra rushed past the free workers, careful to keep a good distance from the grime-coated lowborn. They huddled away from her, too, shocked to see their monarch striding through their wayward district.

Helen bypassed the Lion Gates, heading around the acropolis for the sheltered, and less trafficked, Eastern gate. It was a steady climb, and Nestra made quick work of it, but Helen's flowing chiton stayed frustratingly out of reach. It was as though Hermes maliciously lent her twin His speed, knowing how desperate Nestra was to speak with her.

Where is she going?

That was the pressing question that kept Nestra from calling out to her sister. There was something in the way Helen moved that screamed of secret purpose. Nestra used all the skill she inherited from Tyndareus to track her, careful to stay out of sight.

The eastern entrance was a short distance from the bedrock staircase that fed off the private quarters of the palace. Helen ran up them, taking the steps two at a time.

Nestra cursed. She couldn't possibly keep up, the stitching from her difficult birthing at risk of tearing. Fortunately, Helen had her old maid with her and she had to slow for the woman to catch her breath.

Nestra crept into the cover of a thick patch of cypress trees as they rested. The needle-like leaves poking at her were saturated with a sticky sap. After the manic trek up the hill, and now coated with dust and debris, Clytemnestra knew she must appear wild. But that wildness was nothing compared to the storm raging within her.

Helen had to listen to reason. The Trojan couldn't be trusted. No man could. What Nestra did was in order to save her twin future grief. She had to understand that.

Helen and the maid started up the trail again. In short order, they were up the remainder of the hill and into the private courtyard. Helen's destination was no longer a mystery. Nestra watched as she darted into the servant's walkway, the dim and narrow corridors used by the staff to access the royal apartments. The section she entered belonged to the Trojan prince.

Clytemnestra didn't hesitate. She darted into the tunnel right after Helen, her alarm growing with every step. When she reached the small door that led into the prince's room, she hesitated, her empty hand frozen inches from the latch.

Why is she here?

But Clytemnestra was no innocent. There was only one reason her sister would sneak into the bedchambers of a strange man. A low moan grew in the hollow of her throat and she sank to the stone floor.

She stayed there, crumbled on the ground, as the crushing grip of anxiety pressed down on her. She could scarcely breathe. And somewhere in the midst of her immobilization, the prince returned, his panicked voice breaking through Clytemnestra's trance.

Their voices were muffled, the dense oak of the sally door too thick for anything less than raised voices to penetrate. But the wood was old and chipped around the planks. The holes were wide enough to see into the room if Nestra pressed her eye to the portal.

She hesitated, the sordid image of herself—a queen—

kneeling in a darkened hall and spying into a bedchamber, overwhelming her. This behavior was beneath her. If anyone were to see...?

But Helen was on the other side of that wall. And her desire to protect her sister overpowered any lingering claim of propriety. Clytemnestra rose to her knees and pressed her face to the wood.

What she witnessed was enough to bring her back down to the ground. This was no minor tryst. They clung to each other, an intimacy in their touch that spoke of something beyond the physical. Helen ripped the tunic from his back, ferocious as a jungle cat, a side of her sister Nestra never thought existed. And their coupling... It was violent, demanding, and strangely erotic. Even Agamemnon, in his most robust moments, couldn't match the efforts of Paris with Helen.

Clytemnestra watched it all, a sickly void forming in her heart. She should feel outrage, betrayal... *something*. But kneeling in the dark, an unwelcome participant of their lovemaking, she only felt numb. She was unaware when they left. The outside world had quieted down to a mute whisper as she sat there, head pressed to stiff wood. When she finally stood, her legs tingled painfully, the blood cut off from her lower extremities for too long.

Nestra walked for hours, roaming the halls of the palace, lost in a fog of shock. Helen would be killed for this. Agamemnon would find out. He'd make an example of the princess. And when Helen died, a piece of Clytemnestra would as well.

The sun lowered on the horizon, and still she roamed. Her maids tried to attend her. Administrators called her to council. Eventually the servants announced the evening meal. She ignored them one and all. They were insects buzzing around her head, annoying and insignificant. She had only room in her mind for Helen and the hopeless situation her sister had placed them all in.

Clytemnestra was nearing her own apartments when she

finally ran into her. Helen was walking out of her chambers, looking fresh from the baths, a healthy glow on her cheeks. She smiled at Clytemnestra, a shadow of remorse on her lips.

A shadow? It should be a mountain.

Something snapped within Nestra. She stormed down the remaining space between them, grabbing her sister by the elbow and shoving her back into her apartments.

"Nestra? What are you doing?!"

Now Helen panicked? Now she showed the fear and concern she should have worn for her other dalliances? The hypocrisy fueled Nestra's anger to new heights.

"Get out. All of you!" She screeched at the cadre of young maids filling Helen's bedchamber. They scattered like rats before a torch.

She towed Helen to the bed and tossed her down on the mattress. *"How could you...? Selfish... Traitorous..."* she sputtered, her mind swirling, unable to form a coherent sentence.

Helen cowered on the bed, shrouded in her doe-eyed innocence. Always the eternal victim. Rage boiled in Nestra.

Not this time!

She slapped her twin, knocking Helen over on her side. "Are you insane? Do you want to die? Do you care at all what that would do to me?"

Helen held her hand over her red-tinged cheek, tears streaming down her face. "Nestra, I... I don't understand. Why are you doing this?"

"I told you to end it. I warned you he was trouble. And what do you do? You open your legs to him like a common whore."

Helen tried to back away from her, her panic-stricken face doubling in intensity. "I'd never—"

Nestra grabbed her arms, pulling Helen forward into another brutal slap, the ring on her hand cutting into her sister's lip. "Don't you lie to me. Don't you *ever* lie to me."

She hit her again, and again until Helen was a sobbing crumbled mess on the bed sheets. "I saw you together, fucking like two wild animals." Nestra's voice cracked, a wellspring of outrage pouring out of her by the betrayal. "Why, Helen? *Why?*"

Helen stopped trying to fight her. She pushed herself up, her round eyes—mirrors of Clytemnestra's own—filled with tears. "Because I love him."

The tears cascaded down Helen's pink skin making her appearance lovelier despite her shame. It was unfair that even now, in the thick of her treachery, she could inspire tenderness in Nestra's heart.

"I love him, Nestra." Helen spoke with more confidence. "He is the other half of my soul. I... I am lost without him."

A gaping emptiness of shock-induced fog returned to Clytemnestra. In that fog, her left hand, the flesh of her flesh, soul of her soul, took a dagger and plunged it into her beating heart. Inside the gaping wound, the meaty organ gushed fluid. Not blood, but pools of white-hot rage.

"NO!" She struck at Helen again, backhanding her hard across her head. "He is not your other half. *I am!*"

Helen cried out from the pain, again trying to flee her wrath. But Nestra scrambled onto the bed after her, clawing at her sister.

"Nestra, stop it. Please!" She put her hands helplessly out before her, backed up now to the wall.

Nestra grabbed her twin by the hair and shoved her back down on the mattress. "You stupid beautiful fool. These men desire you, fight to claim you, and you think it love?" She pressed her knee into Helen's stomach, pinning her down. Helen tried to bat her hands away, but Nestra's anger made her strong. She locked her sister's arms above her head.

"I want to see it," she growled, tearing at Helen's chiton the same way she saw her twin doing with her lover. "I want to see what drives these men wild with lust. Kings and princes...," she choked up, "*my own husband...* I want to see it!"

Helen's clothes fell away in pieces. She squirmed under Nestra, naked and sobbing. "Please... stop."

Her skin was flawless, her hips perfectly round, a match for the swelling of her perky breasts. But there was nothing unique, nothing special about her twin's body. It was identical to Nestra's own. She trailed her hand down Helen's chest and down between her legs, cupping her private parts in a tight grip.

"They do not love you, Sister. This—" she tightened her grip, "is not love. It is lust. And when they are done with you they will discard you."

But Helen still fought the truth, her whimpering cries fueling Nestra's anger. "You don't believe me? Are you really that naive?"

"No... please."

Helen tried to escape again, but Nestra was too quick. She backhanded her twin. Helen spun from the blow and her head collided with the post of the bed. She fell on the mattress in a daze.

"This prince doesn't love you." Nestra snarled. "None of them love you. Only I do." She shoved Helen's legs apart, her fingers sliding into her twin's wet crevice. She would show Helen, kicking and screaming if she must. That man was not special. The feelings he stirred were not unique. Anyone could do it.

Clytemnestra pressed harder, stroking deeper, some madness taking control of her faculties. This was her body, flesh of her flesh, it belonged to her, not that greedy prince. She pressed her mouth to Helen's cleft, the folds of her rosebud moist and hot. This was hers, too. She plunged her tongue against the little flab of flesh, sucking and pulling, a warmth burning through her own body.

Some part of her heard Helen begging her to stop, crying and pleading. But those cries only inflamed Nestra to greater violence, to stroke harder, faster.

You're mine... my twin, my love, my only love. The words

became a mantra that she groaned as she laid claim to her twin.

Everyone loved Helen best. Their father, her citizens, even her own husband. It was a bitter truth Clytemnestra had long learned how to cope with. But none of those outsiders could lay claim to Helen's love. Only Clytemnestra held that honor. And no one—*no man*—was going to take that away from her.

Helen's cries had stopped. She had grown still, her head rolling listlessly on her shoulders like a rag doll. Her jeweled eyes became flat mirrors, reflecting nothing. Only small gasps escaped her otherwise motionless lips.

There was a quickening in Nestra's loins as an orgasm rolled over her, the pulsing waves of heat soaking through her body. Exhausted, she leaned into Helen's limp legs. An eerie silence dominated the room.

"You're mine, Helen," Clytemnestra whispered with a growl. "*Mine*."

CHAPTER 24

ABDUCTION

HELEN'S BODY shut off when her sister touched her. She retreated into a corner of her mind, a silent witness to the violation of her heart and soul. It was a terribly dark corner, the shadows pressing down around her threatened to swallow her whole. Helen huddled in that blackness, waiting for it to all be over. What could not be stopped must be endured. A lesson her father had taught her and Menelaus had perfected.

But all was not quiet in those dark shadows. As Nestra ripped the innocence from her body, she was reminded of another rape, one long forgotten. Helen, a girl of eight, and Theseus, a king four times her age. And the faces of her saviors, her older brothers Polydeuces and Castor, who died bravely in the war to reclaim her. A locked cabinet in her mind burst open, flooding her with memories which she neither wanted nor knew how to cope.

It was never-ending, this cycle of rape and brutality. One king led to another, Agamemnon shamelessly abusing her body whenever Menelaus was away. Her husband, in his own cruel way, was a blessing. The absence of his affections was preferable to the lecherous taking the others had subjected her to.

And now Nestra, her twin, her confidante, her safe harbor in a turbulent sea. *Nestra* sought to possess her, too. Helen was adrift in her sister's betrayal, unable to speak or react. She felt more than saw her twin leave her chambers. And she saw more than heard Aethra's cries when she found Helen on the bed, bruised and bloody.

Her matron draped a robe around her shoulders, hiding her nakedness. But Helen was too numb to be shamed by modesty. She stared at Aethra, her pain as naked as her body.

"I was a child. How could he?"

Aethra gasped, a shudder of guilt constricting her face. Theseus was her son, a noble warrior king of many great adventures. And yet he kidnapped Helen to fulfill his sick desires, claiming she was a daughter of Zeus and her innocence a notch on the list of wonders he wanted to possess.

"There is no excuse," Aethra stammered. "It is a madness that takes men when they see your beauty. Your father tried to protect you, as I do now. But some men are... beyond my ability to deflect."

A madness? Helen nearly cried from rage. Her lauded beauty—this supposed gift from Aphrodite that inspired lust and depravation—was no gift. *It was a curse.* She was merely an object, a possession to be tossed back and forth between powerful men.

"Helen, please—" Aethra reached out for her.

"Get away from me!" She kicked off the bed, a dark terror giving her speed.

The room spun. The air was too thick. She needed to get away. Far away. Helen backed up to the sally door of her apartments, spun on her heel, and ran.

"The ship is prepped, our men assembled, but the tide won't turn till after the moon sets." Glaucus informed Paris, the last of their personal affects having long since been packed.

Paris paced their apartments, his hands wringing his cape in knots. They were under royal commands to depart. If he missed the tide, the idle tongue of gossip would wag, and he was under enough suspicion as it was. But Helen had not given her consent to stay or go, and he wasn't going anywhere without her.

Paris had hoped to see her at supper, but she was strangely absent. He had an overwhelming urge to seek her out, that she needed him. But Helen had been explicit; she needed time to consider his proposition. He had to respect her boundaries.

"Tell them to wait." He wrung the fabric tight. "I want them at their stations all night if needs be."

"It will be done." The captain turned to deliver the message.

"And Glaucus, make sure they are all armed. If this turns for the worse, I expect three dead for every Trojan casualty."

"The death toll will be far higher than that." Glaucus cast him a grim smile. He tossed open their chamber door and stumbled chest first into Helen's maid. "My Lady?" Glaucus helped her back to her feet. The poor woman was beside herself.

Paris rushed to her side. "Aethra? What are you doing here? Where's Helen?"

"It was the queen, and my stupid mouth, I should never have said a word... Please, Your Grace. You have to go after her. I'm afraid she will hurt herself." The words tumbled out of the woman like rocks cascading down a cliff, one crashing into another until there was only a piled mess.

"Whoa, slow down." Paris set her down on a chair. "Tell me everything."

The mist had returned. The humid air was so thick that even the western zephyrs blowing in strength did little to disperse it. Helen stood at the temple precipice, her toes hanging off the loose rock. Salt spray from the crashing waves below made her purchase more slippery. A gust of wind or shift of weight could send her to her death, each factor seemingly innocent but holding the power of life or death over the weary princess.

She toyed with it. How easy it would be to just fall, to let the rocks claim her. Her body would be crushed to powder, her soul returned to sea foam. There would be no more fighting on her behalf. Paris could return home. He would not have to squander his life in a never-ending battle over her. In time, he could be happy.

But not her. No amount of time or space could erase what Helen had been through. It was better to end it. Her beauty would reap no more ruin. She spread her arms and whispered a prayer to the Goddess, willing Her to make the final push. The wind gusted like a divine breath. The mist parted.

And Paris was there, an expression of love and concern on his face that pierced her heart.

"Paris!" she cried as she turned to him.

The twisting move crumbled the ground beneath her feet. She slipped over the edge, the wet rock sliding through her grasping hands.

He was at her side like lightning, grabbing her arms before she had fallen too far, and pulled her up to safety. "It's all right. I've got you." He cradled her to his chest. "I'll protect you, my love. You don't have to do this."

Helen moaned, sobbing into his chest. "It won't end." She clung to his tunic, desperate for his heat to stop her ice-numbed shivers. "It doesn't matter where we go. Agamemnon will find me. And if not him, there will be others."

With bloodshed and destruction, they'd come for her, and she would be handed to whoever conquered. It felt like a ghostly prophecy riding on the vespers of the frost-laced fog. She shifted her gaze to look out over the precipice. It was only a short step...

Paris' arms tightened around her and she knew if she took that step, he would follow after. "Don't ask me to let you go."

His voice cracked with emotion. "Not like this. There might be a day when we both must jump, but it's not today. Not when a kingdom and a new life waits for us across the sea."

He sounded so confident, his hope a beacon of light she was afraid to take shelter in. But there was no safe harbor, no distant shore where her curse would not follow them.

"They'll unite to reclaim me. They swore an oath...," she cried. "You can't stop them."

"Yes, I can. *Troy can.*"

"*You can't!*" She tore away from him. "Maybe you can deflect Agamemnon, but when it's your brother or your father who tries to claim me? Will you kill them all? *Can you?*" Her body doubled over in guilt. She would be the death of this man. She turned to the cliff, a groan of despair on her lips. "How many will you fight to keep me free?"

"The whole world if needs be." He shook with the weight of that promise.

She moaned again, her spirit broken. She didn't have the strength to keep fighting. When he wrapped his arms around her again, she let him. He drew her close, buoying her spirit with his own.

"I've spent my entire life making other people happy," he trembled as he confessed in her ear, "hoping, if I tried hard enough, they would love me the way a noble son deserved to be loved. It wasn't until I met you that I realized it was for naught. *I owed them nothing.* And there was nothing they could give that would equal your love."

He pulled her away from the cliff, forcing her to look at him. "You are my light, Helen. I dwelt in darkness before I met you, before you loved me. You are more precious to me than air, and I'll follow you wherever you decide we must go. But there is a better way than death.

"You don't belong to these people. You're life is your own. You get to choose which roads to travel, which future to claim, *not them.* You only have to follow your heart. And when happiness is within your grasp, have the courage to reach for it."

Follow your heart.

The hairs rose on her arms and neck. Helen felt herself at a crossroads, as vividly as she had on the eve of her betrothal. All the multitude of events in her life inevitably led her to this very moment.

Follow your heart... into the depths or to Troy?

She looked up at Paris, his eyes so filled with love, so hopeful. Was it worth risking his life; was it worth shaming everyone that she loved?

They don't love you.

Nestra's harsh voice leaked into Helen's mind. Her twin was right. They didn't love Helen. They loved the *idea of Helen,* not Helen herself. Only this man saw her for who she truly was, and his love was worth a lifetime of pain and suffering. The deep emptiness, that gulf of pain and fear, could not exist in his presence. He was a burning warmth that scorched those dark phantoms away.

"Yes," she gasped, somehow knowing it was the right path to take. Paris' arms tightened around her.

"I'll come with you to Troy."

EPILOGUE

A Distant Shore

HELEN STOOD at the prow of the Trojan longship as fifty oars dipped quietly into the still waters of the Aegean. The moon had barely set below the horizon when she led the Trojan entourage out of the acropolis via the hidden cistern tunnels that burrowed beneath the fortress walls. The mist was an added blessing, masking their departure from the prying eyes of the palace. With any luck, no one would know of her departure until the morning meal.

Aethra sat at the stern, deep in conversation with the Trojan captain. There was no question that her maid would travel with them to Troy; Aethra had made that point clear to Paris before they left the palace grounds. She had a debt to repay and would not leave Helen's side until those old wrongs had been atoned.

Paris joined her at the prow, wrapping his arms around her. The warmth of his cloak was a welcome respite from the chill of the night. Together, they watched in silence as the mist swallowed the tiny harbor lights of Mycenae.

"Do you think if we travelled far enough, it would be like this life never existed?" Helen mused, hoping it was true. "Where I didn't have to be Helen of Sparta?"

A pang of empathy tightened Paris' throat. He cradled her to his chest as the wind picked up. He had spent his entire life on such a journey. "You're not Helen of Sparta any more."

The mist lifted as they oared further out to sea. A dazzling field of stars filled the sky, their brilliant light reflecting back from the waters beneath them. The ship cut through those waters as though navigating the cosmos itself. Troy, and their unknown future, lay before them in the east.

A fear gnawed at Paris' mind. The warmth of their homecoming was uncertain. There was no way of knowing how Priam would react. Paris only knew he was not going to live in shame any longer.

He spun Helen around, the starlight reflecting in her lovely eyes, and kissed her with passion. The force drawing them together was as ancient as the celestial orbs shining down on them from the heavens.

"You're not Helen of Sparta," he whispered to her again. "Now and forever after, you're Helen of Troy."

"Helen of Troy," she whispered breathlessly, melting into his embrace.

The title fit, like a key sliding into a lock. As the winds picked up, she dared to lift her head with hope. A greater destiny awaited her. She was leaving everything she knew behind, trusting the Fates once again for a future filled with purpose and love.

She entwined her fingers with Paris', his tender squeeze reassuring her that this time the journey would end differently. She dared to believe it. So long as Paris was by her side, she had nothing to fear.

AUTHOR'S NOTE

When I set out to write this book, I wanted to bring to life a period of history most people only know about through legend. Any history student is familiar with the concept of "Punctuated Equilibrium". It's a theory that humankind advances, not gradually, but with giant strides forward at pivotal moments. If history was a novel, these periods of advancement are the climatic ending after uncountable pages/years of status-quo. Nothing could be more true than the twilight years of the Bronze Age.

Over the course of *one lifetime*, the greatest empires of the ancient world fell to a mysterious power. Cultures that dominated the Near East and the Mediterranean for a thousand years disappeared virtually overnight. As Moses led the Exodus across the Red Sea and Rameses ruled as Pharaoh over Egypt, the heroes of Greek legend walked the earth. These historical figures were *contemporaries* of each other, their worlds interlinked.

This series is my endeavor to understand that pivotal time in our history under that holistic view. The Mycenaeans were not the awesome power that Homer claimed in verse some 400 years later. They were a small part of a larger world: one dominated by bigger, more powerful realms.

History is written by the victors, and events—like those told by Homer—cannot be fully trusted as truth. Myths told fantastical tales of history, but were also propaganda to support Greek supremacy. As an archaeologist, I was trained to question every source and try to remove cultural bias from my conclusions. While I've taken small liberties in my reconstruction of the Trojan War for dramatic purposes, to the best of my knowledge, the socio-political context of the Mycenaean/Near Eastern worlds are true.

The Greek heroes were honorable, brave, and fierce—but they were also human. And like their descendants, some three thousand years later—we are all made vulnerable by love. I hope this tale ignites your curiosity about the world of our ancestors, and perhaps, through retelling their stories, we can learn from their mistakes.

PHOTO BY: JEFF LORCH

ABOUT ARIA

Inspired at an early age by the adventures of Indiana Jones, Aria Cunningham studied marine archaeology at UC Berkeley. In 2004, she set forth to create her own adventures and helped excavate a Roman palace from 200 AD at Tel Dor, Israel.

Continuing her old world education, she travelled the expansive fjords of Norway, castle hopped from Wales to the Rhineland, and explored the funeral complexes along the Egyptian Nile. She is an avid scuba diver who has navigated shipwrecks on the ocean floor, the immense kelp forests off the Channel Islands, and the legendary Cenote caverns of the Yucatan.

Aria has a Master's degree in the Cinematic Arts from USC and currently lives off the coast of Southern California.

Look for

THE
PRINCESS OF PROPHECY

HEROES OF THE TROJAN WAR
VOL. II

Coming Spring, 2015

Visit the author's website for updates, ancient history facts, and insider information on the series at: www.ariacunningham.com

Made in the USA
Las Vegas, NV
04 January 2026